Mixed Blood

The daughter of a Cherokee woman
and a Scottish trader on the
American frontier tells
her story.

By
JEANEAN DOHERTY

Mixed Blood (The StoryTellers, Book 1)

Published by Quill Hawk Publishing
Edmond, Oklahoma
www.quillhawkpublishing.com

© 2025 by Virginia Jeanean Doherty

www.jeaneandoherty.com

Printed in the United States.

Published 2025

Library of Congress Control Number: 2025909905

ISBN 978-1-965142-44-8 (Paperback)
ISBN 978-1-965142-45-5 (Hardcover)

"What is history
but a fable agreed upon?"
Napoleon Bonaparte

"No amount of white blood can take
away the Cherokee in them."
Chief Charles Hicks
Immediately before the
Removal in 1838

Dedicated to Bob, who believed in me;

Fred, who encouraged me;

and all of Hester and Richard's descendants,

including my children,

Stefanie, Stacy, and Bill,

along with my grandchildren,

Sarah, Audrey, Elizabeth, Carley,

Emma, and Liam.

Contents

Descendants of Headman of Estatoe

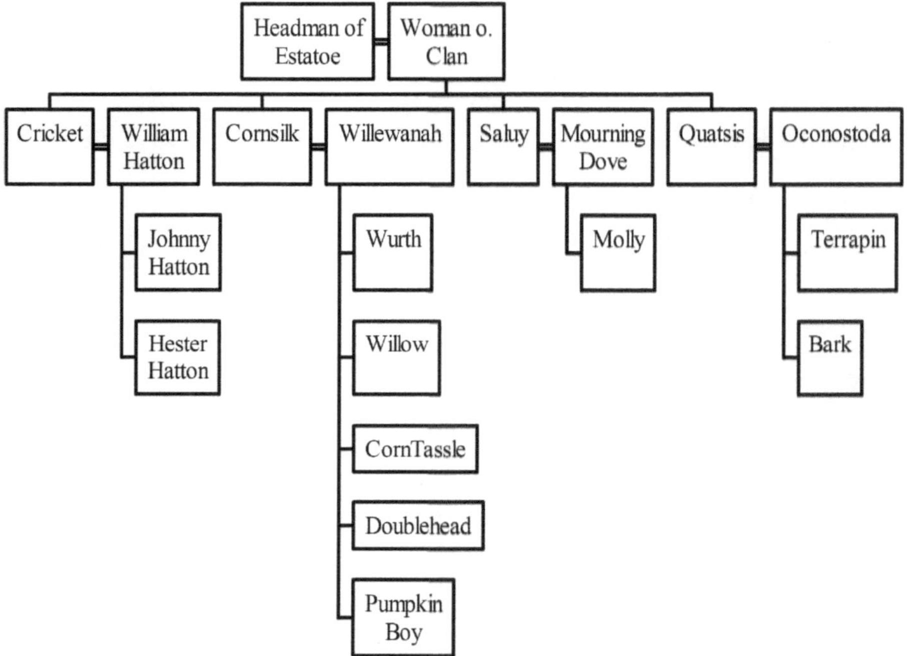

Descendants of Prachey/Hester and Richard Pearis

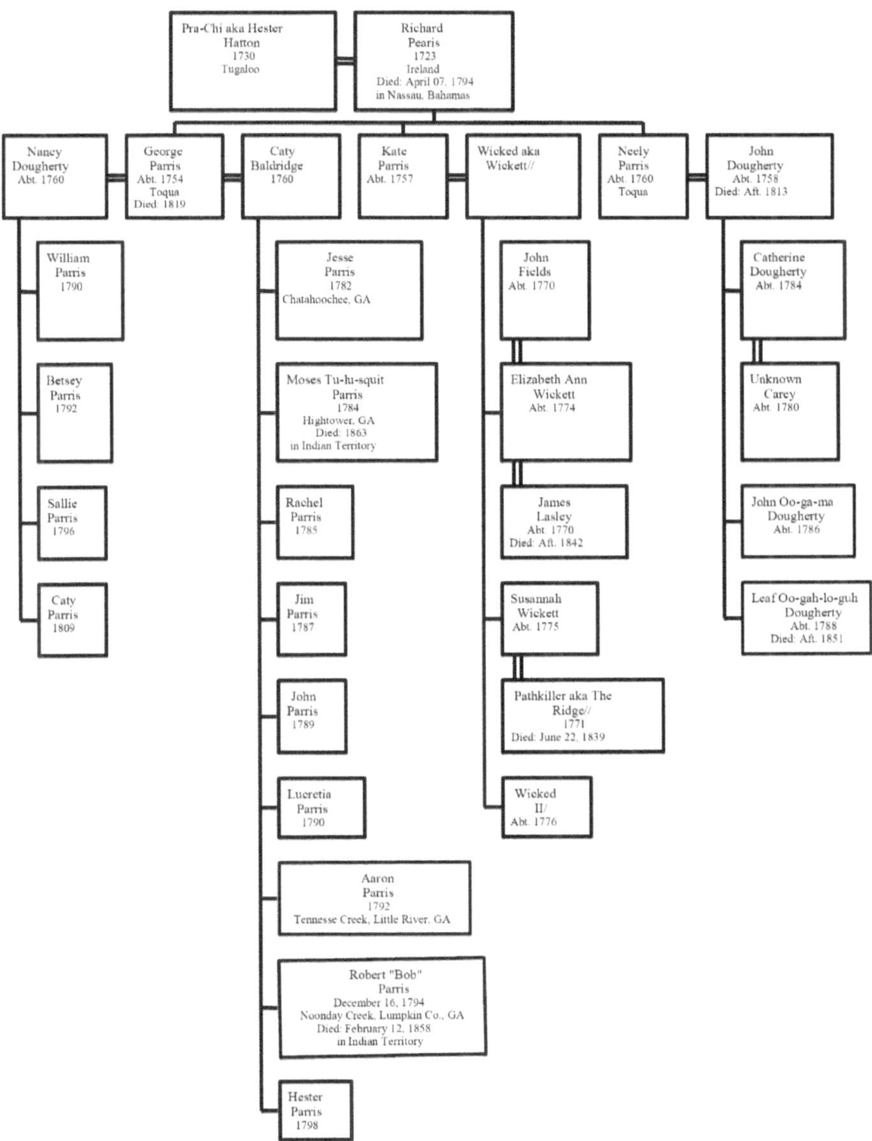

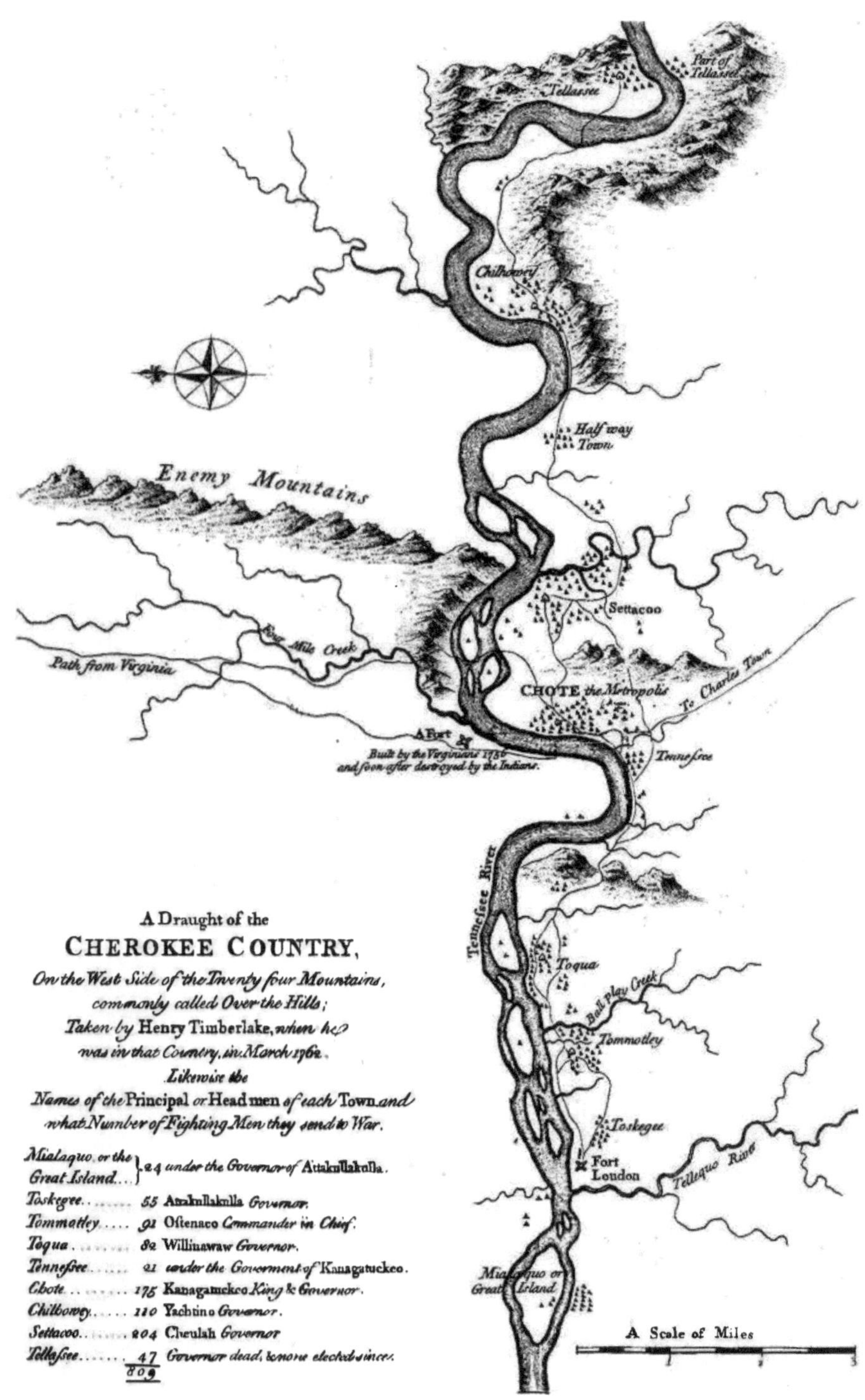

Part of
Tellassee
Tellassee
Chilhowey
Half way
Town
Settacoo
Enemy Mountains
Path from Virginia
Five Mile Creek
CHOTE the Metropolis
To Charles Town
A Fort
Built by the Virginians 1756
and soon after destroyed by the Indians.
Tennessee
Tennessee River
Toqua
Ball play Creek
Tommotley
Toskegee
Fort
Loudon
Tellequo River
Mialaquo or
Great Island
A Scale of Miles
A Draught of the
CHEROKEE COUNTRY,
On the West Side of the Twenty four Mountains,
commonly called Over the Hills;
Taken by Henry Timberlake, when he
was in that Country, in March 1762.
Likewise the
Names of the Principal or Head men of each Town and
what Number of Fighting Men they send to War.
Mialaquo, or the
Great Island... 24 under the Governor of Attakullakulla.
Toskegee........ 55 Attakullakulla Governor.
Tommotley..... 91 Ostenaco Commander in Chief.
Toqua... 82 Willinawaw Governor.
Tennessee...... 21 under the Government of Kanagatuckee.
Chote......... 175 Kanagatuckee King & Governor.
Chilhowey...... 110 Yachtino Governor.
Settacoo........ 204 Cheulah Governor
Tellassee....... 47 Governor dead, & none elected since.
809

The Delegation Of Cherokee Chiefs Who Visited London In 1730
Isaac Basire, engraver, "The Seven Cherokee,"
1730, public domain image.

Oconostota,
Cherokee chief
(1708-1810),
from a painting entitled
"The Great Warrior, Chief
Oconostota-Cunne Shote"
by Francis Parsons, 1762.

Richard Pearis representation at Upcountry
History Museum in Greenville, South Carolina.

My granddaughters, Carley Cate, Audrey Cate, Elizabeth Kelly, and Sarah Kelly along with the life-size representation of Richard Pearis at the Upcountry History Museum in Greenville South Carolina, July 29, 2011.

Preface

While researching my ancestry, I discovered my seven-times great-grand-father, Richard Pearis, who emigrated to the American colonies around 1730. Extensive records detail Richard's westward quest for fame and fortune. He became a trader, transporting goods to the Cherokee Nation deep in the Smoky Mountains. A skilled linguist, he was a trusted interpreter and accompanied Cherokee warriors during treaty negotiations and battles. Although he had a wife and family in Winchester, VA, Richard formed a relationship with a woman likely to be the daughter of a Scottish trader and a Cherokee woman—a "mixed blood." Hester bore him two daughters and a son. I am a descendant of their son, George and their grandson, Robert.

I was captivated by this man who led a remarkable life of adventure and perseverance. Driven to share his story, I immersed myself in obscure books and manuscripts and visited ancestral sites. However, the more I learned about him, the more I realized the profound changes that took place within the Cherokee Nation during the pivotal eighteenth century.

I became fascinated by the mysterious woman—my seven times great-grandmother—who shared his extraordinary life during those turbulent times. There are only a few brief references to her in all the materials concerning Richard, as Native women were viewed as insignificant and invisible.

The historical novel I intended to write about Richard Pearis must be postponed. Hester insists she has waited long enough and demands that her life story be told: a chronicle of the Cherokee Nation's transition from a matriarchal subsistence culture to a patriarchal market-based social system.

Thus, *Mixed Blood* tells the imagined story of an ordinary woman living in extraordinary times. Her narrative unfolds across two timelines: as an elderly woman residing with her son's family, who have adapted to survive in a White man's world, and through the stories she shares with her grandchildren. Like women everywhere, her focus is on community and family. She is determined that her grandchildren know their rich heritage —that the Cherokee Nation survived against unimaginable odds. Most characters in this novel are real individuals who lived and breathed, and the significant events are factual. This is Hester's story, as she may have lived it.

Prologue

A suppressed scream jolts me awake—my fist covers my mouth, attempting to stifle the rising bubble of fear in my chest. Drenched coverings are tangled at my feet as my legs had churned through the night, fleeing from my pursuers. My heart pounds, and I tremble with fear. The acrid smell of dread and sweat stings my nose.

I must remain silent. I must not be seen.

It happened again. Memories I try to push from my mind have resurfaced during the night. Sometimes, my pursuers are clad only in loincloths, their bare chests painted red and black. Other times, they may wear white trousers, while their coats are scarlet red—the color of blood. They might be dressed in belted cotton shirts with knives strapped to their waists. No matter if they are natives, British soldiers, or colonists, they all have faces filled with bloodlust.

I must remain silent. I must not be seen.

Sometimes, in my sleep, I cower in a confined space, the overwhelming smell of dried corn suffocating me. My hands pressed against my ears do not mute the sound of terrified screams and battle cries. Dust motes dance in the dim light. I feel a strong urge to sneeze.

I must remain silent. I must not be seen.

At other times, I run through a wooded area, brambles snagging at my legs as my eyes search for a safe hiding place. I bear the weight of a child I must protect, and the stench of burning buildings and charred flesh urges me to run faster.

I must be silent. I must not be seen.

In my nighttime memories, I may be seated in a dimly lit, smoky room where men talk and determine the fate of those I cherish—my family, my Clan, and the entire Cherokee Nation. I have much to say, but I swallow my words.

I must be silent. I must not be seen.

At other times, I find myself in a crude shelter made of branches, sticks, and brush. We have few coverings to block winter's cold. My stomach growls with hunger. My children remain silent, their eyes wide with fear, and I know their bellies ache with emptiness. I listen, startled by the slightest sound, waiting and fearing what might come from the forest.

I must be silent. I must not be seen.

CHAPTER I

Across Time and Space

November 7, 1794
66 years old
Noonday Creek, GA

My beloved Richard came to me last night, though I slept soundly in my little cabin tucked among the pines surrounding our son George's house. The whispered sound of my name awakened me: *Hester, darling Hester*. There was no one but me snuggled in my bed with thick, hand-stitched patchwork quilts keeping the cold at bay. The fire had burned down to coals, still emitting a steady heat and providing dim light. I listened intently as my heartbeat slowed, not realizing I was holding my breath until I finally inhaled, the cold air burning my lungs. It comes to me that I knew what had awakened me, the one who had called my name in the night: a knowing across time and space that Richard had gone to the Spirit World.

Is Richard Pearis dead? Yes, I know this is true. He died while with his White family on that distant island of his exile. We said our goodbyes when we last lay together, my husband and I, knowing we would never be together again. My aged warrior, weary from the harrowing journey to our remote mountains, held me in his arms throughout that night, talking almost non-stop and telling me about his life since the last time we were together.

Somehow, it seemed to ease the burdens on his soul, this telling of his travails and disappointments—the grief, the voicing of his anger. And, it was fitting that I held him close, taking some of the pain from him, for he and I have a long history, this bedeviled White man and I, a mixed blood Cherokee woman.

Finally, he slept deeply toward dawn and then arose at daybreak, moving quietly about the cabin to not wake me. I kept my eyes closed, breathing easily, pretending to sleep. He knew, of course, that I was awake, for we had frequently played this little pretense to soften the pain of our parting. He was leaving me yet again, returning, as he always did, to his life as an important man in the cities built by men of his race. He was returning once again to his other wife, his European wife, and the family he had made with her, turning his back on me and our mixed blood children and grandchildren, and the life he loved in these beautiful mountains.

When I heard the door close behind him, I rolled to his side of the bed, inhaling deeply, capturing his scent. And then I allowed the tears to flow, easing some of my sorrow, for I knew even then that I would never see my beloved again.

Weeks after I last felt his touch, I sensed Richard's presence in the predawn. His spirit comforts me with the knowledge that he has begun his journey to the Spirit World, and I am to grieve no more, for he is finally at peace.

CHAPTER 2

The Circle of Life

December 16, 1794
66 years old
Noonday Creek, GA

It was no surprise to receive a message from the Bahamas yesterday informing us that Richard Pearis is no longer with us. I have reflected on his death these past weeks, and it was a relief when the messenger finally arrived. Then, long after the expected time and amid the family's mourning, our grandchild chose to leave the shelter of his mother's body. I was reminded that life goes on.

Caty's pains came upon her quickly, and we barely had enough time to prepare. He came eagerly into the world, this little man, crying lustily as his head emerged from the safety of his mother's womb. I knelt between my daughter-in-law's bent knees, encouraging her to push, and she did, thrusting his slick little body into my waiting hands. We laughed at the sight of such a healthy man-child making his presence known as he flailed his arms and legs, seeking the warmth and security he had just left. I wrapped him snugly in a clean blanket and placed him in Caty's outstretched arms. She held him close, and within a heartbeat, his searching mouth clamped down on her breast, quieting his cries.

I sensed Richard's presence at our grandchild's birth and knew he was pleased.

The baby's European name is Robert, but his Cherokee name is Turtle. This name suits the cautious child who waited to enter the world until he felt it was safe, first pushing his head forward from his long neck and then announcing his arrival with a loud cry. This name better reflects this little mixed blood whose birth closely coincided with the death of his grandfather.

Made weary by Caty's labor, I bade the family goodnight and sought the quiet sanctuary of the rocking chair on my cabin's porch. Turtle's birth reminded me that my remaining days are few. Soon enough, I will embark on my journey to the Spirit World. I feel restless— beset by worries for all my grandchildren.

Not so long ago, I was a baby suckling at my mother's breast. Suddenly, it seems, I have become an old woman. The world has turned upside down since my childhood. Little Turtle's life will be vastly different from mine.

When I was just a babe like this newest grandchild, the People lived in communal villages beside beautiful rivers in the mystical Blue Mountains. But in my lifetime, we have had to adapt to European ways and live on separate farms to survive. We must send our children to missionary schools to learn to speak English, even though their language is not as beautiful as ours and does not flow as easily from the tongue. The children must learn to read the talking leaves and write the words for others to read. They need to learn the magical counting symbols and how their sums always benefit the Europeans. But the price for that knowledge is having their heads filled with Christian nonsense.

The missionaries preach to them about the defeat of the heathen Cherokee and the supremacy of White people, making my grandchildren feel inferior. A deep sadness washes over me as I realize these children are unaware of the richness of their heritage.

I tamp a wad of tobacco into my pipe and rise from my chair to light a brand from the candle before extinguishing its flame. Then, inhaling deeply, I touch the brand's tip to the pipe bowl and feel the acrid smoke fill my lungs.

I wonder what the little ones know about their grandfather, my beloved Richard, and my father, Will Hatton, a Scotsman who was one of the first traders to settle with the Cherokee. The blood of the greatest leaders of the proud Cherokee Nation flows through their veins from my own mother. And though they have surely heard the names of her kinsmen, what do they truly understand about them? Do my grandchildren comprehend their noble heritage? What do they know of Old Hop, Attacullaculla, Oconostota, Dragging Canoe, and Willewanah—leaders and warriors of the Real People, as we called ourselves before the Europeans arrived?

In the old days, this knowledge was passed on when elders entertained children with tales of our People. However, due to disease and displacement, storytelling seldom happens today.

Rocking back and forth in the dark, I am barely aware that the lanterns in the big house have been extinguished. All is quiet, blanketed by the hush of a sleeping family. The night has grown chilly, and I pull the shawl across my arms, feeling the rough texture against my goosebumped skin. I feel tired but not quite ready for sleep.

My troubling thoughts gnaw at me like a dog with a bone. I rock slowly throughout the night, occasionally puffing on my pipe and recalling how tobacco was used ceremonially in the past. The burning tobacco—or fire held in the mouth—is an extension of the sacred fire that symbolizes the sun and life itself. The swirling smoke carries our thoughts upward toward the Spirit World.

Deep in thought, my gaze follows the spiraling plume of smoke toward the brilliant stars twinkling in the night sky, enhanced by dim moonlight.

Recalling my journeys to the edge of the Spirit World as a young woman, I clear my mind of burdens and focus on a single luminous star along with my rhythmic breathing. With my body relaxed and distractions forgotten, I sense the inward opening that permits passage to that other realm. I embrace the peace that comes with it.

In that veiled openness between worlds, I become aware of the presence of others—shadowy forms that seem vaguely familiar. I know I am in the presence of ancestors who lived their earthly lives before me and have passed to the other side—to the Spirit World. Without spoken words in the usual sense, we communicate. One by one, they make themselves known and speak to me. *Tell our story*! *Tell our story*!

I am overwhelmed with emotion, tears streaming down my face. Exhausted, I drift into a deep sleep. When I wake, the shawl no longer protects me from the cold night air, leaving me chilled to the bone. At first, I am disoriented, and I try to find my bearings. Eventually, I realize I have fallen asleep in my rocking chair, and it is the dark, cold hour before the dawn of a new day. My neck is stiff and painful from awkwardly leaning to the side. I struggle to get up, and my body protests with stiffness.

I shuffle into bed, welcoming the warmth of last winter's down comforter pulled snugly to my chin. And then I remember the ancestors and their message to me.

Tell our story, they had pleaded. *Tell our story*.

At this moment, I realize what I must do. I offer a silent vow to the ancestors to become a bridge between generations. I am among the few remaining who were born in my time, a generation that spans the arrival of Europeans and the near destruction of our People. My destiny is to teach those who follow about their rich heritage and instill pride in their forebears' legacy. Also, among the first European men who joined with us, we forged a new breed that was not entirely of one race but rather a blending of the best of both—a mixture of bloodlines.

I pledge to my ancestors that I will spend the rest of my days surrounded by young people. I will share what I know of those who came before, ensuring they are not forgotten in the mists of time.

CHAPTER 3

The Trading Post

Early Spring 1734
6 years old
Tugaloo Town

My earliest remembrance is of my father's trading post at Tugaloo Town, where the Chattahoochee begins its journey through the shimmering Blue Mountains. It was the southernmost Cherokee town, located near what is now the meeting place of the imaginary lines marking the borders of Georgia, North Carolina, and South Carolina. Tugaloo was ideally situated on a major trading path that connected the valley and villages over the mountains with the White settlements along the coast. When relations between the Nations were harmonious, our town often served as the meeting place for the neighboring Creek Nation.

A redheaded, burly-chested Scotsman, my father, William Hatton, was among the first adventurous European men to venture into the mountainous homeland of the People. As a young man, he set out on the trade route from Charles Town, a burgeoning port on the South Carolina coast, guiding a train of Natives burdened with trade goods across the mountains deep into Cherokee territory. Back then, trade goods mainly included cloth, beads, shoes, axes, kettles, knives, salt, flint, powder, bullets, and rum.

After traveling from village to village, he would return to Charles Town, the burdeners heavily laden with deerskin and pelts to be transferred to waiting ships bound across the Great Water for nations in the Middle East and Europe. I remember him saying that sometimes goods were traded for captives taken by warring tribes to be sold as slaves on Caribbean sugar plantations, a practice he disliked.

As the volume of trade increased and became more profitable, my father established one of the first permanent trading posts with packhorses replacing the burdeners. Seldom returning to the clangorous city, my father lived among the Cherokee year-round, becoming a trusted friend and adopting many of our traditions. He gained a reputation as an honest man who did not lie and cheat like some traders.

My father was well into middle age when he fell hopelessly in love with a beautiful young Cherokee girl named Cricket, the eldest daughter of the Headman of Estatoe Town. He had been vaguely aware of her growing up, not knowing that she had chosen him as her mate when she was little more than a child. Once my mother reached maturity and set about ensnaring him in earnest, people watched, amused, as she entangled him, knowing he didn't stand a chance.

I remember little of my mother except for the warmth of her careworn hands and the softness of her lap as she soothed a childish hurt. The shape of her face is forever lost to me, though I have tried to recall it many times. Sometimes, I study the faces of my children and grandchildren, searching for a resemblance—a clue that might trigger long-buried memories—but to no avail.

She had long, glossy black hair, which hung nearly to her waist and swung with her movements. But when memories of her hair come to mind, I have learned to quickly push them aside, for they are too painful and still bring tears to my eyes, even after all these years.

Cricket quickly bore several children, and the rooms behind the post overflowed. However, she and my father watched helplessly one winter as the spotted sickness swept through the town like a brush fire, snuffing out lives despite the potions and incantations of our medicine man. The People had no defense against this strange illness known as smallpox. One by one, villagers fell ill and rapidly died. The loss to my parents was immense: all their children except for my brother Johnny were buried on the hillside behind my father's trading post.

I am sure it was a great joy for them when my mother once again felt the flutter of new life in her womb. I was born while her grief was still a raw wound, and she loved me with a fierceness that bore a sharp edge of fear—the fear of losing me as she had lost her other children. She kept me close by her side, never letting me out of her sight, carrying me on her hip long after I should have been running off on my own. I must have wanted for nothing, as my parents and my older brother catered to my every whim.

Our father used to tell my brother and me that he had become more Cherokee than we, a boast that never failed to reduce us to peals of laughter. True, he dressed in buckskin and broadcloth like our kinfolk, but his shock of bright red, curly hair could not have been more different from our glossy black locks. His round face, fringed with a fulsome beard that competed for attention with the hairs on his head, stood in stark contrast to our warriors with high cheekbones and smooth, beardless faces. Naked, his sun-starved backside was as white as winter snow, and we would cover our eyes, pretending to be blinded by the glare. But, the most incredible difference that never failed to impress us was the pelt of hair that grew upon his body, pinkish red and curling, covering him from head to toe.

More Cherokee than us, indeed! For he was a Scotsman, Presbyterian born and bred, and as much as we loved him, we took pride in knowing that we were truly Cherokee.

A practical man, he understood our vulnerability because the borderlands we inhabited often faced conflict. As a result, he had the woods cleared for some distance around the trading post, positioning it in the center of a large meadow while remaining within shouting distance of the enclosure surrounding Tugaloo.

Built of sturdy pine logs, the large storeroom was dark and mysterious, its shelves burdened with trade goods. The few windows opened with shutters that could be securely closed and latched. Strategically placed openings from which a musket could be fired made it a virtual fortress which a handful of men could defend.

A cast iron stove, a rare novelty transported in pieces from Charles Town, sat in the middle of the storeroom. Sitting beside it, he would warm himself in the wintertime. At the rear of the store was the door leading to our living quarters, two rooms with a loft above. The hearth in the main room was the heart of our home, where we often gathered for meals or storytelling.

A barn, smokehouse, slave quarters, corncrib, and other outbuildings clustered around the post, for our home was as much a farm as a trading post. My father kept a few Negro slaves to cultivate the fields and tend the livestock he had imported from the coastal cities. The Indian Commissioner frequently sent letters upbraiding him for having slaves, as he did so in breach of South Carolina law at that time. But Will merely bellowed that he was bedamned if he would till the fields himself. Then he would toss the parchment into the cast iron stove, slamming the door shut with a satisfactory bang that made it bounce on its delicately curved legs.

It is with a heavy heart that I recall my father and Johnny were away on an inland trading venture when a party of Creek warriors raided our town.

CHAPTER 4

Massacre at Tugaloo

Early Spring 1734
6 years old
Tugaloo Town

My mother and I were returning from Tugaloo, crossing the meadow to the trading post a few days after Father and Johnny had left. It was a lovely afternoon, bright with sunshine and smelling fresh after the spring rain that morning. We stopped to admire some wildflowers that had burst into bloom. A butterfly fluttered from one blossom to another, captivating me. My mother laughed at my antics as I tried to catch the delicate creature in my childish hands, but the butterfly continued on its mission, paying no attention to a lively little girl of six winters.

Suddenly, we heard the bloodthirsty war whoops of Creek warriors as they descended upon the town. Gunfire, followed by screams and cries of pain and rage, pierced our ears.

My mother scooped me up into her arms and ran for the safety of the trading post. Clutching me tightly, with my legs wrapped around her waist, she ran as fast as she could. Her calico skirts twisted and hindered her stride.

I hung on tight, feeling her heart pound and smelling the scent of fear, my bottom bouncing on the little mound that was the new life within her womb. Looking over her shoulder, I saw a Creek warrior swing his war club, smashing it into one of our Cherokee defenders' skulls. He fell, the back of his head crushed like an overripe pumpkin.

The warrior paused, sweat glistening on his muscular chest. He spotted my mother just as she cleared the meadow approaching our trading post, safety within reach.

Her steps faltered and slowed as she gasped for air, my weight dragging at her arms. Her strength was fading. The warrior's teeth flashed as he threw back his head, unleashing a piercing war cry while charging after us. My mother held me even tighter, surging forward with renewed energy. But it was too late. The Creek swiftly closed the gap, raised his war club, and brought it down onto my mother's skull.

I will never forget the sickening sound of crushed bone as my mother collapsed in a heap, shielding my body with her own as she died. The warrior stood over us, looking at me appraisingly, perhaps deciding whether I was old enough for the slave market. If not, it would be best to kill me too. His indecision cost him his life and spared mine.

In the seconds it took him to decide and then to raise his war club again, an arrow from a Cherokee warrior found its mark, piercing his chest. He grunted in surprise. His war club dropped to the earth, and the light left his eyes as he fell, his body covering my mother and me, his blood mingling with hers.

Mercifully, I lost consciousness. When I regained my senses, I first became aware of the stickiness of drying blood on my face and arms and then of the weight of their bodies on mine. The battle was over. The Creeks were victorious. The town was in flames. Turning my head, I could see that familiar villagers had been taken prisoner, tied to one another. Among them were the surviving slaves from our household. The stench of blood and death was overpowering, and I swallowed the bile that rose in my throat.

Creek warriors emptied my father's store, loading goods and furs upon their horses. Some moved among the dead and wounded, finishing those Cherokee who still held a breath of life by sinking war clubs into their skulls. The few dead Creeks were tied onto horses to be carried away and buried properly, but the dead villagers and slaves were left as they had fallen.

I must have looked as if I were dead, lying motionless in my faint, covered in blood and brains. But as they approached me, it became clear that they would soon realize I was still alive.

I swallowed a scream of panic. My eyes searched wildly for an escape route; the weight of my dead mother and the warrior suddenly felt more than I could bear. They darted past and then returned to meet those of Hannah, the old slave woman who had helped my mother with household chores. Our eyes locked, and the intensity of her look calmed my panic. Her hands were bound behind her, but she pursed her lips into the familiar "shhh" shape she and my mother had used to quiet me when I became cranky or noisy.

I lay still, not knowing what I should do. Then Hannah jerked her head to her right, staring intently at me. Confused, I questioned her with my eyes. She closed hers, despair etched on her face. She glared at me with renewed determination and jerked her head to the right again. This time, my gaze followed her direction, and I saw the corncrib a short distance away, its door slightly ajar. Comprehension dawned. I looked back at her, my eyes bright with hope.

"Get ready!" she mouthed. Then, being the brave old soul she was, she screamed obscenities at the Creek warriors approaching my direction, causing them to turn away from me.

In the moments she held their attention while they brutally snuffed out her life, I managed to free myself, half running and half crawling to the small storage building. It was elevated off the ground, chest-high for a child like me. I struggled to get my knee up, thrusting my body into its darkness, and pulled the door closed behind me. Then, safe for the moment, I lay quietly as the Creeks celebrated the murder of Hannah, who had sacrificed her life for mine.

Carefully, slowly, I crawled to the darkest recess of the corncrib and burrowed in until only my head was exposed. The walls were made of wide wooden slats spaced three fingerbreadths apart, giving me a full view of the yard in front of our trading post.

Sobbing quietly into my clenched fists, I watched the Creek warriors finish sacking the trading post, trying to avoid looking at my mother's body lying directly in front of me. They found the liquor stores and quickly became intoxicated despite their leaders' warnings. My father's rum saved my life; drunk as they were, they were not as thorough as they might have been.

With a whoop, one of the warriors dashed from the town with a firebrand and, leaping high in the air, hurled it onto the roof of the trading post. Others quickly joined him, turning the burning of the sturdy building into a great sport until it was fully engulfed in flames, with sparks flying. The heat from its destruction was intense, and I feared I would suffocate in the corncrib. However, the trading post completely absorbed their attention, leaving the insignificant corncrib and other outbuildings of the farm standing, thus saving me from roasting as if in an oven.

My terror was so complete that I feared they could hear the thudding of my heart or my muffled sobs as I buried myself deeper into the ears of corn, the dry husks scratching my skin.

I watched helplessly as one of the intoxicated warriors pulled his knife from its sheath and swooped upon my mother's body. With a war whoop, he swiftly removed her beautiful hair. Then, clenching the bloody knife in his teeth and swinging her scalp in an arc above him, he danced around her body, chanting a victory song.

His companions stopped what they were doing to watch and laugh with him. There was some talk among them, with much gesturing and some disagreement. Others moved from body to body, scalping the Cherokee as they went. Hannah was mercifully spared; her nappy head was not a suitable trophy for the warriors.

With their dirty work complete, the Creek warriors gathered the captives and prepared to depart. The Cherokees' hands were bound behind their backs, and they were tied to one another, forming a chain of pain and misery. Tears streamed down my blood-smeared cheeks. Furtive glances toward the corncrib suggested that some had witnessed Hannah's heroism and knew my location. Their encouraging expressions conveyed their hope that I, at the very least, would survive this outrage.

Finally, the Creeks departed, taking their loot and captives with them. Then, it grew suddenly quiet—deathly quiet. The only sound was the crackling and hissing of burning buildings in the damp early evening, with the stench assaulting my nose.

I am unsure how long I stayed in that corncrib, as I lost all sense of time. I remember sharing the space with field mice that woke me by nibbling on the pieces of bone and brain that had dried in my hair. I gasped and brushed them away, suddenly awake but unafraid of those little creatures. It was the two-legged ones I feared. The fear of them returning kept me huddled in the safety of the corncrib.

The next day, a blazing hot noontime caused the temperature inside the tiny building to rise until I thought I would surely die from it. I became hungry and thirsty but was too frightened to leave my sanctuary. I must have lost consciousness again, for the next thing I knew, it was fully dark. Only then did I leave, cautiously opening the door and crawling out. My legs were so weak that I could scarcely walk to the spring, where I quenched my thirst and fell asleep, resting my cheek on the cool grass that lined its edge.

I woke with the dawn and, gripped once again by the fear of returning marauders, made my way to the safety of the corncrib. I carefully avoided my mother's body, still lying in a heap in our yard, now giving off a peculiar stench. Her scalp glistened in the early light. The buzzing of flies disrupted the otherwise quiet yard.

And yet another day passed, or perhaps several for all I know, as I huddled in the corncrib. At times, wild animals and vultures came to feast on the bodies. I left my safe haven just long enough to throw ears of corn at those ravaging my mother's body until, discouraged, they moved on. I could not muffle the horrible sounds of their gorging on the villagers, even with my fingers stuffed tight in my ears. When they were finally done, what remained of poor Hannah's body was recognizable only by the dress she had worn.

And yet, I stayed. I did not know where to go, even if I thought about leaving, so I waited for something I could not name.

I just knew I could not leave my mother or my slat-walled shelter.

CHAPTER 5

Rescue from the Corncrib

Early Spring 1734
6 years old
Tugaloo Town

A bellowing roar and a wail of heartbreaking anguish roused me from a deep stupor. Looking through the slats of my refuge, I saw that my father and brother had arrived. Men leading horses loaded with goods were milling around them, their faces contorted with horror at the grisly scene before them.

My father dismounted his horse slowly, visibly shocked—stunned by the horrifying sight before him. His beloved wife lay dead and mutilated, his prosperous trading post reduced to smoldering rubble, and Tugaloo Town in ruins. He screamed in impotent rage as Johnny wailed in confusion and anguish.

I knew there was safety with my father, but I could not gather the strength to leave the corncrib. Weak from hunger and thirst and drained from my vigil, I found it impossible to go to him. The men began digging graves and gathering the remains of the deceased villagers and slaves for burial while my father sat numbly on the stone steps that had once led into his home. The cast iron stove stood as a silent sentinel amid the smoldering ruins of the trading post.

Johnny saw me first as I cautiously opened the corncrib door and poked my head out from its confines. He screamed in fear, pointing, and my father leaped to his feet, staring at the apparition that was his daughter. What a sight I must have been, still wearing the blood of the warrior who had slain my mother—and hers—my face streaked with their blood and my snot and tears, my hair stiff with the filth that had been my mother's brains.

Recognition came slowly to my father's eyes, and when it finally did, he was incredulous, having believed I was either dead or captured by the Creeks. He closed the distance between us in great strides, scooping me into his arms and holding me in an embrace that took my breath away. Sobbing uncontrollably, the great bear of a man wept with relief at the sight of his baby girl still alive.

I would not leave my father's side. Deep anger controlled him now as he set aside his grief and pain momentarily. All his movements were done with me wrapped around his leg, hanging on for dear life, or clinging to his hip, for I would not be parted from him, nor he from me. Johnny kept us constantly in sight, never far from what remained of his family, his young face tear-streaked, chin jutting in anger.

Finally, the men rested in the cool shade beside the spring, eating the food they had brought or scavenged from the ruins. My father fed me like an infant, offering small bites and sips of refreshing spring water. I was so weak that I could not chew properly. He took food into his mouth, chewed it until it was soft enough for me, and then pushed it into my mouth with his thick, callused fingers, gently encouraging me to chew and swallow. Somehow, I managed to please him; there was only a deep emptiness where there had once been an aching hunger.

He rested against an oak tree with me cradled in his arms, and I closed my eyes. His heartbeat against my ear lulled me into a contented sleep. I dozed intermittently, comforted by the rumble of his deep voice as he and the men made plans.

They knew the Creek warriors had a few days' head start on them, but the tracks revealed signs of captives and heavily loaded horses that would slow them down. The Cherokee who accompanied my father were eager to pursue the Creeks. They believed they could cover ground quickly and were determined to rescue their kinsmen.

The Cherokee were enraged because they knew the fate that awaited the captives. Somehow, word had reached our mountain home, and they knew that captured Natives were often transported to Caribbean sugar plantations, where they spent the rest of their short lives in unimaginable misery as slaves.

My father was furious about the mutilation inflicted upon my mother. The French had placed a bounty on Native scalps while waging war against the northern tribes. They referred to them as "redskins"—those gruesome trophies for which they paid as they would for beaver pelts or deerskins. Their Native allies received the same payment for any scalp, regardless of its origin, because the French could neither tell the difference nor did they care. Whether it was a young warrior, an old woman, a revered leader, or a defenseless child, the price remained constant for a redskin. Thus, my mother's scalp, adorned with the long black hair my father had lovingly caressed at night, would be worn on the belt of a Creek warrior, traded among them, and eventually make its way north to be sold to a Frenchman for the price of a jug of rum.

My father's voice quaked with rage as he vowed to track down the Creek who had taken it from her—to kill him as slowly and painfully as possible. Then, he said, he would return and bury the scalp beside my mother's grave.

My father and his companions shared a common purpose; they were eager to catch up with the Creek warriors and exact their revenge. However, there was one small problem: the child nestled safely in her father's arms.

Their dilemma was complex: They could not overtake the Creeks if they took me with them, yet they could not leave me alone in the ruins of

Tugaloo. On the other hand, if they took me to safety, they would lose valuable time and be unable to catch up with the Creeks. What to do? I stirred against my father, snuggling closer, not fully understanding the problem but somehow knowing I was the cause.

Finally, a solution was found. My brother Johnny would take me to the safety of our mother's brother in the nearby village of Estatoe. Considering himself a man, although he was a few years shy of such, Johnny protested loudly but to no avail. My father was satisfied with this plan. Although the journey from Tugaloo to Estatoe was fraught with danger for two youngsters traveling alone, it not only took care of the issue of what to do with me but also removed Johnny from the coming bloodshed. Will had lost too much already and must have been relieved that his remaining family would be relatively safe. Johnny's wails and protests did him no good. My father turned a deaf ear, and preparations were quickly made to avoid wasting more time.

Johnny mounted a trustworthy horse with the few provisions we needed tied behind him. I clung to my father and cried out as he tried to lift me into my brother's arms. Finally, he had to pry his arm from my grip as one of the Cherokee warriors pulled me away from him, lifting me high and settling me on the horse in front of Johnny.

"It'll be awright, Hester," my father soothed me, "I will come for ye and Johnny in a fortnight." He was not ashamed to wipe tears from his eyes with his buckskin sleeve as Johnny took the reins and signaled the horse to move onto the path leading toward the north. I clung to Johnny, watching my father as long as I could until the trail dipped into the forest, obscuring him from view.

Avoiding the main trading path, Johnny guided our mount along lesser-known footpaths and game trails. Sometimes, the route through the dark forest was so faint that we had to dismount. While holding the reins firmly in his grasp, Johnny would search the dense undergrowth for the barely noticeable trail. Other times, it was so narrow that we had to make ourselves as small as possible, with the sturdy horse forcing her way through a path intended for much smaller creatures.

Finally, we came across the familiar sight of Estatoe Town. Overcome with relief and fatigue, Johnny relaxed his grip on the reins. The horse knew her way to the Council House. Nearby was the home of Mourning Dove, where our mother's brother, Saluy, lived with his wife.

Shocked at the sight of us, Mourning Dove pried me from Johnny's arms and took me into her house. There, she stripped me of the clothes that still bore such an awful burden. Heating a kettle of water, she wrapped me in a soft deerskin and sat with me cradled in her arms, crooning softly and rocking back and forth to quiet my sobs.

She stood me before her and washed my body in warm, sudsy water, cleansing me of the filth that caked my skin and my hair, carefully scrubbing off the dried gore. She wrapped me in a soft trade blanket and laid me upon her sleeping pallet while she disposed of that foul water far from the cabin. Then, filling the tub with fresh water, she cleansed me again, this time with scented soap that left my skin feeling clean and soft.

Someone had brought clothes for me, and Mourning Dove dressed me gently like a newborn. Then, placing me between her legs, she brushed my hair, picking out the debris that still clung to its strands. The fire crackled in the fireplace, and her humming soothed me as she spooned warm broth into my waiting mouth, my chin tilted up like a young bird in its nest. Finally, my eyes grew heavy, and exhaustion overcame me as she lifted me and carried me to her bed, where I fell into a healing sleep.

Chapter 6

Prachey

Early Spring 1734
6 years old
Estatoe Town

Johnny and I stayed at Estatoe until our father arrived for us as promised, his face grim and his expression determined. The Creeks had lingered too long. Feeling the effects of my father's rum and weighed down by their loot and captives, they believed they were safe from retribution, which caused them to move too slowly. The swiftly advancing, vengeful Cherokee overtook them, catching them by surprise at camp, killing those who couldn't escape into the woods, and freeing the captives.

A council was called for the following evening. Messengers were dispatched to nearby villages to announce that my father, Will Hatton, would recount the Tugaloo massacre.

The huge conical Council House stood as an imposing structure on a prominent site in the heart of Estatoe Town. At its center, a sacred fire burned, fueled by seven different types of wood representing the seven clans of the Cherokee. Stripped of bark, the wood burned cleanly, emitting only a faint smoke that billowed lazily through the smoke hole.

In the clearing around the sacred fire sat the Head Man of Estatoe, his councilors, Saluy, the Young Warrior of Estatoe, and Will Hatton. Seven tiers of hewn logs rose up the bowl-shaped interior, one for each of the seven clans. Mourning Dove took my hand, leading me to a place of honor in the front row of the Paint Clan's section. She then joined her own clan in a different section of the Council House.

My father was a skilled orator, and after the usual preliminary ceremonies, he vividly described what he had found upon his return to Tugaloo.

Furtive glances toward me and clucks of dismay and sympathy punctuated the report of his little daughter emerging from the corncrib. Grunts of approval accompanied his recounting of the Creeks being overtaken, the Cherokee's revenge, and the freeing of the captives.

Traditionally, our mother's clan took responsibility for her children instead of her husband. As members of the Paint Clan, Johnny and I had extended family throughout the Cherokee Nation, any of whom would have cared for us in our mother's absence.

It was decided that Johnny would stay in Estatoe with Saluy. In Cherokee tradition, a mother's closest male relative provides guidance and discipline for her sons as they grow into adulthood. Our father could take an interest and be involved if he chose, but the responsibility was not his—it lay with Johnny's uncle, Saluy. As pragmatic people, we Cherokee understand that while husbands and lovers may come and go, a woman's male relatives will always be part of her life.

Once again, the question of what to do with me presented the most significant dilemma. Saluy and Mourning Dove also wanted to adopt me into their home. Mourning Dove pleaded not to separate Johnny and me but to let both of us make Estatoe our home. It was a familiar house, filled with fond memories, and would be a good place for us to live. However, my mother had two sisters who also wanted to take me into their homes. Additionally, Mourning Dove was not part of our clan.

Cornsilk was the obvious choice because she and my mother had always been very close. Wurth, Cornsilk's daughter, and I already shared a sisterly bond. Even though I was three moons older, we were the same size and resembled twins. We formed a close connection as constant companions during our frequent visits to each other's towns. As babies, we nursed from either of the sisters who were our mothers. It was not unusual for one of our mothers to breastfeed both of us, our naked bodies entangled in her lap, our hands clasped as we each suckled at a breast. Cornsilk's second daughter, baby Willow, became a welcome addition to our sisterhood. Not quite a year old, she was starting to toddle from one supporting hand to another, chortling in delight at her newfound independence.

Quatsis, my mother's younger sister, married Oconostota, the Young Warrior of Chota. Two moons ago, messengers reported that their first child was stillborn. Cornsilk's home was filled with healthy children, while her sister Quatsis's arms ached for a child to nurture.

The elders of my clan decided that Quatsis' home was a better option after considering my best interests.

Will Hatton was, I think, relieved that he was not expected to provide care for his children. His wife was dead, and his Tugaloo trading post and home burned to the ground. The responsibility of parenting a half-grown son and a young daughter must have felt like an overwhelming burden for the aging White trader.

So, once again, I found myself lifted into the arms of a waiting horseman. This time, it was my father who cradled me in front of him as we journeyed from Estatoe to the Overhill town of Chota, crossing the mountains veiled in blue mist.

When we arrived, Quatsis took me from my father's arms and held me tightly while my legs clung to her waist. Her tears mingled with mine as we mourned the loss of my mother, her sister. As she held me, she once again felt the sharp edge of pain for the child who had never taken a breath. Oconostota and Will stood aside as we keened our grief. Quatsis dropped to her knees, rocking back and forth with me in a tight embrace.

Then Oconostota came and, kneeling down from his great height, embraced us in his massive arms. Quatsis' wails subsided into sobs, and I, too, quieted as we welcomed the strength and comfort he offered us. Will helped Oconostota assist Quatsis to her feet, as she would not let go of the burden that was her new daughter. Then, with me clinging to her, Quatsis leaned into the supportive embrace of her warrior husband. Finally, with Will closely behind, the three of us made our way through the crowd of well-wishers to my new home.

The following day, Will mounted his horse and headed down the trading path to Charles Town. With his shoulders squared and his chin set, he never looked back at his daughter, who stood in the doorway of her new home clutching her mother's hand.

Although I would retain my European name, Hester, in our tradition, I was given the Cherokee name Prachey, the adopted daughter of Quatsis and Oconostota, Great Warrior of Estatoe Town.

CHAPTER 7

Rebirth

Spring 1795
67 years old
Noonday Creek, GA

As it moves across the sky, the sun's rays create shadows on my porch, waking me from dreams of that other spring sixty years ago when I was just a child. I doze in my rocking chair, which I do more often these days. The warmth feels good on my wrinkled old body. I thought winter would never end; it seemed like the longest and coldest one ever. But my family insists it wasn't remarkable at all.

Finally, winter has come to an end, and spring has burst forth with renewed energy. Green shoots peek through the fallen leaves, signaling a time of renewal. The birds are busy in the trees, tending to their young, their songs a delight to hear. Squirrels dart from branch to branch, chattering as if greeting one another after spending the winter cooped up in their homes, much like I have. Leaves unfurl from their tight buds, stretching toward the sun. That's how I feel—like a newly emerging leaf bud, turning my face to the sun and absorbing its warmth. How wonderful it is!

Turtle is nestled in the curve of my body, resting his fuzzy head against my drooping breasts. He has been fretful, with new teeth pushing through his gums, and has sought the comfort of his Granny's lap. So I sit and rock him in the sun, and he calms, slipping easily into a deep sleep.

How I adore this child—this little replica of my grown son. He resembles George as a baby, and his mannerisms already reflect his father's. Naturally, I cherish all my grandchildren, but the bond with this one is so much stronger that I must be careful not to let it show. I would not want my other grandchildren to think I love them less simply because I love this one more.

Although his sleep is peaceful, I decide to stay in my rocking chair a little longer for fear he might wake if I try to lay him in his cradle. His restlessness last night disturbed the sleep of many in the crowded house. A long nap will ease his crankiness and give his busy mother respite from his unrest. Plus, sitting in the sun and rocking this little babe is quite pleasant.

Soon enough, he will awaken and start rooting at my wrinkled old breasts, searching for what I cannot give him. Then, I will take him to Caty, who is busy planting her spring garden. I can see her from here, her hoe moving swiftly as she uproots the weeds threatening to overtake her precious garden, preparing the soil for the seeds she saved from last fall's harvest. She will be pleased to see us, her breasts heavy with milk.

She will set aside her hoe, smiling with arms outstretched to take this youngest child of her brood. Then, she will sit with him under the elm tree, unbuttoning her blouse to offer him her breast. He's a vigorous nurser, slurping and grunting, suckling as though he fears her milk will run dry before his belly is full. It won't, of course, for she always has plenty of milk for her babies, but he is a sturdy little person who will wholeheartedly embrace all he does in life.

Once he is satisfied, with his little belly rounded and taut, he may be happy enough to play on a blanket under the tree until sleep overtakes him again. Caty will have enjoyed the rest but will be eager to return to work. Clouds forming on the horizon threaten a spring storm this evening, and there is much to do.

Caty always plants a large garden to feed her big family and all the visitors who drop by unexpectedly. She has help, of course. In addition to the older children, the slaves assist her as well, but she prefers to do much of the work herself.

George has adopted the European method of growing field crops. The slaves turn the earth with plows pulled by mules, creating long, straight rows where they drop seeds. However, Caty prefers to plant her kitchen garden in the traditional Cherokee way. She grows various vegetables, but her staple is the Three Sisters: beans, corn, and squash.

She will plant several corn seeds in mounds of earth so that three or four stalks grow together. A fish from the creek will be placed within the mound to provide extra nourishment as the seeds come to life. The beans also planted within the mound will twine around and climb the corn stalks, making them easier to pick when ready. The squash planted between the mounds will spread out on the earth around each corn hill, shading the roots from the hot summer sun. Soon, it will be harvest time, and we will prepare for yet another winter.

Her orchard is the most productive in the valley, featuring peach, cherry, and apple trees. If the weather is favorable, this year's blossoms promise a plentiful harvest for the pies and jellies that Nancy, George's other wife, enjoys making.

My son's two wives make an excellent team. Caty loves working outdoors, growing her produce, and caring for the livestock, while Nancy enjoys cooking and managing the household. Their arrangement works well because they respect each other's space, allowing both to pursue what they enjoy. Having two women in the kitchen is not a good thing. I do my part by staying away when Nancy cooks, thereby avoiding her ire. The same is true with Caty's garden, for, some say, I am a wise woman.

It is fortunate that Caty is both willing and able to manage the farming aspects of this household because, if it were left to George, the garden would grow only weeds, and the livestock would run wild. My son is not a farmer but a charmer—always ready to make a deal, swap a horse, or tell a tall tale. Well-liked by everyone, George's household regularly hosts visitors who stay for days or weeks. Some have been known to linger for months, prompting Nancy to find a subtle way to indicate that it's time for the visit to come to an end. George, of course, would never have noticed, much less cared.

My son often goes on visits himself, riding off on his horse to "take care of business," as he puts it. However, the women in his life know that his business involves catching up on the news, making deals, exchanging stories with his friends, and reminiscing about the battles they fought during the Revolutionary War and its aftermath.

I take pride in the fact that my family has weathered the toughest times and built a good life, even though it differs from my childhood. Still, I recognize the challenges we continue to face as we adapt to the European lifestyle. It is my duty to ease the transition as much as possible. My role is that of Granny, which is an important role to fill—a soft lap, a willing listener, and, most of all, a storyteller.

CHAPTER 8

Guernseys and Jerseys

Spring 1795
67 years old
Noonday Creek, GA

Today, my attention shifts to my older grandson Moses, who appears to be deeply troubled by something. A quiet and serious boy, he has been even more withdrawn these past few days, clearly pondering some issue or another.

He takes his studies at the missionary school seriously, soaking up book learning like a dry creek bed in a spring storm. However, what the missionaries teach him often does not align with what he knows or thinks he knows, and he struggles with it. Unlike his brother Jesse, a carefree youngster, he needs things to fit together and make sense. He is burdened with a sharp sense of justice and believes—unfortunately for him—that what is right will ultimately prevail.

It is clear to me, his Granny, that the missionaries have told him something his busy little mind cannot sort out on his own. I have watched and waited for him to be ready to talk about it, and now, on this beautiful spring afternoon, I sense the time is right.

I ask if I can join him when he brings the cows for the evening milking. It's his responsibility, and he seems to enjoy it; this is the only time he has to himself without a younger brother or sister trailing after him with their constant chatter. However, I have noticed that bringing the cows takes him much longer than necessary. I suspect he lingers, savoring the solitude and thinking his serious thoughts.

I express my concern for Betsey, our Guernsey heifer, who is about to calve for the first time. I tell him I want to make sure she is not hiding from the labor in some underbrush. He sees through me, of course, but since I am midwife for both the livestock and our community, it is a likely reason for his old Granny to walk with him in the woods.

We set out, my gangly, long-legged ten-year-old grandson and I. He walks quickly, swinging his arms widely, but then he notices I'm falling behind and slows to match his pace with mine. So we walk quietly, no conversation necessary just yet, savoring the beauty of our world. Late afternoon is a lovely time of day when the sun's rays slant longer, softening the earth's contours. He has an eye for beauty, this one, and he too appreciates the changes of the season, the greening of the countryside adorned with brilliant bursts of wildflowers.

I let Moses find his way in telling me what troubles him, patiently waiting for him to begin our talk. After a long silence, he asks me the name of a particular plant growing alongside the trail, which leads to talk of its medicinal uses. We continue our walk, chatting about one thing and then another, avoiding what is on his mind. As we draw closer to the pasture where the cows are grazing, however, he is the one who slows our pac e, and I know he is ready to share with me what is troubling him.

"Granny," he finally asks, "how much Cherokee am I?"

His question catches me off guard. "How much?" I ask him. "What on earth is that about? What nonsense are the Europeans up to now?"

Then, he tells me that a visiting missionary instructed the children to line up. He asked them questions one by one, recording their answers in a ledger. He wanted to know their names, ages, and how much Cherokee blood they had.

"What did you say to him?" I ask.

"I knew he did not want to know my Cherokee name, so I told him my White name, Moses Parris. I even spelled my name as Father instructed us. Of course, I know how many years I have, but none of us knew how to answer the question of how much Cherokee we are."

I am surprised he remembered to make sure the ledger man spelled his surname correctly. Richard had insisted George spell it as "Parris" instead of "Pearis." My husband and son harbored the misguided notion that a small change might protect the grandchildren from spiteful Patriots who still despised former Tories like Richard, who had sided with King George.

The ledger man had grown irritated with children like Moses, who did not know how to answer his silly question. He would insult them as "stupid Indians" and curse them for their ignorance. He remarked that Moses looked half-Cherokee, made a mark in his ledger, and told him to move along. But when Jesse, his older brother by two summers, stepped up to him, the ledger man glanced him over, frowned, and said, "Full blood," making his mark on the paper.

"How can Jesse be fully Cherokee while I am only half when we are children of the same parents?" my confused grandson wailed, tears glistening at the corners of his eyes. "Aren't we both Cherokee? If I'm only half Cherokee, what is my other half? And which half is it? I don't understand."

We approach the creek, and I step cautiously on the rocks that bridge it while Moses, always a considerate boy, steadies me. On the other side, we see the cows in the pasture, grazing on the fresh green grass of spring.

"Let us rest," I tell him; although I am not tired, I often walk several miles to visit nearby friends and family. So we sit on a log and watch the creek tumble along its course to the river.

"Well," I ask him, "how much Guernsey do you think Betsey is?" Initially puzzled by my question, he sees the glint in my eye and starts to grasp my way of thinking. We talk about how Betsey is a cow, just as he is a human, and she is called a Guernsey, as he is called Cherokee.

"Betsey and her kind are called Guernseys," I tell him, "because they come from a place across the water with that name. Labeling her as a Guernsey means she looks a certain way and will have certain characteristics like others in her 'tribe, but notice that she is different from Bossy, our Jersey cow. Although both are cows, they differ in that one is a Guernsey and the other a Jersey due to their bloodlines. You are Cherokee not only because of your bloodline but also because you were born into the Cherokee Nation."

We then talk about the racehorses that his grandfather bred at Great Plains, his South Carolina plantation, before the war. He took particular pride in a thoroughbred stallion he imported from England at great expense. The mares were kept secluded during their season so the workhorses would not mount them. Only the expensive stallion was allowed to breed with them. Richard and other wealthy Southerners competed with one another, controlling the breeding of horses with desired characteristics to create a stable of the fastest horses possible.

"They called such stock 'purebred,'" I tell him. "But controlling the mating of people is impossible." We laugh at the thought, and Moses says, "If it were so, the Methodist preacher would be the first to volunteer to be the stallion and breed all the ladies."

"It would be his duty," I suggest somberly. And Moses laughs so hard that he nearly falls off the log.

"All the different races are humans, just as cows are cows and horses are horses. Some of us are White, some are Native, and others are Negro. Within those races are tribes," I tell him. "Members of a tribe have a certain look or characteristics."

We then talk of the Creeks and their differences from the Cherokee or Shawnee—the same as those between Betsey and Bossy, Guernsey and Jersey. I remind him that even among the Europeans, there are tribes.

I said, "Look at the difference between the Irish and the English." And Moses saw that it was so.

"But once different tribes or races come into contact with each other and live close by, they will start to mate with one another, resulting in offspring of mixed blood. That's what you are," I tell him, "a mixed blood."

"Our Jersey bull sired Betsy's calf so that it will be mixed," he says.

"Yes, but now tell me which half will be Jersey and which half will be Guernsey."

It takes him a few seconds to see the humor in it, but when he does, he giggles so hard that tears come to his eyes—tears of relief, I think—and then he does fall off the log.

We keep the silliness going as we round up the cows and follow them to the barn. Moses suggests that he might be Cherokee from the waist up. Or would it be from the waist down? Is his top half Cherokee, or is it his bottom half? I add to the silliness by saying that I think his right half is Cherokee, and his left half is White. And off we go, laughing and shaking our heads at the crazy Whites for even asking such a ridiculous and confusing question.

"Well, Moses," I say, "this matter is even more complicated than it first appears."

He turns to me, his head cocked to the left, just like George does when something commands his full attention.

"You see, my father was a White man. He was one of the first traders in Cherokee country, which makes me half Cherokee—I, too, am of mixed blood."

"But, Granny," Moses asks, his brow knitted in a frown, "if you are half Cherokee, then what does that mean for me?"

"Well, Moses," I reply, "it just shows the silliness of the ledger man's question. If I'm half Cherokee, then your father would be a quarter, making you one-eighth. But that doesn't consider your mother and her family. She's the daughter of a Cherokee woman and Old Dan Baldridge, a White trader. I doubt even your missionary teacher can do the counting signs to figure that out!"

It is clear that Moses is not sure what to think about what I have told him. It confuses him further and sends him into deep thought. We follow the cows across the pasture, crossing the creek before re-entering the woods. The cows know the way and require little attention, so we poke along behind them. I give my serious grandson time to sort out these new details.

I pause and wait beside the path, lifting my heavy hair off my neck to welcome a cooling breeze. Moses walks a short distance ahead before he realizes I am not by his side. I watch him come back to me, his brow furrowed with concern. I reach out to push a lock of hair from his forehead, caressing his chin and then drawing him to me as he lowers his head into the shelter of my embrace.

He now realizes the absurdity of his dilemma, and I can sense a great relief in his mind. We continue following the cows home, our hands intertwined and swinging freely between us.

I tell him that the Whites always want to measure and count, as that is what they do best, and that they are excessively proud of their ability to make marks on paper.

"Men like George Washington came uninvited to our country, bringing glass tubes on long sticks—land stealers, as the Cherokee called them. They would point the tubes at each other from great distances and wave their arms back and forth. 'Surveying,' they called it, to create imaginary lines across the earth.

"Those imaginary lines were drawn on large sheets of paper where they had sketched how the earth appeared to birds in the sky, showing the locations of rivers and mountains. Then, they would tell us that one side of the imaginary line belonged to them and the other to us. Belonged? How could anyone claim to own the earth? Such foolishness!

"They would make a treaty with our leaders, saying, 'You stay on your side of the line, and we will stay on ours,' giving us gifts to seal the agreement. Our ancestors accepted the offered gifts, not knowing they considered it a trade for our ancestral lands.

"The treaty words were scratched on paper, and all the White leaders would make their sign on the paper. Our leaders did not know how to make the sign of their names, so they would draw two lines crossing, and a White man would write their names next to those lines. This writing on paper was supposed to make the agreement and the treaty binding."

I remind my grandson that even though they can draw imaginary lines and write words on talking leaves, they often forget their agreements. Despite all the treaties the Cherokees signed with the Europeans, settlers quickly began farming on our ancestral hunting grounds. Within just a few years, their leaders would return with more land stealers to draw more lines and create new treaties.

"Their leaders must write the words because they are not as intelligent as ours," I tell him. "They cannot remember as well as we can. They believe they are clever to write the words but then cannot remember what they wrote and must write it again."

We arrive at the barnyard, where the cows find their way to the milking stalls, ready for their heavy udders to be emptied. Jacob, the slave who will begin the milking, smiles and shakes his head as he sees a granny and her grandson holding their sides and laughing so hard that we can scarcely walk while shouting silliness back and forth to one another.

CHAPTER 9

Mixtures of Bloodlines

Spring 1795
67 years old
Noonday Creek, GA

It is comforting to see Moses relieved of his burden at supper this evening. Caty smiles at me and touches my shoulder, and we share a look that conveys her understanding of my purpose for accompanying him to fetch the cows. She has noticed his troubled mind and is pleased that our long walk allowed him to unburden himself.

This evening, though, I sit on my porch, rocking in my chair, thinking about what it meant to write words in a journal at the missionary school. How foolish of the Whites to ask how much Cherokee a person is. That's like asking how much American the ledger keeper is!

Now Moses understands that we are citizens of the Cherokee Nation, just as Americans are citizens of the United States. While most are White, they, like the Cherokee, represent a mix of tribes and nationalities that have embraced America as their homeland.

The big house's windows glow with lantern light, allowing me to glimpse the family's movements inside. The murmur of voices drifts into the night air.

I know Nancy is bent over her quilting frame and focused on her work because she loves putting needle and thread into fabric each evening. Caty, a meticulous record keeper, will be making entries in the farm's journals. I can hear the children from the upper floor preparing for bed, with two of the younger ones caught up in some squabble or another.

I think about my grandchildren—each one of them, from Susannah, my eldest granddaughter, a grown woman with a child of her own, to Turtle, the youngest. They are all unique and precious to me. I also consider their mixture of White and Cherokee blood.

At dinner that evening, faces of every hue, from coppery brown to freckled white, crowded the table. Glossy black-haired heads sat side by side with redheaded Betsey. Brown eyes, blue eyes, and the deepest of black were all turned toward their father when he entertained them with a tall tale from his day's adventures. The ledger man was correct in that some of them looked full-blood Cherokee, and some looked full-blood White—but they are all Cherokee.

It occurs to me that part of Moses's confusion stems from the ledger man making him feel that being White is more desirable—that being Cherokee is bad. He felt guilty because, even though he and Jesse share the same parents, the White man suggested that he is somehow superior due to his reddish-brown hair, while Jesse's is black.

I pull my shawl around my shoulders against the night chill as I rock gently, puffing on my pipe. The smoke from my exhalations rises in lazy spirals in the dim light, its acrid fumes stinging my eyes, as always. Nonetheless, I will continue to smoke my pipe.

I remember how surprised Moses was to learn about his grandfather's prized stallion. If Moses, one of the brightest and most curious of my grandchildren, was so misinformed, what about the others? I'm troubled that my grandchildren know so little about their ancestry. With my vow to teach them about their heritage renewed, my eyelids grow heavy, and my mind drifts to another time and place. I find myself a child once again.

CHAPTER 10

Mature Green Corn Festival

Summer 1738
10 years old
Chota Town

"Prachey!" I heard my name echo through the woods, interrupting my play with friends. We paused, tilting our heads to the side to hear better. Water from the pool streamed down our hair and bodies, pooling on the warm rocks at our feet. "Prachey! Where are you?"

I grinned at Sour Mush, his dark eyes crinkling with silent laughter. We acknowledged the voice of his older sister, Walina. We silently melted into the surrounding woods, signaling our playmates to follow suit.

"Prachey. Sour Mush! I know you are here. I heard you noisy children while I was coming down the path. You cannot fool me!"

She was now in sight, daintily picking her way down the steep incline to the spring where we had engaged in a riotous water fight. We watched her stand where we had been moments earlier, hands on her hips, wearing an exasperated expression.

I clamped my hand over my mouth, a giggle almost escaping. Her eyes scanned the surrounding spring landscape and passed over my hiding spot without pausing. She looked down at the puddles on the rock, where the damp imprint of our feet was nearly evaporated by the hot afternoon sun, and shook her head in disgust.

"Oh well," she said to the willow tree, whose limbs dipped gracefully into the water. "I guess they've gone somewhere else, so I can't tell Prachey that Hatton has returned. She'll find out soon enough."

With an exaggerated shrug, she tossed her long hair away from her pretty face and retraced her steps up the path to town.

I looked at Sour Mush, my mouth an O of surprise. My father had been gone so long this time that I had forgotten to miss him.

We children emerged from our hiding spots and gathered on the large rock overlooking the pool. Our desire to prank an older sibling faded in the excitement of her news, which was delivered to the unimpressed willow tree.

The other children hesitated only a moment before following Walina's footsteps up the path, expecting me to join them. However, I held back, reluctant to return to the village just yet, feeling uneasy about the upcoming reunion with my White father.

Sour Mush had started up the path, but when he noticed my hesitation, he returned to my side with a quizzical expression on his face. "What is wrong, Prachey? Do you want to see your father? And your brother Johnny? He will probably be with him. They will likely have packhorses loaded with all kinds of trade goods! And stories of their adventures! I cannot wait to see what they have brought. Come on, hurry!"

"You go ahead," I told him. "I will be there in a little while."

He hesitated for a moment, but the allure of the excitement in the village was too strong, and he dashed off like a streak of lightning to hurry and catch up with the other children.

I scurried down the rock to the pool's edge and crawled into the cool, damp space beneath, pushing aside the willow branches. Snuggling into a hollow formed by the massive roots, I hugged my legs to my suddenly chilled, naked body, resting my chin on my bony knees. Staring blankly through the curtain of willow branches, I watched the little brook created by the spring tumble free from the rocks lining the pool and begin its journey to the river below.

My father had returned, bringing with him the pain and confusion of the Creek massacre and its aftermath.

With the resilience of youth, I quickly adapted to my new life as Quatsis and Oconostota's daughter, a full-fledged member of the Paint Clan in Chota Town. The first few months were difficult; I felt anxious and was haunted by nightmares. I missed my mother terribly. Even though I had spent much time at Tugaloo, which was near our home, living in a Cherokee village instead of the familiar trading post was foreign to me, causing me to be easily upset and tearful. However, Quatsis and the other members of my clan were patient, quietly reassuring me as I healed and adjusted to my new life.

My father, Will Hatton, was off on one trading mission after another, each keeping him away a little longer than the last. Seasons came and went. A year or two passed, and Johnny convinced our uncle and father that he was nearly a man and ready to learn the trading business. So, he, too, rode off on adventures that took them both farther and farther from me.

My mother's sister, Quatsis, was a small woman so full of life that it was impossible to feel gloomy around her. The spring after I moved in with them, she gave birth to a healthy son, and I became a big sister to little Terrapin.

And so, more seasons came and went. As I became a full member of the family, the memories of my previous life and other family began to fade. Sometimes, when I couldn't sleep late at night, I picked at the husk of my mother's memory like a child would pick at a scab. Tears would then well up and roll slowly down my cheeks until I cried myself to sleep. Yet, with the morning's light, the dark ache would have vanished like my nighttime tears.

So now I huddled in the embrace of the willow tree and picked at that old wound once more but found there was naught but a dull ache where once there had been acute pain. I squeezed my eyes shut, trying to wring out a tear or two, but without success. Feeling relieved yet somewhat guilty, I realized the acute pain was no more.

Pushing aside the willow branches, I scampered up the rock, finding toe-holds and fingerholds in its crevices. Its surface felt hot from the midday sun. Dancing with bare feet on its scorching top, I jumped to the cool grass in the dappled shade beside it and, no longer hesitant, followed my playmates to the village to greet my father and brother.

I hurried to Chota, following the dusty path past the community fields, where the corn stood at attention like silent sentinels. Within the palisaded town, smaller paths snaked off the main one, leading to small, gabled houses made of white clay and cane, baking in the noonday sun. Scattered among them were slatted corncribs on posts above the ground and cone-shaped winter houses where families would lie around a smoldering fire during the cold season.

Dogs lounged on their sides in the shade of the cabins, barely acknowledging me, whereas when it was cooler, they would jump up and run alongside No people were present to witness my passage, as everyone had gone to the town Center to greet the trade caravan.

The houses stood closer together as I approached the town Center. The Council House, built on a mound, was the largest in the Nation. Chota was the Mother town, and this Council House served as a gathering place for its townsfolk and others from across the Nation during formal councils, religious ceremonies, or festivals.

My pace slowed as I neared the crowd of townsfolk, their excited chatter blending with the neighing and snorting of packhorses, weary from their journey over the mountains and made anxious from the clatter.

I weaved through the crowd, looking for my friends. Sour Mush grinned as I approached him, silently nodding his head toward the front of the pack train.

There was Will Hatton, my Scottish father, with a red beard that had turned grayer since his last visit. He was earnestly conversing with Cornelius Dougherty, Sour Mush's Irish father, who was the designated trader for South Carolina in Chota. Craning my neck and standing on tiptoe, using Sour Mush's shoulder for support, I scanned the crowd of traders and bearers for my brother, Johnny. It wasn't until he turned toward me that I felt a jolt of recognition; the grown man lifting a heavy load from a horse's back was him. My brother had grown since I last saw him and now stood as tall as our father, though he lacked his bulk.

Suddenly feeling shy, I stood quietly among the gaggle of children, watching first Johnny and then Will. I saw they were surreptitiously scanning the crowd, searching for me, but I continued to wait.

Johnny spotted me first, grinned, and winked before returning to his work. After my father's dealings with Dougherty were finished, he turned and surveyed the crowd with his hands on his hips. His gray eyes passed over me first, then flickered back, widening with delight at the sight of his daughter.

"Hester! Damme, there ye be—Ye naked little heathen! Come give yer old Pa a hug!" He roared. And with that invitation, I vaulted into his waiting arms.

***

On the coming day, visitors from across the Smoky Mountains will begin gathering in Chota for the biggest festival of the year: the Mature Green Corn Festival. There will be feasting and dancing for the next several days, but tonight, my father and brother will be with us, their Cherokee family.

Oconostota and Will lounged beneath the shaded arbor, while Quat-sis busily prepared a squirrel and hominy meal in her outdoor summer kitchen. I was busy looking after Terrapin, her rambunctious son of three summers, my calico shift barely covering my behind.

Like other Cherokee children, I did not bother with clothes in the summer heat. However, when Will was home, Quatsis encouraged me to wear the shifts she made for me. To him, I was still Hester, and although he was glad to see me healthy and happy, Quatsis mentioned that she thought it bothered him to see me running around naked. Therefore, to honor him, I slipped on the scratchy garment, even though I had grown so much that it barely served its purpose.

Johnny stayed with us for a moment, but it was obvious that the charming Walina had caught his eye. He soon left to follow her as Oconostota and Will exchanged knowing looks.

With his belly full from eating from first one wooden bowl and then another, Terrapin tried to curl up in his mother's lap. He became fretful when he realized his little brother, Bark, was already there, greedily tugging at her breast. Shifting the baby, Quatsis made room for both her sons, the eldest still needing cuddling and comfort when he was tired and ready for sleep.

As dusk settled over the village, evening activities slowed, voices hushed, and children made their way to their sleeping pallets. Women gathered at one cabin and then another to plan for the next day. Will's packmen and trade path horsemen had finished unloading the last of the trade goods, filling Dougherty's storehouse. The hardworking horses, freed from their heavy burdens, grazed in the meadow under the watchful eyes of eager young boys, hoping one would allow them to ride.

Relieved of my duties as an elder sister, I sought my father and found him gathered with the men. I curled next to him, relishing his familiar male scent. As was my usual ploy, I made myself still and quiet, even abstaining from tugging at the itchy tunic, pretending to sleep.

Neither Will nor Oconostota was fooled, of course, but they played along with my little pretense. When Quatsis came looking for me, Will motioned her away. Through slitted eyes, I saw them exchange a conspiratorial smile and knew I would once again be permitted to listen to the men's talk.

CHAPTER II

Playing Possum

Summer 1738
10 years old
Chota Town

It is a quirk of old age that we often remember events from long ago with greater clarity than more recent ones. Such is the case with one particular evening; I can recall it so vividly that it feels almost like I am there again. It may be deeply etched in my consciousness because it marked the end of my innocence.

In the deepening darkness of that unusually warm summer evening, men w ho would become the shapers of our Nation's destiny gathered. Old Hop was in the full bloom of his manhood, his blood cooling and the wisd om that would become his genius settling upon him. The brothers Oconostota, Kittagusta, and Willewanah, their cousin Attacullaculla, and others destined to have a profound influence in the upcoming decades were the young warriors of our People, still determining who and what they would be. Sheltered by the towering chestnut trees with a cooling breeze wafting from the river, they began to mark the paths they were destined to tread.

Among those who joined the group was Christian Gottlieb Priber, an adventurer who came to change our people and, as so often happens, was changed himself in the end.

As a young man in his homeland of Germany, he found the Jesuit priesthood unsuitable and sailed to the New World, eventually making his way to the mountainous Cherokee Nation. Dreamy-eyed and idealistic, he became infatuated with our People, whom he called "children of the forest."

As he approached the group that evening, he was greeted with hoots and taunts, causing him to duck his head in embarrassment.

"Here he comes," Oukah-Ulah called out. "The lusty buck has finally left his wife's sleeping pallet to join his friends once again."

"It's a wonder he can even walk!" Clogoillah chimed in. "For his woman has surely exhausted him."

Since his arrival, Priber had been the brunt of many ribald comments, for he had been fully engaged in trying to couple with every Cherokee woman he encountered. But then Clogoillah's young sister caught his attention, and, it was said, he relentlessly pursued her until she caught him.

Grinning sheepishly, he settled beside his new brother-in-law and attempted to steer the conversation in a different direction. He had just returned from Tellico, where he had browbeaten Moytoy, his wife's ambitious father, into granting him the title of "His Majesty's Principal Secretary of State." Now, with his pretentious title and his Cherokee wife, he was nearly unbearable in his fervent zeal to convert others to his way of thinking.

As was their custom, the men listened politely while he embarked on yet another tirade. All Cherokees were to be equal, he preached. Goods were to be held in common, and each Cherokee was to work for the Nation's common good. As always, his listeners grunted and nodded in agreement, for was it not so? Were they not already as one? But then, warming to his subject, he launched into his sermon about the abolition of marriage and making children the property of the Nation.

At this point, the men felt uneasy, as they always did, because this way of thinking was hard to grasp. Men and women came together and separated as they pleased; that was how it had always been and would always be. Children, of course, were the responsibility of their mother and her clan. Therefore, they were full members of the Nation.

How can one person be the property of another, let alone the Nation? Of course, there were the occasional slaves taken in battle. But even those slaves were not kept as property for long. If they showed courage and merit, they were adopted into the tribe. At times, they were traded with other tribes for goods or for Cherokee prisoners, who were also held by warring tribes. Priber's argument about how he believed the Cherokee should change fell on deaf ears, as it was simply the senseless babbling of an unenlightened White man with poor manners.

At the first opportunity, when Priber stopped to catch his breath, Otter Tail turned to Will and inquired what news he brought from Charles Town and the Cherokee villages on his way to the Overhills. Others breathed a sigh of relief and encouraged Will to change the direction of the evening's conversation.

Will informed them that each time he returned to the bustling port of Charles Town, more ships were in the harbor than before. These ships brought trade goods in exchange for Native slaves for the Caribbean slave market, along with pelts and deerskins for the European markets. He had been told that 25,000 deerskins were shipped to Europe just last year alone.

The men murmured and shook their heads in amazement, unable to comprehend such numbers. They all agreed that finding game had become increasingly difficult, and with each passing year, they had to range farther from our traditional hunting grounds.

Each year, their hard-earned pelts and deerskins yielded even less in trade goods. The traders Cornelius and Will took no offense at the complaints, for who knew the truth of the situation better than these two? It wasn't their fault, as the price of trade goods was determined by the merchants in Charles Town, and they had no control over it.

Priber could not stay quiet any longer and launched into another harangue. We had trade agreements with the English, but he insisted to the men that they were being tricked. He urged them to trade with the French to counter English demands for more deerskins in exchange for fewer goods. The French would offer better deals, he claimed.

The discussion became heated as the warriors debated the merits of trading with one nation over the other. Priber was persuasive, and it was evident that many warriors believed we should trade with the French. Oconostota was particularly attentive to the discussion, and I recalled that he had spent many hours in lengthy talks with Priber. However, Attacullaculla led the argument in favor of honoring our trade agreements with the English.

Gray Squirrel, an elder so old that his eyes were barely visible among the creases of his face, warned us about our growing dependence on the White man and his manufactured goods.

"There was a time," he said, "when my father, my father's father, and countless others before me lived off the bounty of Mother Earth. We did not need the White man's muskets or gunpowder to hunt. We took only what game we needed to survive, first thanking them for their lives so that we could live. There was balance in the old ways. There was no waste or greed as seen among the younger generations." His voice grew peevish and quivered with emotion as he shook a bony finger at the young warriors who had joined the group of older men.

They were, of course, too polite to argue with or to disrespect an elder, but it was evident from the glances they exchanged that they considered him as just an old fool who knew nothing of the world.

Who wanted to go back to the old ways? People had grown accustomed to brass arrowheads, iron axes, hoes, kettles, and steel knives. Sure, young men still used bows and arrows, but muskets were the superior weapon, not just for defending against other tribes with muskets but also for bringing in ever-increasing numbers of deerskins for trade. No Cherokee warrior of merit would be content with just a bow and arrow.

Gray Squirrel continued to dress traditionally, donning a deerskin flap and a loose mantle of furs or deerskin, while most Cherokee men chose woolen coats during the colder months. Some of our women still wore short deerskin shifts like their grandmothers, but the young women demanded that their men provide them with colorful calicoes. Our women longed for the glass beads that had replaced the painstakingly crafted shell or porcupine quills, along with the brass earrings that had become fashionable for both men and women.

His talk of the old ways fell on ears that were closed to his words, for even if the men had been willing to live like their ancestors, who was left to teach them? Furthermore, their women would never entertain the idea. We relied on the Europeans to provide us with goods we could not manufacture ourselves, and we needed only to trade pelts and deerskins to obtain them.

When Priber tried to turn the talk back to the French, Attacullaculla was uncharacteristically ill-mannered, interrupting him to remind the men again of his journey to England a few years ago. As one of seven young men to journey across the Great Water to the court of King George II, Attacullaculla never grew tired of recounting the story.

In our midst that night were young warriors from neighboring villages who had heard about the journey, of course—for who in the Cherokee Nation had not? However, they had never heard the entire story from so many participants. Several of the bold seven were present, making it natural for the visitors to encourage them to share their adventure, much to the relief of many in the group who were not in the mood for serious discussions. "Save that for the Council House!" someone murmured just loud enough to be heard during Pribner's last discourse.

Eleazar Wiggan, a trader from Tellico, joined the growing crowd of men. He had arrived early for the Mature Green Corn Festival when he heard about the pack train's arrival loaded with new goods. After locking up his storehouse and mounting his horse, he set off on the short trip to the nearby village, eager to see his old friend Will Hatton.

As a natural storyteller, Wiggan skillfully shifted focus from the escalating conflict between Pribner and Attacullaculla by recounting the arrival of Sir

Alexander Cuming. I nestled closer to Will's warmth against the evening chill, pretending to be an opossum to avoid being noticed, since I had only heard parts of this story.

CHAPTER 12

Power Play

Summer 1738
10 years old
Chota Town

As the night deepened, I listened to the men's melodic voices as they talked among themselves about the events of eight years past. In that way, I came to understand how a meddlesome White man had plunged my People into unprecedented political disarray.

A rapt audience settled onto their robes and blankets, directing their full attention to the old trader Wiggan as he began recounting their adventure. "It was springtime, during the Flower Moon, when the leaves were fully green on the trees, in the year we English call 1730 when Sir Alexander Cuming presented himself to the Council at Keowee." Thus began his familiar prologue to an oft-told story.

Cuming had arrived at the Nation, claiming to be an envoy from King George II of England. Ignoring the advice of traders and armed with guns and swords, he boldly entered the Council House during a meeting of three hundred elders. My father was shocked by Cuming's actions and fully expected the worst.

"If I had nae been there to see it meself, I would na'er believed it." Will chimed in, the rumble of his deep voice carrying across the crowd of attentive warriors. "That little sour-puss Englishman came riding into the wilderness, not knowing his arse from a hole in the ground."

Will detailed how Cuming had knelt in the Council House and demanded that everyone else kneel as he did to acknowledge King George II. His audacity and rudeness somehow overwhelmed the Nation's leaders. On bent knee, they pledged their loyalty to the Crown of England against the French in North America. However, they were likely unaware of what they were giving or to whom they were giving it. They probably did not fully grasp the significance of the European ceremony. But the traders were aware and felt uneasy.

"We were all afeared for our lives. Wiggan's knees were shaking so hard I could hear them rattle all the way across the Council House," Will said with a chuckle as Wiggan ducked his head in embarrassment.

"I would nae been within a hundred miles of the place if I'd known what he would do. It's a wonder all the Whites weren't kilt right then and there, considering how jealous the People have always been of their liberties," the old trader added.

The Peace Chief, or White Chief, had died a few months earlier, but the consecration ceremony for his successor had not yet occurred. Perhaps Cuming believed that the People were without a Peace Chief and saw an opportunity to influence their European allegiance and choice of leader. Had he not been so presumptuous, Cuming would have understood that it was not the Cherokee's way to act with unceremonious haste.

The next White Chief would be Standing Turkey, affectionately known as Old Hop, because of a childhood injury that left him with a distinctive limp. It's more likely that Cuming chose to remain unaware that Old Hop was soon to become the White Chief of all the Cherokee Nation. He preferred someone upon whom he could exert significant influence, someone who would follow his orders. He found ambition equal to his own in Moytoy, the Headman of Tellico Town, and the ambitious younger brother of Old Hop.

My father had been sipping on his own rum, and, as was his wont when he'd had a bit too much to drink, his tongue wagged looser than prudence allowed. "I do nae know how in hell that crazy Englishman did it," he said, "but somehow he managed to sway some o' the headmen to name that weak-livered Moytoy as 'Emperor' of all the Cherokees, whatever in hell that means!"

At his comment, all heads turned to Old Hop, who had quietly seated himself on the edge of the group to observe and listen unobtrusively. "Hmmph," he grunted, embarrassed to have attention drawn to his presence. It was part of his genius to hear more and speak less, to observe rather than be observed, and then, after careful deliberation, he would reach a conclusion or make a statement.

Regardless of how it was done, Moytoy's appointment as the Cherokee representative in trade negotiations with the English upset the balance of power within the well-ordered Cherokee system. The past few months have been disturbing as the previously clear lines of authority have blurred, leaving the People confused about where to place their loyalties.

Despite his persuasive skills, Cuming failed to convince Moytoy to accompany him to England to finalize what he believed was a deal with the Cherokee Nation. He intended to introduce Moytoy to King George II; however, Moytoy refused to go, stating that his wife was too ill for him to leave her side.

A series of chuckles followed that pronouncement, for Moytoy's wife was a robust and energetic woman. "More likely, she wouldn't let him go!" Oukah-Ulah declared. "We all know who rules that family!"

"In any case," Will chuckled, "her recovery was swift, and she rallied shortly after Cuming left the Nation."

More likely, Moytoy understood that his claim to be the "Emperor" of all the Cherokee, as the English referred to him, was tenuous at best and would not last through a lengthy absence.

"The Englishman was having trouble persuading any Cherokee to return to England with him," Wiggan told the men, "and he came to me for help. As for me, I admit I was right fond of the ideer of returning to England with a bigwig like Cuming and meeting the King and all, so I agreed to go with him as an interpreter."

Wiggan approached his friend Attacullaculla about making the journey. The young warrior was intrigued but uncertain. "I thought it too distant from our homeland," Attacullaculla said. "Wiggan reassured me that the distance was exaggerated. He promised I would return by hunting season in the fall, so I agreed to go. Kittagusta insisted that I shouldn't travel alone—he would accompany me and knew two or three others he could persuade to join us. As soon as he convinced them, we began preparing to leave."

One of those who volunteered was Oukah-Ulah, the Headman of Tassetsa. As the highest-ranking Cherokee on the journey, Moytoy appointed him as his representative. The other four young warriors were Kollannah, Tathtowe, Kittagusta, and Clogoittah. Shortly before leaving, Oconostota's request to go was granted. This brought the total to seven Cherokee—a promising sign, as seven is a sacred number.

CHAPTER 13

Across the Great Water

Summer 1738
10 years old
Chota Town

"It were May 4, 1730, I remember," began Wiggan, warming to the narrative as he leaned forward and reached for the jug of rum being passed around, "when I rode into Charles Town with that troop of Cherokee warriors. My, my, but how those overdressed, tight-arsed city folk scurried out of our way!"

Laughter met his statement, for everyone present that night could imagine what a spectacle it must have been: seven young Cherokee warriors bedecked in their loincloths and moccasins, colorful blankets draped over their muscular shoulders, wearing silver medallions and armbands glimmering in the sun. What a sight they must have been to the citizens of Charles Town, as Native visitors to the port city were still a rarity.

Attacullaculla seized this opportunity to tell the men about the journey to England. "We boarded the ship, 'Fox,' for the moon-long journey across the Great Water to London—"

"And I've never been so sick in my life!" Clogoittah interrupted amid great laughter. Evidently, he and Tathtowe had been so ill aboard the ship that they feared for their lives, certain they would not live to set foot on land again. Even when they finally arrived, they could scarcely enjoy their visit for dreading the return voyage.

"It's true!" Tathtowe exclaimed, to the amusement of the men. "I was so fearful of the return journey that I thought of begging the Englishmen to allow me to stay. But, foolish men that they are, they would think I wanted to remain because I loved their stinking city. Hah! 'Twas only because I did not want my body tossed to the huge fish that live in the Great Water."

As the laughter faded, Oukah-Ulah joined in. "The closer we got to London, the more nervous Cuming became. We thought he was an official envoy of King George, but he was just a small fish in a big pond. And he was using us to make a place for himself with the king."

"No wonder he was nervous," Dougherty said between puffs of his pipe. "I sure as hell would not want to get on the bad side of King George or his suckups."

"Well, whatever his intention, it didn't work," Wiggan said. "We saw damn little of the scurrilous bastard once we hit London Town, especially when the bills needed to be paid. And when we set sail to come home, we left his skinny arse on the dock."

An indignant Attacullaculla quickly jumped to his benefactor's defense, and the evening was rent with a chorus of men trying to outtalk each other, telling their versions of what sort of man Cuming was.

"Be that as it may," Will finally roared into the melee, drawing the attention back to the story and causing my ears to ring, "bastard opportunist or benefactor o' the Cherokee, whatever the hell he is, our warriors certainly caught the attention o' those highfalutin Englishmen!"

Attacullaculla sprang to his feet, taking control of the storytelling. He held the entire gathering enthralled that night beneath the chestnut trees, transporting us to a mysterious place across the Great Water. From my vantage point at Will's side, I could see that his fellow travelers were just as spellbound as the rest of us, reliving their incredible experience. He would tell and retell the adventure in many council houses and around many fires for the rest of his life. I heard the story more times than I can count, yet there was something special about that particular evening's narration.

Perhaps it was that night when Attacullaculla realized the full power of his eloquence. A small man and not a particularly skillful hunter or fierce warrior, he grew in stature as he grabbed the attention of that unruly group of men and held them with the power of his words.

In groups of two and three, the women joined the men, their plans for tomorrow's festival finalized, while the little ones settled down for the night. My playmates stopped their rowdy games, quietly joining their parents, drawn by the unfolding drama under the rising moon. We were spellbound and captivated as Attacullaculla described their adventures in London.

With his eloquence as my guide, I could see the harbor teeming with ships of all sizes and shapes, their colorful flags from around the world fluttering in the ocean's breeze. My nose twitched at the stench of open sewers, and my ears buzzed with the clamor of street vendors and the chatter of more people than I could imagine milling through the crowded city streets.

We were amazed as he described streets lined with shops overflowing with manufactured goods spilling onto tables propped against the walls of the buildings. We could envision tradesmen calling out to passersby to browse their wares.

Attacullaculla described being driven through the cobblestone streets of London in small houses mounted on wheels and pulled by four horses. He recounted how they were entertained at festivals, received gifts, and attended fairs. A group of merchants interested in the South Carolina trade hosted them with lavish dinners, during which they drank an intoxicating beverage made from a berry. They competed with the King's archers, astonishing them with their skill in using bows and arrows. They attended plays where actors and acrobats performed to their amazement, visited a place where the insane were chained to the walls, and heard fantastic sounds coming from an instrument called an organ. He described their visits to the Tower, St. James's Park, Westminster Abbey, and the Houses of Parliament.

Attacullaculla grew expansive as he described the English-style garments His Majesty presented to them—rich satin breeches in vivid colors and coats embellished with lace and trimmed in gold. How gorgeous they must have been! We were amazed as he described how they posed for the Duke of Montague, who, using only paint similar to that which they used to decorate their bodies, created their images on large canvases. What magic the English possess!

Not a sound could be heard in the crowd as Attacullaculla described the military power of the English. He spoke of countless warships in London's harbor, the incredible accuracy of their firearms, and the might of enormous cannons. And the soldiers: red-coated English soldiers, wherever they went—far more than our Nation had people.

My favorite part was when Attacullaculla, with his powerful eloquence, transported me to a grand stone building known as Windsor Castle. As a refreshing breeze swept through our secluded mountain valley, I witnessed the ceremonial knighting of three noblemen.

That night, they dressed as they wished but acted according to Cuming's guidance. As Moytoy's representative, Oukah-Ulah wore a scarlet jacket and knee-length satin trousers while carrying a musket. The other warriors wore only loincloths, each adorned with a horse's tail trailing behind, while Tathtowe carried a bow and arrows. Their faces and upper bodies were painted in red, blue, and green, and their shaved heads, featuring a single lock of hair, were decorated with vibrant feathers. Our hearts swelled with pride at the thought of how impressive our Cherokee warriors must have looked as they marched into the grand hall of that imposing castle and knelt before King George, kissing his hand and those of his two sons.

Sir Alexander (as Cuming had instructed them to address him while in England) then presented the King with what he referred to as the "Crown of Cherokee," a wig made from the tail of a female opossum that had been dyed red, along with four scalps from our enemies and five eagles' tails of peace.

"King George seemed pleased enough with our gifts," Kittagusta added, interrupting a disgruntled Attacullaculla, who did not appreciate the disruption of his narrative. "But then, they told us to stand near the King while he was at dinner so he could look at us whenever he wanted; yet, we were never offered anything to eat. So, we had to stand on display while those gluttonous Englishmen gorged themselves."

We were astonished at such rudeness, for a Cherokee would eat only after first offering food to his guests. Such details of their adventure validated our opinion of the strange ways of the English. They were like unmannered children in many ways.

"Well, our Tathtowe put a scare into those nobles, not to mention nearly causing me to die of fright." Wiggan declared.

After their leisurely dinner, still not offering the hungry Cherokee so much as a morsel to eat, the King and his court strolled along the gallery that overlooked the castle terrace. Spotting a huge elk grazing in the park, Tathtowe pulled an arrow from his quiver and, nocking it in his bow, prepared to shoot the stag for the warriors' evening meal.

Wiggan doubled over with laughter as he described the frenzy of excitement among the King's entourage when the furious, almost naked warrior pulled back the bowstring, with the elk in his sights.

"I had to do some quick talking that time, let me tell you!" he chuckled. "And thank God nary a one of those fancy dukes and lords could understand what Tathtowe was really saying. I convinced them he just wanted to impress the King. It's a miracle the King's guards didn't run us through with their swords before I could get us out of that mess."

An embarrassed Tathtowe grinned, scratching the back of his neck as his companions had a good laugh at his expense. Defending his actions, he added: "Well, after that, they took us to a fancy place and fed us the flesh of that stupid animal they call a sheep. It didn't taste nearly as good as that elk would have, but I was so hungry I didn't care."

"And, thanks to Tathtowe, we never missed another meal!" Oukah-Ulah chimed in.

But after about four moons, the young men grew weary of the English. The novelty had worn off for them and their hosts. They longed to return to the misty mountains of their homeland in time for hunting season, as promised. However, their sponsor had lost favor with the King and was nowhere to be found. So, Wiggan used all his powers of persuasion to arrange an audience with the Lords' Commissioners.

Attacullaculla stood before us that night, once again commanding our full attention. As the representative of the seven warriors, he used the limited English he knew to address the bewigged Lords; with great dignity, he repeated that farewell speech.

"We have come here from a dark and mountainous country," he said, "but we are now in a place of light. Our Nation's crown is different from that which our father King George wears, but it is all one. The chain of friendship shall be extended to our people. We regard King George as the sun, our father, and ourselves as his children, for though you are White and we are Brown, our hands and hearts are joined together. When we have shared with our people what we have seen, our children, from generation to generation, will remember it. In war, we shall always stand united with you. The great King's enemies shall be our enemies. His people and ours shall always be as one, and we shall die together."

Dramatically, Attacullaculla pantomimed how he placed the eagle feathers they had brought onto the table before the King's representatives. "This is our way of talking," he said, "which is the same for us as your letters in a book are to you. And to your beloved men, we deliver these feathers to confirm all we have said."

The young men had taken their leave of the English in a dignified way that filled our hearts with pride.

But before they could be permitted to set sail from England, the Lord's Commissioners presented them with a document they called the Articles of Agreement. They demanded that each of the young warriors sign it as a representative of the People.

"I was struck dumb," Wiggan said. "Damme, I thought we were just bidding them farewell, and then we would board a ship fer home. But they had this bedamned document for the fellers to sign. And they made it clear that nobody was leaving fer home until they did!"

"Ah-ha!" cried Pribner, having listened in silence long enough to the stories of English glory all evening. "I've been telling you all along that you can't trust those damned English!"

From my vantage point, nestled against my father, I could see Oconostota stiffen, his attention fully on Priber and a perplexed look on his face. Even after all this time, I am confident that the events that unfolded in the years to come took root that night beneath the towering chestnut trees, when opinions were formed, and conclusions were drawn that would shape the young men gathered there.

Bless his soul, Wiggan could read. Picking up the document, he had read it to the warriors as they gathered around.

He told us that the treaty decreed that the Cherokee would be subordinate to the English and would trade exclusively with English merchants. They would be governed by English law rather than Cherokee law. They were expected to fight against anyone who opposed the English. Most importantly, the treaty called for the English to expand their lands even further.

The seven men refused to sign the document, knowing they lacked the authority to make agreements for the Real People.

They returned to their living quarters to await their journey across the Great Water. However, arrangements still needed to be made to pay for their passage. They had no money, and their sponsor refused to take responsibility for their expenses. The warriors grew increasingly apprehensive because they had been told they would be home by the end of summer or fall. Now it was September, the month of falling leaves, and hunting season was upon them.

The eight of them waited in their living quarters as the flood of invitations suddenly ceased. In the blink of an eye, their status shifted from visiting nobility to that of beggars. The innkeeper began to badger them for payment, threatening to force them to leave if he did not receive the money owed. The tavern keepers would no longer extend credit for meals, often leaving them threatened with starvation. They were stranded in a foreign land, reliant on an indifferent monarch to return to their homes and families.

Weeks passed, and their situation became more desperate each day. Then, their sponsor appeared at their door, asking them to sign the agreement and promising them passage home in return. What choice did they have but to mark where instructed? So, they signed.

Within days, they were aboard a ship, once again sailing across the Great Water, eager to return to the mountains and valleys they cherished.

Chapter 14
London Town

Summer 1738
10 years old
Chota Town

The night had grown late, with the full moon rising above. Most of the women and all the children, except for me, had drifted off to their sleeping pallets. Several of the men were hesitant to leave just yet, so they lingered under the chestnut tree, reflecting on all they had been told that evening. My eyes grew heavy as I curled into a ball, seeking warmth from my father's bulk against the evening chill. But then, in the stillness of the late hour, someone called out, "Tell us about your adventure, Tathtowe!"

Through narrowed eyes, I saw Tathtowe grin and duck his head, pretending embarrassment, although he was likely waiting for such an opportunity.

"Come on, tell us!" the chorus of men urged him.

As he began his story and I recognized where it was heading, all my drowsiness vanished. I pretended to be sound asleep but kept my ears wide open so I would not miss a thing. My Presbyterian father leaned towards being prudish about matters between men and women, much to the amusement of my Cherokee parents. I understood how men and women brought pleasure to one another and that if the woman chose, a baby could result from their union. Will was a lusty man who often engaged in such activities with willing partners, yet he became embarrassed at the thought that I might know about it.

I quickly realized I had not heard about this part of the journey. It had not been shared in the formal setting of the Council House, and I could sense it was a story I did not want to miss.

A master storyteller, Tathtowe began crafting his tale by continuing from where Attacullaculla had left off in his description of London. Having never seen an English town, I could hardly envision the residences he described. Broad cobblestone avenues, filled with horse-drawn carriages of all sizes and shapes, were lined with houses rising three and four stories tall. Narrow alleys that twisted and turned through a maze of such houses led to the Inn at Covent Garden. Their accommodations were on the third floor in three adjoining rooms overlooking the courtyard below.

My nose curled as he described the filth and stench of the city, with horse droppings in the streets and human waste floating in the gutters. There were no clear rivers for the warriors to go to water as we did every morning; the Thames was far away and so filthy that they would not have dared to dip a toe in it, let alone bathe. Dark brown and covered with an oil slick, dead animals and trash swirled in its eddies. At their insistence to bathe, they were given a basin of water every morning, and all seven were expected to cleanse themselves in it, one after the other.

I was embarrassed for them and could not imagine such a thing. But worse than that, he described how the Englishmen expected them to deal with their waste. They were given a handled pot with an ill-fitting lid and instructed to dump the contents out the window after making water or emptying their bowels into it—hopefully, most of it would fall into the gutter below rather than on an unfortunate passerby.

They were mortified, he said, refusing to do such a vile thing. Instead, they would sneak into the stable behind the inn whenever possible. Kollannah was the most fastidious of the seven, and the men laughed as he recounted how his bowels became so blocked that he could not empty them. An English medicine man was finally summoned, and Kollannah was given a physic that turned his bowels to water. After that, even upon his return to his mountain home, he continued to suffer with his bowels and swore that the Englishmen had ruined him.

"What a relief it was," Kollannah said, "when we finally returned home and could bathe in our mountain streams' cool, clear waters. And we could go to the woods to empty our bowels properly!"

A giggle bubbled up and almost escaped, threatening to betray my pretense of sleep. I sensed Will turning to look at me, reminded of his young daughter curled up beside him. I sighed deeply, burrowing further into the shadow of his girth as if disturbed by a dream. Satisfied, he turned his attention back to Tathtowe's story, and I was free to eavesdrop a little longer.

One evening, Tathtowe continued, four elegantly dressed men arrived at their lodgings and engaged Wiggan in a lively discussion. Initially reluctant, then incredulous, and finally amused, Wiggan approached Tathtowe, the fierce warrior who had threatened to shoot King George's elk, grinning as he informed him that he was to accompany the men.

At first, he was alarmed because the seven had not been separated since leaving Charles Town. So why was he being singled out?

"Well, lad," Wiggan told him, "it seems that some well-born lady has a fancy to see what's in your loincloth."

Initially, he was appalled and then curious, but Tathtowe agreed to go with the men because, young and lusty as he was, he had not been with a woman for quite some time.

He described being led through increasingly narrow and dark alleys, eventually arriving at a concealed door where a uniformed guard deliberately turned his back. His escorts guided him through torch-lit stone passages and up twisting stairs to a narrow landing where another hidden door was opened. A wall tapestry was pulled aside, and he was pushed into an elaborately furnished yet dimly lit bedchamber, the door closing firmly behind him.

A beautiful, yellow-haired woman approached him with outstretched hands. He remembered seeing her near the King's dais when he was presented at court. Their eyes had briefly locked, and he had felt a stirring in his loins as she regarded him with downcast eyes.

Her hair was braided and piled upon her head in the English fashion, and she was wearing a long, soft gown that clung to her body, outlining the shape of her legs and hips as she moved toward him, a pleased smile on her pink lips. The gown was cut so low it exposed her breasts to just above the nipples, which he could see were erect, pushing into the filmy fabric of her bodice.

All the men were quiet, holding their breaths, and struck with wonder of the experience Tathtowe was sharing with them.

He told his friends that they didn't speak each other's language, but the language of a man and a woman who desire to be together needs no words to be understood. They soon engaged in exploring each other with their hands and mouths, his masculinity having quickly responded. Her woman attendants appeared from the room's shadows and, as they continued their embrace, let down her hair and removed her gown. Two of them began tugging at his unfamiliar fastenings, but he shrugged them off, unwilling to be disrobed by strange women.

Amused, his partner said something that made them leave the room and quietly close the door behind them. Then, deep within the castle where King George slept, Tathtowe and the yellow-haired English woman shared a night of passionate lovemaking.

Toward dawn, having fallen into a deep slumber, a tap on his shoulder awakened him.

Her women stood beside the bed, holding his discarded clothing, signaling that he was to dress. His lover continued sleeping soundly, her bare limbs tangled in the bedding as he dressed. The tapestry was pulled aside, the concealed door opened, and the four escorts from the night before were waiting for him, ready to guide him back to his lodgings before the light of day.

After that, they shared several nights of passion in her bedchamber. He saw her among the royal attendants at regal events, often seated near King George. But, of course, they did not allow their eyes to meet nor acknowledge their passion for each other on those occasions.

Each of the other young Cherokee warriors soon found themselves engaged in similar liaisons with curious English women. Even Wiggan was in great demand. It was a rare night when more than one or two travelers slept in their chambers at the Covent Garden Inn.

As they sailed back to Charles Town, Wiggan told them the innkeeper had reported coming upon Attacullaculla asleep on the table in the central room. The Englishman had supposed he slept there because he considered himself of a higher station than his traveling companions. They enjoyed a good laugh at that, slapping an embarrassed Attacullaculla on the back and holding their sides as they laughed at his expense.

The truth of the matter was that the previous evening had been spent in the eager embrace of a love-starved woman of generous proportions. She had exhausted the diminutive Attacullaculla so that his back pained him to lie upon the soft sleeping spaces of the bedchamber. He walked bent over for several days after that and could sleep only on the hard tabletop.

The conversation then became increasingly ribald as the young warriors pressed for more details. Unfortunately, no matter how hard I tried, my pretense turned into reality, and I sank into a deep sleep.

I was barely aware of strong arms lifting me from the mat and carrying me to my sleeping furs in Quatsis' house.

CHAPTER 15

Secret Revelation

Summer 1738
10 years old
Chota Town

Daybreak arrived too soon after the storytelling beneath the branches of the towering chestnut tree. I had scarcely burrowed into my sleeping furs when Quatsis called me to hurry. The sun was already turning the eastern sky a rosy pink as it began its journey across the sky. It was time for the going-to-water ceremony with which we began each day.

With a struggle, I crawled from the cozy nest I shared with my little brothers, rubbing my eyes and stretching the stiffness from my gangly arms and legs. Terrapin whined and tugged at my shift, clutching his tiny manhood with his other hand. Fully awake now and laughing at this little one, I hurried him through the door and to the bushes, where we both made water.

Returning quickly to the house before Quatsis became impatient with us, we joined the rest of the family, including Will and a bleary-eyed Johnny.

Other family groups joined us as Oconostota led the way through the town gates and down the path to the beautiful Tennessee river that flowed past Chota. Quatis took the lead at the river, guiding her flock to a favorite spot where the river narrowed and dashed against submerged rocks, creating a joyous sound. Then, facing east, we formed a line at the river's edge, our bare toes dipping into its early morning chill as the men moved upriver to their sacred place.

As the eldest woman in our family, Quatsis came behind each child, clasped our shoulders with her strong hands, and recited a prayer for us. Then, after she held the infant Bark over the rushing stream and repeated her prayer for his benefit, we waded into the frigid water.

Kneeling, I gasped as its coldness enveloped my bare body. Holding my breath, I scrubbed myself with the gritty river sand before reaching over to help Terrapin with his morning bath. When we finished, we turned east again, and just as the sun appeared on the horizon, Quatsis completed the morning prayer, asking the Provider to purify us and bless our family with good health and long life. Thus, we began each day, regardless of the weather, for in this manner, we washed away evil thoughts and physical impurities, starting each day anew.

This morning, Quatsis was anxious for us to return to the village, for she still had much to do before the festivities began. I had hoped to slip away from her scrutiny to play with my friends, but she was too quick. She grasped me by the arm as I tried to sidle out the door and directed me to a multitude of chores she expected. Quatsis still held firm to the belief that I would someday be interested in homemaking and meal preparation. But that expectation was never to be realized.

It was with envy that I watched Sour Mush, Hanging Maw, Cappy, and other boys my age heading for the river to fish or the woods to hunt small game. Bad Water, Moytoy's son, had joined them. My disappointment was forgotten, however, when I saw that Cornsilk, my mother's sister, was among the crowd of visitors arriving at Chota for the Mature Green Corn Festival.

She came from Toqua, bringing my cousins Wurth and Willow and the new baby, Tassel. We three girls were so delighted to see each other that our mothers soon gave up trying to get any meaningful work out of us. The two sisters, Cornsilk and Quatsis, fell into a familiar routine, effortlessly completing last-minute chores after directing us to watch over the little boys.

We were happy to obey, shooing the little ones away from the outdoor kitchen and into the cool recesses of the cabin. We chattered nonstop while playing with the babies until they finally collapsed into a sleepy heap, arms and legs tangled like a litter of puppies.

In the hush of the darkened sleeping room, we grew quiet, huddling close together and whispering to avoid waking the boys from their nap. But then we had to cover our mouths to keep from giggling aloud, for on the other side of the wall, we heard the unmistakable sounds of a man and woman pleasuring each other.

Several years ago, Will and Johnny added a room to Quatsis' cabin to create a dwelling. It was the closest they had to a home since the destruction of the trading post at Tugaloo. The room served as a place to store their personal belongings and entertain guests.

Their living space shared a common wall with the sleeping room of the cabin, but it lacked a connecting door. The only way to access their quarters was through an entrance at the back of the cabin. Consequently, they and their guests could come and go freely, mostly unnoticed by curious neighbors.

At night, I often woke to the sounds of a man and a woman enjoying each other's company. Johnny and our father were lustful men who frequently entertained women who could slip in and out of their quarters without provoking the ire of jealous husbands or lovers.

And now, there was no mistaking Johnny's muffled voice or the nervous giggles of Walina, Sour Mush's pretty older sister and Cornelius Dougherty's daughter. Johnny had been pursuing her for some time and was about to succeed in his seduction from the sound of it.

Our ears pressed against the wall, and our eyes widened with wonder when Quatsis came to investigate the sudden silence in the sleeping room. Unfortunately, she was not in the mood for nosy little girls and gave us a stern scolding in as loud a tone as she could manage without waking the sleeping boys.

"Shoo!" she told us. "Go outside and play, you naughty children! And be quiet about it!"

Of course, we were happy to comply, finally free from the watchful eyes of our busy mothers. We hurried to the woods and down the trail to our favorite swimming hole, where we waited for the rest of our friends to finish their chores.

Willow soon fell asleep beneath a shade tree, tired from the long journey and the day's excitement. Clasping hands and grinning at each other, Wurth and I cherished the joy of having one another completely to ourselves. Our bond was closer than that of sisters; it was almost as if we had shared the same womb.

"Prachey, I have something to tell you!" Wurth confided in a conspiratorial tone that signaled a bit of gossip. Wurth and I shared a lifelong interest in the lives of our mutual acquaintances and never grew tired of discussing what we knew about them. We were both skilled at being unobtrusive and, as a result, were privy to more adult conversations than most girls our age.

We gathered stories and gossip like other girls collected pretty stones or colorful feathers, eagerly anticipating the chance to share our news the next time we met. Then, when we were finally alone, we would relay this snippet of observation or that unguarded comment, and together, we would weave an uncanny perception of the members of our community.

"It is about your mother," she said. The grin faded from my face as I became very still.

"My mother?"

"Yes. It is about your mother," she prattled, hardly aware of my discomfort. "Do you remember we've wondered about Old Hop and why he seems to watch you closely?"

I nodded, for it was true. We had observed that the lame headman frequently cast his gaze in my direction, and he appeared sad or wistful when he thought no one was watching.

"Well, Prachey," she continued, "I overheard my mother talking to Ollie, and guess what?" Then, without waiting for my response, she plunged ahead with her story. "It's so tragic!" she exclaimed, clasping her hands to her chest in that overly dramatic way she always had.

"Old Hop deeply loved your mother and believed they would marry. She was younger than him and the prettiest girl in the whole Nation; everyone said so. My mother said she was as sweet as she was beautiful, always smiling and laughing, and so much fun to be around. Old Hop was her first lover, and even though she took a few other men to her sleeping pallet, she always returned to Old Hop. Everyone thought theirs would be a great match, for she was well-born and beautiful, and he was destined to be the Peace Chief of the Cherokee."

Well, this was shocking news to me—for I never would have thought that my long-dead mother had led such an exciting life.

"But she had secretly been infatuated with the trader William Hatton since she was young," Wurth continued. "Will had bedded many women of the People but never grew serious about any of them. So she pretended to ignore him. My mother said the more he pursued her, the more aloof she became, and all the people of Tugaloo and Estatoe knew he didn't stand a chance." She stifled a giggle, and then we looked hard at each other, for this was good information to have when we grew older and wanted to ensnare a man of our own.

"Their courtship was brief because she would not take him to her bed until they were married, and he resembled a stag in a rut! Before long, they had tied the knot, and she was carrying someone within."

She lowered her voice to a theatrical whisper, "Poor old Hop was heartbroken, for he had been certain she would become his wife."

Well, imagine that! My mother was a heartbreaker. But would he have been my father if she had married Old Hop? No, because in that case, I would not have been myself but someone else. That line of thinking was far too confusing, so we quickly abandoned it and moved on to the story at hand.

"Of course, Old Hop wasn't old back then, nor did he go by 'Hop' because he wasn't lame when he was a young warrior. He was known as Standing Turkey, as he was tall and stately, strutting like a tom attracting hens."

I must have looked incredulous because she added emphatically, "My mother and Ollie agreed that he was as handsome as your mother was beautiful."

"Old Hop? Handsome?" I asked, as that was indeed hard to imagine.

"Very!" she said emphatically. "But he went to battle against the Shawnee soon after he learned about your mother's marriage and was badly wounded. He took a musket ball to the right leg, and despite everything the healers could do, it never healed properly. As a result, he became known as One Who Hops and later as Old Hop."

"Sometime later, he married Su-Wi, who had long yearned for him," she continued, "but everyone knew that he still loved your mother."

That would definitely explain the sad-eyed Su-Wi, who never had a kind word for me, the child of the woman her husband loved.

"And," Wurth added dramatically, pausing to capture my full attention, "Ollie and my mother said you look just like your mother!"

Well! I had heard that before, but now it became clear why our Headman cast such sorrowful gazes at me, for it was the image of his lost love that he saw before him.

We clasped hands and chatted about this exciting drama and its implications. The children of Old Hop and Su-Li were some of our closest playmates, and we wondered if they knew that my mother and their father had almost married.

Wurth suggested that if they had, maybe I would have been their daughter Sookey, a quiet girl our age that we secretly called "Granny" because she acted like such an old woman. Neither of us liked that thought nor the idea of me being Cappy, their son.

Our speculation was interrupted by a swarm of children who had also been relieved of their chores for the day. Pushing such unsettling thoughts aside, we stripped off the little clothing we were wearing and plunged into the cool water.

CHAPTER 16

Gathering of the People

Summer 1738
10 years old
Chota Town

We splashed and swam in the pool until the sun was directly over-head. We knew we had lingered too long and that our mothers would be looking for us. It was time to prepare for the most important ceremony of the year: the Mature Green Corn Festival.

About six weeks ago, we celebrated the New Green Corn Festival, which occurs when the young corn is ready to eat. Now, our main food source was fully ripe, the stalks had grown tall, and the ears of corn were hard and perfectly formed. It was time for a celebration to give thanks.

Hurrying down the path to the village, we were astonished to see how Chota had transformed during our brief absence. Its population had swelled as hundreds of Cherokee traveled from all parts of the Nation to attend the festival. The Tennessee River was lined with log canoes, neatly arranged side by side along its rocky banks. More people were seen making their way down the river, with the late arrivals searching for a place to beach their canoes.

The entrance through the palisaded walls of Chota was crowded with visitors who had arrived via the Tennessee river or various trails leading to the Nation's Capital, their arms burdened with baggage and food containers. Wurth, Willow, Sour Mush, Hanging Maw, and I stood to the side with a small group of friends, our bodies drying in the sun, wet hair dripping down our backs as we watched the parade of visitors streaming into the village.

Once inside, the crowds spread through our once spacious town, which quickly became jammed with ten times its usual population. Townspeople welcomed the visitors with warm greetings, assisted them with their belongings, and directed them to houses and temporary shelters that would serve as their accommodations for the next several days.

Young men and women were assigned to take the baskets and animal hide containers filled with food to the large storehouse behind the Council House, where they would be stored until needed for the festival feast.

After separating from the other children, Wurth, Willow, and I held tightly to each other's hands. Captivated by the scene before us, we paused to stand in the shade of a nearby cabin. Our clothes were bundled and clutched under Wurth's arm, our naked bodies streaked with river water and sweat, and our damp hair in disarray.

Suddenly, Wurth and I felt Cornsilk's sharp fingernails digging into our shoulders as she swooped down on us, her brow knitted with anger.

"There you are!" she hissed. "I've been looking for you everywhere!" And we knew we were in big trouble.

Quatsis was easygoing, even a bit scatterbrained, and easily distracted when I misbehaved. But Cornsilk was different; she was a strict disciplinarian whose attention could not be diverted. Now, I felt her nails digging into my shoulder like a hawk's talons as she pulled the three of us into a small circle, leaning down so we could hear the full force of her fury.

"Prachey, your mother has a house full of guests and two little boys to care for while you play in the woods! Shame on you! And look at the three of you!"

She released her grasp to lean back, better able to examine our pitiful state. Suddenly, I felt very dirty and very, very naked.

"I am very disappointed in both of you," she scolded Wurth and me. "You were responsible for Willow, and just look at her!" Willow wore a look of pure innocence, knowing that Wurth and I would take the blame for her appearance while she remained off the hook.

Cornsilk led the three of us back to the house while we desperately wished for a large hole to open up and swallow us. We felt shame, as even with our eyes downcast, it was evident that everyone was staring at us in our pitiful state.

My mother was, of course, embarrassed to see her filthy daughter walking down the main street of the town, past the Council House and toward her door. The pain on her lovely face and her clear mortification heightened my shame. Even Will and Johnny appeared distressed at the sight of me, and I realized it was because my shift was tucked under Wurth's arm instead of covering my bare body.

Our cousin Molly's knowledge of our disgrace only heightened our humiliation. Saluy, now the Headman of Estatoe, and Mourning Dove had arrived to visit our home during our absence. Molly, their daughter, was only three summers younger but far more mature in her demeanor. A beautiful girl, she was always well-groomed, with never a speck of dirt or grease spot on her. Soft-spoken and graceful, she never misbehaved or caused her parents any distress. Quatsis and Cornsilk often held her up to us as an example of how we should look and behave. Consequently, Wurth and I felt a deep dislike for the child.

That afternoon, we were two very remorseful little girls after quickly bathing and dressing in clean clothes. Will had brought a length of bright yellow calico covered with tiny red flowers, and Quatsis had somehow found the time to create a new shift for me-one that covered my backside.

My shame over my misbehavior deepened when I realized she must have sewn well into the night. I silently vowed never to misbehave again, as it was too painful for both me and those I loved.

Dressed appropriately and with bright ribbons in our shining hair, Wurth and I were once again responsible for the little ones while our mothers could tend to their duties as the wives of leading warriors.

Keeping a watchful eye on Molly, Willow, and Terrapin while carrying the babies Bark and Tassel, we set out to see the remarkable transformation of the familiar Chota Town.

Columns of gray smoke wafted from numerous cooking fires scattered throughout the town. The rich aroma of roasting meat and corn filled the air, making our stomachs growl in anticipation of the feasts to come in the days ahead. As we wandered aimlessly, we found ourselves in a crowd near the town entrance. The people parted to allow a large hunting party, led by seven ceremonially adorned hunters, to make their entrance.

We knew they had been sent out on a six-day hunt, their return tradition-ally timed to coincide with the eve of the festival. Several freshly killed deer were slung from poles carried by the men, their hooves pointing skyward and their heads dangling and bobbing with each step the hunters took. With great solemnity, the hunters paraded down the main thoroughfare to the sacred square before the Council House, which sat atop a high mound of earth.

Other men had cut down a shade tree, brought it into town, and set its trunk in a deep hole in the center of the square. We were surprised by its enormous size, which dominated the usually empty square. Branches trimmed from its wide expanse were used to create an arbor for the Old Hop, the White Chief, and his Council. With great ceremony, the hunters presented the deer to the dignitaries. Throughout the afternoon, men gathered at the sacred square to select a green bough for the next day's ceremony.

In the late afternoon, the People gathered in the square dressed in their finest clothing. Young women chattered gaily, their dark eyes sparkling as they looked around to see who else was there. Their dresses were orna-mented with colorful beads, shimmering feathers, and tiny bells that filled the air with soft musical tinkling as they moved gracefully through the crowd. They had styled their hair elaborately, either piled high upon their heads or in a bun secured with carved bone or shell pins, or they had let it flow freely in glossy streams over their shoulders and down their backs.

Older women were more sedate in their composure, moving regally and with quiet dignity through the crowd. As befitting their status, they were dressed even more elaborately than the younger women. The wives of healers and headmen of other towns were easy to identify, as they were clothed in dazzling white buckskin dresses with their hair piled even higher than that of other women. Touches of the distinctive red, symbolic of war, on otherwise white costumes distinguished the wives of leading warriors.

The warriors moved purposefully and proudly, carrying their shields and weapons, with their upper bodies bare to display their battle scars as marks of distinction. Their costumes also showcased their achievements in battle, featuring silver gorgets and armbands that glistened in the waning sunlight.

At dusk, we gathered with our clan members to watch distinguished women perform a religious dance. My heart swelled with pride as I saw our mothers among the women dancing silently and with great solemnity, moving in a timeless pattern older than anyone could remember. We were encouraged to focus our thoughts on the faithfulness of the Provider who had granted us yet another bountiful crop of life-giving corn, assuring us of food to survive the coming winter.

Later, bonfires were lit, and the women set out large platters and baskets of food. Then, everyone wandered through the town, feasting and socializing until late into the night.

CHAPTER 17

The Festival

Summer, 1738
10 years old
Chota Town

The sunrise the next day signaled the official start of the Festival. After our ritual of going to the water, Wurth, Sour Mush, and I joined the other women and children watching the men perform their dance in the sacred square.

The leader initiated the dance, setting the rhythm with his rattle while the other men followed, each holding a green bough from the sacred tree above their heads. They leaped around, mimicking the green corn that reached upward toward the sun in the fields of virtuous people. Seven times during each of the seven dances that morning, they circled around the trunk and beneath the tree's broad branches, symbolizing the Provider's sheltering arms.

Johnny of Tannasee, the Great Warrior of the Cherokee, joined the men in their triumphant dance. He sat upon a platform, carried around the sacred tree on the shoulders of six of our strongest warriors, including the handsome Tathtowe. As the Red Chief, he appeared suitably fierce, dressed from head to toe in garments dyed the color of war. The War Chief's outfit was completed by a raven's skin fastened around his neck with red strings, eagle feathers striped in red adorning his scalp lock, and his arms covered with otter skins.

Cornsilk came beside us and gently placed her hands on the shoulders she had squeezed so mercilessly the day before. This was her way of showing she was no longer angry with us. "Children, do you know why the number seven is sacred to the People?" she asked.

We were quick to answer, eager to demonstrate what good little girls we had become. "Yes, Mother," Wurth and I answered in unison, for all the women of the Paint Clan were our mothers. "Seven represents the seven directions: east, west, north, south, up, down, and here, where we stand."

"Very good, children," she smiled. "I am proud of you." We understood she meant more than just our correct answers to her questions.

The crowd parted as she moved regally away from us, and I felt a surge of pride in being recognized as one of her family members. She was elegantly dressed in soft white buckskin adorned with elaborate beadwork that caught the sun's rays.

Cornsilk tended to cling to old ways and had yet to adopt the fashion of sewing glass beads from the traders onto her ceremonial garments. Instead, she carefully cut porcupine quills and stained them with colors extracted from plants. Consequently, the colors of her tunic were muted, not as brilliant as those adorned with the colorful glass beads, but no less beautiful.

Sour Mush poked my ribs, bringing my focus back to the arbor, and I gasped at the sight before us. Green boughs from the sacred tree sheltered not one but two groups of dignitaries, all dressed in their finest garments.

Old Hop and his counselors sat under the arbor created by the townsmen the day before. To his right was the solemn Bear Killer, his principal assistant. Flanking them were the seven counselors representing the seven clans, along with his messenger, speaker, and the representatives of the Councils of Beloved Men and Beloved Women.

They were all splendidly dressed, as suited their exalted positions, but the familiar Old Hop of Chota had become an especially regal figure. He was clad in the purest white, including a cape made of white feathers.

This majestic man bore little resemblance to the unobtrusive figure who had sat on the edges of the gathering the previous evening, listening quietly and contributing little. Instead, Old Hop's demeanor was so regal, with his uptilted chin and squared shoulders, that aside from his resplendent attire, there could be no doubt he was a royal personage.

I couldn't help but wonder, if my mother had seen him thus, would she have chosen the burly Scottish trader for her husband? Confusing thoughts overwhelmed me as I stood there staring, my mouth agape. Old Hop must have sensed my gawking, for he turned his implacable gaze toward me. Catching my eye, I noticed the slightest glimmer of amusement. I felt my cheeks burn with embarrassment, for he surely must have known what I was thinking.

Sour Mush nudged me, saying, "Prachey! Look over there!" He jerked his head to indicate the direction since it would have been rude to point at Moytoy, who was sitting nearby under a hastily constructed arbor. Beside him were his counselors, including Christian Priber, who had spoken so forcefully the night before. They were all dressed in costumes that sharply contrasted with those of Old Hop's court. Everything they wore was of English origin.

The People stirred, moved restlessly, and murmured among themselves, for this confusing arrangement caused them great unease.

My tendency to linger around my fathers and their friends had fostered an unusual interest in politics for a child my age. I understood that we were governed by a dual organization that had served us well through alternating periods of war and peace for countless generations. However, Cuming's interference disrupted the power balance, unsettling the people who were unsure where to place their loyalty.

The White Chief presided over each town's governing body when not at war. He would ceremoniously step aside during wartime and defer to the Red Chief or Great Warrior. The national governing body reflected this same structure. Since Chota was the mother town of the Cherokee Nation, Old Hop, as Chota's White Chief, also served as the foremost White Chief of the Nation.

I remembered overhearing that his brother, Moytoy, had held the prestigious position of Great Warrior of Tellico Town before Cuming named him Emperor. This title meant little to the People. Moytoy's new designation had minimal impact on our daily lives, and little attention was given to his posturing. Old Hop could have pressed the issue, but he was a diplomat first and foremost and quietly bided his time.

A few years went by, and Moytoy grew impatient. He had sacrificed the people's respect for a title that carried no real authority within the Nation. King George of England may have recognized him as Emperor of the Cherokee, but even the colonial governors ignored him.

Will grumbled that White men too easily influenced Moytoy, who had listened raptly as Priber extolled the French and the benefits of trading with them instead of the English. French ambassadors had made the long journey from the north, tempting him with rare and unusual gifts while encouraging him to switch his allegiance from the distant King George, who seemed to have forgotten about him.

The increased French activity in the Nation caught the attention of the colonial governments. Concerned about an independent Cherokee Nation aligning with the French, South Carolina had recently recognized Moytoy as the leader of the People. They chose to appoint him to participate in negotiations with their government. Everyone present could see that Moytoy was following Cuming's advice and making an unprecedented effort to gain a more prominent position among the People. As a result, his aides had quickly constructed a poor imitation of the holy arbor where the beloved Old Hop sat.

Old Hop's dignity amid these uneasy circumstances was striking. If anything, he seemed even more stately than during other ceremonial events.

Moytoy, however, fidgeted and squirmed, whispering excessively to his councilors.

As young and inexperienced as I was, it struck me that Moytoy felt uneasy with the title of Emperor since he knew he was just a puppet of the White men. His power derived from our growing dependence on European trade goods, yet he had not garnered the respect of the People as his older brother had. In reality, the governors of the colonies held the power as they controlled trade. I believed he understood this and regretted having dipped his hand into the honeybee's hive, but for now, he did not know how to pull back.

My musings were interrupted when Wurth appeared beside me, jutting her right hip forward to better support Tassel. Unlike Bark, who would ride on our narrow hips by clasping his chubby baby legs around our waists, Tassel sat like a heavy basket with dangling legs, bearing none of his weight. So, even though Bark was the oldest and weighed more, he was the one I rushed to scoop up, leaving the placid Tassel for Wurth to carry. Always gullible, I doubt Wurth was aware of my ruse; otherwise, she would have complained loudly.

"Have you seen our mothers?" she asked, shifting Tassel to her other hip in a vain effort to carry him more comfortably.

"No," I replied, stifling a grin at her discomfort. "I've been watching Moytoy and his followers trying to figure out what they're up to."

"Hmmm," she said, distracted by Tassel reaching for the colorful ribbons in her hair. Despite our closeness, Wurth did not share my interest in politics or the power dynamics among those wielding influence within the Nation.

"It is unprecedented to have two arbors set up this way. So, what are they trying to gain from it? Do you think Moytoy is making a bid for Old Hop's position?"

"Who knows?" she said dismissively, nearly losing her balance as Tassel lunged for one of my hair ribbons.

"That's it, you little weasel!" she scolded, quickly setting him on his sturdy legs. He took a few unsteady steps before plopping down onto the hard-packed earth, after which he puckered his face and let out a pitiful wail.

"I suppose I should have used the carrying cloak, but I didn't want to ruin my tunic," she said, smoothing the colorful glass beads she had sewn onto her deerskin dress. With her hands on her hips, she looked down at her sobbing little brother with exasperation.

"I think he wants to nurse, don't you?" I asked her with a conspiratorial wink.

"What? Oh, yes, I'm sure he does," she said, finally understanding my ploy and picking him up again to search the crowd for our mothers.

We joined them where they congregated with other women of the Paint Clan near Old Hop's arbor. Handing Tassel to their mother, Wurth quickly stepped back as we moved to the crowd's edge to watch the men perform the Mature Green Corn Dance.

The sun reached its zenith as the men stopped dancing. The air was thick with dust, stirred into red-brown swirls by their feet. They placed their green boughs in safe places for easy retrieval the next day. Their women gathered around them with offerings of cool water to quench their thirst. Groups formed and then scattered as the People moved toward their dwellings or temporary shelters, eager for a midday meal followed by a period of rest.

Wurth and I helped our mothers set out the platters and baskets of food. Then, we herded our little brothers and sister into the coolness of the house for a nap. None objected as they were all tired from the morning's exciting activities. Even Terrapin forgot his usual protest. Once everything became quiet, we were free to explore our transformed town.

Despite the hundreds of people within the palisades, the town was surprisingly quiet, burdened by the heaviness of late summer heat. Wurth and I held hands as we wandered through the lanes that separated the houses. Our friends, who had also been freed from their responsibilities, joined us one by one until we formed a sizable crowd. Without discussing it beforehand, we made our way to the center of town, to the Council House.

The cool darkness inside was a welcome relief from the blazing midday sun. We paused at the entrance, letting our eyes adjust to the dimness. Respectfully subdued, as we were in a sacred place, we moved to the center where the elders of the Nation sat on woven mats.

As much as I loved the grandeur of the ceremonial dances, this part of the festival was what I cherished. In the afternoon heat, small children napped, adults gathered in small groups to gossip, and young men and women got to know their future partners. During this time, the elders came together to share the myths and legends of the Cherokee. I loved listening to their stories, sitting enthralled for hours, soaking in every word and committing them to memory.

Gray Squirrel, the eldest of the elders, was a wise, wrinkled man who spoke eloquently and deliberately. He recounted the stories he had heard as a child, often pausing to sip from the gourd at his side. He would then rest, closing his eyes and occasionally nodding as another elder began a different tale.

All the stories were familiar to us since we had heard them many times, and they never varied. Yet, despite their familiarity, they remained entertaining. They were imprinted on our young minds through repetition, shaping who we were—children of the Real People.

Before long, as always, the sun's slanting rays slipped through the Council House door, marking the end of the storytelling, just as the sounds of increasing activity within the town did. Scattering to our homes, we prepared ourselves for the evening celebration.

Women were not allowed to enter the sacred square while men danced during the day; however, after sunset, both men and women participated in social dances. At these dances, married women danced with their husbands, while young women danced with men from other clans, flirting with those who seemed to be suitable mates.

It was a joyful time, marked by a greater sense of informality than the morning's ceremony and filled with laughter from the crowd. The dancers often paused to enjoy the large platters and baskets of food set on trestles. They danced well into the night, hesitant to leave the celebrations. Eventually, fatigue took over, and the ranks of dancers dwindled as the moon rose.

Finally, Wurth and I curled up together, my sleeping place crowded with younger brothers who had already fallen into an exhausted slumber.

"This is my favorite festival," Wurth whispered, careful not to wake the little ones.

"Mine, too," I confided, ignoring that we always made the same remark after each of the six major festivals.

The Cherokee of my childhood gathered at Chota, the national Capitol, six times a year for significant festivals, each with its own distinct purpose and rituals. As always, we whispered excitedly to one another, sharing our observations of the day's activities: I was particularly interested in the implications of who had been seen with whom, while Wurth focused on how certain delicious dishes were prepared or recounted details of the beautiful clothing we had admired. Finally, our thoughts turned to the morning, and we fell into a deep sleep, anticipating yet another three days of festivity.

CHAPTER 18

The School Teacher

Winter 1796
68 years old
Baldridge Creek, GA

I can no longer tell my grandchildren stories of their ancestry, for my rage has rendered me speechless. A white-hot coal of anger has settled in the pit of my stomach and will not cease its burning. Never, in all the years since I first drew breath, have I felt so helpless.

If I were younger, I would mount one of the horses in the paddock and ride through the woods to the house of that despicable man, the school teacher. When he saw me coming, he would know why I was there, and I would laugh at the fear I would see in his eyes. Once I was finished with him—slowly doing what must be done, prolonging his agony as long as possible—he would no longer pose a threat to any of my People.

The Cherokee would understand that justice had been served in the tradition of blood revenge, and there would be no retribution against me. The White authorities would attempt to uncover who committed this act against one of their own, but the People would reveal nothing. If they were to discover it was I, what of it? I am at the end of my life, and it would matter little if they cut it short by a few months or years to satisfy their misguided sense of justice. But all I can do is fantasize about what I would do if I were able while the coal of anger continues to burn, scorching me from the inside out and offering me no peace.

We have moved to a new farm by a creek named after Caty's family, the Baldridges, not far from the White city of Atlanta. This pleases her, as she is closer to her kin than when we lived at Noonday Creek. Numerous families in this valley are descendants of early traders among the Cherokee—mixed bloods, like my family.

There are also more cleared fields along Baldridge Creek for growing crops, which provide the cash flow needed for the manufactured items that George and his wives consider necessities. Of course, more land required slaves to work in the fields. These field slaves aren't part of our extended family like Jacob, who has been with us since we lived on the smaller farm. Instead, they live separately in quarters overseen by Jonas, a low-class white overseer hired by George specifically for that purpose.

I don't like Jonas. Nor do I like the look I see on the faces of the slaves when he draws near. This is not the slavery I knew as a child. These slaves endure lives filled with hopelessness and despair. They know, as do I, that their only release from the ceaseless toil and abuse is death.

My son George turns a blind eye, as does Caty. She still manages the kitchen and herb gardens, which are quite large considering the many mouths to feed. In addition, she planted rows of fruit trees in the meadow by the creek and eagerly anticipates her first crop.

George has built a much larger house, providing ample space for all his children and the numerous visitors he enjoys entertaining. It is an elaborate two-story home—more fitting for a man of his stature, he claims. Many rooms are filled with expensive furnishings. Glass windows invite summer's sunshine but also winter's chill.

George wanted to set aside a little room for me in his new house so that I would be nearby while still having the privacy I crave. However, I declined his generous offer. A little distance is wise, I think. Two women in a house are enough. A third, even one as old as I, would be one too many. Having their Granny separate from their daily lives is suitable for the children. It adds a hint of mystery and privacy, which I like. Any of the children can come to me whenever they wish to share as much or as little as they want, talk to me, or simply be present with me.

Once George's rather pretentious house was built, I persuaded him to build a small one in the old fashion for his mother. I chose a clearing not far from the big house but screened by rhododendrons. Close to the creek, with only a few steps carved from the steep embankment, it is convenient for my morning ritual of welcoming the sun by going to water. It is disappointing that the family no longer observes the old ritual. Occasionally, a grandchild will accompany me—to humor me—but I know it is only out of their love for me. A great many of our traditions are no longer part of their daily life.

We had to search for an elder who remembered how to build the houses of my youth— those of Tugaloo, Estatoe, Chota, and Tellico. Nowadays, the People construct homes in the English style using hewn logs or planed lumber. Few recall how to create a house of woven cane and plaster, those sturdy structures that have sheltered our ancestors since time immemorial.

Then I requested that a summer kitchen be built for those rare occasions when I feel bestirred to prepare a meal in the traditional way. George, being a dutiful son, honored his old mother yet again.

However, I rejected his offer to build a winter house because its design was intended for several inhabitants, not just one old woman. In ancient times, a fire was built in the center of a domed structure that was fashioned from bent cane and encrusted with clay. On the coldest winter nights, entire families would lie within, kept safe and warm by the fire, their furs, and each other's body heat. Within those turtle shell-like structures, small crafts were made, repairs were executed, and stories were shared.

This winter has been unusually cold. When my little summer house became too frigid, I joined my son's family in the big house. Nancy offered me the elaborately furnished bedchamber next to the dining room, the one reserved for overnight guests, as my own. Since it shares the fireplace in the dining room, she thought it would be a warm place for me to sleep. But midway through my first night in its cavernous bed, I made my way up the stairs to the second level and opened the door to the girls' room. In the dim moonlight, I could see three beds lining the wall. Various shapes and different sizes of my granddaughters and visiting nieces marked their presence beneath the mounds of quilts.

Tiptoeing across the icy wooden floor to the braided rug beside the least crowded bed, I lifted the quilts and crawled into the welcoming warmth radiating from their young bodies. And there is where I spend my winter nights: an old crone, my body and soul warmed by these girls who carry the seed of future generations of my People.

This close proximity to the girls and my lifelong observation habit allowed me to see that something was terribly wrong with Rachel.

This granddaughter has always leaned towards introspection. Among the generally rambunctious children in our household, she is a quiet child. Last summer, she came to my house to whisper that she had become a woman.

It was I who had shown this delicate child of my son how to fasten a wide strip of cotton to the front and back of a belt tied around her narrow hips. Into this strap we placed dried moss, which I kept for just such purposes. I helped her as she awkwardly pulled the moss-filled strap between her legs. I gave her an additional supply of straps and moss, instructing her how to cleanse them of the menstrual flow they would absorb and then dry them for reuse.

Of course, she knew about a woman's monthly moon time, but she had listened attentively because my instructions were relevant to her now. Then, one last time, she permitted me to pull her onto my lap and rock her as I had throughout her childhood.

I couldn't help myself. I became a sentimental old granny, lamenting the swift passage of time since I had placed moss between her baby legs to absorb her uncontrolled wetting and soiling, just as I had most recently done for Turtle.

"To think of it," I whispered in her ear, "my little Rachel, a woman grown."

Rachel is likely the most intelligent of George's older children. She is undoubtedly more studious than her elder brothers, Jesse and Moses. Indeed, she has always had a thirst for knowledge, quickly learning to read English words and then devouring every book or pamphlet she could find. She dreams of becoming a teacher, first gaining as much knowledge as possible from the Whites and then teaching the younger children. Her parents support her aspiration, allowing her to attend the mission school with her brothers. Caty has even encouraged George to explore sending her to a school in the East when she is old enough.

However, shortly after our move to Baldridge Creek, she showed less interest in accompanying her brothers to the schoolhouse. We thought little of it at the time, knowing she didn't like the schoolmaster, Mr. Morgan.

A stiff and formal man of medium height, he sported an unusually protuberant abdomen, which the boys snickered made him look as though he carried someone within. Even on the hottest days, he insisted on wearing the starched white shirts, woolen britches, and jackets he had worn in the northeastern state from which he came. Sometimes, his face would grow so red with the heat that the children would bet against each other whether or not he would faint before the end of the school day. At home, the boys make fun of him, describing his strange ways and mimicking his Eastern accent. I am sure Mr. Morgan knows their ridicule, which undoubtedly makes him behave even more obnoxiously.

Aside from his repugnance, I do not like what Mr. Morgan teaches the children. He has been instructed to teach them counting words and to read and write the English talking leaves. But he persists in teaching them the Englishman's version of history, which makes them sound far superior to the Real People. But even worse to my way of thinking, because it is a missionary school, he feels compelled to preach his religion to them. Some of the Cherokee have adopted Christianity, while others have added some parts of the Christian faith to our ancient religious beliefs. But I am not among either of those.

To Mr. Morgan's way of thinking, I am a heathen. And I say, "What of it? The beliefs of my People have stood us in good stead for more generations than can be numbered using the English counting words, and I see no need to change now. Mr. Morgan be damned!"

Therefore, at each evening meal, I ask the children what they learned at school that day, listening carefully to what they say and asking what I think are artful questions. In this fashion, I know what falsehoods he planted in their young minds; the better to root them out quickly with my storytelling.

Thus, when he filled their minds with that preposterous story of a warrior named Adam and a maiden named Eve, I settled beside the evening fire and told them how Mother Earth was really created.

"This is what the elders told me when I was a girl." I began, remembering Gray Squirrel and long afternoons in the Chota Council House, and any children within earshot stopped their play to come to hear my story, for I am a good storyteller. "The earth is a great island floating in a sea of water, suspended at each of the four cardinal points by a cord hanging down from the sky vault, which is of solid rock." I looked up at the ceiling, and each of the children sitting at my feet tipped their chins upward, looking for the cords that held the earth suspended.

"When the world grows old and worn out, the people will die, and the cords will break, letting the earth sink down into the ocean, and all will be water again." I continued with the familiar story.

"When all was water, the animals lived above the arch, but it was very crowded, and they wanted more room. They wondered what was below the water. The little water beetle offered to go and see what was there. It darted in every direction over the water's surface but could not find a firm place to rest. Then, it dived to the bottom and came up with some soft mud, which grew and spread on every side until it became the island we call the Earth.

"At first, the Earth was flat and very soft and wet. The animals were anxious to get down, and they sent out different birds to see if it was dry, but, finding no place to alight, they returned. At last, it was time, and they sent out the Great Buzzard and told him to go and prepare for them. He flew all over the earth, low down near the ground, and it was still soft.

"He was very tired when he reached the Cherokee country, and his wings began to flap and strike the ground. Wherever they hit the earth, there was a valley; where they turned up again, there was a mountain." Here, I extended my arms and bent at the waist, mimicking the Great Buzzard's flight, to the delight of the youngest children.

"When the animals above saw this, they feared that the whole world would be mountains, so they called him back. But the Cherokee country remains full of mountains to this day." And the little ones nodded their heads, for was it not so?

"Once the earth was dry, and the animals came down, it was still dark. So they got the sun and set it in a track to go every day across the island from east to west, just overhead. However, it was too hot this way, and the crawfish's shell scorched a bright red so that his meat was spoiled, and the Cherokee do not eat it." This elicited a pleased giggle from little Betsey, who has an aversion to any creature that crawls upon the earth.

"The conjurers put the sun another handbreadth higher in the air, but it was still too hot. They raised it another time, and yet another, until it was seven handbreadths high and just under the sky arch. Then it was right, and they left it so. Every day, the sun goes under this arch and returns at night on the upper side to the starting place." They nodded in understanding, for they knew this was true. Each morning, we go to water and greet the sun as it rises.

"When the animals and plants were first made, they were told to watch and keep awake for seven nights, just as young men now fast and stay awake when they pray for guidance. They tried to do this, and nearly all were awake through the first night. But the next night, several dropped off to sleep, and the third night, others were asleep, and then others, until the seventh night, of all the animals, only the owl, the panther, and one or two more were still awake. These were given the power to see and go about in the dark and to prey on the birds and animals that must sleep at night.

"Of the trees, only the cedar, the pine, the spruce, the holly, and the laurel were awake to the end. To them, it was given to be always green and to be greatest for medicine, but to the others, it was said: 'Because you have not endured to the end, you shall lose your hair every winter.'" This never failed to bring about a chorus of giggles, for I shook my heavy mane of silvery gray hair, creating a curtain from which I peered at them.

"Men came after the animals and plants. At first, there was only a brother and sister, until he struck her with a fish and told her to multiply, and so it was. A child was born to her in seven days, and after that, every seven days. Their number increased very fast until there was the danger that the world could not keep them. Then it was made that a woman should have only one child in a year if she chooses, and it has been so ever since."

The children clapped and laughed with delight at my story, regardless of whether they had heard it before, as I blended my teaching with entertainment, using gestures and expressions to emphasize the tale. I am engaged in a serious competition with Mr. Morgan, determined that my stories will replace those he delivers at the schoolhouse.

Nor do I like some of the teacher's behaviors my grandsons describe, although they laugh about it and make sport of the telling. Lighthearted Jesse particularly likes to parody Mr. Morgan standing before the class with his hands thrust into his pockets while he lectures them on some subject or another. Moses says he thought the pocket seams must have been ripped out because the more agitated Mr. Morgan becomes with his lectures, the further his hands go into his pockets until he fondles himself as he lectures. George and the boys laugh uproariously at such foolishness while Caty and Nancy shake their heads, smiling, and tell the boys to stop telling such incredible stories.

Lately, however, I have realized that Rachel has ceased to join in with her brothers' silliness. Whenever Mr. Morgan's name is mentioned, she will sit quietly, her face closed, until she finds some reason to leave the room.

CHAPTER 19

Outrage

Winter 1796
68 years old
Baldridge Creek, GA

However, there came a time when even George ceased to be amused by Mr. Morgan's behaviors. Perhaps in response to the children's scorn, Mr. Morgan began punishing them for their infractions. He would take one and then another of the boys to his living quarters, which were attached to the schoolhouse. He made them remove their trousers and grab their ankles. Then, standing behind them, Mr. Morgan beat their bare behinds with a shortened canoe paddle.

We four adults were outraged by the beatings. Cherokees never strike their children. From an early age, they learn appropriate behavior through example. Affection and cooperation among family members are our way of life; children model their behavior accordingly.

Occasionally, if an unruly child does not respond to public ridicule or being ignored, the exasperated mother will give him or her a vigorous dunking in the river. That usually shocks them into better behavior. However, in rare situations when more extreme punishment is necessary, dry scratching with briars or snake teeth will be used as a last resort. In that case, the mother's brother or oldest son will be called upon to complete the task. Certainly, a father will never punish his child, as the child is not of his clan. Mr. Morgan's beating of our children was against all our beliefs and traditions.

One evening, the children told us that Mr. Morgan had taken Rachel into his room and beat her because she had made too many errors while doing her sums. Rachel said her punishment differed from the boys' in that he had bent her over his knees while sitting and paddled her with his hand, allowing her to keep her drawers on. But still, we were angry. It was bad enough to beat our sons, but he should never have beaten our daughter.

George led a delegation of fathers who spoke with Mr. Morgan, chastising him for the beatings of their children. His response angered them, as he insisted it was his duty to impose discipline on the lives of the "heathen savages" by whatever means he deemed appropriate. However, their anger seemed to affect him as the beatings decreased in frequency.

Weeks passed. Jesse and Moses seldom attended school—Jesse because it was hunting season and Moses because he had begun to read the law with a new acquaintance of George's. Rachel and the younger boys, Jim and John, still went, but they no longer entertained the family by ridiculing Mr. Morgan's strange behavior, and we ceased thinking about it.

George was distracted and frequently absent from home during this time. He and Goodwyn, his lawyer, were attempting to recover his South Carolina lands, which had been confiscated at the end of the Revolutionary War. The claims required his presence in Augusta for a longer period of time.

As winter settled upon us, the day arrived when George returned from Augusta, reeking of rum. I noticed he sat loosely on his saddle as he rode directly to the barn. After uncharacteristically leaving the care of his horse to Jacob, he struggled to walk to the house. Clearly, he had tried to drown his sorrow and disappointment in rum. George had never been one to drink heavily; as a young man, he learned that he could not hold his liquor as well as his father could. It was unusual to see him drunk.

The South Carolina government had denied his most recent claim for restitution. He had also learned that Richard's plantation, which the Americans also confiscated, had been awarded to Thomas Brandon, a colonel of the so-called Patriots. Brandon had lived on the property for the past ten years and established a thriving plantation of his own. It was highly unlikely that even Richard's White son would inherit the South Carolina holdings that his father had left him, much less my George, his mixed blood son.

However, ownership of George's adjoining plantation, which included thousands of acres, was more ambiguous. As a young man, George sailed to England to acquire English citizenship through his father. Upon his return, his Cherokee uncles Oconostota, Willewanah, and Saluy granted him a vast tract of land. He then sold part of it to Richard for a nominal fee, retaining the rest for himself. Thus, his holdings were legally the result of Cherokee grants to an Englishman. This unique circumstance gave my son hope that his claim against South Carolina's illegal confiscation would be successful.

Thus far, the ongoing negotiations and litigation through the lawful process of the new republic have only led to more disappointment for him. However, his mother—me—did not sympathize, as it was clear that this battle was a waste of resources. His legal struggles also caused disagreements at home. Caty encouraged him, while Nancy grew frustrated with his stubbornness. It became a significant source of conflict.

An added distraction for the family during autumn and early winter was the new baby Nancy had birthed far too early. Little Sallie was so tiny that she fit in the cupped hands of the midwife, who was her Granny. She occupied all my attention as I drew from my store of medicinal knowledge to help this little one survive those first perilous weeks.

Caring for Sallie became Nancy's full-time occupation. We fashioned a harness from the softest doeskin, lined with rabbit fur, to snuggle the tiny one against her mother's body. There she was, warm and safe, with the familiar sound of her mother's heartbeat soothing her to sleep. When she stirred, Nancy would nurse her as often as the child could muster enough energy to suckle. It fell upon Caty to see to the household, an unfamiliar role for her.

Thus, George's household was in great turmoil that autumn and winter, and concern about Mr. Morgan's behavior was the least of our worries.

One evening, I was particularly fatigued and retired early. As I lay abed, my mind quiet for the first time that busy day, I noticed Rachel preparing for bed. As she disrobed, I saw a telltale spot of blood on her skirt. It struck me as odd because I knew that, within the fortnight, she had come to me for dried moss to replenish her supply. With a sickening jolt, I knew what was wrong with our Rachel.

I slept little that night, remembering how quiet she had become and how she withdrew from the family circle. With a heavy heart, I recognized the emptiness in her eyes, just as I had seen in other women in another time and place. Our women had been subjected to brutal attacks and rape by White men bent on destroying us and pushing us from our homeland. Their lust for land was often equal to their lust for the flesh.

The next day, she eagerly agreed to my suggestion to stay home from school to help me with some tasks at my summer house. It was there, in the privacy of that setting and through my gentle probing, that she revealed what had happened.

She told me that, as an older student and one of the brightest, Mr. Morgan assigned her the first seat in the middle row. Despite her embarrassment, there was no way for her to escape his self-fondling. She became increasingly aware of his staring at her developing breasts and that the touching of himself was in some way directed toward her.

His punishment of her became a dreaded occurrence, something that she could not escape, for it mattered not how diligent she was in her studies; he would find some reason to take her to his lodgings behind the schoolroom and make her lie across his knees.

At first, he had paddled her with his bare hand, her bottom covered by cotton drawers. But then he progressed to first pulling down her drawers, then making her take them off while he paddled her. He expressed concern for the welts that he raised and began applying a soothing ointment after each paddling, the application becoming more caressing each time. It distressed her because she could feel his arousal pressing against her side as he did this thing.

And while his hands were touching her, he would tell her what a bad girl she was, that he was doing what he did for her own good, to save her soul from eternal damnation.

The time came when the paddling was but a brief interlude to the more extended application of the ointment, his hand slipping lower until he had gained entry into her private place. Then abruptly, he would shove her to the floor, making her watch while he finished what he had started, threatening her and her family should she tell anybody what had happened.

I held her to my breast as she sobbed with confusion and shame. With great effort, I quelled my anger and revulsion, fearing she might misconstrue it and, in her delicate state of mind, believe it was she who repulsed me.

And then, her sobs quieted, and with her face pressed against my sodden bodice, she told me the rest of it.

The day before, he once again called her to his room while the other students ate their midday meal. Again, he made her remove her drawers before lying across his lap. With dread, she noticed that his trousers were unbuttoned. He began by paddling her with his bare hands, then quickly dipped his long, bony fingers into the jar of ointment on the table beside him. Applying ointment to the welts he had raised on her delicate skin, his hand moved lower once again, sliding into that place she tried to close against his searching fingers.

Suddenly, she told me, he lifted her from his lap, fumbled with his trousers, and then set her down, impaling her upon his engorged male organ. As he thrust into her, he held one hand over her mouth, whispering into her ear what a bad person she was, a wanton who tempted him beyond reason. He told her he was redeeming her soul by piercing her and that he was leading her down the path of righteousness.

When he finished, the monster threatened her again if she told anyone what had happened. In her confused and bewildered state, she cleansed herself of his discharge and returned to the schoolroom, pretending that nothing beyond the usual paddling had transpired.

Quelling the rage I felt for what she had endured, I acted not so much as her Granny but as a medicine woman. She allowed me to examine her, flinching as I applied a healing herbal ointment to her bruised and torn tissues. Then, I brewed a concoction of herbs that would dislodge his seed had it taken root in her young body, adding willow bark for its sedative effect. Relieved of the burden she had carried alone, she lay in the comfort of my bed, a cheerful fire keeping the winter's cold at bay. I sat with her as she drifted into a healing sleep, tucking the quilts around her chin.

Anger welled in my chest as I strode across the yard and into the big house, where I called for Caty and Nancy to join me. Bewildered, they left their tasks and followed me through the house, Sallie still nestled between Nancy's breasts. I led them to George's office, a room he had set aside to conduct his business affairs. But, in truth, this room had become the place where he wallowed in drink and self-pity.

It was no surprise that, although it was still mid-morning, my son already reeked of rum, with bloodshot eyes and slurred speech. I saw clearly then what I had not seen these past weeks—my son, who had always been so prideful, was unshaven and disheveled, his paunch protruding over his unbuckled belt and his jaw slack with bags under his eyes. His drunkenness only inflamed my anger further. My son, and Richard's, had become naught but a drunken lout!

His drinking buddies were with him: John Vann, George Downing, and Charles Beamer. However, I had seen these middle-aged men grow from naked little boys in the villages of my youth, and I had no qualms about telling them it was time for them to leave. Surprised, they looked to George, but he was as taken aback as they were. So, I waited beside the door, hands on my hips as they skulked out, mounted their horses, and rode away. Caty and Nancy took their places in the vacated chairs beside the fireplace.

To his credit, George immediately sobered when I told him of what had happened to his daughter. Her parents were as upset and angry as I was, and the four of us chastised ourselves more than each other for not being aware of what was happening to the child. Caty berated herself for insisting Rachel went to school when she had asked to stay home to help with the added burdens of the past few weeks. We were consumed by guilt as we remembered a comment, a look, or a clue that should have alerted us to what was happening. It was the always practical Nancy who ended our recrimination by raising the question of what we should do about it.

George found a new purpose in seeking justice for our Rachel. He led a delegation of Cherokee fathers who confronted Mr. Morgan, demanding his resignation. However, the despicable man denied Rachel's claims. In his arrogance, he audaciously suggested that a heathen boy had been with her, claiming it was commonly known that Cherokee women had loose morals. The other fathers had to restrain George from striking him with his fists.

Enraged, the men went to the sheriff and the church authorities, demanding punishment for the teacher. The sheriff told them that Mr. Morgan had faced similar charges at his last school in the far northeastern state from which he had come. The church authorities had swept those accusations under the carpet and sent him west to the Cherokee People.

After going from one authority to another, the men were furious. Weeks went by, and it became clear that our children had no protection under the regulations and laws of the White men. No charges would be brought against Mr. Morgan. Even if there had been, they were told that Rachel would not be allowed to testify against him in a court of law because the Cherokee have no rights in the White man's legal system.

The day came when George called the family together and told us what we were to do. Jesse and Moses were to return to school with the younger Jim and John, but Rachel would not. We were to give up the fight and continue as if nothing had happened.

Seeing that darling girl's expression as she took in her father's words broke my heart. Her shoulders slumped as she tried to disappear into the chair upon which she sat, the vacant look returning to her eyes.

A fury overwhelmed me, and I railed at my son, that burning coal of anger consuming my heart. He held my fists in his hands to prevent me from beating his chest as I screamed the most obscene words I knew in every language I could speak.

"Where are the men?" I screamed. "Have the Parris men lost their manhood?" I pulled my hands free, reaching for his belt. "Let me see!" I shrieked at my son. "Where is that thing between your legs? Have you lost it somewhere? Or has it shriveled to nothing from the rum you've pickled yourself with?"

Jesse and Moses pulled me from their father, but not before I had raked his cheek with my long fingernails, leaving a trail of blood. "Look at him!" I told them. "Look at me!" For their eyes were downcast, and they would not meet my eyes.

I drew my shoulders back, thrust my chin forward, and wrapped my dignity around my bony frame. Then, speaking deliberately and coldly, I addressed my son and his family. "There was a time when the People took care of their own. We did not need the White sheriff or the White churchmen to protect our women and children. Our men protected us."

Still, these men I had once held on my lap would not look at me but glanced furtively at each other. "Elder brothers looked after their sisters and their sisters' children." I told them, "And our clans protected us, for we Cherokee honor justice and balance above all else."

They knew, for I had taught them, that in the olden days, if a wrong had been done to one of ours, the entire clan would demand restitution from the offender's clan. However, our clan system had weakened due to intermarriage with the English and Scotsmen, who traced their descent from their fathers rather than their mothers, as the Cherokee had done for as long as anyone could remember. Even worse, Mr. Morgan had no clan to take responsibility for his crime. Therefore, there was no clan for us to demand justice or restore balance.

Still, George or his sons, Rachel's older brothers, did not respond. They stood passively while I raged, allowing this old woman to vent her anger, which only enraged me further.

Then, I spat at my son's feet, the final insult, symbolically divesting myself of breath and saliva, my life force. Turning, I stalked from the room with as much dignity as I could muster. Still burning with rage and frustration, I veered from my course to my cabin, going into the barn instead.

George's horse was in its stall, enjoying the bucket of oats Jacob had given him. Surprised, the roan looked at me wide-eyed as I threw the blanket over his back. However, the saddle was not as easy; age had sapped me of the strength I once knew. My frustration grew as I struggled to lift the heavy leather trappings, only managing to let them slide to the floor, taking me down with them.

George came up behind me, lifting me into his arms. "Mother," he said quietly, holding my arms against my chest. "Your anger only brings harm to yourself and those you love."

I crumpled against him, my rage washed away by tears of grief and pain. George held me until my sobs ceased, and I leaned into his strength, completely exhausted. He helped me to my cabin, tucking me into bed as though I were a child, and sat beside me as I drifted into a restless sleep.

Chapter 20

Blood Revenge

Mid-Winter 1797
69 years old
Baldridge Creek, GA

The following days and weeks were very strained in our home. The four boys did as their father bade them, going to the hated school each morning. They were quiet of an evening, no longer regaling the family with their high spirits. Caty and Nancy were subdued as well. Caty was intent on her unfamiliar household responsibilities, and Nancy was pre-occupied with the tiny infant who was finally beginning to thrive. Rachel stayed close to home, quieter than usual. She was expressionless, her eyes blank. Our home was no longer a hub of activity. Friends and family kept their distance during these troubled times, and visitors were few and far between.

And that white-hot coal of anger lodged in the pit of my stomach, burning without cease, giving me no rest.

In the depths of winter, when the days grew short, the morning sky dawned dark, heavy with moisture. A biting cold seeped into every crack and crevice of the house. It was difficult to avoid one another, for we were forced to spend the day huddled around the fireplaces. Tension mounted, and it was a relief when the four boys came home from school early. Mr.

Morgan had dismissed them because it was evident that a winter storm was rapidly approaching.

Tension increased as we endured the unusually long evening, with everybody's nerves on edge. At last, Rachel and I took a candle from the mantle and went up the stairs to the bed we shared. I lay awake for a long time, sleep evading my weary body. A lone tear tracked down my cheek as I thought about the sadness that engulfed this family. Finally, I snuggled against the warmth emanating from my granddaughter's young body, welcoming the oblivion of sleep.

I awoke to the sound of footsteps on the staircase landing outside the bedroom door. The house was enveloped in an unusual quietness that magnified the squeak of pine floorboards under someone's stealthy footfall. There was a muffled "Shhh!" followed by a pause, and then I heard the hinges of the boys' room door as it closed. More steps descended the stairs with uncommon caution as if to avoid awakening the household. Yet, I felt a universal holding of breath. Few slept this night.

I could see thick snowflakes falling gently from the dark sky through the window on the opposite wall. Slowly disentangling myself from the sleeping Rachel, I crept out of bed and looked down at the yard. A blanket of snow already hid familiar landmarks.

I watched the barn door open, and three mounted men rode forth. I recognized the shape of my son and my two oldest grandsons. They guided their horses to the tree line where I could barely discern other mounted horsemen through the veil of snow. Together, they turned their horses toward the road leading to the schoolhouse, the sound of their movement muffled by the swirling snow.

I grew cold, though not from the chill seeping through the glass windowpanes. I had been wrong. While I raged at the men, consumed by helpless anger and furious with them for their inaction, they had been biding their time. They had wisely waited for the right opportunity to do what must be done, to do it in a way that would not bring more harm to the family or the People.

And because of my furious fits of rage, it had been safer to keep their plans from me for fear I would give them away.

Relief and shame consumed me as I stood by the window, staring at the swirling snow that concealed their progress to the schoolhouse and the hated Mr. Morgan. A creak signaled my return across the room to the chest, from which I drew a quilt. Then, wrapped snugly in its warmth, I sat beside the window and began a vigil for the safe return of the men of Rachel's clan—her brothers and uncles. And her father, too, although he was not of her clan.

The eastern sky was growing light when Caty tapped me gently on the shoulder. Despite my best intentions, sleep had overtaken me.

"George!" I cried, suddenly awake and filled with fear for his safety.

"He is safe in his bed, Mother," she told me, "as you should be in yours." Then, she helped me find my way to the bed I shared with her daughter.

Rachel recoiled from my cold gown and icy feet, murmuring her protest from the depths of bottomless sleep to which only the young go. No doubt, if she had any thought, it was that her Granny had been to the chamber pot.

Caty bent down to tuck the quilts around us, a tear glistening on her cheek. As our eyes locked, I saw the answer to my unspoken question. I nodded in acknowledgment, and we exchanged a grim smile of satisfaction. Then, she returned to her husband's bed while I cradled their woman-child in my arms.

It snowed heavily all that day and the next, insulating our family from the rest of the world. The boys and men tied ropes around their waists when they went to the barns to tend to the livestock in case they became lost in the blinding whiteness. Our farm was unrecognizable after the storm was spent, with familiar landmarks and buildings obscured by a glistening mantle of snow.

It took a week or more for the road to clear enough for the children to return to school. We were unusually quiet that morning, huddling closely together in the familiar warmth of Nancy's kitchen. Although it felt like a long morning, we spotted the sleigh approaching the lane before noon. Jesse held the reins; his hat was pulled low, but it could not hide his grin. Moses hopped off first to tend to the horse while young John bounded to the house with Jim close behind him.

"Guess what!" he shouted. "Mr. Morgan has gone missing!"

We adults feigned surprise, but Rachel's shocked response was sincere.

We learned the schoolhouse had been in an uproar. When the blizzard was over, Mr. Morgan's neighbors noticed no smoke coming from his chimney. They went to check on him but found he had mysteriously disappeared.

The heavy snow had obliterated any clues as to his whereabouts. The authorities questioned everyone, but he had not been seen since the day the blizzard began.

His quarters behind the schoolroom showed evidence of an evening meal, with dishes still on the table. His few clothes were removed from their pegs, but oddly, his spectacles were found under the bed. All the bed linens, including his pillow, were gone. There was a dark stain at the head of his bed that the Sheriff thought might be dried blood.

But, good old Doc Haverty inspected the stain and declared it was naught but coffee spilled while Mr. Morgan read in bed.

Rachel listened carefully to these details with dawning comprehension. Her father and brothers avoided her questioning eyes for fear of revealing too much. Caty and Nancy suddenly became busy in the kitchen, their eyes downcast, uncharacteristically silent. Whatever Rachel might have suspected, they must protect her innocence. She must not be an accomplice after the deed had been done. She looked at me, her eyebrows raised, but I, of course, knew nothing. Had I not slept with her the night of the blizzard? The snow's white embrace had imprisoned us all.

But, the unusual quietness of her three parents and older brothers confirmed what that precious girl suspected.

I watched as she processed the information and its implications for our family and the People. When I saw the squaring of her shoulders and the tilting of her chin, I knew she had come to a full realization. Slowly, she turned about the room, lovingly caressing each of her protectors with clear eyes that were once again lit from within. In the age-old tradition of blood revenge, balance had been restored.

Justice served.

And, with relief, I felt the burning coal of anger cool and crumble to ash.

CHAPTER 21

Reunion

Late Winter 1797
69 years old
Baldridge Creek, GA

It is a relief to feel this unusually harsh winter coming to an end. The family has been isolated from the community for long periods, confined to the farm as winter storms raged, blocking the roads with mounds of snow and ice. Although still gripped by frigid temperatures, the roads are finally clear, and we have begun to welcome a steady flow of visitors again.

Nothing more is said about Mr. Morgan. It seems as though he has vanished into thin air, and the authorities are making fewer inquiries about his whereabouts as time goes on. The missionaries have already requested a replacement and expect the school to resume by spring.

Rachel carries herself with pride, showing a level of maturity seldom seen in a girl of her years. Her appreciation of the menfolk is sometimes almost excessive, but that will fade with time. Nothing was done on her behalf that did not also benefit our Clan and the People.

Sallie, the youngest member of our family, survived the harsh winter, demonstrating a determined spirit for one so tiny. She will do well. It is I, the eldest of our family, whose life force has been sapped. Although my earthly body goes through the motions of living, my thoughts are more often in the past, reliving events that occurred so long ago.

I both dread and look forward to nighttime. When I rest my head on the pillow, I never know if I will sleep through the night, experience another of the nightmares that plague me, or have sweet dreams of Richard.

As soon as the roads cleared, my youngest daughter, Neely, named for Richard's sister, came to visit, bringing her father-in-law, Sour Mush, with her. Our reunion was joyous, for Sour Mush and I share a long history. We were children together in Chota, offspring of the earliest traders amongst the Real People. Few mixed bloods existed in those days, and although our clans and the People treated us no differently than other children, we felt a special bond.

Sour Mush and I were lovers when we were very young, and we learned how it is between a man and a woman. We enjoyed each other but, in the way of youngsters, became curious and took other lovers, remaining close friends. Our paths have crossed many times, and we share innumerable memories.

The bond of our youth is even more vital in our old age, for we have grandchildren in common. His son, John, married my daughter, Neely, and his daughter, Nancy, is one of George's wives. So we laugh, finding joy in knowing that our seed has joined, although we did not have a child together.

We venture outdoors, relishing the fresh air and warm sunshine—a welcome relief from winter's confinement. Strolling in the woods beside my cabin, we are delighted by a shower of redbud blossoms released by a slight breeze. Overnight, it seems, purple blooms of creeping phlox have appeared in stark contrast to plants still slumbering in their winter dormancy. Soon, the bright white bloodroot flowers will follow—all sure indications of spring. We are approaching the season of renewal.

I show him my summer home, flinging the door wide open to dispel the mustiness. Sour Mush and I are tired from our walk, unaccustomed to physical exertion after being housebound this winter, so we lie together in my bed. Soon, we find ourselves clasped in each other's arms, snuggled under a quilt, giggling about how we had pleasured each other when we were young lovers. But now we find joy simply in holding each other as sleep overtakes us.

Nancy came looking for us, concerned about our safety, and found us there—the quilts pulled up to our chins, her mother-in-law's head resting on her father's shoulder. She scolds us like misbehaving children caught doing something they shouldn't have.

"What would your grandchildren think if they could see the two of you?" she upbraids us. With the same unruliness he had as a boy, Sour Mush replies, "Well, I expect it would give them something to look forward to." Nancy tries to remain angry with us but soon gives in to his mischievous grin.

The adults in our family smirks at the two of us that evening, with Jesse and Moses making snide remarks about how we had spent our afternoon. Of course, we do not bother to tell them we had been fully clothed under the quilt, but we let them think what they will.

After a few days, Neely returned to her home, but Sour Mush stayed here at his daughter's and my son's home, and I am glad. He is frailer than I, but we draw comfort from each other. I gaze upon the wizened face of my old friend, and the years melt away. I see before me once again the bright-eyed, laughing scamp of my youth. Oftentimes, he and I sit together by the fire and reminisce about days long past, savoring each precious remembrance drawn from the depths of our memory, a covey of children gathered around, listening to stories brought to life by our shared experiences.

I see the incredulous looks on the children's faces and am struck by the difference between the childhood we shared and the one our grandchildren are experiencing. Our People's way of life has undergone such a transformation that it is like we live in another world. The old ways are almost gone, soon to be forgotten.

Our storytelling tends to linger overlong on the fall of our tenth year, the time before our world was irrevocably altered. Until then, we believed our lives would continue with the unchanging rhythms of our ancestors. We were so innocent! A heavy mantle of grief descends upon me as I recall how naive we were. Even our leaders were unaware that our People were unwilling pawns in a game of greed and power. Who could have foretold the events of that fall that would change our lives forever?

I feel an even greater sense of urgency to share our People's stories with the next generation. There is so much to tell—and I have so little time remaining.

CHAPTER 22

Startling News

Late Summer 1738
10 years old
Chota Town

With reluctance, Will and Johnny left Chota a few days after the Mature Green Corn Festival. Johnny was thoroughly smitten with Walina, and they were loath to be separated. Even the most casual observer would have recognized the depth of their connection, evident from their furtive hand clasps and the soulful looks they exchanged, revealing their infatuation to all.

Quite often, one would vanish from the village, and then the other would follow. Late one night, when I had slipped into the woods to make water, I saw them coming from the bean fields. Johnny carried a rolled-up blanket under one arm, his other around Walina's shoulder in a loving embrace. The full moon's brightness was no match for the glow radiating from the two of them. I stepped back into the forest's shadows, careful lest I disturb their enchantment.

Will was also reluctant to leave this time. He was getting older, and the long journeys to the Carolina coast were taking their toll. On the morning of their departure, he sat with Oconostota and Dougherty, and I overheard them talking.

He told his friends that he had grown weary of constant travel and was ready to settle down again. He said that with each trip, he was dismayed to see the encroachment of White civilization. Charles Town grew larger yearly, expanding from a small village into a bustling port. Small farms and large plantations encircled the city in an ever-widening arc. Moreover, the trickle of European immigrants was increasing into a steady stream that flooded the Carolina lowlands with land-hungry settlers moving into the Piedmont.

"This journey to Charles Town to transport trade goods between the coast and the backcountry will be my last," he said, drawing deeply on his tobacco-filled pipe. "I'll settle my debts with the merchants, sell my packhorses, and return to live here for a while."

He knew he could not open even a small trading post because all trade was now strictly regulated by the South Carolina Board of Trade, and only licensed traders were permitted to conduct business with the Cherokee.

"That's fine with me. I don't want to have a trading post again," he said, and we all knew he was remembering life with my mother at Tugaloo. But then, he sighed deeply, his shoulders slumping, and continued, "I'm ready to turn it over to younger men."

His comment surprised me because I had not considered my father an old man.

However, looking closely, I saw how the years were beginning to take their toll. His once fiery red hair was now almost completely gray, and his face was etched with deep lines.

Oconostota and Dougherty agreed with Will's plan, assuring him they would be glad of his help in Chota and that it would be good to have him back in time to winter with us.

Thus, on a brisk morning signaling the advancing season, Will and Johnny mounted their horses and began their journey to the coast. Most of the train of packhorses stepped nimbly as their bulky packs were much lighter than those on their inland journey.

On this trip, they carried only a few dressed hides, as it was too early for the fall harvest of pelts and hides. Most of their cargo consisted of nested baskets crafted by Cherokee women. Double-walled and tightly woven, these sturdy baskets were highly prized by European settlers. Not only were they beautifully ornamental, but they were also utilitarian and fetched good prices at the colonial markets.

Several horses carried considerably smaller panniers that were now empty. After crossing the mountains, Will planned to stop in Tugaloo, employing young boys to fill the simple baskets with a special white clay used for pottery.

Will told Dougherty about a young potter, Andrew Duché, whom he had met that spring. Duché, he said, was ecstatic about the beautiful white china he had baked at his Savannah workshop using clay taken from near Tugaloo. This clay contained some unusual ingredient that made porcelain similar to that of a remote tribe known as the Chinese. Duché aimed to establish a business relationship with my father, who would transport the clay to Charles Town for shipment to a London porcelain factory. The two traders had joked about selling earth to an Englishman for shipment to London.

"They want the land of the People so badly, I'll be damned if they won't crate it up and ship it across the ocean to have it," Will declared. However, he agreed to provide the first shipment on his return trip. He confided in Dougherty that this business venture might be worth considering since he was leaving the trading business.

Despite Will's assurance of a prompt return and his promise to winter with us, I bid my father goodbye with a sense of foreboding. From the Council House mound, I watched the pack train wind through the palisaded gate to the trail that skirted the river's edge, turning eastward toward the sheltering embrace of the Smoky Mountains. Feeling my gaze on his back, Will turned once and caught my eye across the distance. Then, touching his fingertips to his forehead, he signaled a reassuring salute before disappearing into the dark forest.

Village life in Chota quickly returned to normal, resuming the ageless pattern of our daily lives. Corn, beans, squash, gourds, and other produce from the communal fields and individual family plots were tended and harvested in their time. This was also the season when the fruit on various trees and bushes ripened. Small groups of women and children left early each morning, returning before the midday heat with their baskets filled to overflowing.

Women of the Paint Clan were known for their medicinal skills, and this was the time of year when they gathered many of the herbs used in their remedies. Meanwhile, the Wild Potato Clan women harvested the foods that grew along the streams, marshes, lakes, and ponds.

Each day, the women fastened their produce to drying racks fashioned from small tree limbs and bound with sinew, which dotted the town's open spaces. Some of the harvest was spread on clean hides in sunny places. The sun shone brightly daily, drawing moisture from the fruits, vegetables, and herbs. Once completely dried, the produce was stored in baskets and gourds that hung from the rafters of houses, safe from pesky rodents.

Soon, it would be time to gather the wide variety of nuts ripening on the trees. The squirrels scurried from tree to tree, their jaws stuffed with nuts destined for their winter stores, while young boys hunted them with blowguns.

Men were not idle during this time of gathering. Hunting season began with the next moon, known as the Nut Moon. The final days of summer served as a time to repair or replace hunting weapons. They played games of skill and daring in preparation for both the hunt and warfare. The Little War, or stickball, was particularly favored. Competition was stiff; the games were fierce and brutal.

My playmates and I also had responsibilities. We were at an age to begin learning the skills and crafts that would contribute to the well-being of the People. We were encouraged to watch our elders as they performed their duties, lending assistance with small tasks when practical. Thus, our particular talents and interests were recognized.

Each of the seven clans had a specific role in village life. The people of the Deer Clan were often fleet-footed and athletic and were known as the runners or messengers of the People. The Long Hair Clan members were gifted storytellers and keepers of our myths and legends. Foreigners or captives were typically adopted into that clan to learn to be Cherokee. The Wolf Clan was known for its members who exhibited strong leadership abilities, and many of our fiercest warriors originated from that clan. The Wild Potato Clan had a gift for growing things, so they were known as keepers of the earth. The Blue Clan was exceptionally skilled with children, and members of the Bird Clan were renowned for using snares and blowguns in hunting. The Paint Clan, to which I was born, was known as medicine people.

Children were not compelled to learn the skills of their clan if their interests were elsewhere. We were, however, expected to become productive citizens of our village.

Thus, Wurth, who had returned to Tellico, was learning the home crafts in which Cornsilk excelled and for which Wurth had a strong inclination. Quatsis was beginning to realize that her efforts to inspire a similar interest in me would not be successful. I wanted to please her, as I loved her very much, so I diligently stayed close by her side, trying to help and listening carefully to her instructions. She had great hopes that I would learn about herbal cures.

"Prachey, my child, what herb is this?" Quatsis asked me patiently as she sorted through her medicine bag.

I groaned inwardly, for I knew this familiar question was just the beginning of yet another attempt to impart knowledge about medicinal herbs to my dull-witted mind. I was expected to know the various herbs and their remedies, the most favorable time to harvest them, and the proper prayers to recite during the process. Without these elements, the plants held no power.

I took a dried leaf from her outstretched hand and crumbled a piece, holding it to my nose and inhaling slowly. The oils released from the crushed leaf reminded me of my favorite dried fruit. Looking again at her cupped hand, I saw a small dried berry as dark as night.

"It is a leaf from a raspberry bush, Mother," I replied smugly, pleased to respond quickly to her question. Both of us pointedly ignored the fact that this particular herb was so commonly used that any child, likely even Terrapin, could have easily identified it.

Smiling with encouragement, my mother asked, "And how is it used, Daughter?"

Warming to the lesson with two easy questions in succession, I quickly recited, "With this herb, we can make teas or syrups that soothe canker sores and sore throats."

"Yes?" she asked expectantly.

There was a long pause as I considered her response. She was obviously expecting me to know of yet another use for this ordinary herb, but try as I might, I couldn't think of anything. Finally, in desperation, I blurted out, "I know! It helps relieve stuffy noses!"

My mother's pained expression told me that was not the answer she expected to hear. "No, my dear," she said, always patient with her reluctant pupil. "It can be used to treat loose stools or diarrhea."

My dropped jaw spoke for me as I considered that remedy. However, I worsened the situation by asking my sweet mother what I believed was a very good question.

"When a person drinks raspberry tea, how does the raspberry know where it is expected to travel—to the bowels or the throat? If the raspberry goes to both parts of the body, it would seem that if a person does not have diarrhea and drinks the tea for a sore throat, they might suffer with sluggish bowels, even though their throat would no longer be sore."

My mother sighed in exasperation and suggested that I check on my little brothers to ensure they stayed away from the drying racks.

Glad to be released from my ordeal so quickly, I rushed to obey her command but then abruptly stopped, for I could not believe what I saw.

Will rode his lathered horse through the town gates at a brisk trot, a stricken look on his face. He headed straight to the house of our headman, ignoring the greetings called out to him and leaving a trail of puzzled villagers behind. Men set aside whatever tasks had occupied them and moved toward Old Hop's house, for it was clear that something important had occurred. Women exchanged anxious glances, fearing what news had unsettled the usually jovial Will Hatton. And it struck me that I recognized his expression; I had seen it once before at Tugaloo when he thought I was dead or captive: it was fear.

I joined the other villagers to wait outside Old Hop's house while he and Will conferred inside. Although it was only a few minutes, the wait felt prolonged before they finally stepped into the bright sunlight.

"Our friend, Will Hatton, brings news of great importance," Old Hop announced to the villagers gathered beside his door, raising his voice louder than usual to be heard by the anxious crowd. "We will have Council at sunset." The two of them then returned to the recesses of his house while the councilors prepared for the gathering later that evening.

Meals were prepared and eaten quickly as anxious parents hushed their children from their usual noisy late afternoon play while glancing at the Council House and Old Hop's home for clues about what was happening. There was much activity, with many of the town's leaders coming and going, their faces grave. I drew his children aside and pestered them with questions, but Cappy and Sookey had been forbidden to enter their home and knew no more than I about what was being discussed.

The benches in the Council House were crowded with townspeople long before the sun dipped below the western mountains and dusk settled over the apprehensive village. Will and Old Hop entered together, with Old Hop settling onto his platform and Will taking his seat in the place reserved for visiting dignitaries.

The usual Council ceremonies were performed, if somewhat perfunctorily, and then my father stepped before the People to tell them the news he had brought. Forgoing his usual flamboyant oratory style, he plunged right into the declaration everyone had been waiting for: "Damme, friends. It's smallpox."

The sudden silence spoke eloquently of the fear that his words brought to the People. In the hush of the crowded Council House, mothers clasped their children to their sides in sheltering embraces while men looked at each other in a communal spasm of helplessness. I felt the cold chill of fear snake down my spine, for I remembered well the stories I had heard of earlier times when the White man's spotted sickness had come to the Cherokee.

This same affliction had claimed my mother's mother and my brothers and sisters before my birth. The fear and anguish on Will's face confirmed that he, too, remembered that terrible time in Tugaloo when he and my birth mother buried one child after another. Only Johnny survived; their other children succumbed to an illness for which our medicine men had no cure.

Quatsis' soft sobs echoed those of other women recalling loved ones who had died in the earlier epidemic, their sobs escalating into wails of distress and renewed grief. With his head bowed and shoulders slumped, Will stood before the People he had come to love more than the tribe to which he had been born. As their cries subsided, he raised his face, suddenly appearing an old man, and stepped forward to speak of what they must know.

He told us that as he approached the familiar landmarks of Tugaloo, there was a strange quietness in the countryside. No women raised their hands in greeting as they paused from harvesting or gathering to watch his packhorse train pass. No children ran to greet him, laughing and calling for treats. His passage was unmarked by men at work, preparing for the fall hunt, nor were they practicing their games of skill and daring on the empty ballfield.

He approached the town's entrance with a sense of foreboding. As he grew near, he saw a white warning banner hanging listlessly from the flagstaff. The unmistakable sound of keening women announced their grief. He knew with certainty what had befallen the town where he had lived for so many years.

He and his packhorse men stood far from the palisaded town, calling out to the townspeople. Soon, a young warrior, well known to them, came to the entrance and confirmed that the village had been stricken with the spotted sickness. He had been among those who journeyed over the mountains to Chota for the Mature Green Corn Festival. Upon returning to Tugaloo and beginning to feel ill, they found a town besieged by the spotted sickness.

Will, Johnny, and the packhorse men set up an overnight camp beside the river, far away from the town's palisade, and debated their next course of action. The following day, they left a fresh supply of game and fish at the gate before parting from their beleaguered friends.

Johnny would continue leading the packhorse train to the coastal cities, but Will was determined to return to his Cherokee family in Chota. On his journey back along the familiar trading path, he stopped again at town after town and found, to his increasing dismay, that the spotted sickness was spreading like wildfire across the mist-covered mountains. With a growing sense of dread, he pushed down his panic and urged his mount to greater speed along the tortuous mountain trails, hurrying to warn his friends and family.

CHAPTER 23

Spotted Sickness

Late Summer 1738
10 years old
Chota Town

When Will finished his somber narrative, a hush descended upon the overcrowded Council House. I could hear his words being repeated to those waiting outside the entrance, followed by total silence. For the span of a few heartbeats, one question loomed unspoken among the villagers of Chota: Would our town be spared?

Now that we knew of the dreaded scourge, what was there to do but wait? We had waged battle against this unseen enemy before, and we knew there was no defense. Neither our fiercest warriors nor our most knowledgeable women had been able to halt its insidious invasion during previous epidemics.

Even the powerful medicine men proved ineffective with their divining crystals and potent prayer formulas. This was a sickness unlike any we had ever known. We understood only that it was highly contagious, often striking entire families while leaving others unscathed. Children and the elderly were particularly susceptible, but all the People were vulnerable.

"What shall we do?" I whispered to my mother. "What can we do?" And my mother looked at me with that same question reflected on her face.

The women of the Paint Clan were highly skilled in the various uses of herbs to treat common ailments of the People. Daughters born into the clan were often as gifted as their mothers in the healing arts, and their training began at an early age. The women of my clan spent many hours at each festival sharing experiences and insights with other women, thereby expanding their knowledge and expertise.

If an illness or injury was beyond their expertise, they would consult a medicine man known for specialized healing practices. In those days, our medicine men served the People as leaders of religious services and esteemed healers. They accompanied our warriors on the warpath to care for those wounded in battle.

Over the centuries, women and medicine men became very competent at treating well-known afflictions with formulas developed through observation, prayer, and ritual. They were skillful at treating the many ailments and illnesses for which they had been trained since childhood, but they had no experience with the diseases of White men. The healers conferred after each of the previous epidemics but could not agree upon their cause or treatment.

We understood that ailments could arise from both natural and supernatural sources. For instance, an individual might sustain a cut from mishandling a knife or fall and break a bone—common accidents that typically don't require specialized knowledge to address. However, most issues stemmed from supernatural causes.

It was generally accepted that physical defects, such as toothaches or abdominal pains, were caused by disregarding taboos or spirits—stemming from some impurity of the patient. Relief from the pain and discomfort of such ailments was usually obtained through a woman's pharmaceutical experience. If the patient did not respond to her ministrations, a request was made to a medicine man known for his competence in treating that ailment.

The medicine man's examination of an afflicted person involved intense questioning about any possible breaking of a taboo and inquiries regarding dreams or omens to determine the actual cause of the ailment. He focused not only on curing the disease but also on discovering and removing its root cause.

We knew that immorality caused contagious diseases. The medicine men told us that the mysterious and inexplicable epidemics of the spotted disease resulted from the evil influences of the Europeans. Smallpox, they said, was caused by malevolent spirits brought by the White men, spirits that did not belong here but in another world far away. Most White men did not die when these spirits entered their bodies. Some never even became ill. But the Cherokee had no power against the invading spirits.

Talks within the Council House continued late into the night as our leaders discussed ways to combat the invisible threat to our safety, but no conclusions were reached. As always, each person was free to weigh the speakers' words and choose a course of action. Some family groups chose to take a few provisions and retreat into the forest, while most decided to remain within the perceived safety of the town.

Black Buffalo, the respected Chota medicine man, and his assistants fasted and began their prayers and incantations to discourage offending spirits. Purification ceremonies were performed in all the houses, and cedar smudges were set around the town's palisades. The villagers attempted to resume regular activity, but fear and anxiety hung over the community like a dark cloud.

Concern for clan and family in other towns grew daily as our once-bustling Chota became increasingly isolated. The constant stream of visitors slowed to a trickle and then stopped altogether.

Mothers anxiously watched their children, alert for the first sign of illness so that even an ordinary throat-clearing cough caused their brows to furrow with concern. I saw Quatsis touching Terrapin and Bark more than usual and knew she was checking that the dreaded heat from within had not yet begun in their sturdy little bodies.

The wait seemed interminable, but it was actually only a few days before it began. The young men who had helped unload the Charles Town trade goods a fortnight ago were the first to become ill, suffering from a burning sensation inside and grievous pain throughout their bones. The pain of the head was such that they could endure no noise nor the least light without crying out in agony.

Word spread throughout the village, and all pretense of work came to a standstill as we waited, hoping this was just a minor complaint that would have gone unnoticed in ordinary times. Night came upon us, and we foolishly refused to believe what we knew to be true.

Our worst fears were confirmed by daybreak when a dozen people had fallen ill and then even more as the sun continued its journey across the sky. By evening, a rash had developed in their mouths, and the flesh on their faces and chests had erupted with angry pustules. Throughout the night, their stomachs rebelled against the evil spirits by continually emptying— draining their bodies of fluids.

It had begun. The dreaded spotted sickness had invaded Chota.

I stayed close to our house, caring for my little brothers, as Quatsis was busy day and night. She went from one house to another, working with the medicine men to comfort the afflicted. Will insisted that we remain isolated, so in her absence, he fetched water from the spring, brought food from the fields, and provided fish or small game for our nourishment.

The days became a blur as the spotted sickness spread throughout the town with ever-increasing ferocity. Quatsis was seldom home. The demands for her healing skills left her little time to eat or rest. I could not sleep at night until I knew she was safely home.

I heard her creep into the sleeping room late one night, moving slowly, her steps heavy with fatigue. I listened to the familiar rustling as Oconostota made room for his wife on their pallet. As I slipped into a deep sleep, I heard the reassuring sound of their murmurs as he folded her into their customary sleeping embrace.

The sun had fully risen when I awoke to an unusually quiet household. My brothers were sleeping soundly, entangled in a knot at my side. Then, turning to look across the sleeping room, I saw the stricken face of my father, Oconostota, a mighty warrior of the Cherokee with Quatsis spooned protectively in his massive arms. I crept silently across the floor, my eyes fastened upon the red splotches on her face and neck.

"Oh no!" I moaned, "No! No! No!" My moans increased to a wail. My mother's eyes fluttered open, and I could see they were burning with the fire from within.

"Daughter," she said, weakly reaching her hand toward me, "you must be strong."

I cared for Quatsis to the best of my ability, fervently wishing I had listened more carefully to her instructions in the healing practices so that I would better know how to comfort her in her distress. Oconostota helped as long as he could, but he, too, had fallen ill, so Will and I had only one but two patients to tend. My father was stalwart and proved to be a tender caretaker for his good friend and this gentle woman who was the sister of his deceased wife, as he had too much experience with this awful disease.

No one could assist us because the entire town, and indeed all of the Nation, was besieged by smallpox. Thus, we isolated ourselves within the house, with Will being the only one who ventured forth to bring fresh water or provisions.

Will insisted that the little boys stay in the chamber that had belonged to him and Johnny, as far away as possible from their ill parents. Despite their young age, they obeyed and remained quietly within the small room's dark confines. When I brought nourishment to them, their eyes were wide, and their faces pale in the dim room. Little Terrapin spooned soup into his baby brother's mouth, who had been weaned too soon from their mother's breast.

First, Quatsis and then Oconostota followed the same course of illness as the young men, all of whom had died. By the second week of their illness, the raised pink rash had spread from their faces and trunks to their arms and legs until their entire bodies were covered. The rash then developed into raised pus-filled bumps that formed crusts and scabs by the third week. Quatsis's delicate skin was especially susceptible, and there was hardly a fingerbreadth of flesh that did not bear awful witness to the affliction consuming her.

The itching from the rash and later skin lesions was intolerable, and we constantly fought our patients to prevent them from scratching themselves raw. The fire within consumed them, causing them to fling their coverings to the floor and thrash about, attempting unsuccessfully to escape the heat.

"We must do something to quench the burning," I told Will, for I could see its coals were devouring what little fluids they could swallow and were consuming their flesh.

"Aye, little one, but what? I have seen your mother and Quatsis prepare many drinks for those who were burning, yet I do not know what herbs they used."

Although I was frustrated by how little I remembered from her teachings, I felt pleased to recall that the magic in the bark of the willow tree could cool a fever and soothe discomfort. However, when I opened her medicine bag, I discovered it was nearly empty. I turned it upside down and shook it, but only a few packets of healing herbs tumbled to the floor—she had used most of her herbal medicine stores.

Mother had explained that she bound each packet with a series of different knots to quickly identify its contents. With trembling fingers, I picked at the unfamiliar knots until the soft deerskin packets opened, revealing unknown contents. Which was from the willow tree?

Tears welled in my eyes as I turned to Will for an explanation.

"She's used all her medicine helping others," he told me. "There's nay left for her."

"Then we must find some more!" I cried, flinging the medicine bag aside as I headed for the door.

I was pulling on the heavy door when Will lifted me off the floor and carried me to the pile of storage baskets across the room, where he set me back on my feet. "I won't have ye going out there," he roared. "It's too dangerous."

Seeing my stricken face, he softened. "Tell me what ye need, Hester, and I'll get it for ye. Ye must stay with yer mother."

I had a pot of water boiling when Will returned with bark from the willow tree. I wasn't sure how much to add, so I kept dropping in chunks of bark until the water turned a deep, rich brown. After removing it from the flame, I sat anxiously as the magic within the bark was transferred to the water. Once it had cooled sufficiently, Will held each of our patients upright in turn as I spooned the potion into their mouths, allowing it to trickle down their parched throats.

Their bodies were a little cooler within a short time, and they appeared to rest. My concoction seemed to relieve them. Will and I watched them closely, repeating our ministrations when the internal fire began to increase once again.

On one of his forays to the river for fresh water, Will returned with some aloe, which we used to make soothing poultices for their skin. I used rabbit fur to fashion mitts for their hands, drawn tight at the wrists with rawhide strips to keep them from digging their fingers into their tormented skin. Yet they would work their fingers free to dig at the unbearable itch.

I was grateful for their delirium, for it spared them awareness of how Will and I tended them like infants as they retched and vomited until they spewed only a weak bile, and their bowels turned to a bloody flux. As the disease followed its course, their skin lay slack as though they had shrunk from within.

Oconostota's great warrior body, whose muscles had rippled beneath his skin, became so weak that he could not raise his head from the pallet. And yet, when he was awake, we quickly learned that the only thing to soothe his restlessness was positioning him so his gaze fell upon his beloved. Quatsis, the sweet and gentle soul who had been the strength of our little family, had fallen into a deep slumber and would not awaken.

We tried to nourish them by dipping soft deerskin into fresh spring water or thin soups, trickling the moisture between their lips. Oconostota took fluid in that manner and then began to suck the end of the deerskin between his lips, drawing the life-giving moisture into his body.

But the fluid flowed in and out of Quatsis' unresponsive lips as her breaths grew more shallow, the pulse of life in her sunken chest weakening.

Black Buffalo came to see about them when they first succumbed to the spotted sickness, performing his prayers and incantations, beseeching the evil spirits to leave them.

"They must go to water and be cleansed of impurities," he instructed Will. "They have brought this upon themselves through immoral conduct that has angered the Provider."

I stood beside Will, taking his hand in mine, for I saw the rage that was about to erupt and knew it was not wise to anger the Medicine Man.

"Immoral conduct be damned!" he roared. "My brother is a warrior who has killed many men in battle, yet he is a good man—none better. And my sister..." His voice broke, and he could not speak until he swallowed his tears. "My sister has done naught but good! Don't ye dare speak to me of immoral conduct, or I'll run ye through with me knife." He reached for the weapon he kept at his waist, but his hand came away empty, a perplexed look on his face.

Looking around the room, he saw I was no longer at his side but standing in the corner, with a forced look of innocence on my face. His knife was safely hidden in the storage baskets.

"Ye little heathen!" he roared. "I'll take my strap to ye!"

But his outbursts roused Quatsis, who whimpered weakly, calling for Oconostota, and we both sprang to her side to soothe her.

The prevailing treatment of the medicine men, we knew, was a common one for almost any illness. The ill person was placed in the hothouse, and water was thrown upon the rocks within, causing steam to rise. Once thoroughly bathed in sweat, they were taken to the river and plunged in. Will had witnessed this therapy during the previous epidemic, which had claimed the lives of my grandmother and his young children. He knew that, more often than not, the patient was dead when pulled from the river.

"I'll be damned if I'll let ye bake 'em like they be a lump of bread and then toss 'em in yon river to die. This little scamp and I will do what we can for 'em, and you can go tend the rest of the town."

The medicine man did not argue, as many more villagers needed his skills as a healer. He had neither the time nor the energy to expend arguing with an angry Scotsman. With a venomous look, he turned on his heel, left the house, and did not return during the course of their illnesses.

CHAPTER 24

Epidemic Aftermath

Autumn 1738
10 years old
Chota Town

Quatsis' spirit left her body early one morning as the sun began its course across the sky. Oconostota had been steadily regaining his strength over the previous day or two. He, along with Will and me, tried to force fluids into her slack lips, entreating her not to give up and to fight the spotted sickness. But the flesh continued to melt from her bones, and, in fact, it was as though she had begun her journey to the Spirit World long before her heart stopped beating.

Will allowed me to bring the little boys from their sleeping chamber so they could see their mother one last time. We had hoped her spirit would hear them calling to her and she would choose to return, but that was not the case. Then, as was our custom because of the uncleanness of death, they were sent away. I held my breath, fearing my fathers would look at me and, seeing another child, bid me to leave—but mercifully, they did not. For the first time, I realized that the terrible smallpox marked the end of my childhood.

Pitiful moans escaped Oconostota's clenched jaws as he rocked Quatsis's frail body to and fro, her arms limp and her head lolling as she drew her last breath. As I had heard my elders at the deaths of others, I began a mournful repetition of grief, keening my anguish.

Will took her from Oconostota, lifting her easily, for she was as light as a feather, and laid her upon the last clean sleeping fur. Every other scrap of dressed hide and fur we possessed had been used to staunch the flow of bodily fluids during their long illnesses. Will had seen me trying to clean a piece of rabbit fur I had used to bathe Quatsis, and he had taken it from me.

"Nay, Hester," he had said, "I believe the evil spirits spoken of by the medicine men reside in the purulence of smallpox. We will nay use these hides and furs again but will burn them."

I was shocked to think of such extravagance, for I knew the time and hard work it took to dress a hide. I had spent many afternoons scraping a hide when I would have preferred fishing, hunting, or otherwise being in the forest. With winter drawing near, what would we use to keep the cold winds at bay? But one glance at Will's stern face warned me that he would brook no impudence from me and burn them we would.

Oconostota scooped a handful of ashes from the fireplace and placed them on his head to symbolize his grief. Then, exhausted, he lay back upon the sleeping-pallet he had shared with his beloved wife, turning his face to the wall. The last of his strength had left him.

Will beckoned me to follow him, and for the first time in weeks, I left the shelter of our house. "'Tis hard times, Daughter," he said as we walked through the town, his hand resting on my shoulder. "'Tis a terrible thing that has befallen the People."

I was having difficulty keeping up with him. The bright sunlight blinded me as accustomed as I was to the dark interior of our house. Blinking rapidly, I rubbed my tear-stained eyes to clear them, then stopped, my mouth agape at what I saw.

Will paused then, realizing that while he had witnessed the town's transformation, I had not. I stood in the clearing before the Council House and turned slowly, absorbing all that was before me.

The once tidy and industrious village was now filled with debris, and weeds grew unchecked where they had quickly taken root. Several smoldering fires consumed piles of furs and hides, spewing forth foul, odorous smoke. Few people were seen in the lanes separating the houses, and they looked as unkempt as we were, their eyes downcast and grief hard upon them. The haunting keening of mourning assaulted my ears from several directions; otherwise, the town was shrouded in a peculiar stillness.

Will drew my bony shoulders to him in an embrace, holding me tightly as if to shield me from what he knew I must see, protecting me while also giving me strength. I realized then that the horror within the sheltering walls of our house had been repeated a hundredfold throughout the capital of Chota.

We walked through the palisade gates, protective ramparts that had proven useless against the unseen enemy. Will guided me to an embankment in a meadow at the forest's edge, where villagers clustered around several mounds of freshly turned earth, their cries rising in crescendos of grief.

Within the nearest group stood the trader Cornelius Dougherty and his son, my dear friend Sour Mush, beside a freshly dug grave that embraced his beloved grandmother, the earth still glistening in the bright morning sunlight. Turning from the knot of mourners, Sour Mush saw me and burst into a fresh deluge of tears. We clasped each other, crying until we had no more tears to shed, and then wandered to the sheltering embrace of an oak tree, its leaves beginning to hint at autumn.

With gut-wrenching sobs, I told him of Quatsis and Oconostota's suffering from the awful illness. I whispered that my mother's spirit had left her disfigured body just a short while ago. Clasping me in a tight embrace, a freshet of new tears mingled on our cheeks; he sobbed that the beautiful Walina had begun her journey to the Spirit World the evening before.

"Black Buffalo did all that he could," Sour Mush told me, and I remembered that he was the uncle of Sour Mush and Walina. "He was angry with her because he said she violated ancient laws and offended the spirits by consorting with Johnny."

"How can that be?" I asked. "Men and women will pleasure each other, no matter, so why would the spirits be offended?"

Sour Mush shrugged, indicating that it was also confusing to him. "I don't know," he mumbled. "But he said they had polluted the bean plots with their coupling in the night."

I remembered the night I had witnessed their return from the fields and the magic aura surrounding them. I wondered how something so beautiful could be offensive to the spirits. It occurred to me that Black Buffalo had been wrong in his accusations even though he was our most revered medicine man. Perhaps he had no answers for the cause of the spotted sickness and had focused on the only thing he could fault in his lovely niece.

I also recalled that he was concerned that Walina might choose Johnny as her mate. I remembered the gossip about his anger years ago when his younger sister married a White trader, claiming that her children's blood would be diluted and made impure by having a Scotsman as their father. Even though Dougherty had been a good husband and father, Black Buffalo did not want his niece to follow the same path. He had been pressuring Walina to discard Johnny and to consider a handsome Cherokee warrior he thought would be a better mate.

I resolved to think about this matter later, as it raised an interesting question: Could his personal bias affect his role as a medicine man? However, I decided these blasphemous thoughts were best examined in private and turned my attention back to Sour Mush and his woeful tale.

"Black Buffalo told our parents that extreme measures were necessary to halt the progress of the disease," Sour Mush continued. "He decided that a cure could be effected in the same location and at the same time as the offense. My father protested, but, of course, it was not his decision to make. So, Walina was laid in the bean plot, exposing her chest to the night dews. Each daybreak, Uncle saw the spotted sickness continue on its dreadful course. Soon, there was congestion in her lungs, and her breathing became more labored."

Overcome with grief, he had to stop, and it took some time for his sobs to quiet enough for him to continue his narrative.

"I stayed beside her, of course, when our mother had to leave to care for other family members who were ill, and I tried to comfort her whenever she called out for Johnny. However, she grew weaker until the coughing spasms became the only sounds she made."

Sour Mush and I sat closely together, clasping hands for comfort. Gazing out at the river and the mountains veiled in blue mist, we deliberately avoided looking at the town and the burial plots. After taking a deep breath, he continued.

"Uncle grew desperate, I believe, for the fire from within had begun to burn in him."

"Had he, too, polluted the bean field?" I interrupted cynically, immediately regretting my outburst. Fortunately, Sour Mush had not understood my meaning.

"Yesterday morning, Uncle poured cold water on her chest while praying and shaking his gourd rattle, yet her condition continued to worsen. By evening, as he himself grew more ill, Uncle decided he must attempt one last treatment for Walina. Under his direction, two men carried her to the hothouse and sweated her; then, they took her to the river and plunged her into the cold water. When they lifted her to the riverbank, her spirit had left her body."

A fresh wave of grief washed over us as we clasped each other, crying while exhaustion overtook us. Our fathers called us to join them on the path that was taking shape, leading from the newly scarred meadow to the town.

At Old Hop's request, as his own home was besieged by illness, a hasty council was convened for those who could attend. After a remarkably brief discussion, a decision was made to follow the advice given by the White traders, our fathers, regarding the burial of the dead.

A huge trench was dug by any of the villagers capable of performing the hard labor, and those who had crossed into the Spirit World were laid within. Relatives washed some of the dead with a purifying mixture made from boiling willow root, but for others, there was no one to undertake that final act of love.

Fortunately, Walina and Quatsis were ritually cleansed and dressed in their finest festival clothing. They were laid side by side within the shallow pit, their favorite possessions beside them, and their bodies entombed with others by placing heaps of rocks and stones.

Black Buffalo and his two assistants had fallen ill with the spotted sickness. No medicine man was available to perform the sacred rituals of burying our dead. Sending messengers to request assistance from other medicine men in nearby towns would be futile since the disease was rampant throughout the Nation. Young men—boys, actually—who had begun their training performed what they knew of the ancient burial ceremonies. However, their training was incomplete. Many traditional prayers and incantations fell victim to smallpox—forever lost to our collective memory.

When Black Buffalo realized he was becoming ill, he threw his gourds, rattles, beads, and divining crystals into the sacred fire of the Council House, crying out that the holy objects had lost their power. His wife and sons helped him return to his home, where he lay on his pallet, refusing any prayers or medications. He said that he would welcome death when it came and that he preferred to go to the Spirit World.

In ordinary circumstances, a medicine man would have eased Quatsis's journey to the Spirit World, but there had been none to aid her. There were no medicine men to perform certain rituals that comforted the bereaved and ceremonially cleansed them of the contamination associated with death. Many traditions that had provided comfort for generations were abandoned due to the brutality of the disease.

No matter how exhausted we were, we did not question the importance of performing purification rituals as best we could. We did our best, those of us who were still healthy, but it was an overwhelming task with so many villagers requiring constant care and attention.

And so it continued, this pestilence that knew no mercy. The weeks stretched into months, the days grew shorter, and winter was hard upon us. Those who were able went hunting, returning with fresh game and skins to help stave off the harshness of the year's coldest months.

Children hunted small game in the nearby forest and fished in the rushing river, its waters growing colder daily. And, of course, the meat had to be butchered and preserved, the hides scraped and cured lest they spoil.

We went to the fields and saved what we could of the forgotten harvest, although most of it had fallen to the earth and rotted. We were able to save some of the late fruit by cutting off the rotten portions and laying them in the waning sun to dry.

The nuts that were a staple of our diet were harder to gather this late in the season because the ground was covered with fallen leaves. Normally, the underbrush would have been burned to facilitate their gathering by groups of laughing women and children on brisk fall days. However, the risk of an out-of-control fire was too great with so few able-bodied villagers. It took much longer and required more energy to scrape the leaves aside in search of the little brown shells that encased the nutritious meat, and ours was a meager harvest that terrible autumn.

And still, the smallpox claimed new victims. Always, there were the ill who required tending and the dead who had to be buried.

And yet, life would go on. Just as the disease peaked and there seemed to be no end to the dying, Tame Doe, the niece of Old Hop and Moytoy and sister of Attakullakulla, gave birth to a little girl. Her husband, Five Killer, a Delaware from the northeastern region, named their beautiful daughter Nanye'hi or Nancy, but her Uncle called her Little Wild Rose because of the soft hue of her delicate skin.

So, amidst the grief and pain brought by the spotted sickness, the people of Chota felt hope for the future and found cause for rejoicing.

CHAPTER 25

Winter's End

Spring 1739
11 years old
Chota Town

The winter of my eleventh year felt as though it would never end. Exposure to extreme cold and meager nourishment only heightened our distress, rendering us even more susceptible to smallpox and other illnesses. Despite what the medicine men had claimed about the cause of the epidemic, I believed that Will was correct in asserting the purulence responsible for the disease.

The budding trees foretold the renewal of spring, lifted our spirits, and offered hope. However, even though the initial fury of the spotted sickness had passed, the pestilence still lingered among us. People continued to contract the illness, though in fewer numbers than during the epidemic's peak. In some respects, it was worse for them because, after surviving the first several months, they began to feel as if they had been spared. They were cruelly surprised when the disease began its now familiar and relentless course.

Each week brought new grief as the rock-covered mounds in the meadow increased in number, sheltering even more bodies of loved ones.

As the sun's journey lengthened once more into longer, warmer spring days, two out of three Cherokees had fallen ill with smallpox. At least half of the Real People perished that year, and many survivors were left blind due to the disease or disfigured by its characteristic circular scars. There were invisible scars for others—deep wounds of the spirit crusted over with protective shields that haunted them for the rest of their lives.

In the shortest days of winter, Johnny returned from the coast, his horse exhausted from the grueling journey over the treacherous mountains. He had hurried from Charles Town, sick with worry for his family and friends—and for Walina. He led a beautiful, delicate pony behind him—a gift for his love. Upon learning of her suffering during her illness and how she had cried out for him in her delirium, Johnny was overcome. The manner of her death tore at his soul. His grief for her was profound, and he felt consumed by guilt when he heard of Black Buffalo's terrible accusations.

"You are not to blame, Brother," I comforted him. "The medicine man was wrong."

"Sister!" He cried out. "You mustn't say such blasphemous things!"

"I'll say what I want," I retorted, "and who is there to stop me? Even the most powerful medicine man in all the Nation was not immune to the spotted sickness." For Black Buffalo had indeed died, as he desired, when overcome with the fire from within.

"I don't think it has anything to do with evil spirits," I continued, despite my brother's shocked look. "I think there is something in the thick white pus of the lesions that causes some of those who come into contact with it to become ill."

"Only 'some'? Why not all?"

"I don't know," I replied, momentarily at a loss for answers—a condition that seldom occurred. "I haven't worked that part out yet." I continued with a saucy tilt to my chin, "But some of us, like Will and me, handled the bodies of those who were ill and remained healthy while others became ill, some of them dying. I don't know why."

And once again, I felt that familiar tug of guilt that overcame me at times: guilt for having remained healthy while others who were more worthy than I had succumbed to the disease. No matter how I tried to work it out, it remained a senseless affliction. The one thing I knew for sure was that my brother should not carry the burden of blame for Walina's death but that I could never convince him.

As the epidemic began to wane, communication between nearby towns resumed, and we were not as isolated as we had been. As did all the villagers, I anxiously watched the town's entrance, hoping for, yet dreading, news of our kinfolk and friends.

It was a great relief when a messenger came from Toqua, and I learned that Willewanah, Cornsilk, Wurth, Willow, and Tassel had become ill but, thankfully, were recovering. Later, a message came that Saluy, Mourning Dove, and Molly survived, although two-thirds of the People of Estatoe had died. Mourning Dove was slowly recovering from the illness but had lost much of her vision. All would forever bear scars on their bodies.

The English trader Adair, who had lived among the Cherokee almost as many years as Dougherty, braved heavy snows blanketing the treacherous paths to Chota to exchange news. He listed many familiar names from the neighboring towns lining the banks of the Ta-na-see whose lives had been claimed by the spotted sickness. My chest ached with his naming of the dead, and I covered my ears to close out his hurtful words. How could this be? How could so many have died in such a short time?

Grief went hand in hand with relief, however, as I learned who had survived the first onslaught of the disease. Attakullakulla, the orator from under the chestnut tree, and his wife Ollie lost several family members, but their lively little son of four summers, the one we called Canoe, still lived. Adair said he had been gravely ill, but the little warrior valiantly fought the disease, refusing to loosen his grasp on life. And, despite the severity of his illness, he lived. His sturdy little body was covered with pockmarks, and they would likely always be with him.

I turned my eyes to Oconostota and saw him fingering the deep facial scars he bore, still red and raw from his illness. Always a handsome and proud man, I recalled the first time he saw the ravages of the disease on his own face.

He had been so consumed with grief for Quatsis that he did not yet realize his own disfigurement. I furtively squirreled away the warrior mirrors he had worn as pendants upon his broad chest, hoping to delay the day he would realize the extent of the damage. But one afternoon, I returned to the house to find him sitting on his sleeping pallet, looking in horror at his reflection. Overturned storage baskets indicated he had found my stash while looking for something. I could protect this proud man no longer.

Anger flashed in his eyes, and he threw the mirror across the room, causing it to shatter against the wall. The terrified wails of Terrapin and the baby, Bark, shifted his focus from himself to his sons, and he took them into his arms, soothing them that all was well and he hadn't meant to frighten them. But I had witnessed the despair on his face and knew that the scars went deeper than his skin.

As he heard Adair's words, I knew he thought of his own disfigurement, and I saw his anger rise again that children so young as Canoe should have their smooth, unbroken skin scarred in such a manner.

Adair told us that smallpox had claimed many medicine men throughout the Nation, and others experienced the same frustration as Black Buffalo. In desperation, they had tried every cure they could think of.

One medicine man, he told us, decided that the buzzard must be immune to sickness because he could devour dead flesh without ill effect. He prepared a soup made of buzzard flesh and bade the people of his village drink it to ward off the spotted sickness. Some people did his bidding, but most did not. It mattered not whether they drank it; the spotted sickness claimed them without favor. Eventually, the medicine man himself became ill and died, although he had consumed great quantities of his horrid concoction.

Adair told us of one elderly medicine man who smashed the consecrated pot he had used for cleansing rituals for decades, declaring that it had lost its power, and another who had thrown away all his holy things, claiming they were polluted. We shook our heads in dismay, words failing us. How could we express the fear and anxiety his news brought us, for if the medicine men were without hope, what hope was there for us?

But the news he brought of Tathtowe broke my young heart, for I had harbored a secret affection for the handsome warrior who had made love to a yellow-haired woman while King George slept in his castle.

Tathtowe, Adair told us, had always been the most prideful of our proud warriors, and we grunted and nodded in agreement with him, for it was so. And rightfully, I thought to myself, for I had loved to look upon his handsome face, which often mirrored the same mischief as mine.

Tathtowe was inconsolable when he recovered from the spotted sickness. His wife and children had died, as well as several other family members. Adding to his grief was the horrible disfigurement of his handsome face. Finally, he became so melancholy that he declared he would choose death rather than live with such grief and shame.

His friends feared he would indeed take his life as others had, for there were rumors of medicine men and warriors who had stabbed themselves or cut their throats out of despair. So, they took all sharp instruments away from him and watched him constantly, hoping he would regain his senses. But, their care only angered him more, and he cursed them vilely and tried to injure himself by beating his head against a wall, but to no avail.

Bad-tempered and foul-mouthed, Tathtowe flung himself upon his sleeping pallet, turned his back on his friends, and refused to eat, saying he would starve himself to death. They stayed with him, Adair said, as much as they could, but they, too, had extreme demands placed upon them, as we all knew.

As soon as he was left alone, Tathtowe arose from his pallet and wedged a thick hoe handle into a soft corner of the floor of his house. Kneeling before it, his hands grasping the handle, he threw himself upon it repeatedly until he forced it down his throat, suffocating in his own blood.

Tears coursed down my cheeks as I heard this story, and I remembered the good-natured man who had winked and flirted with a love-struck little girl.

CHAPTER 26

Trade Blankets

Spring 1740
12 years old
Chota Town

One afternoon, I was clumsily weaving a basket while watching my little brothers playing in a patch of warm sunlight. My fathers and several men from the town huddled close to our fire. Christian Priber had arrived the evening before, bringing news of Tellico. I was focused on the intricate weaving, trying to remember what Quatsis had taught me, but I needed help to succeed because this basket insisted on being lopsided. Then, my fingers stilled as I focused on the men's conversation.

"Yes, Will," Priber said, "I am convinced that smallpox was brought with the trade goods—the bedeviled blankets."

"Damme, man! Do ye really think I would bring that pestilence to the People? To my family? What in God's name are ye saying?" His voice rose with each word, and I could see the red spreading on the back of his neck, a sure sign of impending rage.

"Don't be a fool, Will," the unperturbed Priber said, poking at the coals with a stick. "I know you wouldn't do anything to harm the Cherokee. But think about it. Put aside your feelings and think about how it began and spread throughout the Nation."

The room fell silent as each man reflected on the painful memories of those terrible months, recalling experiences they would rather forget. Priber pushed a floor mat aside and used his stick to draw a small circle in the hard-packed dirt. "Here is Chota," he said, then drew more lines and circles while naming the rivers and towns of the Nation. I set down the basket that would not be and joined the group of men watching him.

"Think of it, friends," he said. "Will, you brought in a load of trade goods just before the Mature Green Corn Festival, did ye not?"

"Yeah," was his hoarse reply.

"Did you stop in any other town on your way across the mountains?"

"Well... yes," he answered hesitantly, beginning to reluctantly understand. All eyes turned toward him, waiting for him to continue. "I stopped at Tugaloo."

"Did you leave them any trade goods?"

"Aye," my father whispered. "I left a few blankets."

Blankets—those European-made, warm, supple woolen coverings rapidly replacing our traditional hide and hand-woven robes.

The word hung heavily in the air, and the implication was evident.

"Friends, how do you think smallpox spreads among the People?" Priber queried, sitting back on his heels, the sketch on the floor momentarily forgotten.

The men broke into a heated discussion, debating the teachings of the medicine men against those of the White traders like Will, who insisted that the purulence from the pustules caused it. Will did not join in this discussion but sat apart, his face a pasty gray.

"Will?" Priber inquired when the discussion had run its course. "What do you think?"

"Ye know what I think."

"Yes, I do. And you are right. Something in the pus causes the disease. I believe the trade blankets you brought from Charles Town were contaminated with smallpox."

Will visibly recoiled from Priber's words as though struck, but he did not answer. I wedged myself between him and the man sitting beside him, needing to feel the strength of his shoulder against mine; however, it was as if his entire body had suddenly grown cold. He knew—we all knew—that Priber was right.

"Look," Priber continued, sketching the route with his stick, "when you returned, you found that the illness had started in Tugaloo. It began there first. That's where the blankets were first left."

He paused expectantly, looking at Will, who could only nod in agreement "And then, a few days later, it began in Chota," he continued, his stick guiding our eyes and thoughts. "Remember, friends. It began in Chota with the young men who unloaded the trade goods."

A cry of distress escaped Dougherty, who had been sitting quietly up to that point. He had chosen the young men to transfer the goods from the packhorses to the storage building and trade house. Unfortunately, all of them had fallen ill, and most had died.

"And," Priber continued, "the blankets were traded and distributed throughout the festival, were they not?"

Both Will and Dougherty mutely nodded their heads.

He continued his damning evidence by using his stick to draw lines from the circle he named Chota to other similarly drawn towns of the Nation. "And then, smallpox broke out almost simultaneously in the other towns. Because... " he paused dramatically, "...because those people had been exposed at the same time—at the Mature Green Corn Festival."

I recalled the opening ceremony, where hundreds of Cherokees gathered in celebration, dressed in their finest clothing and thankful for a bountiful harvest. I also remembered the colorful trade blankets spread on the ground to protect their prized garments from grass stains.

A flood of memories returned of beautiful Cherokee babies napping under a shade tree, their round cheeks pressed against the woolen blankets from Charles Town. Lovely young women catching the eye of handsome warriors and slipping into the forest, a blanket from the trading post draped over one arm. Wrinkled old men and women, their wispy gray hair spiked by the cool evening wind blowing across the river, sitting close together with trade blankets slung over their shoulders.

I knew Will remembered the same things I did: the heavy burden of guilt descending upon him, his shoulders sagging with the weight of it.

"Oh, God, Merciful God! What have I done?" he cried out.

For the first time, I think, Priber realized the effect his damning evidence was having on Will and Dougherty, for at Will's outburst, he turned, a startled look on his face.

"You didn't do it." he said, "You did nothing. It was the English merchants who did it!"

He claimed that the infected trade blankets were a diabolical scheme intended for the extermination of the Cherokee people to open our ancestral lands to settlement by immigrants. With fire in his eyes, Priber stood before us and named the tribes of the south and east that were no more—entire tribes decimated in the face of advancing land-hungry Europeans.

"'Tis likely so," Dougherty added. "Damme, if that isn't what the blighters did to Ireland. The entire population was forced out of fertile lands and into the mountains to starve, making room for English farmers. And now the same is true for the Scottish Highlands, I'm told, where they are grazing bedamned sheep. Wool, they want, for their stinking mills."

Truly, Scottish, Irish, and English immigrants were pouring into the colonies in ever-increasing numbers and spreading further westward each year. They were advancing from the south through Charles Town, and a new wave of advancement had begun from the east. A river of Scotch-Irish immigrants was moving through Pennsylvania and down the Shenandoah Valley in Virginia. Wherever the settlers went, they fenced off farms, burned forests, and built roads, destroying ageless hunting grounds in the process.

Debate raged intensely from that day forward over the motives of the Englishmen, yet an agreement was never reached. However, one thing was certain in my mind and that of many of the Real People: the evil spirits that caused the spotted sickness had originated in Charles Town. Whether intentional or not, many believed the disease spread through the trade blankets.

The events of that terrible winter forever changed the three men in my life.

Will carried the guilt of his role in the near-destruction of the People he loved to his death, trying without success to drown his pain in rum.

Johnny's self-imposed penalty of guilt and shame for Walina's death shifted to a lifelong distrust of all things European. He tried to deny his Scottish ancestry and sought to become more Cherokee than any full-blood. As he grew older, White men would taunt him, goading him into drunken rages by calling him "half-breed Johnny."

Oconostota bore distinctive pox scars upon his face for all to see, but the deeper scars on his soul were revealed to only a chosen few. But, he could never hide anything from me, for I knew him better than he knew himself.

Chapter 27

Fancy

Late Summer 1740
12 years old
Chota Town

My family gathered around the communal pot, dipping our horn spoons into the rabbit stew that had simmered over a bed of coals all afternoon. My friend Cappy was skilled at setting snares and kept us well-supplied with rabbits. After stripping their long, thin bodies of soft fur, which changed from white to dark brown with the lengthening days, I cut the flesh into bite-sized chunks with my knife. Then, tossing the meat into our last brass pot, I added whatever vegetables I could find to make the one meal in which I had any degree of proficiency.

Ordinarily, we followed the Cherokee practice of eating whatever was available whenever our stomachs complained of emptiness. Lately, we had begun to gather around the cooking fire each evening as the sun dipped below the distant mountains. It was as though we needed each other's presence for comfort as much as, or more than, we needed nourishment.

Bark sat in the hollow of my lap, slurping from the shell spoon I offered him. The spoon was smaller and easier for him to handle than the large, bowl-shaped horns. The clan tradition of finding homes for motherless children had fallen into disarray due to the spotted sickness. In fact, I had taken on the role of mother to my little brothers despite my youth. It was quiet, the only sound being the family sharing their evening meal. I couldn't help but remember past times when Quatsis entertained us with stories and gossip about the village happenings that day.

Never at a loss for words, she chattered throughout our evenings, drawing Oconostota out of his usual reserve and causing broad grins to crease his normally stoic face. When he was home, Will joined in her lively conversations, and their banter was quick— a delight to hear, even if I was too young to understand everything they said. But from the glint in their eyes, I sensed that some of their banter held a double meaning.

I still missed my first mother, murdered at the massacre. And now I missed my second mother, dead from smallpox. Their deaths left an emptiness that caused my chest to ache. I longed for Quatsis from when I awoke until I returned to sleep.

But just then, I found myself missing her cooking. She was very skillful with the cooking pot and could turn simple meals into feasts. She had tried to teach me, showing me how to simmer the meat and when to add the vegetables. She even knew which herbs or roots to use for flavoring certain meats. However, I had not paid attention, as I was eager to return outdoors, to prowl through the dark and mysterious forest, to run and play with my friends, or to eavesdrop on the men and their far more interesting conversations.

And now, everything I prepared was either overcooked, nearly unrecognizable, or almost raw. My stews were either too bland or seasoned with a zest that brought quick tears to our eyes. The only meal of mine that was nearly appetizing was rabbit stew. Thus, I fell into the habit of preparing it daily, and I was heartily sick of rabbit stew, especially my rabbit stew.

A sigh escaped me, and I murmured, "I wish I had paid attention when Mother tried to teach me how to cook."

There was a period of silence; then, "And so do we," came a gruff reply to my musing. looked up, surprised, as did Will and Johnny; our eyes turned to Oconostota. We watched spellbound as the twinkle in his eyes traveled to his mouth, which was turning up at the corners, hesitantly at first, before a wide grin transformed his face. We all burst into laughter. This gaiety felt so strange. It was the first time we had laughed since the spotted sickness came to Chota.

Terrapin was startled at first as the unexpected sound frightened him. He began to cry and then, between sobs, laugh with us, looking from one adult to another for validation. Bark's lower lip trembled, his eyes wide as he absorbed the unfamiliar sights and sounds of his family. Their reactions only added to our spontaneity, and we laughed longer and more intensely than Oconostota's little joke warranted.

Once the laughter had quieted and we returned to our meal, we felt we could talk freely for the first time in months. Somehow, the dark cloud under which we lived had dissipated, at least temporarily. The tension was lessened, and a comforting lightness returned to our home.

"Well," I teased, "if you didn't like my cooking, you could have said something."

"And anger you, Little Sister?" Johnny joked. "We men are wiser than to get on the wrong side of Hester for fear she would really punish us with the cooking pot." And so the banter went that evening, and when seasoned with laughter, the taste of the rabbit stew improved.

The following day, Will told us he had an idea. "Not that Hester isn't doing a good job caring for us," he added with a grin. Messages from Estatoe had informed us that although Mourning Dove recovered from the spotted sickness, her vision had disappeared. Will felt that a visit from me might be helpful. "And," he chuckled, "maybe our little woman can learn a few tricks in the summer kitchen."

I was delighted by the prospect of stopping at Toqua on the way to Estatoe to see Wurth and Willow, as we had not been together since the Mature Green Corn Festival —a lifetime ago, it seemed. It was agreed that Will would take me on town business as he rode that way.

I gathered some of my belongings and wrapped them in deerskin, fashioning a pack to carry on my back. In an instant, while Will was still saddling his horse, I stood beside him, ready to ride behind him as always.

"Well, damme, Hester," he said, startled, "I dinna know ye could move so fast."

"I'm ready when you are!" I cried, my excitement barely contained

"Well, but Hester, are the wee ones ready?" he asked.

"The wee ones?" I repeated, not understanding his meaning.

"Terrapin and Bark? Have ye got the wee ones ready for the journey?"

"Oh!" It had not occurred to me that I would take the little boys to Estatoe with me. Instead, I had looked forward to the journey as a chance to escape the burden of being the only woman in our household, even though I had not yet begun my monthly flows.

Tears welled as I selfishly realized that my responsibilities would go on this journey with me. I stamped my foot and wailed, "But I'm too young to be their mother!"

"Aye, Hester, that ye are. That's a fact. And they're too young to be orphans, and there's naught but us since the bedamned smallpox. So what're we ginna do 'bout it?"

He looked over my shoulder, an embarrassed look on his face, and I turned to follow the direction of his gaze. There stood Terrapin, his eyes clouded with hurt, trying to bat away the tears that threatened to fall. Behind him, the baby Bark stood on unsteady legs, holding onto the doorframe for support as he was just learning to walk. When he saw me, Bark's little face broke into a delighted smile, and, holding out his arms, he toddled toward me.

How could I resist these adorable little brothers of mine? And how could I have been so childish—and worse, selfish? A wave of shame and remorse washed over me as I scooped them into my arms and nuzzled their necks, blowing bubbles and making them laugh and squirm until I lost my balance, causing the three of us to slide into a heap of arms and legs.

Arising from the ground, I was intent on brushing the dirt from my tunic and didn't notice Johnny's approach from the town's entrance until he stopped beside Will. Looking up, I saw that he was leading the beautiful pony he had brought as a surprise for Walina. I shifted my gaze from him to Will and then to Oconostota, who had joined them, unsure why all three were grinning at me and looking like conspirators.

"Well, Hester," Will said with mock gruffness, "are ye ginna get ready to go or not?"

"Yeah, Little Sister," Johnny added, trying unsuccessfully to frown at me. "Your horse is saddled and ready, and there you are, still playing in the dirt."

"Well, Prachey, I thought you'd be excited and ready to mount up and go, but there you are, fooling around with the little ones," Oconostota said, grinning from ear to ear.

It took a few seconds for their meaning to sink in, and I was stunned into an uncustomary silence. The pony was mine. I was to have my own horse!

As comprehension set in, I jumped from one man to the other, squeezing the three in tight hugs and smothering them with slobbery kisses. Mine! I have a horse! I never knew of a child having a horse, but my brother was giving me the mount he intended for Walina.

Horses arrived among the Cherokee during my mother's generation, brought by traders to transport goods over the mountains. Before the introduction of horses, young men carried heavy burdens on their backs, a task that proud warriors hesitated to undertake.

As the flow of goods between the coastal cities and our mountain home increased, horses became a welcome innovation, and the Cherokee adapted quickly. Now, numerous horses grazed outside the palisades of all the towns, and most young people had become skilled horsemen.

Some of the elders refused to mount them, stating they had no need for a horse to convey them from place to place. I heard them grumble about the horses' noise and complain loudly about their droppings, which littered the trails and meadows.

"What is the need for haste?" Gray Eagle had asked. "We will arrive when we arrive. And how can one contemplate or anticipate the journey's end if one arrives too quickly?"

"It is not good to be so high off the ground for one cannot read the signs others have imprinted upon Mother Earth," Otter Tail had commented.

A common complaint among the elders was that their two legs had been good enough for their fathers and their fathers' fathers and would, therefore, be good enough for them as well.

Their reluctance to ride horses puzzled younger generations, as the benefits were clear to us. I would never voice such a thought, as it would be disrespectful, but I secretly wondered if their hesitation stemmed from a fear of the horses.

Of course, like all Cherokee children interested in horses, I knew how to ride. We were free to play among the horses as they grazed in the meadow beside the river, and when we could persuade one to stand still long enough, we would mount it bareback and ride until it grew tired of our foolishness and bucked us off.

There had been little time for such frivolity in recent months. Still, I often went to the meadow in the late evening as the sun approached the western mountains for a few moments of solitude. To my delight, the spotted pony intended for Walina had taken to me, and we sought each other's company in the gathering dusk. She became my friend, a being with whom I had formed the habit of confiding fears I did not want to burden my fathers with, for they were overwhelmed enough.

Sometimes, after her mane had absorbed my tears of sorrow for all those who had died, she would shake her head and snort as if to remind me it was time to stop grieving. Then, I would grasp a handful of her mane and spring onto her back, and we would gallop from one end of the meadow to the other and back again, scattering the other horses in our wake.

I always felt better after those encounters, and as dusk descended upon our valley, I would return to our house with a lighter step. My fathers and brother must have noticed our close bond, for they were now saying she was mine.

Later that day, Will and I left Chota, taking the familiar trail to Estatoe. I held tight to Bark, who sat in front of me, gurgling and squealing with delight to be so high off the ground. Terrapin had a firm grip on the back of Will's shirt, his eyes wide with wonder at sitting behind the horseman like a boy instead of in front as babies did.

I tried not to appear too prideful, as that would have been ill-mannered, but I could not refrain from grinning at my friends Cappy, Sookie, and Sour Mush as they ran alongside us while we rode through the town gates.

As we traveled along the trail by the river's edge, I stroked my pony's neck and crooned, "Aren't you the fancy one?" And that became her name, Fancy.

CHAPTER 28

A Lost Sailor

Autumn 1798
70 years old
Baldridge Creek, GA

George's house is full to overflowing with my descendants, as he has invited his sisters and their husbands to meet with him and Goodwyn. The lawyer has come from Augusta with news of the latest attempts to reclaim George's South Carolina land. It was unsuccessful, of course, and I grow weary of George's tenacity. He has inherited his father's stubbornness. Richard was equally blind to what was evident to me when it didn't suit him.

George wants Kate and Neely to file a claim against Richard's adjoining property, the flourishing plantation and trade post that was seized after the war. He and Goodwyn have devised a scheme whereby George will make yet another claim. They think that, somehow, the two coming simultaneously will garner the attention of the South Carolina government. One hundred fifty thousand acres of prime land are at stake, and they believe the size of the claims will force the Americans to seriously consider George's charge of unlawful seizure.

He feels encouraged because much of his property remains vacant. South Carolina seems hesitant to divide it into grants. Richard's property, however, is densely settled, and there is a thriving little town called Greenville on the site of his Great Plains plantation by the Reedy River Falls. However, I think their scheme is just more of Goodwyn's hot air. Whites have never returned lands taken from the Cherokee, and they aren't about to start now.

When I tell George this, he becomes angry and says, "But the Cherokee granted me the land as a British citizen."

"Yes, I know—I was there. But in the eyes of the South Carolinians, you are Cherokee," I remind him, "and they will not recognize your dual citizenship or return the land to you. Besides, you fought on the side of the British during the Revolutionary War—a Loyalist. They will never forgive you for that."

We frequently argue back and forth, neither of us gaining ground, until George or I grow weary of the same old debate and walk away from each other. Of course, we hold no grudges after such arguments, as that would be foolish. Besides, George and I have always spoken freely to one another.

His wives will not discuss it with him, as they have heard his tirades too many times. Even Caty, who initially supported his fight for inheritance, has grown weary of the battle. Now, when he starts, they find an excuse to leave the room, leaving him to mutter to himself or to the tankard of whiskey that has become his constant companion.

His sisters have come as he bade them, but I know they will not join him in this latest endeavor. They and their husbands are unwilling to commit their time and resources to a futile battle with South Carolina's stubborn governor. However, to honor their elder brother, they loaded their children and grandchildren into wagons and traveled to George's farm here on Baldridge Creek. I am glad to see Sour Mush, who lives with Neely, accompanied them. While George talks his silly law talk, we enjoy a wonderful time in each other's company.

Or, we were—until the past couple of days, when a cold rain set in. The children have been housebound for too long and are growing restless, their bickering escalating to blows and, at times, hair-pulling. Their mothers are also weary of the confinement and are becoming a bit testy themselves. My stories of the olden days are falling on closed ears, and even Sour Mush cannot capture their interest.

Finally, as the rain turns to sleet, I call Rachel to help me. "Fetch an old quilt, granddaughter, and bring it to the dining room."

Curious, the children follow us, watching as I spread the quilt on the table while Rachel carries a large basin of water from the kitchen and sets it on top. Rachel's eyes shine with excitement because I have confided my plan to her, and she hurries from the room to gather the rest of the materials we need.

"Why did you put a quilt on the table, Granny?" four-year-old Turtle asks. "Are you going to sleep there?"

The other children titter, but he asks the question they want answered, so they grow quiet for the first time today.

"No, Turtle, that table is too hard for your Granny's old bones," I tell him. "But the quilt will absorb the water, so we won't make too big a mess and cause Nancy to be angry with us."

With their quarrels behind them, the children grow excited for the adventure that awaits them. The room is filled with their questions and laughter. "What are you doing, Granny?" Betsey asks, her red curls bouncing as she climbs onto a chair.

"I'm going to make a doll for Baby Sallie," I declare. As I hope, my announcement is greeted with a chorus of children's voices crying out, "Me, too!" "Can I make a doll, Granny?" "Will you help me, Granny?"

This is how we spend this dreary fall day, with the offspring of my children and my grandchildren, making dolls out of cornhusks, just as I did in my own childhood.

The older children assist the younger ones, who are focused on their creations, by demonstrating how to shape the cornhusks softened from soaking in the basin of water. They create their doll's heads by draping the pliable cornhusk over a carefully chosen walnut and securing it with a piece of twine. At the ends of the cornhusk, they tie together three or four additional husks to form the body, shaping them to be full. Next, they tie a tightly rolled husk at both ends and place it sideways, within the body, to give their doll arms. Another piece of twine at the waist holds everything together, creating a skirt.

I watch Rachel as she helps Turtle make a doll. His bottom lip sticks out, just like his grandfather's did when he concentrated on a task. This child of my son reminds me so much of my beloved Richard. "Turtle," I murmur, reaching across the table to caress his downy cheek. He glances up and smiles at me, proud of the doll he is making.

"Granny, do you know how to make a boy doll?" he asks me.

"A warrior?" I inquire.

"Yes… Oh yes!" he breathes.

I show him how to tie the body into two sections to fashion legs, thus transforming the "maiden" doll wearing skirts into a "warrior."

"Here, Turtle, let me show you how to place a feather on your warrior's head," Rachel says, taking her little brother's hand as he slides off the chair and follows her to the corner where Nancy has a supply of scraps for the children's play.

Oh, how they chatter and giggle, these babies of mine, as they create their dolls. Then, using the scraps of fabric left from Nancy's needlework, they fashion little aprons, dresses, and hats for their dolls. Like them, each cornhusk doll is unique and unlike any other. They decide that each doll must have a name and display the same creativity in how they name their make-believe children.

Lucretia's doll has a peculiar name, I think—one I have not heard before. "Co-lum-bus?" I ask as she leans against my knee, proudly showing me her creation, her eyes shining joyfully at her accomplishment. "That's an interesting name. What does it mean?"

"You know, Granny," she says, carefully pronouncing it again for me. "Co-lum-bus. The man who discovered America."

"The man who did what?" I ask her, trying to disguise my dismay.

"The man who discovered America," she replies, with growing self-importance. "The teacher told us about him. He knew that the world was round instead of flat like people said and that he could sail around the world. Others had warned him that he would fall off the edge of the earth, but he was very smart and knew better.

"He convinced the rich Queen Isabel of Spain, and she gave him the money to buy three ships so that he and his men could sail across the ocean. They were looking for a place called In-de-a, which has many riches, but found America instead."

Her little chest swells with pride at being the one to impart such exciting news to her Granny, who did not have the benefit of an education in the White men's school as she does and is, therefore, ignorant of these things.

Sour Mush has entered the dining room and, seeing the anger building within me, places his hand on my shoulder. "Hester," he warns quietly, giving my shoulder a squeeze.

I pat his hand with mine, then slip it within his grasp, taking deep breaths to calm myself before speaking. "And so, Lucretia, this Columbus who discovered America—what about the people who were living here when he 'discovered' them?"

The older children grow quiet as they recognize the warning signs, while the younger ones chatter happily, eager to display their knowledge of the world as taught to them at the missionary school in a class called World History.

Sour Mush and I listen as our descendants tell of a European hero who accidentally stumbled upon our land while searching for a route to another.

My ears burn as they tell me of ignorant savages and heathens who populated the land by coming from the frozen north and moving south across the continent. Some traveled to Mexico, they report, and even farther south. Others, the children's teachers said, went to the mountains of blue mist, our ancestral home, and then some of those went northeast or to the southern coast. They say Columbus was the first White man to walk upon this land, and had it not been for his bravery, the continent's inhabitants would still be living in ignorance.

I am appalled. George and the other parents allowed the Christians to come and teach our children, but they were cautioned against preaching their religion. They were instructed to teach our children to read and write English words and to do sums with counting signs. This history of our People's migration and Columbus discovering us was something we had never considered.

"And so, was he lost? This Columbus?" I murmur innocently, yet my overly sweet demeanor does not deceive Rachel and the older children, who regard me with questioning looks.

"Well… yes, I guess he was," Lucretia answers, a puzzled look on her pretty face. "I guess he was lost. But," she brightens, "isn't it a good thing he found us?"

Sour Mush is once again squeezing my shoulder, much like Corn Silk did when I was an unruly child. It has the desired effect: I do not throw Sallie's doll across the room and commence cursing this hero of the Americans who took our land from us, this Columbus.

"The Whites do have some interesting myths," Sour Mush begins, giving me a warning look. I notice Caty and Nancy standing in the doorway, with Kate and Neely crowding behind them, and I know they overheard the children recounting our history as taught by the White missionaries. They, too, are angry.

Why won't the Europeans do what they are paid to do: teach our children what we ask and not pollute their minds? Their tendency to meddle where they have no business is beyond comprehension. My fury rises again, and Sour Mush speaks just as I open my mouth, once more quelling me with a look.

"Yes, indeed," he said to the children. "The Whites have some very interesting myths, and I'm sure they believe in them. However, this is our ancestral land. It belonged to our grandfathers and their grandfathers long before

Columbus arrived, and our elders have shared the truth of how our people came to be here: our true history."

The children turn to him, momentarily putting their dolls aside. They are eager to hear a new story about the Cherokee that they have not yet heard.

"This is what the elders told me when I was a boy," Sour Mush begins with the timeless introduction to storytelling that we heard as children. I close my eyes and lean back in my chair, allowing his melodious voice to wash over me. It feels as if the past has become the present, and I hear Gray Squirrel's voice; Sour Mush and I are children once more, gathered around the elders in Chota's Council House.

"Our ancestors lived on mountainous land surrounded by water that was undrinkable," Sour Mush tells the children. "One day, our ancestors' island home began to tremble and shake; rumbles echoed, cracks opened on the land, and the air thickened with a dreadful odor. They were terrified, for they did not know what was happening.

"Seven traveling groups that became our clans were formed to leave the island and journey to safety on the mainland. They traveled for several days, and on the fourth day, they reached the summit of a great mountain. Looking back to where they had come from, they saw the island that had once been their home. They were astonished to see the tallest peak of their island erupt, unleashing vast plumes of dark smoke rising into the sky before it exploded, spewing fire and ash into the heavens as their island home sank beneath the water.

"Some of the People stayed in this new land, and their descendants are still there. However, our ancestors moved further inland and traveled northward. They crossed numerous rivers during their journey and encountered many strange sights: animals and plants they had not known on the island. In one place where they lingered, and some chose to stay, there were herds of animals with large humps on their backs, which they killed for meat and hides.

"Generations passed as they continued their journey northward until they reached a place where the water turned white in winter. It was very cold, and the elders said, 'We cannot stay here.' Thus, they changed their direction and traveled east, toward where the sun rises.

"After crossing a long river, broader than any they had crossed before, they encountered the Mound Builders—people who had inhabited their land for many generations. This tribe performed sacrifices—taking the lives of their own people—to honor their higher beings.

"Our elders stayed with the Mound Builders for a while but then continued their journey east. They lived among the Iroquois for some time but eventually broke away and moved south until they reached the mountains that touched the clouds. This was where we lived when the Europeans arrived."

All is quiet as the children consider Sour Mush's teachings. They realize that the Cherokees have a very long history that spans more generations than can be counted and that the history recorded by the markings on the White man's talking leaves is very recent by comparison.

This cold and rainy autumn afternoon, we discuss it for a long time, with children of all ages, from the youngest to the nearly grown, alongside the adults who have joined us—my family—gathered around the quilt-covered table. Laughter rises up and spills out into the gathering dusk as large hands assist smaller ones in shaping dolls made of cornhusks, and we talk about the true migration history of the Real People.

I am glad when George pauses his scheming with Goodwyn long enough to join us, assuming his rightful role as an elder. He also reminds us of ancient legends about other Whites who visited our land long before Columbus: large, hairy men who wore horns on their heads and called themselves Vikings.

Several times, they arrived on our eastern shores in great sailing vessels. They sent out parties of men to explore deep into this land and then returned to their ships, sailing back to their homeland. Often, they burdened their ships with trees harvested from the vast eastern forests. Because of their visits, which had only aroused curiosity among the native people, the eastern tribes were not surprised to see hairy, pale-faced men in sailing vessels arriving once more—the Europeans. But these white men did not leave.

The children talk among themselves and ask the adults questions, pondering what they have been told while continuing to create a village of cornhusk dolls. I am pleased to see that they understand the essence of the lesson: they must balance the missionaries' teachings with those of their elders, as scratchings on talking leaves are not always as reliable as the oral traditions of our People.

Later, while the women of my family sort out the various sleeping arrangements in the crowded house, Rachel and I clear the table of its clutter. Soaked from the wet cornhusks, the quilt is set aside until a sunny day, when we will spread it out to dry.

As I fold it, my fingers trace the outline of its design, and I remember the items of clothing the fabric once was. Here is a shirt George wore as a young man, and the bright blue fabric was Susannah's skirt when she was a child. In a sense, this tattered quilt is a chronicle of my family's history, for while touching these remnants of fabric, I recall the events of our lives.

My hands smooth the worn fabric as I reflect on how we learned to make patchwork coverings when I was a girl. I remember it was born out of necessity and frugality.

My grandmothers used thick, luxurious furs on their sleeping pallets to stay warm on cold nights. However, with the arrival of traders came a dependence on European manufactured goods. Our furs were too valuable for such ordinary use, so in my mothers' time, sleeping furs were gradually replaced with woolen trade blankets.

However, after the terrible winter of 1738-39, when more than half of our people died from smallpox, many Cherokee women refused to let trade blankets come near their loved ones. Many believed, as I do, that the colorful woolen blankets were tainted with evil spirits that caused the disease.

By then, we had become reliant on trade goods for our survival, making it impractical to return to using the fur of large animals for warmth, especially during the first year or two after the epidemic that severely disrupted our lives. Resourceful women like Wurth began sewing the fur of small animals, such as rabbits and squirrels, into warm coverings for the children, allowing more of the larger furs to be available for barter with the traders.

Then, they began stitching together bits and pieces of European fabrics, utilizing every scrap left from a length of material after making garments for their loved ones. Intact pieces of fabric from clothing that were too worn to wear were incorporated into quilts. Smaller pieces were joined to create larger sections, which were then connected with a layer of insulation to form a covering for the sleeping pallet.

Later, with the luxury of leisure time, some of our women began creating designs with the fabrics, much like they did with their baskets. Thus, while some of the quilts were simply utilitarian, others were beautiful works of art. Nancy was one of those clever women, and all her quilts were highly prized.

I set the damp quilt aside and rose to search for my sleeping place for the night. *It is true.* I think as I bank the fire, *I stand in the middle of a span of women who lived in different worlds.* My grandmothers knew only fur coverings to hold the cold of night at bay, but my granddaughters will only know of quilts. There are few left who know the pleasures of both.

But replacing furs with quilts was just one of the many changes brought about by misguided European men who "discovered" us while searching for one thing and unwittingly found another. And most of those changes occurred after the catastrophic smallpox epidemic of my youth in the winter of 1738-39.

CHAPTER 29

Secrets of the Wild Carrot

Autumn 1741
13 years old
Estatoe Town

As the seasons changed in my thirteenth year, many transformations turned me from a gangly girl into a woman. I grew suddenly taller, towering over my mother, Mourning Dove. With longer arms and the unfamiliar swing of my body, throwing a spear felt different and affected my accuracy. I was especially annoyed by the breasts that emerged from my chest. I had to learn how to hold my bow slightly differently before releasing arrows, as those soft, tender protrusions hindered my aim. Even in the heat of summer, I had abandoned the near-nakedness of my youth and began wearing a shift for modesty.

Mourning Dove was often exasperated with me for no fault of my own, and we quarreled over minor infractions. She claimed I was temperamental and moody. At times, I felt she treated me like a child, while at other times, she treated me like a grown woman. Often, I would storm out of the cabin in tears, only to regret the harsh words we exchanged and return to apologize.

I noticed remarkable changes in Sour Mush's body, too. He had suddenly grown much taller, but the rest of his body had not yet caught up with his height, making him appear as if he were built of sticks— all legs and arms with huge feet and hands. He, too, gave up the freedom of going without clothes. However, the most concerning aspect was our newfound shyness toward one another. It troubled me that even Sour Mush treated me differently.

Although I was constantly surrounded by people, I often felt over-whelmed by loneliness and sadness, weeping at the slightest snub. Then, unexpectedly, I would become giddy with joy, giggling and acting like a silly little girl again. I hardly knew what to do with myself from one moment to the next.

Earlier in the year, when the first buds were forming on bare tree limbs, Mourning Dove had bade me to sit with her in the darkened recesses of our home. I silenced a groan when I saw her bring forth her medicine bag, thinking it would be yet another frustrating lesson. But I scooted forward on the mat to see what she pulled from her deerskin bag.

She spread out multiple bundles of soft doeskin in various sizes, stitched with rawhide and secured with intricate knots. I knew the knots had a language of their own that told of the contents within. My mother sorted through her collection, discarding some bags and setting aside others until she was satisfied with what lay before us.

After making her selection, she took a pinch from a bag and sprinkled it into the small bowl of rendered fat placed between us. Then, she mixed it with a wooden pestle, creating a fragrant cream, and handed the bowl to me.

"You can apply this to the hairs that have begun to grow between your legs and other parts of your body. Soon, they will loosen their hold on your skin and begin to fall away."

I knew, of course, that Cherokee people regarded body hair unsightly, unclean, and even unhealthy and would not permit it. European men, some with almost bear-like pelts, were a source of wonder to us—but it was their aversion to bathing that we found most offensive.

I was unaware of this magical concoction and silently vowed to pay closer attention to Mother's lessons. Surely, there were even more secrets to uncover in her medicine bag.

"Those hairs that may remain will be loose and can be easily removed," she had continued. From the recesses of another bag she pulled from behind her, she presented me with a curved seashell. Holding it against her leg, she demonstrated how I could scrape the remaining offending sprouts of hair from my body.

Then, she presented me with a packet containing a soft deerskin strap and dried moss. "Soon, your first moon time will come upon you," Mother explained with a small smile. I saw the glint of moisture in her eyes. "Then, my little girl will be a woman."

She instructed me on how to fasten the belt around my waist to secure a leather thong between my legs. Dried moss held within the thong would absorb the blood flowing from my body during my moon times. I was responsible for keeping the packet's contents clean and replacing the moss as necessary.

She added a small doeskin packet containing the inner layer of willow bark which was for me to chew when needed to ease the occasional discomfort of those times.

Bursting with pride, I held these things close to my chest, knowing I would be ready when my moon time came upon me.

But later, on a warm autumn afternoon, Mourning Dove bade me walk with her to the meadow. She had regained some of the vision lost to smallpox but still could not see clearly. I didn't want to go but felt guilty because I had been disrespectful that morning. She had scolded me for leaving my sleeping pallet askew on the floor, with my belongings scattered around. My mother kept a tidy cabin, and we children learned from an early age to roll up our pallets and hang them from their pegs on the wall. Personal belongings were to be returned to their baskets when not in use. She did not tolerate clutter.

Molly, of course, never left her sleeping pallet in disarray but always hung it from its proper peg. Indeed, she was always neat and tidy and never disrespectful to our Mother. She and I obviously had little in common and spent as little time together as possible.

I knew my laziness would irritate Mourning Dove, yet I still dawdled until she became angry, and we exchanged harsh words. Her invitation for me to accompany her was less a request for help because of her impaired vision and more a means for us to heal the wounds caused by words spoken in anger.

"Daughter," she began as we left town and walked toward a wooded meadow. "Now that you are a fully grown woman, there are some things you should know." My interest in the walk increased because I was curious about what she would share.

As we walked, I noticed her squinting as she gazed across the meadow, straining to find particular plants. When she spotted them, she broke into a grin and led me to a cluster of tall plants with delicate white caps. Of course, I was familiar with wild carrots, a staple vegetable in their season. However, I failed to grasp its appeal now that the slim, crunchy root had passed its prime and would likely taste bitter to the tongue.

"They make pretty flowers, but I don't think they will taste good, do you?" I ventured a question of doubt to Mother.

"No, my daughter," she laughed as she embraced me. "But soon, it will be the season to collect the secrets of wild carrots."

Secrets? Secrets! What young girl doesn't want to know secrets? Mother had my undivided attention as she spread her cloak on the ground for us to sit.

"Look here within the flower," she instructed. And there, I could see tiny seedlets clinging to the safety of the enfolding petals. She continued, gesturing toward the cluster of plants nodding in the afternoon sun. "In a few weeks, these flowers will begin to turn brown as they complete their season. Then, when the moon is in the correct phase, women will come in the early morning while the dew is still on the ground. We will ask permission of the plants to harvest and, if given, will give an offering of sacred tobacco. Then we will chant the proper medicine song as we remove the flower from its stalk." And she taught me the incantations I was to sing when I harvested my own wild carrot seeds.

"We give thanks to the wild carrot for its gift and take only what we need, leaving more for others."

The flower heads were stored in a tightly woven basket, but not so tight that they could not breathe. Thus, as they lost moisture, the seeds would loosen and fall into the basket.

"It is the dried seeds that hold the magic—the secret—that gives women the power to choose when and if to allow a child to grow within their bodies."

My mouth must have made an "0" of surprise, my eyes widening as understanding dawned. Many mornings, I saw women preparing a special tea using an herb from beautifully beaded bags, but I hadn't known its importance.

"When you are mated with one man—or, for that matter, have coupled with several men—you must drink the tea every day to prevent a child. But, if you are caught unaware or suspect you may be carrying someone within, you must chew a pinch or two of seeds every day until your moon time comes upon you. In this way, you can prevent a man's seed from taking root."

Then, she withdrew a delicately beaded bag from her pouch and placed it in my hands. "I prepared this for you long ago," she said, a glint of tears in her eyes, "and now that I see how things are with you and Sour Mush, it is time I give it to you."

I felt myself flush bright red, as I thought nobody knew about those strange sensations I had recently experienced around him. The evening before, he and I reached for something at the same time, and when our hands touched, I felt a burst of fire deep in my belly. He must have felt the same jolt as we both jerked our hands apart and, stammering, parted ways.

To cover my embarrassment, Mourning Dove chattered casually about how it should be between a man and a woman—that pleasure was to be given and received. And then, she described some things that could increase the pleasure of joining.

My embarrassment faded. I asked questions, and she answered—sometimes with more detail than I truly wanted. I knew about the coupling of animals and humans, of course, but these details sparked a new level of curiosity. Could it be true? Had she and Saluy really done those things with each other? My father must have done such things with my mother, or I would not have been born. I pushed those thoughts away, unable to imagine such elderly people being in the throes of passion.

Smiling as if she understood my thoughts, Mourning Dove continued, "You will likely be curious for a while and want to lie with men other than Sour Mush." She advised me with an even more startling disclosure.

"There will come a time, however, when you will wish to mate with only one man and bear his children. When such a man walks in your soul, you will not want to couple with other men—only with the one..." As I was thinking of this, imagining who I would choose as my mate, I heard a soft chuckle, and my mother added "...most of the time."

CHAPTER 30

False Promises

Spring 1742
14 years old
Chota Town

In the years since smallpox claimed the lives of half our People and disrupted our traditional way of life, I have enjoyed more freedom than usual for a Cherokee youngster. I rode Fancy freely from Toqua to any of our Nation's towns, carrying messages or delivering packages. The People were accustomed to seeing me here, there, and everywhere, and they paid little heed.

It was my habit to sit quietly where men gathered to smoke their pipes and talk as men do. I learned to make myself small so they would not notice my presence. I found their boasts of bravery in battles and discussions about the politics of the People far more interesting than the women's gossip.

Both Johnny and I had spoken English words with our father since infancy—often colorful curse words that had no equivalent in our musical Cherokee language. As children at the trading post in Tugaloo, we learned

Creek, Choctaw, and Shawnee words as people from other tribes came to trade with our father. It was easy for me to learn these various languages—a gift to compensate for my lack of cooking skills.

By listening closely, I became adept at understanding many of the languages spoken in our villages. In this way, I learned a great deal about the leaders and warriors of my People—and our European visitors.

Wise beyond my years, I did not boast to the other children about my knowledge, nor did I interrupt or correct an elder when he stated something I knew to be different from what I had overheard. To do so would be extremely rude. I kept my knowledge to myself—known only to me for fear of drawing attention to my presence. If the warriors and elders knew I was listening to their conversations—that I was not merely a sleepy girl—I could be sent away and not permitted to sit in their presence.

It was my determination to learn French by listening to Christian Priber that compelled me to break my silence and inform Old Hop about what I overheard.

In his arrogance, the English-loving Moytoy of Tellico, whom Cuming had named the Emperor of the Cherokee, appointed Priber as Secretary of State for the Cherokee People. Priber believed he could control the Real People through Moytoy. Although I was young, I understood his duplicity. In typical European fashion, he continued what Cuming had initiated and fostered division between Old Hop, the true Headman of the Cherokee, and Moytoy, his ambitious younger brother.

When Moytoy died in battle against the Creeks two years earlier, Priber attempted to position Moytoy's thirteen-year-old son as Emperor. The boy had been one of my playmates and was known as Dreadful Water, a name that suited him due to his foul temperament. His royal title held little influence within the Nation and was primarily symbolic in relation to the Europeans. We knew that Priber desired to be the real power and to rule the Cherokee People.

Frustrated by the slippery politics of what he thought were simple people, like Cuming before him, Priber disrupted our orderly traditions, fostered division between our leaders and the governors of the English colonies bordering our east and south, and encouraged friendship with the French to our north.

Old Hop wisely refrained from supplanting Priber, granting him free rein among the People. His silence stemmed not from weakness but from the cunning that was his genius.

He permitted the disruption due to promises Priber made that would lessen our dependence on all Europeans.

I had been present at a Council meeting when, shortly after his arrival, Priber vowed to bring someone who understood the secret of making gunpowder to our misty mountains. With this knowledge, we would no longer be at the mercy of English or French traders for something that had become essential.

"The merchants in Charles Town purchase gunpowder from Europe and bring it to our shores across the Great Water," he had said to our leaders. "Importing it is costly, and then they must hire men to transport it across the mountains to the People."

"We understand that… " Attakullakulla had replied testily, "But each hunting season, they demand more deerskins for less powder and shot. As we take more deer, fewer remain in our hunting grounds. We must travel farther each season to hunt what we need for trade."

"Ah, and they will continue to raise the price of gunpowder because they know you depend on it," Priber gloated.

The elders had chorused their objections, wishing we would return to the old ways. They argued that the People had survived countless generations without the metal tools, muskets, and gunpowder, which had been introduced as novelties but had become essential. There was disagreement among the elders and warriors on this subject. The younger men liked having a musket not only for hunting but also for warfare.

"Our enemies wield the White man's fire sticks, and we must do the same," argued Beaver Tail, a fierce warrior. "We cannot go to battle with bows and arrows when Creeks fire upon us with muskets. We need guns and gunpowder for our own protection."

As usual, the men heatedly discussed whether to return to the old ways or continue bargaining with traders for guns and ammunition.

I remembered how Priber had quieted the discussion and commanded their attention when, in his booming voice, he announced, "What if you made your own gunpowder?"

"How could that be?" many had chorused.

Pribner then explained that the ingredients necessary for making gunpowder were present in our mountains. He pointed out that saltpeter is the main component, which can be produced from bat droppings found in the caves that crisscross the mountain valleys.

"Bat shit makes gunpowder!" Beaver Tail had exclaimed. "What magic is that?"

"It isn't magic," Priber replied, "but simple science for those who know how to do it." He then explained that the soil beneath the bat's resting place in caves could be shoveled into wooden troughs. Water from a nearby stream could be poured over the soil, and after it evaporated, the remaining residue would be saltpeter.

"The other two ingredients, sulfur and charcoal, are easily found in these mountains," he told us, gesturing widely. "It can be done. Then the People will no longer have to bargain with the English for gunpowder."

I remembered how the elders had been silenced by a chorus of joyous exclamations from those who did not want to return to the old ways. The majority of People were excited about making our own gunpowder.

"I will bring an expert from England to teach you how to do this," Priber promised.

But years passed, and nothing progressed despite the People's frequent inquiries. Priber became increasingly evasive about when this would happen. Thus, Old Hop continued to tolerate Priber's ever more offensive behavior because he wanted the People to learn how to make gunpowder and become less dependent on Europeans—both French and English.

But it was I who discovered Priber's duplicity while I occupied myself carving a toy for Creat, his little daughter by Moytoy's daughter, while eavesdropping on Priber and three Frenchmen who had come to Toqua to trade.

I had been curious about this odd man since his arrival among us and took every opportunity to observe him. It was not unusual for me to position myself nearby and appear focused on a task when French traders gathered around the fire outside Clogoittah's cabin.

Priber did not know that I had gained a rudimentary grasp of the language by listening to him and the French traders. I was careful that none realized I understood much of what they said. Therefore, they were accustomed to speaking freely among themselves, and, as a result, I learned what they did not want the Cherokee People to know.

"Priber, you fool. Are you really that daft?" chided Guillaume Potier, one of the Frenchmen. "We make our best profit by trading gunpowder to the Indians."

"And we don't want them to have an endless supply of the stuff," Jean Arlut muttered, scratching the belly that hung over his belt.

Pierre Albert added, "Remember, Priber, as long as we control the heathens' access to gunpowder, we control who they wage war on."

"We damn sure don't want them using their muskets on Frenchies." Potier chuckled. "It's best they rely on us to sell them just enough gunpowder but not too much."

"I'm not a fool," Priber bristled. "Are ye forgetting I get a percentage of the profit ye make trading with the Cherokee? It is not to my advantage for them to trade with the English."

I did not understand the meaning of the word 'percentage,' but as they continued talking, I could grasp enough to realize that Priber was acting in his own best interests, not those of the People, as he claimed.

"I ain't gonna bring anybody here to teach them how to make gunpowder. That would be stupid. And I ain't stupid," he bragged to his companions.

Some lighthearted teasing and back-slapping among the four of them provided me with a moment to reflect on what I had heard. Was it true? This man, whom the People had welcomed into their community—a man who had married one of us and had a child with her—was motivated by his own selfish interests.

As if he sensed my disbelief, I felt rather than saw his glance at me. I kept my eyes downcast, focused on delicately carving the face of the wooden doll I was making for his daughter. Satisfied that I could not grasp what was being said, the four of them continued discussing how to increase Cherokee trade with the French and sow discord among the English.

They spoke so rapidly and over each other in their excitement that I could not grasp much of what was said. It was enough, however, to understand their intention of profiting from the People.

"I guess that applies to your promise to teach them how to make iron-works, too," Arlut challenged Priber.

"Damme, man! These Injuns are too ignorant to master something as complicated as a steelyard. Granted, everything they need is here in these mountains," he exclaimed, gesturing widely to emphasize his point. "There are plenty of rivers for water power, forests for charcoal, and lime-stone and iron ore are easily found. Yet, I would prefer we sell them the goods rather than see them making their own."

"We're glad to hear you say that," Arlut boomed, a broad grin visible through his bushy beard. "But I must admit, you worried us for a while."

"No need to worry," Priber boasted, scratching his backside. "Moytoy may be dead now, but I have Dreadful Water and Old Hop in the palm of my hand. We'll soon break ties with British traders, and there will be more business for you Frenchies. And more profit for me."

I was so upset that it was hard to continue carving. But I didn't dare get up to leave, for I didn't want to draw attention to myself. They must not know I had been listening and that I understood much of what was said.

With Old Hop's quiet, courteous mannerisms, Priber believed he was a simple man he could control. Little did he know of Cherokee politics.

It was a great relief when two Cherokee warriors approached and interrupted their conversation. I silently slipped away as quickly as possible and hurried to find Old Hop. I was sure he would want to hear what I had overheard.

CHAPTER 31

Old Hop's Little Flea

Spring 1742
14 years old
Chota Town

That same afternoon, I told Mourning Dove I needed to travel to Chota. She was so busy with her endless chores that she did not question my urgency, likely thinking it was unimportant. Indeed, everyone was used to my coming and going as I pleased, traveling from one town to the next. I simply had to show respect by informing her of my destination. I gathered a few essentials in my pack and mounted Fancy. If I left immediately, I could reach a town along the trail in time for a meal and a place to sleep for the night. The next day, I would reveal my secret—and that of Priber to Old Hop.

Although Chota was our largest village, Old Hop was always easy to find. He preferred to be near the Council House in some capacity, ensuring he was available to anyone who wished to speak with him. Due to his even temperament and approachable nature, the People kept him well-informed about even the smallest details of life in our mountain home. I often observed him listening carefully and patiently to the most tedious gossip. He reminded me of a squirrel saving nuts for later, but in his case, it was information.

As I expected, he was seated at the entrance to the Council House, engaged in conversation with Attakullakulla, his sister's son. This was good fortune for me, as I knew Attakullakulla also needed to hear this news.

I approached the two men shyly, as I had been bashful around Old Hop since learning of his love for my mother. I was also aware of his quiet interest in me—the daughter he might have had with the woman he loved.

I squatted nearby, within their sight, and waited for one to notice me. Old Hop saw me but said nothing. Attakullakulla sensed the direction of his gaze and cheerfully called out to me, "Prachey, what mischief have you been up to this day?"

"None," I replied with a grin, as Attakullakulla and I were good friends who often teased each other. I moved closer to them and, lowering my voice for their ears only, said, "I have news of great importance."

"What important news could our Prachey have to bring her all the distance from Toqua?"

"It is news that I must share privately," I said with a brazen jut to my chin. It was unusual for a young woman to be so bold with our leaders.

Old Hop studied me for a moment and then invited me to walk with them. We three casually strolled through Chota, past a gauntlet of greetings, to the edge of the forest. We settled ourselves comfortably on fallen logs, and both men turned to me with anticipation.

I appreciated the honor they had bestowed upon me— despite my youth, my request for a private audience was not questioned. Because they recognized my worthiness, the initial nervousness I felt dissipated.

"What news do you have for me, Little Flea?" Old Hop asked with one of his rare grins. I realized that while I thought my eavesdropping was a secret, there was someone who had noticed a quiet girl listening and absorbing everything that was said.

I settled beside them in the shade of a giant oak and quickly, scarcely pau sing for breath, told them the words I had heard exchanged between the th ree Frenchmen and Priber.

Attakullakulla did not question my account, but he expressed surprise that I could understand their conversation. Old Hop, however, showed no surprise. He winked at me and said, "I always knew this one would accidentally overhear something of import. I am glad she has wisdom beyond her years and knew to inform us of Priber's duplicity."

Old Hop had taken Pribner's full measure long ago and was not surprised to learn of his collusion with the French. Colonial authorities suspected him of inciting trouble, and twice, they had sent soldiers to Tellico to apprehend Pribner. To their frustration, Moytoy's warriors turned them away on both occasions. Moytoy had declared Priber a friend of the People and would not surrender him without a fight.

Being the wise diplomat he was, Old Hop called a Council of advisors. After many pipes had been smoked amid much discussion, they decided that Priber must be made to leave our midst. However, this must be done without his knowledge or that of the French. It should not appear that Old Hop and his advisors had been instrumental in removing him from our mountain home. We would find a way to turn him over to the English.

Old Hop called for Priber to join the Elders in their Council, and he was asked to accompany several of our warriors to parley with the Creeks. Unfortunately, there had been a recurrence of border skirmishes that disrupted trade. Priber's ego was inflated by the flattery heaped upon him. He was told that his skill as a negotiator was needed to broker a peace agreement. Bristling with pride at what he perceived as his importance, he was eager to go.

CHAPTER 32

Duplicity Returned

Spring 1742
14 years old
On the Trade Path

I was pleased to accompany Saluy, Johnny, Priber, and several warriors on the trade path to meet with a Creek delegation after we had sent word of our intentions. We knew that the Creeks would inform the South Carolina authorities that Priber would soon be within their reach.

Our journey proceeded without incident. The warriors were unusually quiet as Priber continued to rant about one thing after another. He was unaware that we intended to allow the English to capture him. His duplicity had inspired our own.

After we set up a makeshift camp for the night, I pulled a fallen log closer to the fire and settled onto it, wrapping warm furs tighter around my shoulders as the evening dampness grew chill. Fancy snorted and stomped her feet from where she was tethered with the other horses. She, too, felt the cold from our long journey that day. I reached for the pile of firewood and tossed more onto the flames, making them leap, dance, and sizzle while providing considerably more warmth. Smoke billowed from the fire, causing my eyes to water. Yet I loved the sharp scent of burning wood.

"Damme, Hester, if ye haven't built a White man's fire!" Johnny teased, mimicking our father's brogue as he silently emerged from the forest, a brace of rabbits dangling from his belt. He tossed them in my direction, a not-so-subtle hint that it was my responsibility to clean and prepare them for our supper.

Reluctantly, but because I wanted to impress my adored brother with my worthiness, I left the comfort of my log and the fire, took the still-warm, furry bodies to the creek a stone's throw away, and hurriedly set to work.

When I returned with the rabbits skewered on green limbs, ready to position over the coals, I was pleased to see more of our fellow travelers silently settling around the fire. I admired how quietly they moved through the forest without so much as a snapped twig. Of course, Sour Mush and I had played survival games in the woods with our friends, as all Cherokee children do, but the warriors impressed me with their stealth. I vowed to watch and learn how to mimic their skills.

It was important for me to prove my value to this small band of Cherokee warriors and not be a burden. I had wheedled my way into their midst; some were not overly pleased with my presence. The one ability I offered to justify my presence was my gift as a linguist—my capacity to interpret the words spoken by White men and people from other tribes.

"It is good that we brought a woman with us," Saluy said, interrupting my thoughts with his teasing. "Her way with this rabbit is surely better than Johnny's."

I felt a rush of pride at the rare praise, as compliments were infrequent among the People. Uncle was aware of my discomfort during this journey and that some of our traveling companions had not welcomed me. A full belly after a hard day's travel would help them accept me. I was grateful that Corn Silk had taught me to stuff the rabbits' cavities with wild onions found beside the creek and a bit of salt from my pack, making them tender and flavorful.

Although I spent as little time as possible with the women of my village, a small amount of their teaching had taken root. Still, we all knew that while the rabbits would make a passable meal, they would likely be burned on one side and raw on the other.

"Tell us once more what you know about the English, Priber," Saluy asked the only White man traveling with us. He added more wood to the fire, stirring the coals and revealing their glowing red underbellies.

"Easy enough, monsieur," Priber replied in Cherokee and halting English, mixed with a touch of French, as was his tendency.

As the logs caught fire, flames leaped, and sparks flew toward the stars, illuminating our campsite nestled in a grove of chestnut trees a short distance from the trading path. Priber gathered his furs and moved closer to the warmth, not only to fend off the night's chill but also to be better heard, for he always had much to say.

"The English cannot be trusted," he said emphatically, drawing the fox pelt around his shoulders. "They are greedy people and will cheat you at every opportunity."

Grunts of agreement followed his statement, as the warriors were aware of or had experienced unscrupulous traders. Some traders, like my father, established a permanent storehouse near a Cherokee village and treated the People fairly and honestly. It would follow that such a trader formed a bond with a woman and soon started a family, becoming trusted members of the community. Others traveled from the coastal cities, their pack trains laden with goods as they moved from village to village. While some were honest men, too many were greedy, aiming to acquire as many deerskins as possible in exchange for the least amount of goods.

Since my grandfather's generation, the Real People have depended on rifles, ammunition, and other European innovations brought to our misty mountains. Our warriors have always hunted in the fall and winter, but only enough game for our needs was taken in the olden days. A prayer of thanks was given to the animal whose life was sacrificed for ours. However, as our dependence grew on tools made of metal, glass, and cloth, our men began hunting deer solely for their hides.

The People lamented the waste of meat, bone, and sinew, but it could not be helped. The deer would be killed and skinned where it fell, for a deerskin was easier to transport than a carcass. As our need for trade goods grew, the men had to hunt farther from the villages since deer were becoming increasingly scarce. There were frequent bloody clashes as hunters ventured into hunting grounds claimed by other tribes.

Otter Tail, settling comfortably into his furs, cursed the English for the harm they had inflicted on our People. "Firewater is destroying our young men," he lamented. "They lose their senses and act foolishly, yet they drink the cursed rum at every opportunity."

Murmurs of agreement followed, and the conversation shifted to a new problem that had emerged since the smallpox epidemic: many of our men had developed a taste for firewater—rum, the same drink my father had used to drown his grief when my mothers died. Some men would lose all sense when consuming the firewater provided by the traders. Evil spirits seemed to overtake them as they cursed, quarreled, and even exchanged blows with one another.

"I remember when Turkey Feather, one of our bravest warriors, drank to excess, staggered around the fire, and fell into it, badly burning one side of his body," Johnny contributed, shaking his head with disbelief. "The stench of his burning flesh remains with me to this day."

"Ah, yes. I was there," Otter Tail said. "He was so severely disfigured by the burns that he could no longer hold a rifle or a bow and arrow. The rum was the cause, but he blamed it on their White man's God and called it an evil spirit."

The men chuckled, remembering how his cursing of their God had terrified the unscrupulous traders, who feared a lightning bolt from the sky would strike them down.

Holding his belly as he laughed, Johnny retold the story we had all heard many times before. But we loved hearing it once again. "I heard it myself—Turkey Feather shook his fist in the air and shouted, 'I am a beloved warrior and not afraid to die. I shall piss upon you!' The traders were so scared that they dropped their rum kegs, mounted their horses, and hurried down the trade path back to Charles Town, leaving the deerskins behind."

"The rum-selling traders knew that the elders would be angry with them for what had happened," Otter Tail added as the laughter died down. "They had been forbidden to bring rum into our mountains, yet they still chose to do so."

"Yes, the worst of the lot waits near the path the hunters take to return to their village. The traders will entice them with a little rum and then offer to trade their deerskins for more firewater," Spotted Deer added. "And when the falling down sickness caused by the rum has passed, the hunters must return to their town with no skins to bargain for what their families need from the trading post."

The men fell silent, contemplating the trouble caused by the wicked drink introduced to our mountains by White men. Priber seized this moment, as I knew he would, for the man reveled in the sound of his own voice. "As I keep saying, the English cannot be trusted. It's not just the traders with their rum but also the men in the cities who offer you goods in exchange for your land."

My kinsmen murmured among themselves, for this White man's concept of buying and selling land was something they could not grasp. How could anyone own the land on which we lived? Was it not meant for all the creatures that called it home and relied on it for food and shelter? Could one truly own the air? Or the rivers flowing freely with life-giving water? It was incomprehensible.

"Haven't I told you about William Penn and his son?" Priber asked, eager to recount the story once more. We weren't yet ready for our sleeping robes, and we were glad to remain by the fire's coals, still giving off a little warmth, picking at rabbit bones and listening to yet another tale of thievery committed by a White man.

Even in our remote mountain villages, we knew of a White man named William Penn. He had negotiated with European royalty to purchase lands far to the east, where the Delaware People once lived. They signed one of those talking leaves—a treaty—but had yet to learn that Penn would bring more Europeans than could be counted across the Great Water to settle in their ancient homeland. Thus, their hunting grounds were overrun by these strange people.

The Europeans scattered across the countryside like ants erupting from an anthill, extending beyond the borders of Penn's purchase. Wherever they went, they cut down healthy trees to create clearings in the forest, disturbing all the creatures living there. Some trees were used to build their log dwellings, while others were wastefully burned, plumes of smoke marking each assault on their homeland. They ravaged the earth with metal plows and planted crops in rows instead of our sensible seed hills. The cows, chickens, and hogs they brought polluted the land and assaulted the ears. Pushed out of their traditional hunting grounds, the Delaware People became even more dependent on the White man's trade goods for survival.

Recent news reached the Overhills about yet another affront to Native peoples. Priber was delighted to recount that story repeatedly as an example of English duplicity.

Thomas Penn, son of William Penn, wanted more than the vast expanse of land his father had taken from the Delaware and sold to European settlers. His father's treaty stipulated that no man could buy more land from the Native peoples than he could walk in a day and a half. Therefore, Thomas hired three of the fastest runners he could find, paying them handsomely to run in different directions while ensuring their path was cleared of obstacles. By this means of duplicity, he acquired yet another vast expanse of Delaware ancestral lands—land that now bore his father's name: Pennsylvania.

Not surprisingly, even more fragile wooden vessels sailed across the Great Water, heavily laden with land-hungry European families eager to purchase those stolen lands from Thomas Penn. Meanwhile, the Delaware were pushed even farther from their homeland and into the territories of other tribes.

Thus, it was all around our mountain enclave—border skirmishes with neighboring tribes, including the one that destroyed our home in Tugaloo and led to my mother's death. The White settlers pressed in on us from all sides, constantly seeking more land than the treaties agreed upon.

My traveling companions grew silent as they absorbed this oft-told story—yet another example of the Europeans' devious ways. Quietly, we gathered our robes around us and, with the fire banked for the night, positioned ourselves around it as closely as we dared for warmth from the coals. In my drowsy state, I became aware of the men discussing who would stand watch over our campsite during the night as I drifted into sleep.

The sun peeked over the eastern mountains, awakening us, and there was general stirring as men rose to make their way to the forest to relieve themselves of night water. I waited for their return to the campsite before venturing into the heavily dewed foliage surrounding our camp, seeking privacy to meet my own needs.

We continued our journey, and by midday, we arrived at Tallapoosa Town, where the inhabitants warmly welcomed us, aware of the true purpose of our visit. Moments after our arrival, traders from neighboring Creek towns approached, disarmed Priber, and took him into custody. He was outraged, of course, and then dumbfounded when his Cherokee traveling companions turned their backs on him. He had assumed we would protect him once again, But we did not.

We lingered just long enough to see a detachment of soldiers approach the town. We watched silently from the edge of the forest as Priber was bound and, surrounded by armed English soldiers, led out from the town. A second mount carried the bundle of manuscripts he always kept close by. We learned years later that he had been confined in prison at Fort Frederica in Georgia, where he died far from our mountain refuge.

The disruption he caused among the People was soon forgotten, his daughter Creat being the only reminder. However, his influence on divisions within the People remained. Oconostota's distrust of all things English deepened, while Attakullakulla saw merit in siding with the English in their power struggles against the French.

As for me, I relished my newfound role as Old Hop's Little Flea, as he had come to call me. I continued quietly listening and observing, whispering bits of important information to the man who once loved my mother.

It pleased me to accompany the warriors and headmen on their journeys to the towns of the White men. In their arrogance, those smelly, rude creatures placed little value on women and even less on young girls. Thus, I became privy to their talk when they thought they were speaking in private among themselves.

CHAPTER 33

Assimilation

Spring 1799
71 years old
Baldridge Creek, GA

Freed from the stifling winter chill that had kept me indoors, I invite my grandson, Jim, to join me in exploring the outer fields and meadows of George's new farm here on Baldridge Creek

Jim is a quiet twelve-year-old who often gets overlooked because of his older brothers, Jesse and Moses, and his lively younger brother, John. Not to mention his sisters and the new baby. He is approaching manhood, a confusing time, and I want to spend some time alone with him. The fact that I might need a strong shoulder to lean on from time to time has nothing to do with my invitation.

I am reassured to see that the farm has prospered in the few years since we moved from Noonday Creek. I was not entirely pleased to leave that homestead, as we have too often had to pull up our roots and replant ourselves in another location.

With the acquisition of European trinkets—for that is how I view those things on which my family has become dependent—moving a family as large as ours has become increasingly difficult. I told my daughters-in-law that in the old days, we had few possessions, and moving from one place to another was done quickly and with ease. I noticed the look the two of them exchanged, dismissing my comment as that of a whining old woman, and I retreated to my cabin to let them continue with their packing.

Belatedly, I realize that my silent musing while Jim and I walk the farm's perimeter has caused me to neglect this boy, though that was not my intention. We come upon the creek, swollen with water flowing from a spring rain.

"We should have brought a pole," I tell my grandson. "We could have surprised Nancy with a string of fish for supper tonight." Indeed, the flash of fish can be seen against the rocky bottom of the shallow place where we are stopped.

"Come, Granny," he says with delight. "I know what to do." I let this precious youth guide me along the creek bank, fraught with hazards for someone as unsteady as I am, to a small pool carved out of the soil.

The clever boy selects a sapling of suitable length and strength, freeing it from its neighbors with the knife sheathed at his belt. Then, he pulls out a coil of cord from his pocket and attaches it to one end of his new fishing pole. "What now?" I ask, pleased by his ingenuity.

He grins sheepishly, reaches into his pocket again, and produces a small piece of fabric with a secured fishhook. "Well done!" I exclaim.

Jim patiently helps me settle into a comfortable nook among the roots of an overhanging tree before he begins searching for worms and grasshoppers for bait. Then, my grandson and I relax beside the rushing creek, determined to catch a few fish for the family's evening meal.

"This is a good place," I tell him. "You've done well to find it and to be prepared should an opportunity to fish present itself." He grins sheepishly, ducking his head in embarrassment. I realize I need to give this boy more attention in the future, as the quiet ones are often overlooked in a large family like ours.

In the peacefulness of a warm spring afternoon, as songbirds serenade us, he chatters on, telling me that he enjoys attending the Moravian School and getting to know the Baldridge and Daugherty families. They are his mothers' kin, who have also made homes in this small valley carved by a meandering creek.

Jim grows quiet, focused on watching his fishing line, jerking it at just the right moment and landing one catfish after another. From that miraculous pocket of his, he pulls out another coil of twine and crafts a way to secure the fish through their gills before lowering them back into the water. There, they will wait while he entices more of their brethren onto his baited hook. He is an excellent fisherman. And since silence is essential for good fishing, I, too, remain quiet, enjoying the warmth of the sun, which has released the fragrance of nearby wildflowers.

I rouse from a doze, startled until I remember where I am. My old bones feel stiff and reluctant to shift my position. The afternoon has grown warm, and Jim has put aside his fishing pole to tease crawdads in the shallows. In my drowsy state, through slitted eyes, the lanky boy reminds me of someone from my younger days—Canoe, one of the Real People who was scarred by smallpox long ago.

I smile as I remember when Canoe was Jim's age and had pestered his father, Attacullaculla, that he was old enough to go on a hunt. As pairs of hunters carried their canoes to the river, the young boy continued begging to join them. Exasperated, his father told him, "If you are strong enough to carry your own canoe, you can go."

Villagers watched as the excited boy tugged repeatedly at a heavy canoe resting on the shore, but it barely moved. The men pushed off, preparing to depart.

"Wait for me!" he shouted. The hunters paused, laughing, as the determined boy struggled and finally seized the hemp lashing used for tying, dragging the canoe to the water's edge. Having demonstrated such strength of will and determination, he was permitted to go on the hunt and became known as Dragging Canoe.

The strong-willed youth became one of the People's fiercest Red Chiefs and was present at the Henderson Purchase in 1775, just as the Revolutionary War simmered in the backcountry. Richard and I were there as interpreters while Richard Henderson and Daniel Boone negotiated the purchase of a vast expanse of land that now comprises the states of Tennessee and Kentucky.

Richard was one of the traders who advised our Cherokee leaders against making the deal. Dragging Canoe refused to agree to the treaty even though his father, Attakullakulla, and the great war leader, Oconostota, had signed it. An irate Dragging Canoe predicted that the Europeans would find the settlement "dark and bloody."

Frustrated at the outset of the Revolutionary War, amid the destruction of so many of our towns and the massacres of our People, Dragging Canoe led many displaced people further west. They established towns where the Great Warpath crossed the Chickamauga Creek and, thus, became known as the Chickamauga.

My son, then known as Cherokee George, often fought beside his father, who ascended to the rank of Colonel in the British army. At other times, George was one of the warriors who descended from the Chickamauga encampment on Lookout Mountain, above what is now called Chattanooga, to defend our People. From there, the Chickamauga fulfilled Dragging Canoe's prophecy—they terrorized settlers and committed atrocities, killing them in their fields or burning them alive in their pitiful log cabins.

The rage of the Chickamauga was returned tenfold upon any Native — whether warrior, woman, old man, or child. Our villages were similarly raided, atrocities committed, homes burned, and fields destroyed as they stood. Defenseless women, children, and the elderly were cast out to fend for themselves without food or shelter during the winter months. The settlers suffered, but the People's suffering was of greater magnitude. We were not the invaders; we only wanted to live our lives in peace on our land.

The lives of pioneers on the frontier were made so miserable that one would think it would have slowed the tide of immigrants; however, it did not. The flood of new immigrants was unceasing. Their thirst for more land to deface was unquenched despite the Chickamauga's attacks on settlements.

After the Revolutionary War, when Richard was exiled to the Bahamas, he reestablished connections with trade partners and smuggled goods to the besieged Chickamauga through Spanish-held Florida. Our home at Noonday Creek, located near the growing city of Atlanta, was crucial in transporting goods to Lookout Mountain, which overlooks the Tennessee River.

For me, his smuggling of goods inland provided a rare opportunity to reunite with my beloved Richard from time to time as he undertook the arduous journey from the Bahamas to the mountain retreat of my kinsmen.

Distracted by my thoughts of the past, I become aware that Jim had grown weary of tormenting the crawdads; the allure of a rushing creek is too strong to resist. He removes his britches and slips into the cool, refreshing water, splashing and creating such a noise that any remaining catfish surely seek shelter deep in the muddy bottom. I, too, find the creek irresistible, take off my cotton dress—for I have adopted the European style of dress—and join him. We splash each other and laugh. He dives under and resurfaces behind me, and I pretend to be frightened, causing him to laugh with glee.

He helps me ashore as I stumble on the uneven ground and put my dress back on, welcoming its softness against my damp skin. I rest in the shade of a willow that hangs over the creek. The boy has not yet tired of our outing, so I settle deeper among the sheltering branches and let my thoughts drift back to days long past.

Despite being advanced in age, my language skills remained valuable, and I attended the signing of the Treaty of Holston on July 2, 1791. This treaty aimed to further the destruction of our People. The new American President, George Washington, and William Blount, now Governor of the Southwest Territories, convened with over one thousand Cherokee men and women on the riverbank at White's Fort, a small settlement on the Tennessee River, now known as Knoxville.

The Americans, as I must now refer to them, had done their best to destroy us, yet we persevered. Therefore, they determined that those who had survived must become like them: we were to "assimilate." This was a new word to me, but I soon understood its meaning. We were to turn our backs on our traditional way of life and fully adopt the European lifestyle.

Dragging Canoe urged the elders not to sign, but his pleas were in vain. This treaty forced our people to surrender even more of our land, which settlers had already overrun. In return, we would receive the tools needed to become like the Europeans.

We were to be given cattle and sheep as individual owners, a new concept that differed from our communal ownership. Plows and agricultural tools were to be supplied, along with blacksmiths to maintain them. Thus, our hunters and warriors were to transition into farmers.

Women were to be given spinning wheels and looms to make articles of clothing from sheep's woolen covering or cotton. Growing cotton required clearing forests, defiling the Earth's surface with plows, and planting cotton seeds. It demanded many hours of hard labor under an unforgiving sun—a task unsuitable for warriors. Thus, I was disheartened to witness more of my People adopting the White way of enslaving others to toil in their fields.

The intention was that by adopting these methods of sustenance, our hunting grounds would be open to White settlers. Extensive territories would no longer be necessary for our hunting grounds to provide food, clothing, and deerskins for trade. We would live on individual farms instead of in our communal villages.

We would become White.

As part of the agreement, the Americans were permitted to construct a road through Cherokee territory—a travesty, in my view, that further divided us and made encroachment even easier for settlers.

But even worse, "we," the Cherokee People, were to receive an annual cash award. "Who is the 'we'?" I had asked repeatedly, as there was no provision for the disbursement of the anticipated windfall—if it were actually to happen. The money would end up in the pockets of a few influential men.

Greed had become a new pox upon our Nation.

The borders were drawn—yet again—on their maps. However, as before, this did not prevent the invasion of settlers. They remained blind to the invisible lines that separated the new United States from our Nation. There was no stopping them.

A few months after the Treaty of Holston, messengers informed us that Dragging Canoe had died suddenly following a night of celebration with the Creek and Choctaw Nations, during which he danced all night. I, for one, do not believe that Dragging Canoe died from exhaustion. More likely, he succumbed to a broken heart. I still grieve deeply for that little boy I knew so many years ago, who grew into one of our greatest warriors.

Richard's death two years later disrupted the flow of smuggled goods to Lookout Mountain, further weakening the Chickamauga.

And they are no more.

Therefore, when Caty's brother, Robert, visited our home on Noonday Creek to share news about the settlement of mixed blood family and friends in what was becoming known as Baldridge Creek, it wasn't long before George and Caty persuaded Nancy to make the move. She agreed upon hearing about the region's rich soil—ready for planting. We all felt crowded by the increasing number of White settlers around the nearby town of Atlanta and were eager to leave for northern Georgia's peaceful, unspoiled region.

Jim retrieves his string of fish from the creek, rousing me from my reflection. The afternoon wanes as we begin a roundabout return to the house. As we go back, I ponder all I have seen of George's new farmstead: furrowed fields and a hay meadow with cows and horses grazing, a newly planted orchard beside the fenced garden, hogs penned with free-roaming chickens, a large barn with a hay loft, his house featuring glass window panes, my small cabin behind it, and a small row of newly built cabins for slaves.

"It is good," I mutter to myself. "This is not the life I wanted for my family, but it is good. With kinfolk nearby, they will be safe on this farmstead—a part of, yet separate from, the world of White people. For here, in the gentle hills of northern Georgia, my family can find safety from the land lust of Europeans."

My initial misgivings were unfounded, and I recognize the wisdom of the move. The only darkness that I see is its too-close proximity to James Vann and his bedeviled tavern.

CHAPTER 34

Battle with Firewater

Spring 1799
71 years old
Baldridge Creek, GA

I pull the heavy layers of quilts over my shoulders and burrow deeper into the tangled nest I made during my restless night. The fireplace emits little heat in the early morning, its coals promising a warm fire should I bestir myself. However, I am reluctant to start this day, disturbed by the memory of the evening before.

It isn't just the early spring coldness of night that creeps under the door-frame nor the dampness that frosts the one glass window in my cabin that chills me—it is the realization that my son George is naught but a drunken lout.

His wives and I are relieved that he resisted James Vann's repeated requests to join him in various business ventures. James and George share a long history; both are children of a Cherokee woman and a White man. Perhaps because of Richard's influence on the boy—for he had doted on him—George weathered their tumultuous childhoods and grew into a son I could take pride in. James, on the other hand, chose a dark path.

Vann is the wealthiest man in the Cherokee Nation due to his often un-scrupulous business dealings. He owns taverns and ferry boats along the heavily traveled Federal Road and is constructing an enormous two-story brick home on his vast plantation. His cruelty toward his hundred or so slaves and the dire treatment of his several wives are well known.

Yet this man I have known since he was a babe is not just mean but evil. The latest outrage is that he beat one of his pregnant wives to death—a horrendous crime for any man, especially a Cherokee. Our men have always revered women, and such behavior was unheard of in the olden days. A man would never dare raise a hand to his wife, for her clansmen would seek retribution. Furthermore, a husband who misbehaved or displeased his wife would be put out of her home for, indeed, the house and children were hers, and it was her decision with whom she would cohabit.

But James fears nothing from his wives, as the age-old clan system has weakened; indeed, it has nearly vanished. The incessant wars, displacement, and diseases introduced by White people have disrupted many of our traditions. Men like Vann abandoned the fight against Europeans and chose to adopt their basest values—lust for greater wealth, physical abuse of slaves and wives, and an insatiable thirst for whiskey.

Our George resisted joining him in business, but they often drink that mind-numbing concoction of firewater until he can no longer sit on horseback and must wallow at the tavern until Jacob is sent to fetch him home in the wagon.

George is consumed by self-pity as he realizes he will never reclaim the lost estates that once belonged to him and his father. The site of Richard's Great Plains plantation along the banks of the Reedy River has now become the heart of a growing city known as Greenville. However, the South Carolina government remains uncertain about what to do with the adjacent lands owned by our son. We have received word that the Americans refer to the most prominent feature as Paris Mountain, a clear indication that they acknowledge to whom it belongs, although they choose to misspell its name.

My son has wasted too many days and far too much money trying to reclaim what was his, and he has finally realized that it is futile. Meanwhile, the move to this farm on Baldridge Creek a few years ago has proven to be quite profitable, largely due to his wives' efforts.

Caty manages the farming operation with little help from her husband, who laments that he is a warrior, not a farmer. He is loath to plow a furrow or harvest a crop but will find a need to take up his rifle to hunt for the scarce game in these woods—or, more often, saddle his horse to ride to Vann's tavern to drink and swap war stories with other men.

Nancy maintains the big house while also developing a profitable business venture with her family, descendants of the trader Cornelius Dougherty, and Caty's family, descendants of yet another early trader, Old Dan Baldridge.

Washington's plan for the Cherokee to "assimilate" with the Whites was taken to heart by resilient Cherokee women once they received the promised tools. Their hard work generates income for their cash-strapped families—and fabric to make clothing.

Our centuries-old system of bartering for our needs becomes less effective each year. We increasingly rely on coins or even paper money to fulfill those needs. I fail to see the value in either. We have always found a use for whatever we might trade or barter, be it furs, meat, baskets, or beads. But what use is a small, round piece of metal? It cannot be eaten, nor can it be planted in the soil to regenerate. Coins create a pleasant jingle when attached to ceremonial robes. But paper money? Bah! Its only purpose is as kindling to start a warm fire on a winter night. Yet, we must have it to survive in this modern world.

Old Dan Baldridge first settled on this creek and encouraged his extended family to join him over time. Now, it is a strong knit community of mixed bloods scattered among the hills and valleys of northern Georgia near the Tennessee border—the Buffingtons, Fields, McLaughlins, Emorys, and Downings, among others. A few families keep sheep on the steeper farms, where the grazing is too poor for cattle. Caty and George will not permit sheep on our farm, for it is well known that those stupid creatures do not pasture well with other four-legged livestock.

In their season, the sheep are sheared of fleece, their woolly covering—again, a nasty task my George would not deign to perform. Blocks of fleece are carted to strong-armed women who are paid to clean the wool of mud, twigs, and sheep shit. They stretch a pad of raw wool upon a block of wood and, with a large brush featuring iron teeth, brush up and down with firm, tireless strokes. Once cleaned and the fibers disentangled, the wool is twisted into a loose rope.

That is a task Nancy doesn't want in her tidy house, much less near the children. Instead, sacks of cleaned wool are brought to her for spinning into yarn. She has become quite industrious with the spinning wheel she set up next to the fireplace in the large room.

Indeed, she seems to enjoy the mindless task of working the pedal with her foot while watching the long strands of yarn wind onto bobbins. I often see her gazing into the distance, dreaming of who knows what. But then, the spinning abruptly stops, and she takes a misbehaving child to task or cuddles an unhappy one on her generous lap. Later, another woman in our community weaves those bobbins of yarn into strips of cloth.

Thus, hardworking women among the Cherokee earn coins and paper money to help support their families in this new European fashion. They also have the opportunity to share news and gossip as the wool, yarn, and fabric move from cabin to cabin in our little settlement. But, it is a poor substitute for when women worked side by side, as they did in my youth.

Even I, in my old age, contribute to the family's well-being by taking over the care of the chickens. They used to roam freely, pecking at plants and bugs such as caterpillars, beetles, and ants. However, their incessant pecking at the soil for morsels quickly damaged Caty's prized garden. Their eggs were often hard to find—a task assigned to the youngest children—and the chickens frequently became prey to woodland creatures. I particularly disliked how they soiled the ground with droppings wherever they went. When I stepped on a particularly large deposit with my bare foot, I declared an end to their freedom.

My grandsons built a sturdy enclosure using straight tree limbs bound together with freshly cut willow whips woven through the staves like a basket. As the willow dried, it secured and stabilized the fence, ensuring the chickens were confined and protected from foxes and raccoons. Chickens can fly to the top of a fence, pause, and then fly away from the enclosure; therefore, the sticks were pointed and stood on end, leaving no place for them to perch.

Jacob built a small house for them, complete with boxes of straw for the laying hens and a designated area for perching and sleeping. Naturally, their droppings quickly soil the little house, and my grandchildren have to clean it out weekly—a task none of them like, as nothing is messier than chicken shit.

However, their eggs are much easier to find. My grandson, Turtle, is happy to be responsible for collecting the eggs twice a day and brings them to me in a special basket woven by his mother. I nest the eggs we don't eat in boxes of straw and send them to market to sell, adding to the family's resources.

Thus, the family's prosperity is largely due to others, with little contribution from my son. He has become a disappointment to me, and I know Richard would be disheartened as well.

Weary from my musings as I lay abed, I finally rouse myself enough to clamber out from under the warm quilts. My bare feet on the cold wooden floor prompt me to take quick steps to the fireplace, which emits a touch of welcoming heat. I place a few logs over the bed of coals and coax them into flame, creating a dance of warmth for my creaky old bones. Not yet ready for the day ahead, I return to the comfort of my bed to let the cabin warm before breaking my fast.

My heart is heavy as I recall the events of the previous night at the big house. How has it come to this? Is my son destined to continue down this dark path? What will happen to the family if he does not set aside the grief and anger that are consuming his soul?

As usual, the family ate the evening meal together at the big table that dominated the main room. That morning, George saddled his horse and rode off without telling anyone where he was going or when he would return. His dark mood cast a shadow over the family even though he was not present.

The girls were clearing the table when the door burst open, and George staggered in, clearly very drunk. "Where's my supper?" he had demanded, his words slurring as he swayed and reached for a chair to steady himself.

"In the slop bucket," Caty snapped, pointing to the wooden bucket where food scraps were collected to feed the hogs.

Startled by her unusual sass, George straightened and glared at her. "What! Woman, do you dare insult me?"

"You insult the family with your drunken presence," Caty declared, standing with hands on her hips and fire in her eyes.

And George did the unthinkable.

He raised a hand to his wife and struck her across the cheek. The sound of the blow echoed in my heart as I realized the depth of depravity to which my son had sunk. The children were stunned to silence, their eyes wide with fear. The littlest ones began to wail and seek comfort from their older brothers and sisters. Nancy stepped forward and took her sister-wife in her arms, daring their husband to strike her as well.

Surprised by his actions and perhaps embarrassed, George stood slack-jawed and trembling, glancing around at his family. Understanding washed over him as he saw their expressions of fear and loathing. He turned and staggered into his room, a jug of whisky in hand, closing the door behind him.

And now, despite the heaviness in my heart, I must rise from my bed and prepare to face the day. What comes next? Is he to become as beastly as Vann? My feet are hesitant to carry me the short distance from my cabin in the woods to the big house.

I open the door to an unusually quiet house. At this hour, the older children have left for school as usual. However, the younger ones, with their cheerful chatter, are also absent. My questioning gaze shifts from one daughter-in-law to another.

"Do not worry, Mother," Caty reassures me. "The little ones are staying with our Baldridge relatives while we sort it out."

Sort it out? What does she mean? She gestures toward the open door to George's room, and realization dawns.

My son is sprawled upon his bed, fully clothed, lost in a bottomless sleep. On the floor beside him is the whiskey jug, but it is smashed to pieces, its contents leaving a dark stain on the wood floor. He will know upon awakening what his wives have done. Despite the illness that consumes him after a drunken spree, he will have no relief with more firewater.

Caty and Nancy busy themselves with household chores, never leaving the house or their husband unattended. Jacob comes and tells us he has done as instructed: George's prized horse is now loose with the other four-legged creatures in the pasture, and his fine leather saddle is hidden where he will never find it. All the whiskey stores Jacob knows of are destroyed. The women search the house for more, but none are found. Even in his despicable state, George knew better than to hide whiskey in the house.

Around midday, we hear groans coming from his room, and we three determined women exchange satisfied glances, recognizing that the battle is about to begin.

And a battle it is—a battle of wills, at least, as George makes no further attempts to strike either of his wives. He roars and yells, then begs and pleads throughout the day and into the night, but our ears remain closed to him. He regains enough strength to stagger to the barn and back, railing at us because his horse and saddle are missing.

"They are not missing, husband," Nancy scolds him. "They, like your children, are in a safe place."

"The White man's firewater has stolen your soul," Caty admonishes him. "You will stay with us, your women, until the firewater has left your body."

I stand beside my son's wives, a solid wall of determined women who will ensure he returns to himself, whether he likes it or not.

The four of us engage in a battle of wills. However, we women remain united against the evil that has overtaken George. I am grateful to his wives for their wisdom in sending the children away. They should not witness their beloved father in this state: soiling himself, begging for whiskey, ranting and threatening, and falling into a deep sleep from which we are unsure he will awaken.

Several days pass as he gradually returns to himself. His eyes are free from the bloodshot, bleary gaze to which we had become accustomed. He begins to eat the meals prepared by Nancy. We see him walking the farmstead as if reacquainting himself with this property, his home. Finally, the day arrives when he joins us for the noon meal with a freshly shaved face, having bathed and dressed in clean clothes. The firewater has left his body.

But will he have the strength to resist temptation in the future? We do not know the answer to that. He is allowed back as head of this household, but with the clear understanding that we, the three women of his world, will not tolerate such foolishness again.

At last, word is sent, and the older children return home from school later than usual, having collected their younger brothers and sisters. It must pain George to see how they give him a wide berth, uncertain about this stranger who used to be their father—at least, I hope it pains him as much as his behavior has pained all of us.

Baby Hester, named after me, toddles to him with open arms, bringing tears to his eyes as he settles her onto his lap. He has to coax three-year-old Sallie to come to him, and it takes her a moment to lean against his knee. He must regain their trust and that of their older siblings.

Our family has been damaged, but my son's strong wives have united to force their husband to sobriety. He sees now what he almost lost. It is up to him to avoid the firewater and the destructive influence of his friend, James Vann.

I reflect on the differences in the lives of my descendants and how their experiences contrast with mine. Each generation carries the burden of living in its own time, and none are easy, although some are more challenging than others. However, the bond of family strengthens each of us, and together, we will endure.

CHAPTER 35

Transformation

Spring 1745
17 years old
Estatoe Town

There was great excitement in my home in Estatoe, for I was to accompany a delegation of our most prestigious headmen and warriors to Charles Town. My mother, Mourning Dove, took it upon herself to make sure I would bring pride to the People. Other women of our clan also helped, working diligently and providing colorful ribbons, feathers, beads, mirrors, and tiny bells to embellish the soft, white doeskin dress and moccasins she had sewn for me.

Wurth came from Toqua and was pleased to contribute to the unfolding drama. She brought a rawhide container filled with various items intended to transform me into a prideful woman. Despite my protest, I was taught how to scrub my face with finely ground corn to remove impurities. "Do you do this?" I asked my sister, noting that I could feel my facial skin glowing, though it felt raw and dry.

"Yes, of course," she scolded with exasperation as she rummaged through her parfleche. "If you had not been so busy riding from place to place on Fancy and listening to the talk of men, you would have noticed that wom en who take pride in themselves care for their skin."

Chastened, I admitted that the incessant prattle among girls and women about such matters held little interest for me. Their chatter about ornamental headdresses and beaded belts, along with their obsession with various hairstyles, did not captivate me as much as the conversations among men. However, since I was to accompany Old Hop to Charles Town, I needed to learn how to look my best to spare my fellow travelers any embarrassment.

"Here it is," she muttered, pulling a small lidded pot from her bag of mysteries.

"Ah," we both sighed as she lifted the lid, releasing a delightful fragrance that filled our noses. "This is from the aloe plant," she explained, dipping her finger into the creamy substance. "I peeled away the prickly skin to get to its sticky inside part."

Before I could react, she smeared the substance on my cheeks and rubbed it into my face. I wanted to protest, but it actually felt good, so I leaned forward to make it easier for her to reach me.

She giggled at my reaction and continued to explain, "I mix that part of the plant with a little honey to keep it fresh and ready for use, and it has a pleasant smell." I sighed with contentment, thinking that becoming a vain woman might not be so bad after all.

But she was not finished with my transformation. My sister shook her head in dismay at the state of my hair. From within her parfleche, she withdrew a small rawhide bundle containing the root of Aloe vera.

Mother had silently watched Wurth's ministrations, as did Molly, but then she brought forth a basin of warm water. She rubbed the root in the water to create suds, and before I could protest, they were both washing my hair with great vigor. I resisted, of course, but to no avail.

"If you would only brush and braid your hair as I've tried to show you, it would not be tangled like a squirrel's nest," Mother scolded. It seemed that she scrubbed my scalp and hair with more enthusiasm than was necessary.

"You can do the same thing when you bathe in the river, just like our mothers do when bathing the little ones," Wurth explained. "Instead of merely splashing around as you usually do, this will ensure that you are truly clean and will also make you smell good."

I felt the sting of her rebuke, for it was true; my bathing in the river usually consisted of a quick dip or water fights with friends. I swallowed a sharp rebuttal, asking if my scent was so offensive, knowing her reply would be honest, and I did not want to hear the answer. Perhaps I should take more care when bathing—if I could find the time.

Pleased with her efforts, Mother handed Wurth a doeskin bundle tied with intricate knots. "Ah, yes, this is perfect," Wurth exclaimed as she opened it. Even I could identify its contents as the roots of the evergreen juniper bush. Mother often prepared concoctions of this for someone with a complaining stomach—which I did not have. So, what now?

Wurth carefully selected a few roots and placed them in a clay bowl to soak while she worked on my tangled tresses with a brush made from a dried porcupine tail, its quills still attached. I fidgeted as she worked out the snarls with the brush and smoothed my hair with a comb. Molly had been silently watching the whole time, but my wailing caused her to smirk, which silenced my protests.

"Here, dry your tears," Wurth scolded, having untangled my long, dark hair from its offending knots. "I made this comb for you."

When I took it from her, I marveled at its beauty. My sister had carved a beautiful tortoiseshell comb, even adding fanciful scrolling to its handle. "You made this for me?" I murmured, my protests forgotten.

"Yes, for you," she said, smiling as she embraced me warmly. "And Corn-silk made this for your journey." She reached into her parfleche again and handed me a smaller rawhide bag. Inside were containers similar to Wurth's that held the same herbal remedies she had just used.

Mother knelt before us, her smug smile evident as she set down a clay bowl filled with juniper roots. "Perhaps you would like to use your new comb after we rinse your hair with this sweet-smelling water." Indeed, it had a delightful fragrance. It felt refreshing, too, and even I could tell that my hair gleamed with newfound brilliance after rinsing it.

I believed that what had been done was sufficient, but not for my dearest friend. Indeed, Wurth taught me various ways to style my hair, instead of my usual messy knot tied with a strip of rawhide. I noticed Molly was paying close attention; undoubtedly, she would soon be styling her hair more fashionably.

Once they had finished their ministrations, I was made to look at myself in one of Willewanah's mirrored medallions. I could hardly believe the woman gazing back at me, as I still considered myself a gangly, pointy-faced girl.

"You are beautiful, my sister," Wurth assured me. "You will bring pride to the People."

"Well, okay, if you say so. I just want to see all the sights of Charles Town. Can you believe I am to go?"

That day, I received another surprise. Molly, the perfect child I had tried my best to ignore all her life, approached me with a bundle wrapped in doeskin. I asked, "What is this, Little Sister?"

"Open it, please," she replied, her pretty face flushed with pride. Indeed, she had reason to feel proud, for the child must have worked hours fastening tiny colorful beads onto a strip of soft doeskin in a most pleasing pattern. She had created a beautiful belt that would complement my new dress, made especially for me.

"It is beautiful!" I exclaimed, pulling her close to my chest. "I will wear this belt with pride when in Charles Town—and I will think of you when I do." It occurred to me that perhaps I had been unfair in my treatment of her. I promised to be kinder in the future.

I was overwhelmed by the love and generosity of my family, and I did not notice my brother Johnny's silent entry into the cabin. Grinning broadly, he said, "Hester, look what I've made for your grand entry into the white man's city." He presented me with a beautifully braided, elaborately decorated bridle for my pony. Fancy would truly live up to her name.

I dispensed hugs and slobbery kisses to my family, who had shown confidence in me. I vowed to be on my best behavior and make them proud. Then, with clasped hands and giggling with glee, Wurth and I hurried to our quiet spot in the shade of a hemlock tree to speculate about the adventures that awaited me.

"I was surprised when Old Hop said I was to go," I confided to Wurth. She knew that I had accompanied delegations throughout our Nation as Old Hop's Little Flea over the past few years. Women often traveled with the men, but it was unusual for a young girl like me to join them. However, I frequently gleaned helpful information for my mentor by unobtrusively listening to the men as they talked among themselves. I believe Old Hop enjoyed the bits of gossip I brought him. The fact that I resembled Mother, the woman he had loved, may have contributed to his tenderness toward me.

Thus, Old Hop nodded at me during the last Council and, with a wink, stated that I would accompany the delegation escorting Dreadful Water to greet the new Governor of South Carolina, James Glen. He was only two years older than I, yet the English, in their arrogance, had named him Emperor of the Cherokee after his father, Moytoy, was killed in battle. His title, like his father's before, was merely ceremonial, as the Nation's real power resided with our traditional chief, Old Hop.

I was honored to be included in the delegation. I also understood that my mentor, Old Hop, expected me to gather helpful information to benefit his leadership of the People. Humbled by the trust placed in me, I vowed to conduct myself well and make my People proud.

Cherokee Trade Path

Summer 1745
17 years old
Keowee Town

Finally, we were on our way to Charles Town. I had to restrain my impatience, for it felt like the headmen and warriors talked over long at numerous Councils. How hard can it be? I often wondered as I dared not express any displeasure with the arrangements. I knew all too well that my invitation to accompany the delegation could easily be revoked. Thus, I bit my tongue and endured the endless conversations about the journey to the capital of South Carolina—the source of most trade goods brought to my mountain home.

There were discussions about what each delegate would wear, the order of presentation, and the speeches to the new governor were practiced and refined. Our White traders offered an abundance of advice—too much, in my opinion—regarding the habits and traditions of the White people of Charles Town. Little was known about the new governor, James Glen, yet the headmen held great expectations that he would be an honorable man.

We gathered at Keowee, one of our southernmost towns, for a final Council. I must admit that the impressive delegation left me speechless. Over two hundred Cherokee warriors and headmen would attend. Dreadful Water and his court were set to give the impression of leading the delegation since the English had taken it upon themselves to name him Emperor of the Cherokee—whatever that meant. Although the delegation included many of Dreadful Water's followers, numerous members supported the traditional governance of our Nation. He would be closely watched and restricted to a purely ceremonial role.

At long last, I mounted Fancy and joined the long line of travelers, riding not far behind Old Hop, as he had subtly indicated with a nod. I had secured our finery in a large parfleche and placed it, along with others, on the back of a packhorse. Mourning Dove had accompanied me to Keowee and had carefully packed my belongings.

"Not that I don't trust you to be careful," she placated me, "but these delicate garments and accessories must be packed in a way that ensures such a long journey won't damage them."

Although I pretended to be offended, I was secretly pleased she had chosen to do so. I watched intently as she folded them just so, and I noticed the care with which she placed them in the parfleche. I would do the same for the return journey. I vowed to make her proud of me when I returned home. She would see that my carelessness had not damaged any of the precious things.

At first light, we formed a procession and set forth on the well-worn trader's path to Charles Town. As we approached a cane break, a sudden burst of color made me laugh with delight. A flock of gorgeous birds in brilliant shades of green, yellow, and orange clouded the sky with their numbers. Their raucous cries and vibrant feathers brightened the dim forest path as we left the valley.

"Estatoe," Johnny said as he rode up beside me, gesturing toward the beautiful birds. "White men call them parakeets." Of course, I knew the birds shared the same name as the village, for who did not? I am always grateful for Johnny tutoring me in the White man's tongue. Yet, in my usual private musings, I wondered which came first: the name of the bird or the name of the village. I often heard them referred to as the Yellow Birds of Estatoe.

Lost in such thoughts that had no answer, I marveled as they swooped low above the shadowed river, alighting here and there on overhanging vines and branches, darting in and out of the dense stand of cane that was their home. There were so many that, at times, their flock darkened the sky as if night were approaching.

The beautiful birds had an insatiable hunger for the seeds of our fields and gardens. They ravaged our mothers' fruit trees, dropping the fruit to the ground and consuming only the seeds. Corn was their favorite staple, greatly annoying the villagers who tended our fields. Yet, their brilliant plumage was a vital addition to our ceremonial clothing and headdresses. So, in my opinion, it was a fair trade. However, I was not among those who tended the fields, gardens, and orchards; otherwise, I might have thought differently.

Their raucous cries seemed to celebrate our delegation and promised well for our journey, making me laugh with joy and anticipation.

By midday, we had ventured farther than I had ever gone from the trails that Fancy and I had traversed countless times. As the sun arced from east to west, the mountains behind us diminished in the distance, shrouded in a blue mist.

My carefree mood was dampened the farther we traveled from our home-land, for I could now see what had been spoken of at the Council and around the evening fire where warriors gathered. I was appalled by the encroachment of White settlements.

We remained silent as we rode through their villages or passed houses and taverns along the trade path, a major thoroughfare worn down by many travelers. Many emerged from their hovels or set down their hoes to stare as we passed in procession. My People looked straight ahead and made no chatter. We proceeded with great dignity, looking straight ahead and did not engage with them.

Johnny rode alongside and remarked that there seemed to be more of these dwellings each time he made the journey. "They assault my eyes," he complained. And indeed, they were a pitiful sight. "Hester, look at how poorly made their cabins are. They are hastily thrown together with green poplar trees that have not been debarked or aged."

Our uncle Saluy joined us and commented, "Those flimsy cabins will not last the winter, as the unseasoned logs will rot under the bark. They will shrink, become smaller, and leave large gaps between the logs."

"That will surely happen," Johnny agreed. "And the leaves, cloth, and mud they pack into the cracks will do little to keep out the winter cold." Indeed, the settlers were clearly unprepared to survive harsh weather.

"And yet they continue to pop up overnight, much like a mushroom on the forest floor," Saluy lamented, shaking his head in dismay. After nudging his horse's flank with his heel, he rode ahead to voice his complaints to another companion.

Still, the settlers kept coming—more and more of them each season—men alone and those with families. I pitied the dirty, scrawny children running and hiding in fear when they caught a glimpse of passing Cherokee warriors.

"Why do they defile the earth in this way?" I asked Johnny as our horses carried us steadily down the worn trade path.

"They are like children who don't know any better," was his disgruntled reply. "They believe it is their right to clear patches of forest and plant their pitiful gardens and fields, thinking, in their ignorance, that they can tame the forest."

I was amazed at the crops planted in wavering rows around the stumps of trees in scrubby, isolated, hastily cleared patches of the vast forest.

"Why are the trees in the field dying?" I asked my brother. Indeed, some majestic trees stood tall, yet their branches were dead at the time of year when they should have been clothed in bright new leaves, reaching toward the life-giving sun.

"When a White man claims a patch of forest for his own, he will girdle the trees, cutting off their life force, and they will die slowly over time. Then, the man will cut it down for his use," he explained.

We both sighed, grieving for the healthy trees despoiled and the creatures who depended on them for food and shelter. We Cherokee knew the forest was not to be destroyed by fire and ax but to be respected and not desecrated.

As we traveled further south, the sun hung heavily in the sky, and its journey to the nightland seemed slower than at home. The heat became oppressive, and we stopped often to rest the horses and ourselves as we were unaccustomed to the moist air.

Large fields were flooded with water flowing through small creeks that were constructed by men, as they were straight and purposeful rather than meandering with the earth's contours like our creeks. These creeks carried water to fields of some sort, where rows of green vegetation were visible. Ebony-skinned men were bent over their labor, pulling weeds from the waterlogged fields. White men on horseback rode along the embankments of the creeks, occasionally shouting instructions to the laborers—or even, on a few occasions, striking them with a whip.

"That's rice," Johnny said. "It is a food highly valued by Europeans."

I was distressed to see this thing. Why would they scar the earth to grow a crop requiring such labor? Johnny, long accustomed to my inquisitive nature, explained that rice is a cash crop for the Whites of this region.

"They cannot do the labor themselves, for they are too weak. Therefore they import Negroes, from far, far away, to work in their fields—slaves."

I was aware of slavery, of course, as the Cherokee, like other nations, often enslaved captives from rival tribes. They were subjected to harsh tasks and beatings when necessary. If they proved themselves worthy, they could be adopted into the tribe or traded in exchange. This European system of slavery horrified me.

"What is a cash crop?" I asked my brother, who, in my view, knew everything.

"Money, Little Sister. They use some of the rice for themselves, but most of it is shipped to Europe in exchange for money. The plantation owners—for that is what they call these large holdings—are growing very rich from the labor of their slaves."

He chuckled sadly and added, "But it seems that no matter how wealthy they become, it is never enough. They always grasp and claw to accumulate more riches."

In the distance, streams of smoke signaled more settlers staking their claims. The farther we traveled, the more of them we encountered. It was as the traders who frequently traveled this path often said—there was a relentless influx of Europeans arriving from across the Great Water to settle upon our lands.

From listening to the men's talk, I understood this was one of the reasons for our visit to the South Carolina governor. The settlers were overrunning our hunting grounds, forcing the deer, buffalo, foxes, bears, and other furred creatures to migrate westward and deeper into the mountains. Their numbers dwindled each hunting season, while our need for their hides and furs grew with our reliance on the goods provided by English or French traders.

Skirmishes and wars erupted with neighboring tribes, who also felt the intrusion of Europeans into their traditional hunting grounds. It was during one such battle with the Creeks that Moytoy lost his life. We faced pressure from all sides, and violence was occurring with increasing frequency.

The headmen wished to greet the new Governor and discuss the Creeks' ongoing treaty and trade violations. They hoped for a Cherokee boundary that would prevent settlers from crossing into Cherokee country.

They planned to urge him to honor previous treaties with the South Carolina government as a representative of King George, but they had little expectation that this would happen.

However, they would still attempt to negotiate with the White men for a treaty to bring peace to our homeland.

CHAPTER 37

Goose Creek

Summer 1745
17 years old
Goose Creek, SC

We encamped near Charles Town, at a place called Goose Creek, to await the ceremony with Governor Glen and Dreadful Water's entourage. This large meadow was set aside for visiting Native peoples and was equipped with rude shelters, firewood, and food. I quickly found my precious parfleche and stored it in the shelter I would share with other women. Fancy was happily grazing in the meadow with others of her kind.

After tending to my responsibilities, I wandered the grounds, marveling at how different it was from my homeland. Towering trees with sprawling branches were draped in moss. Egrets with slender legs darted their beaks in the shallow water at the shore, spearing their dinner. Johnny pointed out a peculiar creature that appeared to be sunning itself at the water's edge.

"That'll be an alligator," he warned me. "Ye stay well away from creatures such as that. I've heard tell they can run as fast as a horse to take a man down and drag him into their lair beneath the water."

That was all the warning I needed to give the ugly creature with a long snout, short legs, and a deadly-looking tail a wide berth. The horrible creature raised its head to stare at us with beady eyes, and without saying a word, Johnny took my arm as we backed away, safely out of reach—or so we hoped.

I marveled at the strange new sights and smells, my skin clammy from the heavy afternoon heat and humidity. I sniffed, and the tang of the nearby ocean tickled my nose. Remembering the stories of those who had traversed the Great Water to see King George, I felt compelled to experience it myself.

Accustomed to coming and going as I pleased, I left Fancy tethered with the other mounts and walked to a barge crossing the river to the nearby city. I noticed people giving a man coins to board, but I had none. Undaunted, I managed to slip in with a crowd just as it reached full capacity and pushed away from the dock.

Charles Town appeared to be much as London had been described by those who had traveled there a few years ago, although much smaller. I did not venture into the city's interior but stayed on the broad street that followed the river's course as it widened into a bay. My destination was the ocean. I longed to see the Great Water that separated our home from that of the Europeans.

Soaring ship masts and the cawing of circling white birds led me to the wharf, which was lined with large buildings. Their cavernous interiors were filled with goods being unloaded from enormous ships swaying in the gentle surf. The pungent smell of fish and offal assaulted my nose. An occasional ocean breeze brought relief with a salty tang.

I wandered aimlessly, marveling at the different sizes and shapes of the wooden water vessels, broad-bottomed with limbless trees rooted in their bellies. Huge ropes secured one thing to another. I realized that the enormous fabric rolled up and secured to the crossbeams must be the sails

Attacullaculla described around the Council fire—material that, when unfurled, would tame the wind and propel the ship forward.

Dirty, barefoot men scurried around the ships and the pier, shouting in a cacophony of tongues. Baskets of rope held bales of goods that were swung off the vessel and guided to the wharf, where other men untied the baskets and began carting the bales into the buildings. I came upon a warehouse with broad double doors propped open. Curious, I peeked inside.

"Give way, laddie," a sailor shouted, narrowly missing me as he carried in a massive bale of canvas-covered goods slung over his shoulder.

"That's no laddie; she's a lassie." Another one leered, looking up from beneath the heavy bale that had doubled him over.

"Aye, she is," the first sailor agreed. "And a young one, too."

Suddenly, I became aware of the danger I had put myself in. I was alone in this foreign city with no one to protect me. None of my traveling companions knew where I had ventured. How foolish of me to have left the safety of my People! Shuddering, I recalled tales of beasts such as these taking women by force. Rape—such an act was called—was unknown to the People, for our women were revered.

Dropping their burdens, the men advanced toward me. I sought sanctuary in the building, but they followed me into the dark interior. Realizing the danger, I attempted to dart back to the wharf, but they blocked my exit. I stopped and faced them defiantly, fists clenched at my sides, ready to defend myself.

The door to a small room just inside the entrance opened, and a White woman, unlike any I had ever seen, stepped forward, positioning herself between me and those horrible men. She stood as tall as a man, with broad shoulders and hips encased in a black dress that covered her from neck to feet and shoulder to wrist. Wisps of dark brown hair peeked out from beneath a black cap, its severity softened by a delicate trim of white lace along the edges. Her weathered face wore a stern expression that quelled the men, causing them to back away from me.

"Away with ye," she barked at them. "Leave this little Indian wench alone. When ye've finished unloading the ship, ye can slake your lust at the whorehouse, for surely ye know your way there."

The men turned, hurrying to the ship where their mates were tasked with unloading bales of goods, their pursuit of me forgotten.

"What brings ye here?" the woman asked me kindly. "Do ye not know how dangerous it is for a lassie to go about unaccompanied in Charles Town?"

I was so startled by the encounter with the men and this woman's presence that I was uncharacteristically speechless. "Do ye speak the King's English?" she inquired, stepping closer with a hand outstretched in welcome.

"Aye, and many other tongues," I boasted to demonstrate my value to the woman I sought to impress, though I was uncertain of the reason.

She laughed and, taking my hand, led me into the small room that she called her office.

"Aren't ye a feisty one? What brings you here, unaccompanied as ye are?"

Something about her demeanor inspired confidence, and settling upon the stool she motioned me to, I told her of my presence with the Cherokee delegation as she set a kettle of water on a small brazier.

"Aye, I know of this, forby they be staying on my property at Goose Creek." She placed a tray on the small table beside me and settled into an oversized upholstered chair like none I had ever seen. "Tea?" she asked, with an arched brow.

"What is tea?" I asked, intrigued to learn more about this imposing woman.

"Of course, ye know nothing of tea, being an uncivilized heathen," she said with a smile. Somehow, I knew she was only jesting and took no offense.

She demonstrated how to place the tea leaves in delicate floral cups with handles. When the kettle burbled, she poured the hot water into the cups. The aroma that wafted toward me made me sniff, trying to take in as much of the pleasant scent as possible. "And now, we add a little sugar," she said, emptying paper twists of a white substance into the cups.

Mimicking her, I stirred the white stuff into the tea with a tiny silver spoon, watching it disappear. Then, lifting the cup to my lips, I blew on the hot tea to cool it. Taking a sip, I exclaimed, "It is delicious!"

"Aye, 'tis," she laughed. "No doubt ye will be wanting yer tea every day like a proper Englishwoman."

Well, I had my doubts about that—how could it even be possible after returning home? However, I made no argument as I settled more comfortably on the stool and sipped contentedly from this new concoction.

"I've been rude, child, and I have not introduced myself," she said. "I am Sarah Emory, the wife and business partner of John."

Thus, we sat in the warm comfort of a new friendship, my first with a White woman. I spoke candidly, surprised by how at ease I felt, and shared stories about my life in the Cherokee Nation. I even revealed my role as Old Hop's Little Flea, which made her laugh heartily.

"Of course that old rascal would gladly welcome any snippets of news that an observant child like you might overhear. I know him well; he is a wise man who gathers information much like a squirrel gathers nuts, ready to use it at the right moment."

To my great delight, she asked me to serve us both another cup of tea, and I did so as if I had handled the teapot and delicate cups numerous times before.

As the afternoon light waned, promising dusk, I realized I had not yet seen the Great Water. "Is it far?" I asked Sarah, for she had requested that I address her by her Christian name.

"Not far at all, child, although what you see here is a deep harbor," she replied, setting her cup back on its matching plate. "But let us save that discovery for another time. It will soon be dark, and I wish to see you safely with your traveling companions." After my encounter with the unruly sailors, I admitted to feeling grateful for her generous offer.

I was so engrossed in our conversation and my new experience that I failed to notice the transfer of goods from the ship to the warehouse had been completed. As we left her office, a man with a sheaf of papers approached her, announcing that the manifest was complete. She introduced me to her husband, and they spoke while reviewing the papers. I sensed a coldness and tension between them and observed how she held herself apart as much as possible. This husband and wife did not seem to like each other. If she were Cherokee, she could set his things outside their cabin and be done with him. Did White people do such?

"We shall go now to Goose Creek to check that all is well with the delegation," she addressed both of us, turning her back on John. He watched her, a sorrowful expression on his face, as she guided me to the door and out to the wharf.

Not far from the warehouse, we approached a small boat—a skiff, she called it—that was secured to the pier. A large, heavily muscled Negro appeared and helped us aboard.

"Thank you, Horace," she said, smiling at him, and it was clear there was affection between them. He ensured she was seated safely and comfortably before pushing off from the pier and rowing out to the middle of the channel.

I was surprised to see that the water level had risen, and the boat appeared to be moving of its own accord, with Horace merely guiding its direction with the oars. "How is this?" I asked, looking from side to side in wonder.

"The tide is coming in," Horace explained with a deep chuckle. He then told me a fantastic story about the moon so far above, causing the Great Water to rise and fall. Of course, I knew this was just a fable to entertain children, but it was amusing to hear.

We soon arrived at the small pier that serviced the Goose Creek encampment, and when I took leave of the skiff, a great shout went up. People rushed toward me, calling my name with joy. Johnny enveloped me in a bear hug, lifting me off the ground as he had when I was a child, and I saw tears leaking from his eyes. "Where have ye been, Prachey? We've been so worried."

I was informed that many had been searching everywhere for me, worried that I had come to harm. Johnny's greatest fear was that, due to my relentless curiosity, I had approached the alligator, which likely pulled me into the water.

"I was frightened for your safety," he scolded. "But I knew that if an alligator did grab you, it would bear the brunt of the encounter, for you would burn its ears with your questions."

Chastened, I made my apology and promised not to leave the encampment without telling him again. He and I both knew I was not likely to keep that promise, but it seemed the right thing to say at the moment.

As the crowd dispersed, he draped a protective arm over my shoulder, and we made our way toward the encampment. I noticed an unfamiliar White man dressed in buckskin leggings and a loose cotton shirt, his auburn hair tied back with a leather strap, standing apart. He leaned casually on his rifle, a slight grin creasing his handsome face. His eyes pierced mine, and I felt an unfamiliar jolt.

He approached us, and Johnny said, "Prachey, meet my new friend, Richard Pearis."

CHAPTER 38

Sarah

Summer 1745
17 years old
Goose Creek, SC

As the sun made its descent, a tangy breeze hinting at the ocean cooled our sweaty bodies. A few logs had been laid upon the coals of scattered fireplaces, lighting the pathways and providing gathering places. An ebony-skinned woman with a bright kerchief tied around her nappy head tended a large kettle over the central fire. Her muscular arms strained as she stirred its contents with a large paddle.

Men and women of all ages and races gathered around to receive a serving of rice, that exotic crop that grows in water, spooned into their bowls. Then, a delicious-smelling stew of sea creatures was ladled on top. What strange food this is, I thought. But always ready for a new experience, I gave it a try and exclaimed in surprise at how tasty it was. Another Negro woman stood at a table handing out hunks of fresh oven-baked bread. We were well-fed that night, thanks to Governor Glen.

Sated, my belly distended from such rich food, I sought the glow of a nearby fire and settled onto one of the logs encircling it. Johnny's friend, Richard Pearis, had been watching me all evening. I knew this because I had been pretending not to notice, yet I had actually been keenly aware of his presence. Twice, our eyes met, and I felt that jolt again. It unnerved me, and I was greatly relieved when Sarah approached and directed Horace, who was following her, to place a four-legged chair similar to the one in her office beside me.

"Damned if I'm going to sit on a log," she exclaimed with a grin. "I keep a chair in one of the storage buildings for nights such as this." She then reached for a stick to poke at the logs, sending a spray of sparks flying toward the stars.

"What say ye, child? What do ye think of Charles Town so far?" she asked, gesturing to her slave. He left, soon returning, handing her a flask of whiskey.

"Do ye want a dram?" she asked me with her head cocked inquisitively.

"Nay," I declined, knowing Saluy would be very disappointed if I accepted her offer. He refused to drink firewater himself and encouraged others to do the same. We had witnessed too many of our warriors consumed by it.

And so we sat, two women from different worlds, both blessed—or cursed—with curious minds. We talked at length about one thing and then another. She had many questions about my People and our way of life, and I, likewise, had many for her.

Sarah and I were set apart from others who came and went from group to group. Most of them spoke in the Cherokee's musical tongue, although some conversed in English and Scottish. None showed any interest in our conversation, and we felt at ease with each other, sharing confidences.

As the night grew late and the fire dwindled, we added one log after another, reluctant to part. A full moon rose, dimming the brightness of the scattered stars, and the campground grew quiet. Our companions sought their sleeping places, and soon, it was only the two of us warmed by the fire and our friendship.

That is, except for Richard Pearis, as I could see his form leaning casually against a tree across the grounds from where we sat. But close enough that I sensed his presence and knew he was watching us. Watching me.

Sarah often drank from the flask, but the firewater had little ill effect other than her words sometimes stepped over each other. Late in the evening, her demeanor turned sorrowful, and in the dim firelight, I noticed her wipe a tear from her cheek.

"Tell me, child, do ye not wonder why I'm dressed in black while my husband still draws breath?" she asked, taking another swig from the flask.

I was perplexed. Why shouldn't she wear whatever color she wanted? What did her husband have to do with it? Wearing black seemed to carry some significance for her that I did not understand.

"Well, noooooo." was my hesitant response. "But I did wonder why you wear so many clothes and cover yourself from head to toe in this heat."

Sarah burst into laughter, slapping her hand against her knee and rocking back and forth. "Damme, if you haven't stated the real truth of the matter."

She explained that it was a European tradition for a wife to wear black in memory of her husband for at least a year after his death. She said the layers of clothing were fashion. After that, she needed to explain what "fashion" meant.

"Oh, I understand now. This is similar to why the girls and young women of my People spend much time deciding what to wear—particularly which belts, ribbons, or accessories to use on their tunics and hair."

"Yes, I suppose it is something like that. Women are the same no matter where they live."

"But if your husband is not dead, since you introduced me to him today, why are you dressed in black like a widow?"

"Because that bastard is dead to me," she exclaimed, pounding her hand on her knee. "I gave that rascal my youth, birthed five babies, traveled halfway around the world for him, and kept his—our—business running while he went off gallivanting."

Then, in a torrent of words, expletives, and tears, she revealed what grieved her, even though her husband still drew breath.

"We've established a foothold in the Indian trade business, with me acquiring trade goods here in Charles Town and him going into Cherokee country as a licensed trader. Besides that, I manage this property for the governor, providing hospitality for visiting Natives," she added. "The South Carolina government pays me handsomely for that."

I was surprised that someone would be paid to provide food and shelter for travelers. It was yet another of the many European traditions I found difficult to understand.

"But John and some other traders decided to mine silver on Cherokee land."

"Mine silver? On Cherokee land? Could they actually do that?" I was surprised, as I knew that the coins the Europeans valued so highly were made of silver or gold.

"Not legally, they couldn't. But when do laws prevent men from seeking their fortunes?" And she tossed another log on the fire, causing it to flame up, seemingly to match her fury.

"You know them, child. Dougherty and Grant were involved in the scheme, as was Thomas Nightengale, one of my trading partners here in Charles Town. However, after John invested heavily in the project, the silver ore turned out to be of such low grade that it would not be profitable. We had frequently argued about it, and I warned him all along that it was a bad idea—the rights belonged to the Crown, not a group of greedy traders. The king would be angry had they proceeded."

She shook the nearly empty flask and drained it, wiping her mouth with the back of her hand before handing it to Horace, who hovered nearby.

"But, damme, if the old fool didn't take up with an Indian girl while tramping around in those woods—Mary Moore, the mixed-blood daughter of the trader James Moore. And she bore him a son. The idiot had the nerve to bring the wench and her bastard to Charles Town, thinking I would turn a blind eye." Her anger—indeed, her pain—was palpable, and I hurt for her.

"The fool had to pour salt in my wound: he named the babe after himself—John Emory—lest there be any doubt about who had sired him."

She was silent for a few minutes before adding, "Two years ago, my sons, William and John Robert, received their licenses to trade with the Cherokee. They traveled with the Scottish trader Ludovic Grant to his Cherokee town of Tomatly. I haven't seen them since. Now, I must manage here alone."

This was not news to me, as I knew these young traders, although I had not realized they were her sons. It appeared she was unaware that they had formed relationships with Grant's two mixed-blood daughters—and that they had fathered children.

I knew this because, of course, I made it my business to stay informed about much of what was happening in the Cherokee Nation. However, I decided then and there that, as warmly as I felt toward this White woman, it was not my place to tell her that she had grandchildren in the Cherokee Nation who were the same age as her husband's mixed blood child.

There was no need to add to this woman's pain. Instead, I made soothing sounds of sympathy and hoped Horace would soon arrive to guide her safely to her bed.

I realized that even though she portrayed herself as a strong woman managing what is typically a man's business, she experienced the pain common to any woman whose men disappointed her. Like their love for fashion, women are the same no matter where they live.

Being a Little Flea sometimes presents problems, for often I know more than I wish.

CHAPTER 39

Choices in a Beaded Bag

Summer 1799
71 years old
Baldridge Creek, GA

My ability to listen and observe has served me well over the years, especially as a grandmother. Therefore, I was not surprised when my granddaughter Lucretia came to me for the same reason Mourning Dove had once asked me to walk with her to the meadow all those years ago. The ways of a woman with a man remain unchanged despite wars and displacement.

I brew two cups of tea that I've come to cherish, thanks to my long-ago friend Sarah, and invite her to sit with me on the porch. The rose bushes lining my stoop have faded under August's unrelenting heat, their leaves curling and turning the same brown as the soil. I have long admired the thorny plants that bloom every spring. They bring me such joy that, after asking their permission, I moved four of them closer to my cabin to enjoy them better. Perhaps I can persuade one of my energetic grandchildren to carry a bucket of life-giving water to these plants.

We fan ourselves, opening the tops of our blouses to direct a slight breeze to the sweat that has gathered between our breasts—mine elongated and flat, hers still small and pert with youth. Dust coats the porch planks, settling on our bare feet with the slightest movement. Even the birds are silent, seeking shelter from the oppressive heat. I consider moving inside, but it is slightly cooler here in the shade of the pine trees than in the stifling cabin.

Lucretia cares little where we sit to sip our tea, for her rocking chair will hardly contain her joy. My granddaughter eagerly confides that she has fallen in love with Ignatius Chisholm. I pretend to be surprised, but I have noticed the long, soulful glances they exchange when they think nobody is looking. I saw that at least twice recently, and she quietly left a gathering of friends and family. Soon thereafter, her beau discretely slipped outside as well.

How well I know the familiar maneuver of lovers seeking privacy, thinking none but they know of the feelings they are experiencing. I have observed many such pairings in my dozens of years—and experienced a few myself.

My granddaughter—so suddenly a woman when just yesterday she was but a babe—gushes as she confides her feelings in this first flush of love for a man. She describes how she thinks of him constantly and longs for his kisses and touch. They have not yet fully lain together as a man and a woman, but I sense they are close to that first coupling. Lucretia, a wise young woman, comes to me because she does not wish to bear his child just yet.

The man she has chosen is White, and she understands that his view of their union may differ greatly from hers. Traditionally, our Cherokee People revere and respect women, viewing them as equals, while in European cultures, men dominate women.

In the old days, a woman of the Real People could enjoy a lover of her choosing, but the decision was solely hers. A Cherokee man would never impose his attention on a woman, as that would be highly disrespectful. When a woman selected a man to be her mate and to have children with, her brothers, uncles, and other men from her clan would construct a house for her. It was and would always remain her home. If she grew weary of her mate, she would place his belongings outside her cabin, signifying the end of their marriage. Any children from that union would remain in her house with the mother and her clan.

However, European men of all nationalities regard their wives and children as possessions, much like the mules they use to prepare their fields for planting seeds. A man builds a house, and the woman may reside in it as long as he allows. A White man can force his wife to leave her home to survive as best she can whenever she displeases him. He alone decides whether to keep the children or cast them out as well.

Such a family system is so fraught with problems that it amazed me when I first learned it had been their way for more years than could be counted and was not something new to this country. However, after pondering it a few years ago, I came to understand that European men ruling over women are the primary reason they are such disturbed people.

I am concerned about my granddaughters, like Lucretia, and my sons' wives. If George were to seek the oblivion of firewater again—and become an evil man like James Vann—my daughters-in-law would not be able to put him away as they could in the old days. We live on his farm, and they would have no recourse. They have no power in American courts of law and are dependent on his goodwill.

Our people's traditions were practical: women were in charge of farming, property, and family, while men hunted and engaged in warfare when necessary. While men predominantly made political decisions for the Nation, women influenced social matters. The headman of each Town was typically a man, but women of outstanding wisdom and merit also held leadership roles. Women participated in the Town Councils and the Nation's Council. Beloved Women, recognized for their exceptional wisdom and experience, attended every war council. They were the ones who either urged the men to go to war or advocated for peace. Occasionally, women joined the men in battle. These women were respected and honored for their courage and were known as war women.

Attakullkulla's niece, Little Wild Rose, born during the height of the 1738 smallpox epidemic and inspiring hope, was indeed such a woman. She accompanied her husband, Kingfisher, at the Battle of Taliwa, chewing his bullets before he loaded his gun to ensure the jagged edges would inflict greater damage. When he was killed in battle, she picked up his rifle and led the Cherokee warriors to victory. Later, she married a White man and became known as Nancy Ward. She rose to the position of Beloved Woman and represented our women in various treaty negotiations.

I was present when my People met with John Sevier, representing the settlers in what became the state of Tennessee, in 1785 at Little Pigeon River. My heart soared when she stepped forward to speak. Her words resonated with me so profoundly that I can still recall them word for word. She said, "You know that women are always looked upon as nothing, but we are your mothers; you are our sons. Our cry is all for peace; let it continue. This peace must last forever. Let your women's sons be ours; our sons be yours. Let your women hear our words."

Christians have confused our views of a woman's free choice with their ideas of chastity—at least chastity for women. Not so for the White men, as they will rut with whatever is available, willing or not, for they are quick to force a woman. Some even consort with animals, I am told, especially men who have those despicable creatures they call "sheep," which are undoubtedly the most stupid creatures on Earth.

We have even heard tales of White trappers who live alone in the mountains during the winter finding a knothole in a tree at the appropriate height. They fasten a scrap of beaver pelt around it and proceed to do with it what they would do with a woman if one were available. I was unbelieving when I first heard about this defilement, but it has proven to be true. The appetites of some White men are impossible to understand.

However, White missionaries still preach that men and women should come together only after marriage and solely as husband and wife—as if such a thing were feasible!

In a relatively short time, many traditions once held sacred by our ancestors have been lost to us. That is why Lucretia is seeking her Granny. She knows that I remember when women and men were equal in many ways, but a woman had the power to make choices about her body and her future. She knows that I will remember what had given women such power and that I will share that knowledge with her.

There was a time when a Cherokee woman not only decided with whom to share her bed but she also chose when to give birth to a child. Women could space their children in a way that benefited the People. We did not have more children than our town could support. Our women chose not to start a family when food was scarce, whether due to excessive rain or drought. When times were good, if she wished, she would allow a pregnancy with the man of her choice.

Nowadays, many desire more pregnancies to help our population grow. More children are desired because many die during infancy or when very young. Also, more people are needed in a family to handle the work of individual farms instead of the communal farms of the past. My George is doing his part to repopulate the Nation. He has so thoroughly adopted the ways of the White man that both his wives are perpetually pregnant, and his brood increases each year.

This granddaughter of mine comes to me, her Granny, to learn the old ways. Her mothers could have taught her as mine did, perhaps—if they remember, that is—but they are busy caring for their large household and farm. They no longer collect the secrets of the wild carrot. They do not brew the special tea to prevent a child. If, on occasion, one has chewed the seeds to bring on her moon time, I am unaware of it. It is to me that this woman/child has come.

And so, as my mother did for me at another time, I take her hand and bid her to come walk with me to a nearby meadow, where I will share the knowledge my mother gave me many years ago.

Later, as we return to the cabin, a breeze caresses us, and the late afternoon sun casts a golden glow on my little cabin among the pines. I am not surprised to see that the long-suffering rose bushes have perked up after being mysteriously watered. Once curled down upon weakened stems, spent blossoms have been removed, and a few flowers remain. Bees, drunk on pollen lust, wallow in their petals, their buzzing a happy chorus that promises honey this fall. A dear grandchild, or perhaps two, has visited their Granny.

Dutiful as she is, Lucretia takes my elbow to guide my step onto the porch. I can manage on my own, but I welcome this small courtesy—a demonstration of her love for me.

"Come inside," I invite her. She follows me into the dim recesses of my home and waits patiently while I rummage through a small chest of treasures tucked in a dark corner until I find what I have sought. It surprises me that I struggle to rise from my crouch, finding myself wobbling and dangerously close to falling over. It is a relief to feel Lucretia's steady hand on my back as she helps me rise to my feet without a word to embarrass me.

I take both her hands and place in them the beaded bag filled with wild carrot seeds that I prepared long ago for this occasion. Then, I ask her to recite the lessons taught in the meadow today: when to harvest the herb, to ask permission from the plants, which magic chants to sing, how to brew tea, when to drink it, and when to eat the seeds alone.

Satisfied that she has listened well, I embrace her warmly, surprised that I must stretch to reach her cheek for a kiss. I wonder again at the passage of time.

After she has gone, cradling her gift of choices in a beaded bag, her frank talk about her feelings for this young Chisholm brings back memories of Richard—my beloved.

Thus, it was for us when we were young—a fire from within that could only be extinguished by lying together, by joining as one, our souls intertwined.

As I ponder how it was with us, I remember that such an unquenchable passion was not limited to our youth. Long past gray hairs, paunches, and sagging breasts, our mutual desire never wavered.

I lie upon my soft mattress, covered in quilts sewn by my daughters-in-law and granddaughters, in this snug cabin built by my son and grandsons, reflecting on my youth. It seems as though it were only yesterday—and yet, another lifetime—-that my body was slim and supple, my breasts firm, and my legs long and strong. In my youth, I never considered that age would overtake me and that my body would betray me as it has.

It was not so long ago, and yet a lifetime, that I was young like Lucretia.

CHAPTER 40

Richard

Summer 1799
71 years old
Baldridge Creek, GA

There are some memories of my life that I choose to keep private. My grandchildren will have their own experiences to cherish. They will understand why I share no details about my first encounter with their grandfather.

It was as though Richard and I were alone among the hundreds of people assembled at the Goose Creek campground. I was always aware of his presence and knew it was the same for him. He and Johnny had become good friends and were frequently together; thus, it was natural that we began to speak to each other. Oddly, because I was usually never at a loss for words, I was shy with him. My tongue became thick, and I found it hard to form words.

It further surprised me that I was glad for Wurth and Mourning Dove's instruction. I opened the small bundle in my parfleche and slipped away to the creek to do those things I had been taught. If Johnny noticed that my tunic was clean, my cheeks glowed, I smelled good, and my hair was shiny and styled in a becoming manner, he chose not to comment. For that, I was grateful. I did not want him to tease me about my change in grooming habits.

Our careful dance of awareness and avoidance ended in a rush of sensations when I saw Richard lift a heavy bundle from a packhorse. His chest was bare, with rivulets of sweat coursing down his muscular back. I realized I had stopped in my tracks, staring at him.

He must have been aware of my presence, for he turned, and his eyes immediately went to where I stood. Our eyes locked, and then his gaze dropped as he looked me over from head to toe. I felt myself blush but did not lower my eyes. Instead, I boldly returned his stare and allowed myself to take in the sight of all of him. He grinned, nodded at me, and resumed unloading the packhorse. Without words in either of our languages, we communicated our mutual interest.

And I felt the strangest sensation in my belly. A new feeling deep within, somehow associated with this particular White trader.

Why, I later wondered over time, was it Richard whose soul walked with mine? My life would have been much easier had I not loved him. If only I had simply satisfied my curiosity that first time I crawled under his bedroll and left it at that.

The poor man appeared surprised and awkward—almost like a virgin. Apparently, White men were not accustomed to women choosing who to couple with. Our joining was so quick that it was over almost before it began, much to my disappointment. Was that truly how White men and women engaged in the act of joining their bodies? *If that is the case, I thought then, it is no wonder they are often so angry and frustrated.*

Perhaps that is why I returned to his bedroll the following evening. He had much to learn about our Cherokee ways, and who better to teach him?

CHAPTER 41

Of Birds and Buffalo

Summer 1799
71 years old
Baldridge Creek, GA

At times, I grow weary of these memories of times gone by, yet it heartens me to know that the young ones are learning about their heritage through my storytelling. They are kept busy attending missionary school and doing their chores at home, but then they will find time to come to my little cabin in the woods and ask me to tell an "Old Times Story," as they call it. Lucretia is astonished to learn that her Granny was once as young and fearless as she.

"You went to Charles Town alone? That's where you met our Grandfather Richard?" she exclaims when I tell them that story. "What happened, Granny? That sounds so exciting!"

Her bright, probing eyes beg me for more details.

"Sarah Emory seems like a formidable yet kind woman," Rachel remarks. "I am glad she looked after you."

"Somebody needed to, from the sounds of it," Jim scolds with a fierce scowl. "You could have come to harm being alone with those White men."

I smile, pleased by their interest. "Sarah was a remarkable woman who taught me a great deal about the thoughts and actions of White women like her. We spent time together whenever I was in Charles Town, and over the years, she confided in me as she would in a woman of her age—as an equal, a friend. Perhaps you should know that many of our mixed-blood friends and family are descended from this White woman."

A chorus of exclamations fills the small space of my home as the children want to know of their connection to such an extraordinary woman.

"It pleases me that many of our kin and friends share her bloodline: the Buffingtons, Hembrees, Emorys, and Stuarts are her descendants through her sons who married Cherokee women. Even John Jolly, one of our most revered wise men." This sparks much speculation about their neighbors and playmates, which is my intention. I want them to understand their connection to the past and their relationships with others in the Nation.

A flurry of questions rises in my tiny cabin, where I sit with my darling grandchildren gathered at my feet. Moses settles on the floor by my side, leaning into my knee as if he needs my touch, even though he is a grown man studying the law. I run my bony fingers through his hair, scratching his scalp. If he were a barn cat, he would purr.

"Tell us more, Granny," a chorus of youthful voices fills the cabin.

"Granny, were there really that many Yellow Birds of Estatoe that they blocked the sun while in flight?" Aaron asks, his brow furrowing with concern. "What happened to them? Why don't we see as many as you did?"

"Like many creatures that were once abundant in my childhood—deer, foxes, rabbits, and buffalo—they have dwindled in number as the population of settlers has grown."

"Why did they go?" this inquisitive one asks.

"There are many reasons," I explain, knowing that the missionary school teachers will not share this information with them. In fact, since the teachers are immigrants or the children of immigrants, they likely do not know what was lost—or value it.

"Our people lived harmoniously with other creatures of the earth, taking only what we needed to sustain ourselves and giving thanks when we did."

"Yes, Granny, when I kill a deer—or any creature for that matter—I say a prayer thanking it for giving its life for mine and that of my family," Jesse boasts.

"Good, for that is our way. However, Europeans kill for sport, not always for the meat for their families. They are wasteful. And so, Aaron, when the yellow birds, the parakeets, ate the seeds of fruit or the kernels of corn, they would kill them. They do not understand that the creatures of the earth have as much right to the corn or the peaches as they do, even though they planted them for their use.

"The parakeets, as they called those beautiful birds, were easy to kill in large numbers, for they, like us, had a kinship with their kind."

"What do you mean, Granny?" my quiet little Sallie asks. Although small for her age, she is healthy for someone who arrived in this world much too early.

"When a member of their family fell to the ground from a gunshot, others would gather around as if trying to help it take flight again. This made them easy targets for destruction in large numbers, which many Europeans would carry out.

"And then, of course, as countless settlers polluted the land, the birds' homes were destroyed. We once had vast expanses of cane fields where they liked to live and raise their young. But soon they, like many creatures, had fewer places to build their homes."

The mood darkens as my grandchildren reflect on the fate of the Yellow Bird of Estatoe, their population diminished by senseless killing.

"That's what the Europeans have tried to do to us," Moses reflects quietly. All eyes turn to him, questioning his meaning. "We, the Cherokee People, have also been killed in large numbers for greed, and even sometimes for sport, and our homeland has been destroyed. Our numbers are diminished too."

Sensing the rising tide of anxiety in the children, I agree with Moses; he is correct in his statement. However, I comfort them by reminding them that the People endured—the Cherokee have adapted to their changing world and survived.

"You are evidence of that," I tell them. "Each of you carries the blood of those who came before, and you will pass it on to the next generations. Our People will change our way of life but keep as many traditions as we can. We will make our home wherever fortune dictates, but our family and our People will remain strong."

As an elder, I am doing my duty to educate the young about their heritage and encourage them to look to the future. But then Moses, who reads, studies, and ponders deeply, reminds us of the buffalo.

"I've heard old men talk of the large herds of buffalo in the Old Days—back when their fathers and fathers' fathers hunted them. Buffalo are much larger than deer and provide good meat and a lot of tallow. Their hides, I've heard, were large and kept our People warm during harsh winters. But they, like our People, have moved further west to escape the Europeans. Their numbers are few now in our mountains and valleys," he says, his shoulders slumped.

"Yes," Jesse adds. "Big Will said that when he traveled west a few years ago, he saw White men shooting buffalo and taking only their tongues as a delicacy and their humps for tallow. The rest they left for the scavenger animals and insects. Their bodies were left to rot in the sun." The younger children cried out at such waste. How could that be, they wondered.

"Not only that," Jesse continues, much to their distress, "when they killed a cow, her calf would stay nearby, crying for its mother. They did not kill the calves, as they had little to offer. The calves were left to suffer and starve."

Sensitive little Betsey cries in sympathy for the orphaned buffalo calf, and we realize our talk has upset her. I take her onto my lap for comfort and, rocking back and forth, try to ease her distress. But words fail me.

Turtle comes to my rescue by asking, "I've never seen a buffalo, Granny. What do they look like?" Thankfully, the older children, who have seen one or two, chatter away, describing the beast.

Jim, always a jokester, jumps up and pantomimes for them what they look like. "They are as tall as this," he gestures far above his head. "With heads this big," he cups his hands widely around his head and hunches forward. "And they have a long beard like this," he adds as he gestures. "And short but deadly horns that turn back. And beady little eyes." Then he squints and scowls at Betsey, causing her to squeal with pretend fear.

And so it goes, the mood lightening and laughter resounding in the cabin until Nancy rings the large bell she placed on the porch to call her brood home for a meal.

My little cabin resonates with their chatter: "Tell us more, Granny!" "What was Charles Town like?" "Did you see the Great Water?" "Tell us more about when you met our Grandfather."

"Was it love at first sight, Granny?" romantic Lucretia swoons, making the older boys snort and roll their eyes.

"I will tell you more tomorrow after your lessons and chores. But for now we must go to supper, or Nancy will be cross with us."

As their attention shifts to their bellies and the meal Nancy has prepared on the large table in their home, they scramble around, tripping over one another, giggling and squealing as they hurry out the door.

The cabin falls suddenly quiet. I sigh, take my pipe down from the mantle, and choose to savor the silence for a moment before joining my family.

Tomorrow, I will tell them about Goose Creek and their grandfather.

CHAPTER 42

The Great Water

Summer 1799
71 years old
Baldridge Creek, GA

When I return to my cabin after supper, my thoughts are filled with Richard and our time together. Yes, I will tell them about Goose Creek tomorrow or the next day. However, I hold another precious memory close to my heart—one I will not share with my family. They will create their own such memories, but there are some things I prefer to keep private.

"Come with me tomorrow, Hester; let me show you the ocean as it should be seen," Richard had whispered as we lay together in his sleeping roll. That night, so long ago, I curled against him, relishing the feel of his body against mine, his maleness limp against my thigh. Since our first coupling, we had stolen as many private moments together as possible, and each time we parted, I longed for our next joining.

Discussions among the Cherokee headmen and the governor of South Carolina continued, leading to a treaty that might provide my People some relief. Soon, there would be the ceremonial crowning of Dreadful Water and the formality of signing the White man's paper—a new treaty—and then my People would return to our mountain home.

Richard had tightened his embrace and kissed my forehead. "I want to show you the world," he murmured. "I can't bear to think of our parting."

"I know," I whispered into his chest, for we had to be quiet with our joining and our talks. The campground was crowded with our delegation and those of other nations who had come to see the governor, as well as traders and packmen. "What do you want to do?"

"Just have Fancy ready after the midday meal, and we will go for a ride, just the two of us. I'll show you when we get there."

As the sun rose, I sought out my brother, Johnny, to inform him that I would be leaving the encampment with his friend Richard. He made no objections but cast me a stern look. "Take care, Little Sister. I've seen how it is with you. Soon, he will return to his people, as will you."

"I know, but we just want some time alone before we part," I reassured him. But my heart already ached with the thought of never seeing Richard again.

Later that day, we tried to slip away discreetly, but none of our acquaintances were deceived as we rode out on our horses. We did not follow the river as I had anticipated, knowing it widened into a harbor that led to the ocean. Instead, he guided us along paths winding through marshland to roads that passed by small farms and dwellings. The air grew heavier with moisture as we traveled, and the salty tang tickled my nose. I could hear a distant rhythmic roar that intensified as we progressed.

We crested a dune crowned with clumps of spiky grass, and there before me lay a vast stretch of white sand... and beyond: the ocean, in all its glory. I had not known what to expect, but certainly not something of this grandeur. The water shimmered in varying shades of blue and green, sparkling in the sun, with crests of white on the waves surging forward, crashing upon the shore, and disappearing only to be replaced by yet another wave. The sound was hypnotic, unceasing, and somehow timeless, echoing my beating heart.

I prodded Fancy to the edge, laughing with delight, and slid off her back to feel the sand between my toes. I danced around, splashing wet sand and sprays of salt water, drenching my tunic. Footprints were quickly erased by incoming waves, leaving a brief expanse of sand marked by bits of shell and seaweed before the next wave found the shore.

Without hesitation, I peeled off my tunic and ran into the water. Soon, I was swimming out to sea and relishing the buoyancy of the salt water, floating and treading water as I would in the river at home.

"Hester, damme! What are you doing? Ye'll drown!" Richard shouted from the edge of the Great Water. "What if someone comes and sees ye nekkid like that?"

"Come join me," I called to him, but he would not. He advanced and then retreated as each wave pounded the shore, drenching his boots and leggings.

Understanding that this White man was not as accustomed to water as I was—perhaps even afraid of it—I returned to the shore, standing when I felt the bottom beneath my feet. Richard's mouth was agape as he stared at me. I realized he had not yet seen my body. Later, I learned he had never seen a naked woman before, not even his wife.

Seeing his discomfiture and noting the bulge in his trousers, I advanced slowly to him, trying to keep my balance in the surge of the waves. It wasn't easy to look seductive while being thrust about so, but still, it had the desired effect. The man was spellbound and speechless. When I reached him, I enfolded him in an embrace, my wet body against his.

He returned my embrace but paused to scan the beach for onlookers. "Here, Hester, put your clothes back on," he instructed, his face crimson, as he handed me my sodden shift.

Laughing, we strolled hand in hand, captivated by the beauty of the ocean and our feelings for each other. Richard took the blanket he had brought and spread it in a small space carved by ocean storms in the dune, enclosed on three sides yet open to the beach. Enjoying its privacy, we lay together and began to explore each other's bodies.

I peeled his shirt up and over, relieving him of it and revealing his bare chest. It was a joy to stroke him for the first time, twining my fingers in the curly reddish hair. I could not resist and bent my head to that broad, muscled expanse. His nipples immediately stood at attention, and I laughed as I tickled them with my tongue. I placed one hand on his maleness and felt it increase in size as I played with his chest, marveling at the lushness of the pelt of hairs shielding his private place. "Damme, woman! What are you doin'?" he groaned.

"Relax," I reassured him as I tugged off his trousers and freed his maleness of its confines. I straddled his thighs then and bade him watch as I slowly brought my wet shift up over my hips and waist. I held it at my breast and leaned down to kiss him, feeling his maleness thrusting against my belly.

As his excitement grew, so did mine, and the shift was soon tossed aside, making my breasts available to his hungry mouth. I felt a burning need as never before, and I raised myself above his arching hips, and then, taking his maleness in my hand, I guided him into that place that ached for him.

Our joining was fierce, his thrusts meeting mine in a joyous rhythm that intensified as our passion reached a climax, leaving both of us crying out in ecstasy as I collapsed against him.

Sated, we lay curled into each other, the blanket long since rendered useless against the sand. Richard chuckled, "Thank goodness no one came upon us rutting in broad daylight. And all nekkid as we are."

Suddenly aware of our state, he scrambled for the blanket to cover us, scanning the beach for onlookers. Seeing none, he dressed himself and urged me to hurry and put on my shift.

"I will," I said to him, "but first, I need to bathe."

The poor man was shocked to see me return to the ocean to cleanse myself of his seed and the sand that had made its way into every crevice. But as he stood and walked to the shore, he realized the discomfort of sand in his trousers and returned to our love nest to remove them.

He shook them vigorously to remove the sand and then peeked out from the privacy of the carved-out dune as naked as the day he was born. Seeing no one on the beach, he sprinted to the ocean, covering his maleness with both hands.

We laughed and frolicked in the water, ducking under to rinse our hair of sand. We stopped often to embrace and exchange passionate kisses.

"Hester, this is the first time I've ever had me whole body in water," he confessed as he held me in an embrace, my legs locked around his waist.

Shocked, I asked him, "Do you not bathe?"

"Well, of course I do! Do you think I'm a heathen? But with a basin, one body part at a time. That's how my people do it."

I did not want to insult him, but that clearly explained why White people carried a stench with them wherever they went. To his credit, Richard adopted our way and soon saw the merit of regularly washing his entire body—especially when he wished to lie with me.

He scanned the beach, seeing no one, and decided it was safe for us to leave the privacy of the ocean. I found it amusing to notice that as we retrieved our clothes, Richard once again modestly cupped his hands over his maleness.

Thoroughly wet and still with sand in unusual places, we dressed and mounted our patient horses. Before returning to the encampment, we put our heels on the horses' flanks and rode in the surf parallel to the shore.

I was young and naive, with much to learn about life and love—especially the challenges of loving a White man. The years that followed were tumultuous—sometimes joyful and sometimes painful—but I never regretted loving my Richard.

I miss him still.

Chapter 43

Making Treaty

Summer 1745
17 years old
Goose Creek, SC

I quietly slipped into the shelter of the arbor that served as a temporary Council House. The elders gathered here periodically to discuss the details of the new treaty with Governor Glen's spokespersons. Old Hop and Saluy silently acknowledged my presence with nods of approval. Both spoke English for daily conversation, but they understood how slippery that language could be. Europeans were often tricksters, twisting the words spoken in the Council to suit their interests in the treaty documents. A clerk sat with parchment and quill, ready to record what had been agreed upon during their discussions. From this, the treaty would be drafted and prepared for signing at the formal ceremony with Governor Glen tomorrow.

I watched and listened from the fringe, moving closer to where the White men sat on benches, whispering to one another between conversations with the elders. They paid me no mind, for Native women were invisible to those men unless they were objects of lust. Thus, I could hear useful bits of information to share with Old Hop and Saluy.

A British officer in a red coat named Williams, who seemed to be the leader of Governor Glen's delegation, stood and announced, "Well, then, it appears we have reached an agreement." Pointing to the clerk, he added, "Smith here will formalize the document and have it ready to sign tomorrow after Dreadful Water has been crowned."

"Ah, yes," Old Hop said with a smile, "but first, of course, we will read the document after he has prepared it."

"You?" Williams seemed perturbed. "You wish to read the treaty?"

"We are confident it will align with our agreement this afternoon, but we will review it before signing." His gaze was steady, making it clear he would tolerate no obstacles.

"Humph! I didn't know redskins could read," Williams muttered, obviously perplexed. "Well, so be it." He directed his man Smith to take the treaty to Old Hop once he had scribed it.

The elders gathered with Ludovic Grant and Sarah Emory within a few hours. They took turns reading the document aloud, allowing time for discussion of each passage and examination for hidden meanings. I felt a surge of pride when, while discussing an obscure passage, Saluy turned to his friend and my lover, Richard, to ask for his opinion.

Richard did not hesitate or stammer when singled out; he was ready to explain how that particular passage could be interpreted unfavorably. He suggested minor adjustments in the wording that would clarify its intent and eliminate doubt. Old Hop grunted in agreement, and with nods from the other elders, he instructed the scribe to rewrite the passage.

Thus, it was done: a document written with the entire agreement of our elders, reflecting what had been discussed and agreed upon with Governor Glen's representatives. Our hearts were uplifted, and we expected an end to the bloody Creek War that had raged off and on for a generation, the cessation of immigrants moving unlawfully onto our land, and favorable trade terms for our People.

CHAPTER 44

A Caribbean Pirate

Summer 1745
17 years old
Goose Creek, SC

"Why are you here, Richard?" I asked this White man who had captivated me. "You are not a trader or even a packman. Nor are you a merchant. What brought you to this gathering?"

"Ah," he acknowledged, running a finger down my cheek. "Neither fish nor fowl, am I?"

We had left the crowd at the gathering, which was busy with last-minute preparations for next morning's ceremony. At the edge of the clearing stood a cluster of bushes adorned with brilliant pink blooms, which he said was called "azalea." It was very similar, though much smaller, to the rhododendron I knew in the mountains. I appreciated that he had spread a blanket on the soft green grass near these plants that reminded me of home. We were visible to curious onlookers, yet this lovely, secluded spot felt intimate.

"No, it seems you are neither. So what brought you here for the gathering?"

"'Tis a long story, darling Hester, but I'll tell you the gist of it."

Thrilled that he called me what I believed to be an endearment for the first time, though hopefully not the last, I settled comfortably on the blanket, resting my head in his lap. "Speak!" I demanded with a grin.

He laughed, causing my head to bob, then grew serious. "I will tell you something I have never told a soul." He hesitated, unsure or perhaps gathering his thoughts. For once, I had the good sense to remain silent. Taking a deep breath as if a decision had been made, he quietly stated, "I believe to my bones I am destined to do great things."

I was surprised by such a profound statement and waited patiently. Seeing only curiosity instead of ridicule, he gazed deeply at me, opened his heart, and began to share his story.

He told me that his family had initially been English and had been involved in trade for many generations. They had business connections that spanned continents. Trade partners encouraged their sons and daughters to marry. "Keeping business in the family is a common practice," he elaborated, "which is how Rhoda and I came to wed."

I maintained a neutral expression, as this was my first realization of his marriage. He has a wife! I thought, quickly dismissing the pang of discomfort and planning to reflect on it later.

"My granda was a pirate," he said, expressing a blend of pride and embarrassment. He paused for my reaction, but I remained silent, awaiting further details.

"Do you even know what a pirate is?" he finally asked me, sensing that I wasn't commenting until I knew more. I waited, my brows raised in question.

He sighed and launched into a lengthy, detailed description of the Trade Triangle. Goods were transported from England to West Africa, where they were exchanged with local chiefs and English colonists for African slaves. The enslaved people were considered cheap labor and easily replaceable. They were taken to the West Indies, primarily to an island called Barbados, and traded for rum and sugar to be sent to England. Thus, he sketched the three points of a triangle in the bare dirt beneath the bushes with a stick.

The sugar and rum produced in Barbados required backbreaking labor under extreme heat, resulting in the rapid death of many slaves. I winced at this, recalling stories of Native people being sold into slavery in those regions. I thought Slavery is evil and should never be permitted. Unaware of my disapproval, Richard continued narrating his story.

His great-grandda and several relatives left England to establish sugar plantations in Barbados, producing rum from the sugar they grew. However, they were unhappy with the taxes they had to pay to the English king, who lived so far away. Consequently, Richard's grandda, who was named George, just like his father, became a pirate, shipping rum and sugar directly to Africa and trading for slaves to bring to Barbados, thereby evading the English tax.

I was aware of these dark-skinned people, referred to as Negroes, as even during my ancestors' time, a few had escaped enslavement and found their way to our mountain home. In our tradition, they were adopted and became Cherokee if they proved worthy. But here, in this humid land so close to the Great Water, I saw hundreds, or even thousands, of them. It seemed to me that there were more of the Negro people than of the White. They were laboring in the fields and rice paddies, working at the bidding of their owners.

"Why must the Negroes labor so while their White owners live in luxury?" I asked Richard, causing him to pause in his narrative about his grandda. He appeared puzzled by my question, and his reply was less than satisfying.

"Well, Hester," he finally replied, recognizing that I would await his answer. "That's just how the world works. Some people, especially those of us with European blood, are destined to rule over those who are less fortunate. My father, a devout Presbyterian, explains it well with a passage from the Bible about someone named Ham, but I'm unclear about the details."

I wondered what a "Presbyterian" was but decided not to interrupt his train of thought to ask. He paused, and I waited, allowing him to sort out his thoughts. "We are superior in every way to them... and the Negroes are essential to the economy of the colonies and England."

"Ah, there it is!" I exclaimed, indignant. "Must it always get back to greed and avarice of the Europeans—at the expense of others, like the Negroes... and my People."

Richard defended his pirate grandda's actions in the slave trade: "Damme, Hester, those people would have been transported to plantations in the New World regardless. There was good profit to be made in the business. It's how my grandda built the family fortune."

However, he told me that the English authorities became aware of his duplicity in evading British taxes and put a price on his head. To escape execution, he moved his family to Ireland and adopted the guise of a respectable businessman. Using his small slave ship, he began ferrying men, some with families, from England to Ireland. He claimed this business was even more profitable, as fewer men died in transit than the Negroes from Africa did.

I struggled to keep up with this story since it involved places I had never heard of and sounded exceedingly complicated. Moreover, simply being in his presence was distracting. "Why did he move people from England to this place called Ireland?" I asked as he paused to drink from a flask.

"That, too, is a long story for another time," he said with a faraway look. "Suffice it to say that there was a war, and England subjugated the Irish people. Those who survived were forced off their land and into the hills. The productive farmland was divided into plantations and given to British soldiers as payment for fighting for England. They were to settle and turn Ireland into a profitable English colony."

This caused me distress, as it resembled what was happening in the American Colonies. Only it was my people being pushed off their homeland to make room for English settlers. "What happened to the Irish?" I asked, sitting up as if to distance myself from him.

He shifted uncomfortably, frowning at my question. "Well, many more died because they could not survive in the uplands of Ireland, where growing crops is difficult. Those who had some means emigrated to the American Colonies. But if they had no money, they found passage as indentured servants."

He then must explain to me what an indentured servant was, for I had never heard of such a thing. "Irish people would subject themselves to slavery for a period of years? Willingly?" I asked, unable to grasp the desperation of those people.

"Aye. As were the convicts transported from England to the colonies."

The law courts in England, I learned, convicted men, women, and children of crimes such as stealing to death by hanging. As an alternative, they could be transported to the colonies with an obligation to do seven years of unpaid labor.

This was disturbing as it helped explain the influx of immigrants to my homeland. Some of the interlopers were seizing our land because the British had forcibly taken their own, or they came to escape the hangman's noose. That explained their desperation to settle against all odds.

"The English government paid five pounds per head to the ship owner," he elaborated as I tried to grasp the implications of moving people from one place to another. "Upon arrival in the New World, they were sold as slaves for seven years. Men fetched ten to fifteen pounds in English sterling, women eight or nine, and children less. With 130 to 140 people packed into the ship's hold, my Grandda could make a profit of two thousand pounds on a single voyage—enough to purchase another boat and transport more displaced Irish or English convicts."

I challenged him for more details, and it was clear that Richard felt uncomfortable with my constant questions and confusion about this information. Nevertheless, he persisted and patiently explained these unusual traditions of the Europeans until I had no more questions—at least for the time being.

He left our private place to relieve himself, and returned with a platter of victuals and a flask of water for us to share.

"Back to Grandda," he began, resuming the story and avoiding discussing the displacement of people from one land to another in the name of greed. "He didn't just transport slaves or convicts, you know. Don't think too badly of him—or me. He made enough money to own a small fleet of ships. He also transported sugar and rum from Barbados to the Colonies, returning with trade goods for the Barbadians. All the trees on the island had been cut down, and the land converted into sugar cane fields. The inhabitants relied on goods produced elsewhere to survive, as importing food and timber was less expensive than growing it."

I remembered my new friend Sarah opening a paper packet and pouring a white substance into our tea—sugar. Its sweetness was sublime, and I understood how someone might desire more of such a delicacy. But was it worth the decimation of an island and the subjugation of people? I decided then and there that I would not succumb to the lure of its sweetness.

He had become lost in storytelling and failed to realize the discomfort it caused me. It was all too similar to my own people's plight in developing a growing dependence on trade goods. This conversation was interesting, and I was pleased that he shared it with me. However, I found it disturbing and wondered how to explain it to Old Hop. Sensing that he was only increasing my concern, he returned to telling me more about his grandda.

"Grandda married my Granny, an English woman who was the daughter of one of his merchant business partners. They established their home in Ireland, where she bore him several children. Their son, my Da, married my mother, Sarah, an Irishwoman from a trading family as well. My older brother, George, my sister, Christian, and I were all born in Ireland, making us as much Irish as we are English."

"That's a lot of Georges," I interrupted, gnawing on a fried chicken leg. This meat was new to me—a bird raised for its eggs and later butchered. It seemed more convenient than hunting fowl with a slingshot or snare. I was developing a taste for the meat and also for the eggs frequently served at the encampment.

"Yes, I guess it is," he said, reaching for the water flask. "My great-grandda, my grandda, my da, and then my brother are all named George. It is our tradition to name children after their ancestors, and usually, the firstborn son is named after his da, while the second is given the same name as his grandda."

I explained to him that our way of giving a child a name unique to them is much more sensible and that their name could change as life events dictate. Already in the Nation, some children had both a Cherokee name and a White name, as did I. As events unfolded over the years, his first son, with Rhoda, was named Richard after him, while his second son—and mine—was named George.

"But why are you here instead of in Ireland?" I asked, redirecting him to my original question. I could see the sun descending toward the west, and our private time would soon come to an end. I wanted to learn more about this man who had captured my heart.

"That is a long story for another time," he said, glancing toward the lengthening shadows, "but after my grandda died, my da decided to leave Ireland and move our family to the American colonies. He had become acquainted with William Penn while Grandda was transporting Quakers to the colonies. Penn held a large land grant in Pennsylvania and sold some property along a main pathway to Da, where he established a tavern."

He began to tell me about William Penn, a man named Fox, and the Quakers, but I was eager for him to get to the point. I had already heard about those avaricious White men while listening to men talk at the Council House. I felt a pang of discomfort to think Richard was a party to the displacement of the Delaware People. I quickly asked questions to steer him away from a lengthy discussion on that subject.

"Da sold the tavern on the Pennsylvania Pike, and we moved further west, settling in the growing town of Winchester, Virginia. We acquired considerable property there and established ourselves within the community. Our families arranged a marriage of convenience between Rhoda and me; she's the daughter of a business acquaintance of my father. But I was curious about what lay beyond—the wilderness and lands yet to be explored."

Explored by White men, I thought cynically. We Native peoples have explored it for countless generations.

He paused to drink from the water flask and, finding it empty, tossed it aside, stretching his long frame and scratching his backside. I remained quiet, not wanting to disturb his train of thought by peppering him with questions.

"Word reached me that many of my family's Barbadian relatives and business partners have relocated to the Carolina colony and settled here in Goose Creek. Charles Town is becoming an important port for trade, extending beyond just England. I came to meet with them to discuss the business opportunities we can pursue together.

"When I heard about the gathering of a large delegation of Cherokee coming down from the mountains, I went to see it for myself. There was such a hullabaloo that I couldn't believe it. One of their women had gone missing, and everyone was scurrying around trying to find her."

I ducked my head in embarrassment, knowing of whom he spoke, and he grinned, pulling me into an embrace.

"And then, thar she was, surprised that she had been missed whilst she went adventuring." He kissed the top of my head nestled in his arms and continued.

"I was gut-struck, Hester, when I saw you step out of that boat onto the pier. I knew then that you were a woman whose acquaintance I must make."

I curled into him, purring with contentment, and we remained silent together, basking in the new sensation of being exactly where we belonged—together.

"I feel—nay, I know—my destiny lies out there," he murmured, making a sweeping motion toward my homeland—toward the mountains capped with blue mist.

He was lost to me then, gazing into the distance, dreaming of his future and imagining his destiny. I began to wonder about my own destiny. Was it intertwined with his? Or would we part in two days hence, our paths never to cross again?

CHAPTER 45

Governor James Glen

Summer 1745
17 years old
Charles Town, SC

The women and girls who shared a cramped cabin with me began to stir, stretch, and yawn as dim light heralded the approaching dawn. I had not been the only one searching for her bedroll in the darkest hours of the night; many had shared pleasures with the men of their choosing, just as I had. Exchanging sly glances, we slipped into our shifts and prepared for the morning ritual of going to water.

Quietly, we threaded through the campground toward the small stream that fed Goose Creek. Many of the Native men were doing the same while the White men continued their slumber. We women made our way to a pleasant eddy upstream from the men, shielded by a stand of willows. As has been our ritual since we were babes, we greeted the sun rising over the horizon with our morning prayers. Then, we removed our shifts to cleanse ourselves in the still-warm waters of the pebbled creek.

"How different this water is from ours," Sweet Grass exclaimed as she emerged from the water. "Our water is never this warm, even in summer."

"I believe I could get used to this," Sookey agreed.

"Not me!" exclaimed Yellow Bird as she started applying aloe to her long hair. "I welcome the cold—it makes my skin tingle."

"Did your lover not make your skin tingle last night?" Sweet Grass teased. Thus, the laughter and sharing that began each day continued as we helped one another wash and rinse our hair.

Back at our primitive lodging, we nibbled on warm bread from the earthen oven, overseen by the same kerchiefed woman from our first day. It was soft and sweet, quite different from the bread we ate at home, and we agreed that we would miss it.

The sun quickly rose, warming the campground and evaporating the morning dew. Fortunately, today would be sunny, as we would be dressed in our finest ceremonial attire. Rain would have undermined our intended effect as we officially entered Charles Town to meet Governor Glen.

We helped one another dress in our finest clothing and style our hair elaborately. I especially needed assistance with my hair, as I had not yet mastered that art—nor would I ever. A simple braid or rawhide tie would suffice for my entire life.

We left our shelter with pride, striding forth with our heads held high and a great sense of solemnity, leaving the giggles behind. I was amused to see the expression on Dreadful Water's face when he spotted me. I must be beautiful, I thought, for his expression first lit with desire and then swiftly shifted to a disgruntled frown. I wondered if he would stick out his tongue at me as he had when we were children.

It was no secret that he had made advances toward me several times, assuming I would lie with him for no other reason than his exalted status as emperor. He had not taken my rejections graciously and was now greatly displeased that everyone in the encampment knew I was sharing pleasures with a White man, Richard Pearis.

It was Richard's expression that warmed my soul. He appeared stunned to see me in the white deerskin beaded dress my mother had made, paired with the white leggings. My face gleamed, and my hair was styled in an elaborate and flattering manner. Our eyes locked, and once again, I felt that strange sensation in my belly that only he could provoke.

Fancy came to me when I whistled, leaving her companions to graze in the pasture, her step lively and tail swishing. I laughed to see her, both of us still happy from our excursion to the Great Water the day before. I brought her an extra portion of grain as consolation for not riding her in the procession. We had been advised to leave our horses at the encampment as they were not accustomed to the noise of a large cheering crowd or cannon fire. But, to ease our disappointment, I promised she would wear the fancy halter Johnny had made when we left the city on the morrow.

There were additional barges to transport such a large group to the entrance of Charles Town, where we gathered before beginning our procession. Sarah had informed me that the governor intended to elevate the ceremonial naming of Dreadful Water as emperor by staging a display worthy of royalty. Surely, he understood that the true power resided with our traditional headman, Old Hop. However, we Cherokees cherished pageantry, so we were more than willing to engage in the pretense. Perhaps the only one present who didn't grasp the truth was Dreadful Water, as he was unbearably pompous.

As the congregation approached the city's wall, Dreadful Water was ensconced in an elaborate wagon with sides and a roof, called a coach. Six horses of equal size and color stamped their feet, ready to pull the wagon forward. As the door closed behind him, he grew pale and looked startled, and I almost felt sorry for him.

The headmen, then our warriors, painted and adorned in their finest attire, marched proudly behind the coach as it proceeded down Broad Street, the main thoroughfare. I was grateful to have been warned about the noise as cannons boomed from the city walls and ships in the harbor. The loud sounds would have made our horses skittish.

Although I was with the women who followed the procession, all dressed in our finery, I still had a good view of the events when the coach arrived at the British Council House, an impressive stone building.

Dreadful Water and his entourage were led into the interior, which was disappointing because I wanted to see what was happening.

Undeterred, I slipped into a knot of headmen and warriors, acting as though I were where I was expected to be. The men were accustomed to my appearing in unexpected places and paid no attention, making room for me in their midst as they entered.

I witnessed Dreadful Water kneel before the governor, who wore the distinctive red coat of a British soldier adorned with a dazzling array of medals on his chest. Governor Glen placed a silk and fur crown on Dreadful Water's head, declaring him Emperor of the Cherokee. This was followed by a ceremonial reception of Cherokee headmen from various towns and many expressions of love and friendship for one another—which soon became rather dull.

Finally, the governor presented the treaty signed in London in 1730. He concluded the ceremonies by reminding the Cherokees to behave and adhere to the treaty. However, we knew it was not a legitimate treaty. It was signed under duress by the seven Cherokee warriors who traveled to London and had to affix their names to ensure their passage home.

They had known that they were not tribal elders and had no authority to speak for the Nation. If the English chose to ignore that reality, then so be it. We would, too. What mattered was the treaty the elders would sign that day with Glen. But would he "be on good behavior" and abide by this treaty that bore his signature? Only time would tell.

That night, still in our regalia, traditional dancing took place around a central fire. Some townspeople, including Sarah, stood on the fringes to watch what must have seemed exotic to them. During the men's celebration dance, Saluy motioned to Richard, inviting him to join them. Watching him quickly learn the steps and blend in with my People made my heart swell.

The night stretched long as a full moon rose, obscuring the stars with its brilliance. One by one, men drifted off, some accompanied by their women. Sarah and the townspeople went to the pier to secure their passage to the city, glancing over their shoulders with what I perceived as longing—a desire to belong to our community.

Richard came to me and held out his hand. I took it and drew him to me in an embrace, once again feeling the heat rise between us.

"One last time," I whispered as we made our way to the protective woods, Richard's blanket draped over one arm while the other held me close. At dawn, I would begin my journey back to the mountains shrouded in blue mist.

"I'll find you," he whispered in the night. "I'll come, for I cannot live without you."

But I knew that was not meant to be. He had a life in Winchester with his wife and the people of his kind, while I had a life in my mountain home. Our paths would never cross again.

Thus, as dawn overcame the night, I mounted Fancy and turned my back on Goose Creek—and the White man who had captivated my soul.

CHAPTER 46

Embargo

Autumn 1750
22 years old
Estatoe Town

Mother immediately noticed a change in me upon our return. She embraced me warmly as I dismounted Fancy, weary and dusty from the long trek through the winding trails that led from the valley towns. It must have been evident that my experiences in Charles Town had profoundly affected me. I was no longer a rambunctious girl but a fully grown woman.

I had experienced a broader world than most of my People. I witnessed the Europeans' peculiar customs and their insatiable greed. I had walked the streets of a grand city. The Great Water was no longer a mystery to imagine but something my body had known and rejoiced in. I had paraded ceremoniously with the warriors and elders of my people and sat with them during a significant meeting with the governor of South Carolina. I formed a friendship with a European woman, and we shared secrets, much like

Wurth and I did. But most of all, I had walked with the soul of a White man, and thoughts of him brought me no peace.

Dreams of him haunted me at night. No matter how hard I tried to push thoughts of him away, my mind would return to every moment we had spent together, and I would long for him. Mother saw how it was with me and kept me busy with tasks. But often throughout the day, I would awaken as from a trance and realize I had been staring into the distance, dreaming of him.

I kept my eye on the trails leading into Toqua, or whatever town I was in, always alert to anyone entering the palisade, hoping it would be Richard. But it never was.

Fortunately, with the resilience of youth and the passage of time, the pain of our parting faded to a dull ache, and eventually, I was free of it. I took other lovers when I wished, but none matched the passion I had experienced with Richard.

Events in our Nation left little time to grieve lost love or to dream of a life with a man who could never be. Our relatively calm life in the Smoky Mountains had become a thing of the past as tensions escalated with increasing violence.

The French stirred up conflicts on both the South Carolina and Virginia frontiers. European settlers on our borders and Native peoples from several nations clashed, destroying their settlements and villages—the violence spilling over into our towns.

Just one year after the signing of the White man's treaty intended to resolve our issues, I accompanied Old Hop to yet another conference with Governor Glen at the settlement of Ninety-Six, located midway to Charles Town. Glen sought permission to build a fort in Cherokee territory. Old Hop consulted with the elders and refused.

It seemed unwise to invite armed military men into our homeland. Our warriors would protect us. Governor Glen must uphold his promise to prevent Europeans, as well as neighboring Creek and Choctaw, from defiling our hunting grounds and raiding our lower towns.

As if it weren't enough that our lower towns along the borders of South Carolina and Virginia had to struggle to survive, the French-supported Iroquois Nation began raiding our towns in the backcountry, deep in the mountains—what had been the safest part of our nation.

We were being assaulted from all sides.

Angered by our refusal to permit a fort in our southern territories, Governor Glen imposed a trade embargo. We found ourselves not only besieged on all sides but also deprived of access to the European goods and ammunition we had come to rely on.

There were heated discussions in the Council House at Chota, the principal town of the Cherokee Nation. Our elders wished to return to the old ways of survival, forgoing trade with both the English and French alike.

But the younger men and warriors knew that this was not possible. The game was scarce for such, having been hunted and slaughtered for decades. The neighboring Native peoples were being displaced from their ancestral lands by European settlers and were trying to move onto ours. Our warriors argued that their enemies used the firearms of the White men and that we must also use them to defend our homeland. The bloody Creek War had resumed, and we were almost defenseless without ammunition for the firearms.

In the span of one or two generations, we were more dependent upon trade with the English than they were upon our skins and hides.

Once again, I accompanied a delegation to meet with Governor Glen. One hundred sixty proud Cherokee warriors and one equally proud young woman rode into Charles Town to meet the governor and present our case. By then, I was well acquainted with this trade path and no longer felt overawed. However, each time, I was amazed by the city's growth and the expansion of the surrounding settlements.

As was our custom, I sought out my friend Sarah Emory and drank tea with her in the English fashion. She had become aware of her mixed blood grandchildren. We never spoke of it, but I suspected she knew I had known about them at our first meeting—and understood that I did not mention them out of kindness. Nowadays, she would ask me, and I would share stories of the last time I had seen them. It seemed to warm her heart to know that her sons had healthy children living among the Cherokee.

Willewanah, my uncle and Wurth's father, the War Chief of Keowee, represented the Cherokee Nation at the Charles Town conference. His eloquence filled me with pride. Gone was the gruff jokester who had enjoyed teasing and playing pranks on us children. Instead, I saw a handsome warrior with his chest bared to proudly display battle scars, silver armbands glistening in the sun, and an eagle feather dangling from his scalp lock.

At the Council, a lengthy discussion ensued, growing rather tiresome. I sometimes struggled to stay awake since the outcome had already been decided. Nevertheless, men enjoy engaging in word games and negotiating back and forth. The scribe had difficulty keeping pace with them until, finally, an agreement was reached.

The Cherokee agreed to return what was called "plunder" from the raids and to punish the "murderers." However, the method for accomplishing this was not specified. The so-called "plunder" had long been distributed among the People and either consumed or otherwise utilized. The "murderers" were our warriors—the defenders of our People. Nonetheless, it sounded good in the treaty—and that satisfied Governor Glen. He was pleased that he had taught us a lesson and agreed to lift the embargo.

In return, Willewanah promised our People to assist Glen in constructing an English fort near the lower Keowee Town—his home.

We would allow armed soldiers to take root in Cherokee country and build their detested "Fort Prince George."

CHAPTER 47

Independence

Autumn 1799
71 years old
Baldridge Creek, GA

My nose welcomes the scent of pine trees bathed in moisture, releasing their resin, as I awaken to the sound of soft rain pelting my little cabin in the woods. I arise and slip on my moccasins, for I have not adopted wearing European-style leather shoes, as most of my family has. I prefer the softness of worked hide that protects my feet but allows me to feel the earth's contours.

I wrap a shawl around my shoulders, covering my thin cotton shift, in preparation to welcome the dawn by going to water. My son and I argue about this tradition of mine. Recently, he told me that I was too old to navigate the narrow trail through the woods and manage the steps carved into the creek's embankment.

"You could fall and break a bone," he had warned me.

"What is this!" I exclaimed. "The son telling his mother what she can and cannot do."

"I mention it only because I care about you," he said, softening the insult. "You aren't as spry as you used to be, and that embankment is steep and slippery, especially after it has rained."

Often, we argue back and forth, my pride assaulted by his concerns for my safety. Caty and Nancy merely shake their heads and continue their tasks, unwilling to come to my rescue.

Yes, my back is stooped, and it pains me constantly. My hips are stiff and slow to move as I direct them. I am unsteady on my feet and often reach for walls, furniture, or a grandchild to steady myself. My spirit refuses to acknowledge that my body is failing me. I don't need my son to remind me that I am no longer the lithe girl of my youth but am becoming an old crone. I reminded him that it was I who suckled him at my breast and changed the moss in his wrappings.

"That's my point," he agreed. "Look at this babe you birthed. I, too, am growing old."

"Bah!" I retorted, for it is a truth I do not want to face. To me, he will always be my baby boy, even though he is now a gray-haired man sporting a paunch and deep creases lining his face.

A few days after our latest argument, I found a beautifully crafted walking stick leaning against my cabin when I stepped onto my porch for my morning ritual. I knew this was a gift to my pride from my grandson, Jim, who is a skilled woodcarver. It was made from a chestnut branch and featured beautiful carvings, sanded smooth with river sand, and sealed with buffalo fat. The clever boy had even fashioned a small handle shaped like a Yellow Bird of Estatoe. It was a welcome gift as it lessened the indignity of my impaired mobility.

As I step onto my porch this morning—ready to greet the sun, even though it hides behind clouds—my darling Rachel stands prepared to escort me. We exchange greetings, and she walks beside me, ready to offer her arm when we encounter a treacherous tree root. Without a word, she leads me down the embankment—when did it get so steep?—and offers her hand to steady my descent.

Thus, with the support and love of my grandchildren, I can continue the traditions of my mothers and grandmothers through the mists of time and go to water to greet the day.

This day begins with heavy clouds followed by a soft rain but soon progresses to a steady downpour. Sleet follows as the temperature drops. It is a good day for everyone to gather in the house. Moses and Jesse come in, shedding their coats and leaving puddles on Nancy's clean floor. She tsks at them, scolding them to leave their wet things on the porch before entering. They grin and pay her little mind as they warm their backsides by the blazing fireplace.

"How does the pen fare?" George asks his sons, scratching his belly, which is full from a hearty breakfast.

They began working on the fence early this morning, hoping to make progress before the worst of the fall storm arrived. They were expanding the hog pen next to the barn. Next spring, George plans to buy shoats from a farmer down the road to fatten for butchering next fall.

A hog pen. I think it but dare not say. *My son, once a proud Cherokee warrior, is now naught but a hog farmer.* I hold my tongue, for though we frequently spar, I know such harsh words would wound him.

Lucretia pulls my rocking chair near the fire and hands me a cup of the milk I have come to crave. I still find it amazing that such a drink pulled from a cow's teat—white with flecks of rich yellow cream—can be such a satisfying way to start the day. It seems that I willingly adopted some European ways but rejected others out of hand.

And so this day progresses, my son, his wives, and their children—even their grandchildren now, my great-grandchildren—going about their indoor tasks as I warm my old bones beside the fire. Content, I doze off, as I am wont to do more often these days.

"Granny, tell us more stories from the Old Times," Sallie pleads, her eyes bright with curiosity, rousing me from my slumber.

A chorus of voices encourages me and warms my heart. I am pleased that my grandchildren still enjoy stories of olden times, though several are now young adults.

"Tell us about what happened after you met Grandfather Richard," Lucretia begs.

Always the romantic, she hopes for a sweet tale of blossoming love and romance. But in truth, I can not indulge her with such nonsense—for that is not how it was for me and Richard.

"Where was I when we last spoke about this?" I ask, having forgotten where I left off.

"You had met at Goose Creek, became lovers, and then parted. You thought you would never see him again. But we know you were reunited, or we would not be here." She gestures around the room, filled with the descendants of mine and Richard's.

"Ah, yes. I remember." I settle deeper into my rocker, close my eyes, and drift back to another time.

CHAPTER 48

Refugees

Autumn 1750
22 years old
Estatoe Town

I came from the river, a string of fat catfish dangling from my hand, leaving a wet trail in the dust. Mourning Dove would be pleased with my contribution to the family meal, and perhaps I would not be scolded for my absence while hides were being scraped. I detested the messy task of tanning the skins of deer, wolf, beaver, or whatever game the hunters had brought back from their last expedition to the hunting grounds.

It fell to women and children to scrape the skins clean of flesh and, at times, fur, depending on their intended use, in preparation for the tanning process. Each creature's brain yielded just enough material to tan its hide or pelt. Producing a buckskin or fur pelt was hard work. I wasn't lazy; I knew my skills were better applied elsewhere—by the river, fishing, or in the forest, hunting. Or eavesdropping on men's conversations to report to our Nation's leaders.

Thus, I approached the home I shared with Mourning Dove and Saluy, a fearsome warrior who was now Estatoe's Red Chief. He had earned that designation from the bravery and skill he had shown in fierce battles these past few years. We had known little peace in our town near the southern border of our Nation.

"Oh, good, Prachey," my mother greeted me as I approached her outdoor kitchen. "I am glad to have such a fine catch of catfish, as we have more guests than expected."

Guests? What did she mean? Then, I noticed the bedraggled, frightened woman with three small children clinging to her. They huddled in the deepest shade of the nearby cabin, not only to escape the sun but also to avoid being seen. They were refugees—yet more refugees from another one of our towns that had been raided.

I smiled a welcome to her, knowing Mother was trying to make this little family feel less like a burden. When she tentatively returned my smile, I squatted before them and offered my hand to the little girl of about four summers. With my coaxing, she allowed me to take her onto my lap, giving her mother a moment of respite as she nursed her infant.

I engaged the young mother in casual conversation with soft, gentle tones, feeling pleased to see her relax and grow less frightened. My mother nodded in appreciation as she started working on the catfish—another messy task I tried to avoid whenever possible.

Starlight, as she was called, did not need to share the specifics of what had happened to her family, as it was a tragically common occurrence. Hostilities had escalated along our border with the Creeks, and the situation in the lower villages was more desperate than ever. Once an area unsettled by either nation, the careful use of fire had cleared large swaths of underbrush, creating a welcome space for deer to graze—and making hunting easier. But now, the deer were fewer in number every year, turning the hunting grounds into sites of bloody conflict.

Thus, the Creeks raided and destroyed our outlying villages, just as I had experienced in my childhood at Tugaloo Town. Refugees from the devastated villages fled further into the mountains, seeking shelter at other towns. We welcomed them, of course, but this placed a tremendous burden on the villages that escaped the wrath of the Creek warriors. Our own warriors responded to hostility with hostility, and both nations suffered.

I knew that she and her children had witnessed much of what I experienced during the Tugaloo massacre as a child—memories that would haunt them for their entire lives.

She seemed to need to unburden herself—to tell Mother and me what had transpired. So we sat beside her as she recounted the events between sobs.

My People had learned to anticipate and prepare for raids such as this. Boys and elderly women were tasked to keep watch at strategic locations around the grounds and the palisade to warn of an impending attack. Our defenses consisted of vertical logs forming a circular barrier. Double walls at the entrance slowed entry into the village. This design provided protection against unwanted intrusions, although it limited escape routes for the villagers. Therefore, secret panels were created in the palisade walls, allowing mothers to escape with their children.

Despite the lookouts, there was little warning when the neighboring Native warriors, clad only in loincloths and with their bodies painted red—the color of war—descended upon her town, screaming terrifying battle cries. They hurled torches onto the roofs of homes, setting them ablaze. Anyone within reach of a war club or an arrow became a victim.

Any of her village's warriors who were not out on the fall hunt rushed to defend their home—many struck down before they could notch an arrow. Elderly men, boys, and young women took up arms, rushing toward the invaders and providing cover for mothers and children to escape to the forest.

Starlight fled to safety with her three children. The mothers knew to scatter and blend into the forest. Even the youngest child, like the one at Starlight's breast, was trained to maintain absolute silence—quiet like a fawn, the baby deer, camouflaged by dense foliage. The marauders rarely pursued them into the forest, as they were kept busy enough with the villagers who did not escape and with the destruction of the town.

When the sounds from the village signaled that the raid was over, Starlight left her young son in charge of her two youngest children and crept back to the town. The raiding party had left, but the torched homes still smoldered, and the scent of burning wood and flesh filled the air. There were no wounded to tend, for, as at Tugaloo, they had all been killed or taken as slaves.

The survivors began to emerge from their hiding places in the village and, like her, from the surrounding forest. The sounds of lamenting women and crying children pierced the air. As dusk deepened, the remaining men and women wandered about, trying to determine what to do. They set about gathering the dead, preparing them for burial in the morning.

Starlight's home was nothing but ashes; most of her belongings and those of her family had been consumed by the flames. Her husband was out on the fall hunt. Her clan and village were grieving and trying to reorganize to cope with their loss. After a traumatic night in the destroyed village, Starlight, like many untethered mothers, departed from the smoldering town at daybreak to seek refuge in nearby Estatoe.

Once again, our town faced another influx of refugees; however, we would welcome them, and together, we would endure this latest assault on our Nation.

"Come with me, Feather," I coaxed the tear-streaked little girl. "I believe I saw a cornhusk doll in our cabin that needs someone to love." Starlight's daughter allowed me to lift her into my arms. Her eyes brightened, and the beginnings of a smile touched her rosebud lips before she buried her face in my neck.

With Feather clinging to my hip, I strode from Mother's outdoor kitchen and nearly collided with Richard Pearis.

I don't know who was more startled—him or me. "Damme, Hester! I didn't know," he exclaimed.

My initial reaction was joy at finally seeing him again. However, that quickly shifted to a surge of anger. How dare he come now? Now! After all these years, when I had finally moved on from loving him, why did he have to show up now?

I shifted Feather to the opposite hip and turned away from him, walking as fast as I could. But he followed me, his long legs quickly closing the distance.

"I had no idea. If I'd known, I would have tried to come to you sooner, but I had no word of a bairn."

A "bairn?" Even in my anger, I wondered what he meant. My grasp of English was good, but I didn't understand what a barn had to do with anything. He had just confirmed, once again, how crazy Europeans are.

When I reached our cabin, I hurried inside and shut the door behind me. Surely, even a rude European knew that a closed door was meant to turn him away. He didn't leave. Instead, he stood outside, talking nonstop. My ears were closed to him because I was so angry. I busied myself searching for the doll for Feather and rummaging through various baskets for clean clothing that might fit Starlight and her children.

It grew quiet, and I thought the crazy White man had left. I dried the tears that had come unbidden and unexpectedly. Why would my eyes betray me? Why was my heart racing so? Did my body not know what I told myself—that I no longer loved him? Ours had been a simple joining for mutual pleasure and nothing more. I had enjoyed many such brief relationships.

So why did I have such an overwhelming urge to either rush into his arms and smother him with kisses or pick up the nearest branch and give him a good thrashing? These conflicting feelings made no sense.

When I opened the cabin door, Feather clutched her new doll in one hand and my skirt in the other while my arms were burdened with clothing for her family. Richard had not left after all; he emerged from the shelter of a nearby tree and rushed forward.

"Hester, darling Hester," he exclaimed. "I've longed to see you again."

My rebellious heart melted, and before I knew it, he knelt before the child and spoke to her in that sing-song way that people of all races tend to use with small children. She did not understand his English words, of course, but she grasped his message of kindness and allowed him to pick her up.

"She's beautiful, Hester," he grinned at me. "And she looks just like you."

I couldn't help but laugh. That explained his first outburst. He had come looking for me, and when he saw a child of the appropriate age clinging to me, his first thought was that I had given birth to her after our encounters at Goose Creek. He believed she was his daughter.

My anger melted away with the warmth of laughter, and he walked with me to my mother and the forlorn Starlight. Mother and I exchanged glances; her raised eyebrows signaled approval. Smiling, she suggested I take the grief-stricken family to our favorite bathing spot in the river. Cleansing themselves of the ashes of their burned town, putting on fresh clothes, and filling their bellies would aid in their healing. There would be much for them and others who had fled to the relative safety of our town to sort out.

Once I had fulfilled my responsibilities to our guests, Richard and I walked to a nearby clearing surrounded by towering oak trees. He swiftly embraced me, and a flame of passion ignited as soon as our bodies touched. "Not here. Not now." I cautioned him, as I did not want anyone to come upon us in our fervor.

"I know, Hester. This isn't the right time or place. I just want to look at you and hold you once more."

And, of course, I melted into him, as I always would.

We sat on a fallen log under an oak bathed in crimson leaves as the sun traveled across the sky and the chill of dusk came upon us. We had much to say to each other. I needed to tell him how it had been for the Cherokee Nation and my family these past five years, and, finally, he would tell me what had delayed his coming to me.

CHAPTER 49

Reunion

Autumn 1750
22 years old
Estatoe Town

We joined my family and our guest, Starlight, for the night's communal meal. Bark and Terrapin were delighted in their attempts to teach the peculiar European how to speak our musical language, laughing uproariously at how his tongue struggled with what came so easily to them. Molly was her usual decorous self, immaculately groomed and possessing delicate mannerisms—a stark contrast to me.

But tonight, I did not resent her perfection, for it was evident to all that Richard had eyes only for me. As soon as it was appropriate, we signaled that it was time to find a private space. And I knew where to go.

The previous fall, Mourning Dove had asked my uncles to build a private room at the back of her house—the same arrangement that had been made for my father and brother at Quatis' house a few years earlier. Such private spaces were common and were often used by a woman and the man she considered a mate. This allowed the couple privacy while the young woman did not bear the full burden of maintaining her own household. If she chose to let her mate's seed take root and bear his child, her uncles and kinsmen would construct a separate house for her new family.

My private room was a result of my status in the Nation. Mourning Dove said that if I were to accompany the elders here and there, interpreting for them, I should have my own space when I was home—a separate room to confer with whomever I needed. She looked at me, keeping her face expressionless, for she and I knew the double meaning of "confer."

Without a doubt, my uncles understood as well. However, they raised no objections, and soon, I had a small corner of the world to store my possessions, contemplate quietly, and discuss matters privately with whomever I chose. Thus, I took Richard to my space, where he immediately embraced me passionately. We talked very little because our lovemaking was wild and intense, just as it had been when we first met. He raised my shift over my hips, over my head, and upstretched arms, tossing it into the corner.

I stepped back and smiled, allowing him to look upon my nakedness, as I knew this was a novelty for him. He moaned and pulled me close, and I felt the length of his arousal pressing against my belly. Laughing, I took off his shirt.

His buckskin pants were more difficult to manage because he couldn't untie his leather shoes. I laughed as I watched him hopping around my small room, naked except for his britches gathered at his ankles while he attempted to kick off his shoes. Frustrated, he collapsed onto my sleeping pallet while I began the task of untying his laces as he explored the contours of my back and hips, circling around to my breasts.

When he caressed a nipple, a jolt ran through me, and I jerked the last shoestring free, tossing first one and then the other shoe to the side. He toed off his pants as I rolled him onto his back and set about pleasuring him—and myself.

He shushed me when I moaned with passion for fear those in the cabin would hear. I cupped my hand over his mouth when he cried out as he reached his climax. Then we collapsed together, chuckling, kissing deeply and gently, savoring the feel of each other.

Our passion momentarily satisfied, I curled against him, my ear pressed to his chest, relishing the sound of his heartbeat and the feel of his breath on my forehead.

"Tell me," I urged him. "Tell me everything."

We dozed on and off throughout the night, taking turns discussing what had happened during our time apart. He knew much of what had occurred in the Nation, but I had no news about him.

He told me that his family had settled in Winchester, Virginia. He said his older brother, George, was a disappointment to their father, who had counted on his firstborn son to carry on the Pearis legacy brought from England and Ireland and expected to thrive in the New World. His younger brother, Robert, had a better head for business and was taking responsibility for the considerable land holdings the family had acquired since their arrival on the western frontier of the colonies. They had purchased large tracts of land and divided them into smaller parcels to sell to emigrants fleeing the incessant wars in Europe, eager to cultivate farms.

"The family is doing quite well, Hester," he murmured, nuzzling my neck. "However, I believe we can do even better. This land is so rich; it's there for the taking by a smart man."

"And that smart man is you, I suppose," I teased him. Yet, even then, I didn't doubt he would do what it took to realize his dream.

On that first night of his return to me, he shared his dream—that one day, he would own a plantation to rival those of the Tidewater aristocracy, like the ones I had seen around Charles Town. He mentioned that his wife, Rhoda, also shared this dream, having been born into an affluent merchant family and yearning to be the mistress of a grand estate.

I admit feeling jealous that he could talk so freely about his wife to me, his lover. Such talk caused a sharp pain in my heart, and I wanted to lash out at him. But, for once, I swallowed the harsh words I might have spoken and instead encouraged him to tell me more about his life in Winchester, for I was indeed curious.

He told me that Rhoda had given birth to a daughter named Sarah two years ago. Just before he left Winchester, she also had a son whom he named Richard Jr. The dynasty he dreamed of was taking shape.

Dynasty? What talk was this? Was it not our purpose to see all our community healthy and prospering, with no one family better off than another? This was yet another of the European ways of thinking that I could never understand. At that time, I believed their inability to view their people as a whole—rather than just families or those related by blood—would be their downfall. But in time, I would be proven wrong.

Finally, as the night deepened and dawn approached, we slept, our limbs intertwined and our hearts filled with a profound sense of completion.

CHAPTER 50

Dreams of Dynasty

Autumn 1750
22 years old
Estatoe Town

Richard had not ventured into our mountain home unaccompanied—nor without grand plans for his advancement. He introduced the lanky, sour-faced Nathaniel Gist as his business partner. Both were ambitious young men focused on amassing their fortunes through trade with the Cherokee Nation and the rapidly growing colonies of Virginia and South Carolina. They shared similar aspirations for advancement among White men, yet they could not have been more different otherwise.

I learned that Nathaniel was the son of colonial aristocracy and, perhaps because of that, was haughty and arrogant. I confess I disliked the man from the beginning. He was often rude to me and my People and had no interest in learning or adapting to our customs. On the other hand, Richard exhibited great curiosity about the traditions of the Cherokee and was diligent in becoming proficient in learning our language.

In time, Richard would become as gifted a linguist as I and would often serve as an interpreter at official meetings. We learned that the Europeans do not honor women as much as we do. Therefore, my role as interpreter was unofficial and unrecognized by the Whites. It served its purpose, though, in that I could sit quietly and listen when the Europeans were unaware of my presence. Indeed, to them, I was invisible. And then, I would report to Old Hop, or whoever I was accompanying, what I had overheard as the Europeans talked amongst themselves. Thus, my earlier status as Old Hop's "Little Flea" continued, though not only to him.

Richard and I spent as much time together as possible on those first days of our reunion, nestled in my room behind Mourning Dove's house. Aside from the joyous joining of our bodies, we had much information to share.

"I've found an ideal location for a trading post," Richard told me. "With my family's trading connections in Winchester and Charles Town and Gist's ties to the aristocracy further east, we have the opportunity to establish a profitable foothold in trade with the Native people."

I quickly saw the advantage of this for my People. "Trading with both South Carolina and Virginia, we should be able to negotiate better terms."

"Aye, Hester, you see the benefit to the Cherokee. But even if Gist and I give better terms for deer hides and pelts, there's still a big margin of profit. We'll do well on this venture, giving me the means for other ideas I have. I'll be a rich man someday."

I snuggled against him in the comfort of the furs that lined my sleeping pad, his excitement making me smile. This talk of profit and advancement mattered greatly to men of his race but held little value for me or mine. Our community was where we placed our value, not the manufactured goods that wealth could buy.

However, I realized that those values had changed dramatically in recent years. Women desired more trade goods that they believed made their lives easier. Some men were adopting European clothing styles. And, of course, guns and ammunition had become a necessity—no longer a rarity.

He confided, "We've chosen a spot on the Long Island of the Holston River to establish our trading post."

"I know where that is. I know it well. It's near the forks of the Holston and where the Great Warrior Path connects our southern lands to the north. And that is also where the Great Trading Path to the Ohio country begins."

"Aye, Hester, 'tis the perfect place where travelers from all directions converge on their journeys. They will want to purchase goods from us."

I grew quiet, pondering what he had revealed to me while he chattered about his grand plans for the future.

He surely knew that not only was it a strategic location but also that many nations had long regarded Long Island as a sacred place. It is part of our hunting grounds, teeming with wildlife in a pristine, untouched forest. Because all rivers flow into the Great Water, they hold spiritual significance for us. Large islands like this one serve as resting spots in these holy waterways. Discussions and treaties held on Long Island of the Holston were thought to be blessed by the Great Spirit. It was such an important place to us—even sacred—that I doubted the elders would allow a trading post to be established there.

He continued with details of their grandiose plans, which I found disturbing. Finally, I excused myself, telling him Mother needed me to help with the refugees. I sought a quiet place to think about this.

It was unsettling to think that perhaps Richard was attracted to me not so much for who I was but for my close ties to Old Hop and my kinsmen Saluy and Oconostota, as well as my friend Attacullaculla. Perhaps he anticipated that I could influence their decision to permit him to establish a trading post on our sacred island.

Confused about my feelings for him, which conflicted with practical thoughts, I sought my mother's advice. Mourning Dove quickly recognized the essence of what troubled me.

"I am proud that your eyes are open," she told me. "But you can put your mind at ease. As much as you are esteemed, the elders would not allow a trading post to exist on Long Island if it did not benefit the People."

Thus reassured, I joined my lover in his plans to establish a foothold in the lucrative trade of White man's goods for Cherokee deerskins and pelts.

CHAPTER 51

Recollection

Autumn 1810
82 years old
Baldridge Creek, GA

An early snowfall has blanketed the road connecting our farm to the outside world, making travel by wagon difficult. The family was initially pleased with the unexpected holiday but grew restless by the third day of confinement. My cabin was shuttered, its fireplace cold, as I took refuge with the family in the big house.

After a hearty breakfast of oatmeal and biscuits slathered with butter and jelly made from Caty's peach orchard, Moses sets aside his law book and bids me tell stories of the Old Times.

"Yes, please, Granny," a chorus of voices pleads from the children. "Tell us how it was when you were young." "Tell us more about our grandfather, Richard."

"Yes, Granny," Nancy chimes in, smiling. "Please do something to entertain these unruly children so that I can do my work."

"Very well," I agree and shuffle to the rocking chair my son has positioned as close as possible to the fireplace, for I find the cold eats at my bones. The colorful stuffed cotton pads Nancy has sewn for the seat and back provide a welcome relief to my bony backside, as all my body fat has somehow shifted to my belly. Darling Rachel drapes a vivid red and yellow blanket she crocheted over my lap, tucking it around my feet. Lucretia brings a cup of warm milk, which was once a rare luxury but is now a morning ritual.

Warmed inside and out by the loving attentions of my family, I settle comfortably, sipping the milk and considering what story to share with them. There is so much I want them to know that it is difficult to choose. They sit or stand quietly, allowing me to gather my thoughts. Nancy begins baking something for an afternoon treat for the children. Caty busies herself with seed catalogs. I see George occupied with a book in his room through the open door, but he sets it aside when I begin to speak.

"I've told you many stories of my youth," I begin. "But today, I will speak of when I was a young woman and of the early years with Richard."

I sigh and shift in my chair, made uncomfortable not so much by its wooden enclosure as by surfacing memories.

"I will speak of these things—of that time—for you must know the truth of it."

CHAPTER 52

Painful Memories

Autumn 1810
82 years old
Baldridge Creek, GA

I have regaled my grandchildren, and now great-grandchildren, with tales of my youth so they will know their heritage. However, I have buried the events of my years with Richard so deeply in the recesses of my mind that I have no desire to resurrect them; it is too painful. Now, with their prodding, the memory of that time is as vivid as though it were yesterday. *Where should I start?* I wonder? *How much should I tell them?*

My family is quiet with expectation. My silence unsettles them as I rock, lost in thought. They wait for me to begin.

"What happened next, Granny?" Lucretia encourages me. "What happened after Grandfather Richard came to you?"

"Yes, Granny, please tell us about the trading post on Long Island," Sallie pleads.

"That place you mention is no longer referred to as the Long Island of the Holston River," Moses states. He has traveled east occasionally and is familiar with such matters. "There is a large town there now, called Kingsport, in the state named Tennessee. Our People no longer go there for meetings and treaty-making, as it is completely overrun with the White settlement."

My heart grows heavy with this news, even though I knew it must have changed over the many years since my youth. Still, I wish to remember how it was when I went there with Richard. It was on the banks of that sacred place that we began our life together. There, I allowed his seed to take root, and I carried within me someone who would become our son, George.

Disturbed by the reminder of the changes wrought by time and displacement, I am reluctant to discuss events from that period of my life. However, my family is growing restless with being confined to the house. The snowfall has turned to sleet, encasing the farm in a layer of ice. Apart from the essential care of the livestock, no outside chores will take place today, as walking outside is treacherous even for the most nimble.

"What happened next?" "Tell us more about Long Island." "When did Grandfather Richard build his estate?" "Did you ever meet his White wife, Rhoda?" I am pelted with stinging questions, much like the sleet that continues to assault the house.

Querulously, I begin speaking, silencing their questions. "What shall I tell you?" I ask. "Should I tell of Wurth visiting us on Long Island and how Gist immediately took advantage of her good nature and took her as his wife? I was not pleased, as my distrust of him only grew over time. We established a dwelling and trading post on Long Island, but his mistreatment of her was painful for me.

"She, too, allowed his seed to take root, and the two of us watched our bellies expand with the lives within. Her son, who became known as Sequoyah, was like a brother to my son. And just as we had done with our mothers when we were babies, they suckled from both of us."

"Sequoyah?" John asks. "Is that the same Sequoyah we know now? That strange man who mutters to himself and scratches symbols in the dirt?"

"Yes, that is he. It was a relief to me when Wurth left Gist and returned to her village with her little boy, although I missed her terribly."

I pause, closing my eyes to their expectant faces, waiting for further revelations. "Their venture on Long Island failed, and my suspicion of Gist proved justified. He was disloyal to Richard, sowing seeds of distrust among the elders of my People to advance himself.

"I returned to my room behind Mourning Dove's cabin. Richard had gained stature with my kinsmen, not only because of our bond but also due to his eagerness to learn the skills of a Cherokee warrior. He became one of the rare individuals who moved freely between both the European and Cherokee worlds. He was equally at home in our Council Houses as the drawing rooms of influential White men.

"Richard was with me often, but there were long absences when he returned to his family in Winchester. There, he became acquainted with George Washington, who was little more than a boy at his first military post in Winchester. Now, Washington has risen to the highest office of the new United States. However, when they were both young men, Richard declined Washington's request to gather Cherokee warriors to accompany him in the expulsion of the French from the Ohio River Valley.

"Richard knew Washington well enough to know that he was too inexperienced to lead such an expedition. He also knew that in his arrogance, Washington would not listen to advice from Richard or his Cherokee allies on negotiating peace—or waging war, should it come to that. His judgment proved sound, as Washington's bungling led to what became known as the French and Indian War, which, I have since learned, also fueled wars among European nations.

"I believe Washington still harbors resentment toward Richard and the Cherokee People because of that initial clash from his youth."

"Grandfather Richard knew President Washington!" Moses whispers, sounding impressed by the revelation.

"Yes," I answered, "Richard knew many powerful men of the Colonies. His family connections in Winchester and on the East Coast earned him favor with Governor Robert Dinwiddie of Virginia. His relationship with me and his ties to Cherokee leaders made him a valuable ally for Dinwiddie.

The governor was a small, rude man who did not acknowledge me on the occasions when our paths crossed—to him, I was invisible."

I pause, and they wait expectantly. Everyone is silent. Even George left his office and came to sit at Nancy's table to listen to me. However, I pay them no mind, pausing only to reach for my pipe and tamp its bowl with tobacco. I struggle to leave my rocker, but James quickly lights a brand from the fireplace and puts it to the tobacco. Its acrid smoke isn't the only reason tears well up in my eyes.

"Richard returned to our home in Estatoe infrequently, and he would tell me of his adventures. Thus, I relived the harrowing Sandy Creek expedition. Dinwiddie had tasked him with leading Virginia soldiers and Cherokee warriors in a raid against the Shawnees who were raiding the colony's frontier."

I pause to puff on my pipe, my mind crowded with memories I have pushed aside for many years. My boys and men would savor the tales he shared about serving with British General John Forbes when he captured Fort Duquesne. Richard often boasted that he was the first British subject to enter the fort, now the site of a town called Pittsburgh. Perhaps I will share that story with them another time. But not this day.

"It was when he accepted a post as the Indian agent for the colony of Maryland that we experienced our first major falling out. Before he left on that mission, he approached me bearing a document I was to keep in a safe place should I need it. He knew he might meet his death during this assignment. The raids on our towns were becoming more frequent, and life was precarious; our mountain home was no longer a sanctuary. George was a small boy. Neely was still a toddler, and I was carrying someone within who would be our daughter, Kate."

I hear exclamations from my daughters-in-law and the girls. How did they not know how close in age George and his sisters are? They express surprise that I allowed Richard's seed to take root so often that I bore these children in close succession. I pause to reflect on this and decide to tell them how it was.

"Those were unimaginably difficult times. When our villages were raided and our homes burned to the ground, our packets of wild carrot seeds, meant to prevent a child, were also turned to ash. It wasn't only our traditional enemies who destroyed our towns; the settlers were now determined to crush us until we ceased to exist.

"These men were ruthless and showed no mercy. Women were raped, their breasts cut off and saved as souvenirs; babies were tossed in the air and bayoneted as they fell to the ground; the manhoods of young boys were cut off, and they were left to bleed to death. Our fields were torched, and food stores were destroyed. We who survived such vicious onslaught entered the winter months without shelter or food."

I pause; my voice is hoarse with emotion, yet my eyes do not see my family gathered around this snug kitchen, where the aroma of a hearty breakfast still permeates the air. Instead, I look inward at the visions I have pushed from my consciousness for decades.

"Mourning Dove was such a woman—one of ours who was raped and left to die in pools of her own blood as her home was set aflame."

I pause to drink from the cup of milk held in my trembling hand.

"Like other warriors, when Richard returned to find me in such a state, it was natural for us to seek comfort by joining with each other. Even if I had the magic of the wild carrot seed, I do not know if I would have used it. Women ached from the loss of so many of our People, and it was a comfort to know that life would go on amid such despair."

My daughters-in-law nod their heads in agreement. They, too, have found comfort in this way. Uniting hearts and bodies during times of grief is natural.

"The document Richard asked me to keep safe was a copy of his will. I later realized that Richard had an attorney draft it to protect me. European men valued these documents to guide their families in managing their inherited wealth. In his will, Richard named an Indian woman named Prachey—me—to be given to his daughter, Margaret, in the event of his death. He assured me he had chosen her instead of his wife to prevent

Rhoda from selling me. *Selling* me, he said. *Selling me!* As if I were his property!

"I was furious with him. After all his time with my People, did he not understand that I was not chattel? I was not his responsibility but my own and that of my Clan. Should he die in battle, my Clan would care for me and our children. I would not be subjected to seeking protection for our children with his White family. I tore the paper in half, cast it into the fire, and turned my back on him. I would not acknowledge him as he left our town for his assignment in faraway Maryland. Indeed, I thought I was done with that arrogant man."

My family's exclamations of surprise and distress validate my anger. What could have possessed him to do such a thing, they wondered?

"But when he returned with only scars from his battles, I had moved past my anger and welcomed him into the home my uncles built for me and our children," I continue.

"He had become a respected leader among his Cherokee brethren, leading them in battle. Out of necessity, our warriors had become mercenaries, no longer hunting scarce game for survival but instead receiving trade goods to fight one tribe of Whites on behalf of another.

"Although I acknowledged the necessity, I opposed this because, like most of my people, we simply wished for the Europeans to depart from our mountain home and let us live in peace. The warriors' battles against one faction incited retribution from another. The Europeans needed little justification to raid and plunder our villages—typically when the warriors were away, leaving women, elderly men, and children vulnerable."

I cannot speak, for the painful memory of that time has stilled my tongue. My family remains silent, allowing me to compose myself before continuing.

"Richard assured me that this would pass, as yet another treaty had been made with the Colonies to establish a 'boundary line' between them and the Cherokee Nation. He planned to create a plantation and trade post on the border. 'It will serve as a buffer to protect the People,' he reassured me.

However, I had my doubts, for I knew the Whites would never respect a line drawn on a map.

"But Richard boasted about the wealth he and Rhoda would accumulate from his 'plantation' and trading post. His greed angered me, and I turned my back on him again."

Even after all this time, I feel the outrage rising and realize that I am rocking furiously in my chair. Taking deep breaths, I calm myself and continue. My family needs to hear about this, and I will tell it only once.

"Due to his high standing with the Cherokee leaders and with Saluy's assistance, Richard obtained approval from the elders at Chota for a land grant of twelve square miles—by White men's measurement—just within the Boundary Line in exchange for the cancellation of their trading debts. There, he would establish his plantation.

"However, the South Carolina Superintendent of Indian Affairs, John Stuart, complained to the governor. Stuart, a redheaded Scotsman like my father, had formed a relationship with Mollie, that little girl from my childhood—my sister. His thick hair stood out as though he were alarmed. The Native people called him "Bushyhead," and the name stuck for him and the children Mollie bore him before she died prematurely in childbirth."

I sense a rustling among the children. They knew of the Bushyhead family but were unaware of the reason for their name or their connection to my sister, Mollie. The room remains hushed as I rock, sip, and reflect on days gone by.

"Richard told me that Stuart came from aristocracy, while he came from trade, leading to Stuart's higher status in the White world. Once again, the distinction among Europeans is incomprehensible—evaluated by birth rather than by actions!

"Although Stuart also engaged in land speculation, he was not punished due to his high standing. However, the English court found Richard guilty of acquiring Indian land in violation of their laws. He surrendered the deed, but the following month, he obtained another deed from our Cherokee leaders that granted our son, George—instead of Richard—those exact twelve square miles.

"Richard was nothing, if not tenacious—he would have what he wanted no matter!

"George, by then a young man, traveled to England, where Richard's family connections aided him in acquiring British citizenship. Upon his return, our son, now a citizen of both England and the Cherokee Nation, transferred all but a small portion of the land to his father. Of course, Richard's cleverness only further infuriated the governor."

My grandchildren are surprised by this news, as their father has never mentioned that he once sailed to England and back. "Tell us about your trip, Father," several exclaims.

"Hush now, that was long ago in another time. This is your Granny's story. Perhaps I will tell you of mine someday."

I pause for a moment and then continue. "He chose the most significant location, the falls of the Reedy River, as the site for his plantation, 'Great Plains.' He brought his White family—Rhoda and their three children—along with twelve slaves to clear large areas for planting orchards and plowing the land for grain crops. He hired men from a place called Italy to build a grand house, a trading post, and barns. A gristmill and sawmill were established along the river.

"It angered me because my lover was doing exactly what those other Europeans had done: claiming what was ours for himself. It did not matter if he told me it was for the good of the Cherokee, for I did not believe him. It was for greed—the accumulation of wealth by which White men measure their worth.

"His wife, Rhoda, ignored my children and me, pretending we did not exist. However, our two sons, so close in age, quickly became fast friends, as children often do. My daughters sensed the disdain from his two daughters alongside Rhoda, and although the four girls were of similar ages, they avoided any contact with each other. As did she and I.

"Even after all this time, Richard understood very little about Cherokee women. He offered to build a small house in the traditional style for me and our children. I was angry with him for still not grasping our ways—the traditions of the Cherokee people. As the construction of his plantation progressed, I returned to Chota and the cabin built for me by my uncles.

"George, however, visited Great Plains frequently. I wondered how Rhoda coped with seeing how close her husband was to the son of his so-called 'side wife.' It must have annoyed her, but I did not care. Instead, I settled into our routine of living apart and welcomed Richard whenever he came to me, Rhoda be damned."

I sense George's discomfort with his children's and wives' questioning looks. They are curious about his life before their time, and he will soon have to tell his story.

"Richard established himself as what the Europeans call the 'gentry,' but I chose to remain with my People while the American Colonies moved towards separating from England. Richard urged me to live on the plantation he built, believing I would be safer from the depredations of White men on our villages; however, I disagreed. My mother's teachings on the healing properties of herbs had become invaluable, and to my surprise, I was sought after as a medicine woman. My People needed me.

"Richard sided with the British during rising tensions as the Colonies separated from England. He became a Tory captain, leading Cherokee warriors in skirmishes against the so-called Patriots. It angered me that he now fought alongside those same red-coated soldiers who had destroyed our towns. Men's loyalties in war are fluid—changing with what suits their momentary needs.

"At the outbreak of what became known as the Revolutionary War, he was captured and held in chains in Charles Town for nine months. His house and plantation buildings were destroyed by Patriots—his neighbors—and his livestock and expensive horses were confiscated. Rhoda and her daughters were turned out and forced to fend for themselves.

"As you surely know, those lands seized by the South Carolina government are the lands that George has worked so diligently to reclaim."

All my family looks to George, comprehension dawning. They have indeed heard him rant about the lost estate of Great Plains, especially when rum ruled his tongue, but now they have a greater understanding of what that place meant to him. They will pester him to learn more about his time with his father and his White brother, Richard Jr.

"When I heard the news of the assault on his family, I rushed to see what could be done to help my rival, but she had fled to safety with friends in Augusta. It was just as well, as my People were under attack by the 'regulators,' as they called themselves—men who used the war to justify their own avarice—who were declaring all-out war against what remained of the Cherokee People.

"Those were dreadful times. The raids on Cherokee villages were relentless. Richard was seldom with me, as he was a British officer fighting against the Patriots—often accompanied by one or both of his sons while he led Cherokee warriors into battle."

I pause momentarily, my voice growing hoarse, and note that my grand-children look at their father with amazement. It is undoubtedly hard for them to imagine their father, now a man of many years, as a youth fighting alongside Cherokee warriors and British soldiers. George will be pressured to share his stories in the months and years to come. They may give me rest and shift their focus to their father.

But for now, even though I am exhausted, I continue. "After the war, the British granted the Loyalists land grants and pensions in the Bahamas, where Richard spent his final years. We were separated not only by his life as an influential White man with a family but also by great distance and the Caribbean Sea."

Lucretia sighs, her eyes brimming with tears. "Did you think you would never see him again, Granny?"

"Indeed, I thought I would not. I believed he would be just a memory—a memory of great love that made my heart ache. But no, he would return to me when I least expected it."

Lucretia smiles wistfully, her desire for romance satisfied. But I can not let her have that illusion, for she is a nearly grown woman who must know the truth of it.

"Those years just before and during the war were terrible for the People. Settlers began moving into areas that had been our towns—destroyed by neighboring nations, settlers and English soldiers alike. They were pleased to discover land that was already cleared for building their log cabins, along with fields lying fallow and ready for planting since the previous inhabitants— my People—had been displaced.

"Any of us who survived the war went further west, as did my family and I, those who still drew breath."

I pause, the room hushed, as I think of our warriors who died by violence trying to protect us from European men. Attacullaculla. Oconostota. Saluy. Willewanah. Terrapin. Bark. So many of our brave men dead before their time.

The room remains quiet, allowing me to dwell on my thoughts. Tears streaming down my cheeks dampened my bodice. I take a deep breath and continue. "I bore yet another child during that time before the Revolutionary War," I whispered, for I had never spoken of the tiny girl buried beside an unnamed stream somewhere deep in the mountains.

"We had allowed them to build forts intended to protect us, but they only brought more grief to the People, serving as places of safety for the redcoats between attacks on my People."

I paused, allowing a memory to surface. "I cannot speak of that detested Fort Prince George, where the British killed twelve of our beloved men, for it is too painful."

I pause again, reflecting on that terrible time and all that was lost. "Our warriors sought retribution by massacring English soldiers at Fort Loudoun, but that only served to enrage them further. In their fury, they destroyed Estatoe Town—my home.

"We had little warning before the soldiers descended upon us with no warriors for our defense. Once more, as was typical for them, they killed indiscriminately. Many unarmed women, children, and the elderly died horrible deaths. Our village was burned to the ground, offering inadequate protection against winter's harshness. Our food stores were destroyed, and we survivors were left to starve.

"After they left and we buried the dead, we built crude shelters to the best of our ability. We scavenged insufficient food from the fields that had been set ablaze. We snared and trapped any rabbits and squirrels we could as the game had retreated deep into the forest. The surviving elderly men and women refused to eat, giving their share to children or nursing mothers. They willingly sacrificed themselves so that the young could survive.

"I was carrying someone within, but my first priority was to feed my three little children so they might survive the winter. My skin lay slack on bone, and there was little in my body to nourish the newest babe nestled in my womb.

"We thought we were safe from marauders in that small valley where we had sought shelter, a cluster of women and children with only a few elderly men. But they found us. We posed no danger to them, yet we had become a sport for those evil men who had no cause to destroy us.

"They descended upon us, catching us off guard during an early morning raid. Their horses trampled many as they fled toward the safety of the forest. They shot at us, and when their guns ran out of bullets, they leaped off their horses and pursued us with bayonets.

"All that saved me and my children was that I had awakened early, my stomach aching in that familiar way, and I took my children to the forest to relieve themselves. When the raid began, I rushed them to a small copse overrun with blackberry bushes.

"'Hurry,'" I urged them. Although the pains were growing stronger, I led them deep into the tangled vegetation, out of sight of the wicked ones. 'Hush,' I whispered, and they remained silent despite the wounds from the blackberry bushes on their tender skin. We Cherokee mothers taught our children from an early age to be quiet like a fawn.

"The pains continued, and I knew it was too early. The child was arriving far too soon. I found a stick to hold between my teeth to muffle my moans as we could hear the marauders crashing through the woods, searching for those of us who had escaped the village.

"Indeed, my labor was brief, for she was so small. She slipped out from my body, though I tried not to push but to keep her safe within. She was tiny and covered with fine hair and a thick white substance. Her head fit in my cupped hand as I lifted her to my breast, the birth cord still attached to me.

"I thought she was dead. She lay so still and lifeless. But with a gasp, she drew in a breath and let out a faint cry."

"'What's that?' I heard on the other side of the blackberry bramble.

"They were nearby."

"I held her delicate face against my breast, guiding her rosebud mouth to my nipple. She rooted weakly, searching for the lifeline that even the youngest babies will suckle. The children watched with round eyes full of amazement at this child who had just emerged from their mother. Fearful of the sounds of men thrashing so close to the place where we hid, they held each other tightly and remained silent.

"The baby was weak, her limbs splayed and her breathing ragged. She made only soft mewing sounds as she nuzzled my breast, trying to latch on to my nipple. I heard the sound of a man stepping softly just a short distance from where we were cowering.

"My child opened her mouth to wail. I had no choice. I placed my fingers over her nose and pinched, as we do when teaching our children not to cry.

"'Do you see anything?' I heard a man say, so close to our hiding place that his stench reached my nose.

"'I could swear I heard what sounded like a baby,' a second one replied.

"'Humph,' his companion snorted. 'Are you sure it wasn't a rabbit caught in a snare?'

"'Damme, man, I know the difference between rabbits and babies. A wench is hiding around here with her bairn.'

"'We'll find the squaw and have some fun with her, whadda you say.'

"And they laughed as we cowered, remaining still and barely breathing.

"It felt like hours as we listened to them moving around, chatting with one another and boasting about what they would do to me when they caught me. However, their voices eventually grew fainter as they drifted away from our hiding spot.

"We took deep breaths once we knew they had gone, and I removed my fingers from the baby's nose. But she was limp and blue.

"She did not cry. She did not breathe. She had gone to the Spirit World as I held her in my arms, my own fingers suffocating her."

CHAPTER 53

No More

Autumn 1810
82 years old
Baldridge Creek, GA

Weakened and hoarse, I wrap Rachel's blanket around my shoulders. "That is enough for today, Mother," the ever-practical Nancy gently scolds, taking a bowl of cooled soup from my lap. "Perhaps you should rest before the evening meal."

As if awakening from a trance, I look around the room and see the faces of my grandchildren and great-grandchildren, turned to me like sunflowers to the sun. Varying degrees of distress and amazement are on their youthful faces, and I realize they have been listening to my talk throughout the day. Vaguely, I recall Nancy and Caty calling the family to a mid-day meal of soup and placing a bowl and spoon in my lap. Occasionally, I was handed a mug of fresh water to sip. But the soup went untasted, and now my mouth is dry again. Furthermore, I am in desperate need of the privy.

I struggle to push myself from the rocking chair that is reluctant to release me from its embrace. Standing, Rachel's blanket pools around my feet, and the urge to go to the privy is overshadowed by the realization that I will not make it. The chamber pot tucked under my bed would serve as a practical solution. Yet, my back refuses to straighten, nor will my feet move.

George notices my distress and scoops me into his arms like a child. He carries me to my room, and Caty, always considerate, helps me on and off the chamber pot. I am relieved when that warm, pungent stream is released into the waiting receptacle. I also feel relief that I did not soil myself like a child.

I welcome their attentions as I am helped to my bed, which Nancy has warmed with coals from the fireplace in a brass bedwarmer, and layers of quilts are tucked around me.

"Rest now, Mother," George urges me. "The evening meal will be ready when you awaken. I know there is much more to tell, but only in the fullness of time."

At the evening meal, I find myself ravenous and ask for seconds. The children are careful not to mention what I told them; instead, they chatter about their friends and school, which is the main interest of the young. I am grateful for their thoughtfulness, as the heaviness of my heart is lightened by the normalcy of their banter this evening. It began to snow again in the afternoon, the flakes now falling with greater ferocity as night overtakes the countryside. There will be no school again tomorrow.

In the quietness of the night, once again nestled in the warm cocoon of my bed, my thoughts revisit memories of the past, and grief overcomes me. Tears soak the down pillow on which I rest my head. I grieve for the child I lost to save those who lived.

I have told them the truths they must know. I will speak of it no more.

CHAPTER 54

Snow Hill

Autumn 1818
90 years old
Snow Hill, SC

With great relief, I hear the sound of metal striking metal—the clang of a blacksmith's shop—an early sign that we are approaching our destination. Shifting my sore backside in the saddle, I straighten my back and square my shoulders as my mount gingerly picks her way along the wagon-rutted road to the Snow Hill trading post.

This sturdy horse from George's stable knows her way to the water trough, requiring no guidance from me. This is fortunate, for I am in no condition to attend to her needs, faithful companion though she may be. Now that the journey is over, it is all I can do to remain upright on her back.

My son and our traveling companions dismount and exchange friendly greetings with LeRoy Hammond, the owner of this trading post overlooking the Savannah River at the border between Georgia and South Carolina.

I, too, would love to stand and stretch, arching my back and extending my arms overhead as the men do, but my old body refuses to cooperate, and pride prevents me from asking for help. To hide my reluctance to dismount, I lean into the horse's neck, scratching behind her ears as she shakes her head and snorts, annoyed at being distracted from quenching her thirst.

I shift my weight in the stirrups, releasing my feet, and attempt to swing my right leg over the horse's back, but my hip joints have been spread to their maximum for so long that they are locked in place and refuse to cooperate. Once again, my body fails me. Finally, George sees my dilemma and, being a good son, comes to my rescue. Though his body has grown slack, he is strong. He effortlessly releases me from captivity, placing my feet firmly on the dusty ground.

My legs are reluctant to bear the weight of my body, and I grasp George's arm to avoid staggering like a foolish old woman. He steadies me with an embrace around my shoulders, pulling me to him as he calls out to Hammond, "Hey LeRoy, you remember my mother, Hester, don't you?"

"Good Lord, Hester," LeRoy exclaims as he approaches me. "I can't believe you've traveled all this distance at your age!"

Bristling, I give George a warning glance and shift away from him, suddenly unwilling to appear in need of his support. He suppresses a chuckle and steps forward to grasp Hammond's outstretched hand.

"LeRoy, there's no convincing this old woman once she sets her mind on something. Nothing would suffice; she had to come with us. And on horseback, no less!"

"How old are you, Hester? You've been an old woman for as long as I've known you," the idiot has the nerve to ask me. Why do younger people think their elders have no feelings? That they can say anything they wish? The scathing look I cast his way makes his cheeks flush with embarrassment. I hope he feels the sting of my rebuke.

"Mother is as tough as seasoned leather," George boasts, drawing me into the circle of his arm, perhaps to prevent me from scratching out LeRoy's eyes. "As far as we can estimate, she must be comin' on to ninety years these days. Still, she lives alone, takes care of herself, and walks miles across the countryside to visit friends and family. We could all hope for such a healthy state at that age."

Feeling somewhat mollified by his praise, I release LeRoy from my scorching gaze and move toward the nearest rocking chair on the porch, seeking refuge from the sun.

As if I were not here, George continues his praise of me. "She still has her wits about her, too. I swear her memory is sharper than mine, and she's as strong-willed as ever."

Indeed, he and I battled fiercely when I announced my intention to accompany him to the Snow Hill trading post one more time. I might not have made such a fuss, but Caty and Nancy told me I was too old to make the trip. Their objections only strengthened my resolve.

Too old! Ha! I was determined to show them and the whole family that I could still sit a horse as well as ever. My pride compelled me to ride the bedamned horse the entire way when I could have sat upon a nest of furs and blankets in the back of the wagon that followed us. Once committed to that prideful path, I refused to permit myself a comfortable journey, even after we were out of sight of George's house and its watchful women.

LeRoy and George each grasp one of my elbows, shortening their stride while easily chatting above my head, and walk slowly to the porch that extends the length of Hammond's trading post. They pause as I navigate the steps carefully, their conversation about the weather uninterrupted, before continuing their pride-saving support to the rocking chair beside the door.

What relief to sit! My body assumes its more natural alignment and settles into the padded seat and shaped back of this hand-hewn oaken marvel. Gratefully, I accept the cup of cool spring water offered by LeRoy. The men move away, their talk turning to more serious topics of hunts and politics, and I lean my head back, a sigh of relief escaping.

I awaken from a doze, and the pain in my hips has eased. With my eyes half-closed, I enjoy the warmth of the late afternoon sun on my face, the shade having vanished. I am comforted by the familiar sound of men's voices speaking softly in our fluid Cherokee language, chuckling at some teasing remark as they exchange news and speculate on politics. It never changes, this talk of men. It is always of politics. And I never tire of listening to them.

Turtle, that sweet baby I helped bring into the world when news of Richard's death in the Bahamas arrived, comes to me with a plate of victuals and a cup of coffee. I find, surprisingly, that I am ravenous. Considerate as he is, I know he has been watching to see when I would awaken so he could come unbidden with food for his Granny. I smile at him, for our roles have reversed, and he is now the caretaker while I am the one who is provided for.

I quickly devour the beans and squash, handing him the empty bowl to return to our companions who have set up camp near the creek alongside other travelers. We will spend the night at the trading post and return to our home on Baldridge Creek at daybreak.

"Have you finished your chores?" I ask him. "Then come, sit by your old Granny." His warmth leaning into my leg offers comfort against the late afternoon chill. I rub his scalp with my bony fingertips, and he stills beside me just as his father, my George, always did.

From this vantage point, I can see the rutted road winding along the contours of the land, busy with more travelers seeking shelter for the evening. The angry curses of a drover, whose squealing hogs have been scattered by dogs chasing a bitch in heat, catch our attention. Turtle and I smile at his antics as he runs to and fro, brandishing a stick, trying to herd the hogs into a makeshift pen for the night.

At my gentle nudge, Turtle races forward to help, his nimble legs darting this way and that as he redirects the path of one heading for the safety of the nearby woods. The herdsman purchased these summer-fattened hogs from Georgia farmers and will take them to the city market to sell for a profit, following a trail that was once familiar to me.

I recall that the Great Trading Path wound along rivers and valleys toward Philadelphia. Tributaries to the south lead to the coastal cities of Charleston, Williamsburg, Washington, and other European settlements. Northward branches lead to the mountainous homeland of the Cherokee, the Real People.

"There was a time," I murmur to Turtle as he settles beside me again, "when I was young like you. I traveled the length and breadth of this country. I knew this trail and all its branches like the back of my hand, for I traversed them many times."

I brush a lock of hair from his forehead as he gazes at me quizzically, and I can tell it is hard for him to imagine his stooped old Granny as a young girl eager for adventure. I smile, for it is always so: the young believe they are the first to encounter the thrill of new experiences.

"It is so," I tell him. "I do not lie." But then I smile and add, "However, tomorrow, when we return home, I will ride in the wagon."

***

I am glad to make the return trip in the wagon, snug in a nest made of bags of flour. However, the wagon jostled over deep ruts in the road carved by previous travelers. The contraption often tilts precariously, tossing me into an unsuspecting crate or barrel. Splashes of muddy water from the road startle me from an unexpected doze. A recent rainstorm has made the slick Georgia clay soil difficult for the horses to pull the wagon, which is heavily laden with European goods my son and his family consider essential.

"Ha! Could they survive if they suddenly became dependent on the old ways?" I mutter, then hush myself with a hand over my mouth. I have developed the habit of talking to myself, a trait I associate with the elderly. Even worse, when I was alone in my cabin the other day, I heard myself not only ask a question aloud but answer it as well.

I manage to wiggle into a more comfortable position in the wagon, shifting my view from Jacob's rear end to the countryside we pass. Although Jacob has been George's slave for many years, he feels more like family than property. I wonder why George does not free him with emancipation papers. Perhaps he believes Jacob and the family he has created within ours are safer by remaining George's property.

Without that protection, he would be vulnerable to capture by slave catchers and sold to a southern cotton plantation. On the other hand, his nappy gray hair and stooped back might afford him some protection from enslavement by another. Still... I disapprove of this notion of one man "owning" another.

From my improved vantage point in the wagon, I watch the countryside roll by much better than I could on horseback. Back then, my focus was on staying upright in the saddle. Now, from the comfort of the wagon bed, I can fully appreciate the changes since I last made this journey several years ago.

The landscape along the well-traveled road is dotted with the homesteads of White settlers. Plumes of smoke in the distance indicate other cabins carved from the countryside. There has been no easing of ships bringing immigrants from Europe—the land-hungry White men continue to pour into this new United States like an unending river. And, as they will, they invade our peaceful countryside with Conestoga wagons filled with farming utensils to defile the earth, as if we had not lived since time began without destroying everything in our path.

My family has settled in the valley formed by Baldridge Creek alongside other mixed-blood families. They have fully adapted to the European way of life to blend in—attempting to be unnoticed in this new world.

It heartens me to know that some families—mostly full-bloods—escaped into the formidable mountains known as Snowbird during those terrible times. The trails leading into that region are too rugged for horses, and the White men were too lazy to risk the treacherous footpaths and hunt them down as they did the rest of us. Due to their isolation, those Cherokee managed to survive mainly by relying on what they could remember from the old ways—living off the land and not engaging in trade for European goods.

At times, I wish we had done so, and I wonder if it is possible to hide in plain sight among the Europeans.

I grow weary from such thoughts. My eyes are sore from seeing this defilement. I burrow deeper into the soft bags of my makeshift nest and close my eyes as sleep overcomes me.

CHAPTER 55

News from Snow Hill

Spring 1820
92 years old
Baldridge Creek, GA

I sit quietly on my porch, enjoying my pipe and watching the distant trees darken in the deepening dusk. The men have come from the cornfield, laying down their hoes and washing up at the basin beside the door, taking off their boots before stepping onto Nancy's clean wood floor. I wait patiently, knowing my son will soon join me. Once a fierce Cherokee warrior, he is now a farmer, toiling in the fields alongside his sons and slaves.

Soon, I see him crossing the short distance from the main house, his steps heavy. Although his arms are empty, his shoulders slump under an unseen burden. Wordlessly, he leans down to kiss me on the forehead, placing his hand on my shoulder. He enters my cabin, and I hear him rustling around. I welcome the mug of water he brings me.

"Is the corn planted?" I ask as he settles into the second rocking chair on my porch.

"'Tis done. Ready for the next spring rain."

We sit quietly, basking in each other's company in this ritual, which is our habit in fair weather. We watch lanterns illuminate the windows of the big meal. We smile at each other as two of his small grandchildren engage in a quarrel over a toy they both want. A firm, no-nonsense Nancy quickly solves the dispute.

George returned from LeRoy's trading post at Snow Hill late yesterday and was unusually quiet last night. I wait, and when he is ready, my son unburdens himself to me just like his father did.

He is concerned, and rightfully so, because recently, White men have become excited about discovering gold in our streams and rivers. The Cherokee have known about this unremarkable mineral for generations—ever since that Spaniard, DeSoto, wandered through our mountains in search of it. He showed our ancestors samples of what he was seeking and asked if they knew where to find more. They, of course, told him they did not to encourage the brash man to continue on his way.

Others have followed his path over the years, searching rivers and streams for the elusive stone they desire. We cannot understand their obsession; after all, what good is it? It cannot be eaten, and it is too soft to be crafted into a tool. While we have seen jewelry and coins made of gold, we still do not understand the White man's obsession with this rock.

Thus, yesterday, the men chuckled at LeRoy's story about a young boy, Conrad Reed, who found a peculiar stone while fishing in a stream near his father's farm just over the border in South Carolina. Curious about the large rock's unusual color, he took it home, where his mother was glad to use it as a doorstop. The stone sat there for several years until, out of curiosity, his father took it to a jeweler.

LeRoy told them that the jeweler refined the gold from the stone into an eight-inch gold bar and unscrupulously bought it from Reed for a paltry sum. Once John Reed realized he had been duped, he began gold panning in the streams of his farm. Recently, he started digging a hole in the ground, known as a "mine," in search of more gold-encrusted stones.

Soon, word spread, and others did the same. Recently, a slave found an even larger gold nugget, but this one was dangerously close to the border between South Carolina and Georgia, alarmingly close to our home.

Word of gold in our streams and rivers spread through the East like wildfire. LeRoy told the men he had sold all the picks, shovels, and shallow pans in his store to strangers who came to pan for gold. These men do not arrive in Conestoga wagons with farm tools and families. At most, LeRoy mentioned, they ride horses with a mule trailing behind, carrying camping gear. They're not here to stay; they come to make their fortunes.

George was not one of the men laughing at their foolishness, for he had seen such lust in White men before. "There will be more coming," he told those gathered on the trading post porch, "and they will not stop. They take our land and claim it belongs to them. Why would our rivers and streams be any different? If White men see something they desire, they find a way to take it."

The men fell silent at George's proclamation, for they saw the truth of it. But then, one of their midst added an even more sobering bit of news. White men have found an easy way to establish homesteads in Georgia.

He told them that he had heard about a White man who displaced a Cherokee family from their homestead by setting fire to their home and farm buildings. As the family sought shelter elsewhere, the White man and his family quickly moved in and repaired the buildings, claiming the property as their own. Thus, he immediately possessed an established farm, complete with fields and orchards.

So far, there is no indication that the Georgia government will nullify his claim. Indeed, the government seems to support such outright thievery. The men speculated that such assaults would continue since Cherokees have no legal rights in the state.

In fact, my son tells me that the Georgia legislature has recently passed laws aimed at abolishing Cherokee laws and our government. They plan to seize our remaining lands and sell them to White Georgians through a lottery. There's a rumor that they will buy individual farms if the Cherokee agree to move to a distant place called Ark-in-saw.

"The fight has gone out of me, Mother, for there is no way forward. We have all labored to make a comfortable life for our family. Should I sell this farm we have worked so hard to establish for less than it's worth? Should

I move the family west and start over—again? I am unwilling to leave this homestead."

His shoulders slumped, and he whispered, "Will the Europeans ever give us peace?"

I have no answer for my son. Both he and I know that we cannot stop the advancing tide of White men.

CHAPTER 56

Full Circle

Spring 1820
92 years old
Baldridge Creek, GA

It surprises me this morning to awaken, as I was sure last night that my time would come before dawn. But no, another day breaks and disturbs my slumber, and I realize I am still alive. Old age is taking its toll on me, making it increasingly difficult to make the short journey down the path to the creek for my morning ritual. Instead, I stand before a basin of water, cold from the night, my gnarled feet stinging on the bare wood floor. I face east and offer my morning prayers.

After bathing, I return to the comfort and warmth of my bed, where Sallie finds me as the sun begins its ascent. The sweet girl brings me a crust of bread and a slice of cooked bacon to break my fast. Shortly after, George enters my cabin to check on me. I can tell he is relieved to find me up and poking at the coals from last night's fire.

"Here, Mother," he gently scolds. "Let me take care of that for you." I gratefully settle into my rocking chair as he rekindles the fire. Its cheerful flames swiftly chase away the early morning chill, offering welcome relief for my aching bones.

George tells me that the family will go to a gathering of the People at Vann's plantation as they try to keep the old traditions alive. Of course, it will not be the same as the festivals of my youth, but I am pleased that periodically, the remnants of the Cherokee Nation come together in such a manner to celebrate the seasons.

"Will you go with us?" he asks, fully aware that I will decline, which I inevitably do. Consequently, we argue, as he is hesitant to leave me alone while I am intent on staying in the comfort of my home.

He is so focused on changing my mind that he is unaware his wives have entered the cabin and are busy preparing for my stay. The chamber pot has been emptied, and fresh water has been brought from the spring. Firewood and kindling are laid out, and enough food to feed a field hand is on my table.

He suggests that a family member stay with me, but I feign anger and refuse his offer. "They must participate in any gathering of the People," I scold my son. "I can manage on my own for a day."

"Then, Jacob can stay with you," he says.

But I also refuse that offer. Jacob and his family should go with him as the Negroes will have their own gathering. Jacob has friends and family among Vann's hundred or so slaves and will welcome the chance to visit them.

George shakes his head in exasperation at my stubbornness, but my son knows I will have my way as usual. He kisses my forehead and tells me to rest. The family will return late tonight. The milk cow is no longer producing milk for us but will soon deliver her calf. There's no need to hurry home to relieve her of the burden of teats heavy with milk.

I muster enough energy to walk with him to the clearing where the horse is hitched to the wagon. My daughters-in-law, their younger children, visiting sons and daughters with their mates, and grandchildren chatter happily as they load blankets and baskets of food into the wagon before clambering on themselves.

I smile and wave as they leave the homestead and head to Vann's place for the gathering. Then, I gratefully return to my bed, which has grown cold without my body's warmth. Soon, the fire dwindles to nothing, but the morning chill has faded, and once again, sleep overtakes me.

I wake to the sound of a horse snorting and stomping its feet. "Who could that be?" I wonder before remembering that there is no one to answer; George's slaves have gone with him to the gathering. I am alone, just as I insisted.

When I rouse myself to open the door of my cabin, I startle a filthy White man tying his horse to the porch railing. A firebrand, ready to be lit, rests against the post.

"Damme," he exclaims. "I thought all you damned injuns had left." And I realize, too late, that this man is up to no good. "Old Hester, why didn't you go with your family?" he asks, stepping closer to the porch. It dawns on me that this foul-smelling man knows me, even though I don't recognize him. That is not surprising, as many of these creatures look and sound alike.

"What do you want?" I ask, trying to speak forcefully and hide my concern. I realize this man, barely more than a boy, must have heard about the illegal seizure of Cherokee homesteads. And now, he's come to seek his fortune.

"I'm here to stake my claim on this property," he boasts, confirming my suspicions, and I am chilled to the bone with the knowledge of what he intends to do. He knew about the gathering and, expecting the farm to be unattended, had waited and watched nearby. He had not anticipated an elderly woman opening the door to greet him.

"You should have gone with your family, for I'm going to burn this place down—and you along with it if need be," he growls menacingly, hitching his threadbare pants on his skinny frame. Yet I notice a hint of uncertainty in his demeanor.

Outrage burns away the chill in my body, but I keep my face expressionless and fake a quiver as I reply, "I see what you are about, and I am too old and weak to stop you. But, please, allow me to enter my son's home to remove the family Bible before you burn down his house."

It is a ruse, of course, because while some Real People have embraced the Christian doctrine, or at least parts of it, George has not. He never allowed a Bible or any symbols of Christian ideology in his home. However, I have observed that even the most sinful White men are subdued by thoughts of their God and his son Jesus. Indeed, their ability to reason suffers as a result of their conviction. Therefore, I plead for a small mercy from him before he destroys my family's home.

I sense his hesitation and bewilderment. Not waiting for a reply, I drop the quilt around my shoulders and start for the steps—determination quelling the bubble of fear that threatens to paralyze me.

"Damme, old woman," he mutters as he steps aside. "Go on. Get the damned Bible." Even in these circumstances, I am furious at being called an old woman. How dare he! Suppressing my anger, I exaggerate my frailty by hobbling the short distance from my porch to George's house while he follows me.

Once I am inside and out of his sight, a surge of energy sends me to the fireplace mantle where George's French-made rifle hangs on pegs. It is one of his favorite rifles: a trade rifle he has owned since his youth when he fought against the rebels—those so-called Patriots. Shorter and lighter than the Kentucky rifle, it is perfect for hunting game—or men. I know it's loaded, as George insists on keeping it that way. From the violence of his youth and early adulthood, he knows it's best not to be caught off guard. I struggle a bit to free it from its resting place, but I'm re-energized once I feel its familiar weight.

"Hurry up, old woman," he calls out impatiently. His voice is clear, alerting me that he is just outside the door. I smell the burning pitch and see flickering flames reflected through the window by the door. I know he has ignited the firebrand and is prepared to toss his flaming torch into the dwelling.

"I'm coming," I call out as I raise the rifle to my shoulder, knowing he can not see me in the dark recesses of the house. Then, without hesitation, I stride to the open door, ready to fire straight into his chest.

The rifle is heavy, and in the moments that I struggle to steady it against my right shoulder, I hear him shout, "Shit fire!" as he drops the firebrand and lifts his weapon, which had been resting on the porch rail. Then, I hear the crack of his rifle and feel the searing heat of a bullet pierce my left side.

His eyes widen as he realizes that, despite my severe wounds, I am not yet dead. He doesn't have time to reload and backs away as if preparing to flee. But I manage to steady George's rifle and quickly fire in those brief seconds. My skills from long ago serve me well as the bullet slams into his chest. He grunts as he falls at my feet, dead before hitting the ground, no longer a threat to my family.

All is quiet in the yard. The despicable man's horse is still tied to my porch. I wonder why it has not bolted, but then I realize she must be used to gunfire. "Well, then, so be it," I mutter, flinging George's rifle aside and grateful that his mount has patiently waited for him to carry out his wicked deed.

The horse skittered briefly before calming down and allowing me to tie one end of the dead man's rope around his torso, knotting the other end around the saddle's pommel. Walking alongside her, I take the halter and lead the horse to the hog pen, dragging the corpse behind.

My dilemma is getting his body into the pen with the hogs that George is fattening for the fall butchering.

My strength wanes as blood from the bullet wound flows unchecked down my left leg. Although I pull and push, I can not lift the flaccid body, slight though he is. In a flash of ingenuity, I loop the middle of the rope around the fence post to create a fulcrum. The horse cooperates by backing up at my command while I hold the bridle and steady the pommel. As I hoped, that despicable man's body rises to almost a standing position against the waist-high timbered hog pen.

With great difficulty and a significant loss of blood from my wound, I lift one of his arms and then a leg over the top rail. The rest of his body topples in after a mighty push, causing a sudden rush of more blood, soaking my dress. The hogs rush forward, squealing in a frenzy with the scent of blood—mine and his.

"That should make for some good pork roast," I giggle as the hogs get to work, destroying the evidence of what happened.

I ponder the wisdom of hiding the valuable horse and saddle in the barn, but I realize that only family should know what I have done. Reluctantly, I thank her for her help, slap her rump with the reins, and send her running down the road. Whoever finds her will wonder about the missing rider, but chances are, they will not bother to investigate.

With the little strength I have left, I make my way back to my cabin. Leaning against the now-cold fireplace, I attempt to staunch the bleeding with an old shift. A wave of relief washes over me as I lie back on my bed and faintly wonder if what happened was just a dream.

And now, a heaviness descends upon me—my wounded body draining blood onto the bed linens I enjoyed only a short time ago. A coldness unlike any I have known envelops me, for very little life-sustaining blood remains in my weary body. Like a candle flickering in the darkness of night, my awareness ebbs and flows.

"Is this how I am to die?" I ask the bedstead. There is no answer, of course—nor anyone to call for help—no one to come through the door to tend to me, for I am alone as I insisted.

The family will immediately see what is amiss when they return late this evening—the door to the big house left ajar and two rifles flung aside, their bullets spent. There is a great deal of blood in the yard, evidence of carnage. They will follow the horse tracks and drag marks to the hog pen. There, they will find remnants of the man's clothing in the trampled mud, for even hogs have limits to what they will consume. And they will know what has been done.

When they come through the open door of my cabin, they will find me lying under the crimson-stained quilts on my bed. I smile, amused, as I think about my beloved family's reaction to their Granny's final act. Yes, it is my time, and I feel no fear—only curiosity about what lies beyond the veil of death.

I think of these things as my life force weakens, comforted by the thought that my family is safe from White opportunists—at least for now.

I must have dozed off or lost consciousness... or perhaps I have died. No, not yet, for breath still flows through my lungs, although faintly. My wound no longer bleeds my life force, as indeed, the last of my blood has surely drained from my body. A lightness descends upon me, a weightlessness. I sense Richard's presence, and I feel at peace.

"Have you come for me?" I ask.

"Yes, my darling Hester. It is time."

And I push out the last air from my lungs and allow my spirit to leave my body.

About The Author

Born and raised in Oklahoma, Jeanean's elementary school education reflected the typical whitewashing of that era. Although the state is heavily populated with Native Americans from hundreds of tribes, the school curriculum was Eurocentric. Movies and television, primary sources shaping opinions in impressionable minds, consistently portrayed pioneers and cowboys as the good guys trying to survive against onslaughts from bloodthirsty Indians. She and her childhood friends often played "cowboys and Indians." All the kids wanted to be cowboys or pioneers because they were the clever ones who always won. When playmates took their turn to portray an Indian, they did so with a lot of prancing, threatening yells, and waving of pretend tomahawks.

Her family did not discuss the implications of her beloved grandfather, Henry Parris, being Cherokee. While some people of Cherokee descent quietly maintained remnants of their ancestors' culture, most of her contemporaries only vaguely understood their heritage. In recent years, she has witnessed a resurgence of the Cherokee Nation and feels grateful for those who have kept the culture alive.

It wasn't until she was in her thirties that she completed the application to become a Cherokee citizen based on her grandfather's registration on the Dawes Rolls. However, even then, having Cherokee DNA held little significance for her. In her fifties, she began ancestral research that ignited her curiosity about her Native roots. Much of what she learned deeply resonated with her. The more she learned, the more she appreciated what it meant to be Cherokee.

Mixed Blood is a thoroughly researched historical novel that tells the imagined story of Jeanean's seven-time great-grandmother. Like women everywhere, she would have focused on family and community as they navigated events on the American frontier that irrevocably altered the Cherokee Nation.

Like Hester, Jeanean employs storytelling to foster a deeper understanding of the Cherokee Nation's rich history and the resilience of the "Real People," as they called themselves. This is Hester's story, as she may have lived it.